REINTEGRATION

Eden S. French

Dedication

For Li, every word,
and especially the words we learned together

CHAPTER 1

Music droned beneath her, a sonic lure that held the promise of drinking, dancing, and sex. The crime lord who owned the club below was one of Lexi's regular associates, and the bouncers never gave her any trouble, even though she caused plenty of it herself.

The distant music coaxed her down a hall plastered with posters from a bygone century: musicians long dead, films banned and burned, world tours to countries that no longer existed. She slinked into the lounge, blinked at the strobing confusion of the dance floor, and caught an incoming high-five.

"Yo, Lexi!" said the high-fiver.

Lexi squinted to make out the grinning face of the man who'd accosted her. He was a scrawny gangster with bad breath and a stupid nickname Lexi could never remember—the Cobra or the Viper, something dumb like that. "How you doing, Anaconda?"

"Viper." The gangster—it was hard to think of him as the Viper, no matter how charitable Lexi might be feeling—scratched his tattooed cheek, his grin already replaced by a peevish frown. "C'mon, you knew that."

Behind him, the dance floor teemed with shadows and bodies twisting together within a thick hum of bass. Colored light broke the darkness at erratic intervals, bright enough to spill into the lounges and dapple the faces of patrons drinking and chatting in booths and on couches. Any of them would be more interesting company than this guy.

"Sure, I knew that," said Lexi. "Tell me, is your girlfriend here tonight?"

"Yeah, yeah. She's here."

"What's she look like?"

The gangster's grin returned with enhanced smugness. "Tall brunette, black minidress. She's got the tightest ass in the city." He made a cupping gesture with both hands to emphasize the tightness of the ass in question.

"I'll bet she does. Where's she at?"

"Over by the bar with... Oh, hell no. Lexi, don't you hit on my girlfriend. Don't you fucking do that to me. Come on."

Lexi smirked. "Later, Mamba."

She strode toward the dance floor, ignoring the gangster's increasingly desperate protests. Of course, she wasn't really going to hit on his girlfriend—unless he wasn't exaggerating about her ass, in which case all bets were off—but he had good reason to be worried.

As she crossed the seedy carpet of the lounge, heads turned and appreciative gazes lingered. Lexi slowed to a cocky saunter, giving her admirers all the time they needed to soak in the view.

She'd never gotten the hang of humility, and who could blame her? Her handsome features drew attention wherever she went, as did the way she wore her hair—dyed snow white, gelled into loose spikes and shaved on the left side. Of course, clothing mattered too. Tonight, she'd matched a dark leather jacket with a white dress shirt and a clinging pair of black jeans that flaunted her narrow hips and long legs.

The scents and sounds of the dance floor enveloped her. The haze of cheap perfume and body odor she could have done without, but the music had the kind of sensual rhythm that made hips move of their own volition.

Tempting though it was to stop and wiggle, Lexi wasn't the kind to dance alone, and she pressed through the mass in the direction of the bar.

It was busy tonight; every stool occupied and the bartenders struggling to keep up. A bouncer waited nearby, a fist in a suit with another ridiculous nickname—the Shark, or maybe the Dolphin, who the hell knew?

As Lexi neared the silver curve of the bar, the Marine Animal advanced toward her, moving with all the speed of a shifting continent.

"Lexi," he said. "You know our boss has been looking for you?"

"Is that right?" Lexi folded her arms as the bouncer lumbered to a halt. "Why doesn't he just call me?"

"He's looking for you." It seemed the big guy wasn't interested in the finer details. "That's all. Wants to see you as soon as possible."

"I'll get around to it." Lexi looked up into the meaty slab of concentration that constituted his face. "What's your name, anyway?"

"The Squid."

Classic. Among all the city's gangs, the Menagerie was definitely the stupidest. "Why? Because you're good at escaping from little plastic mazes?"

"He wants to see you. Just remember." The Squid slunk back to his corner and stood there wrapped in idiot menace.

Whatever his brain-dead employer wanted, it could wait. Lexi descended upon the bar, and a chorus of excited voices greeted her.

"Lexi!" A fragrant, wobbly young woman caught her by the arm and stared into her face, blinking at manic speed. "Are you here by yourself?"

"Not for long." Lexi eased the woman's hand from her wrist. Damn drunken, grabby clubbers. "Do you usually sway on your feet like that?"

"My friend is here!" The clubber indicated a group of equally inebriated young women clustered at the end of the bar. "Her boyfriend broke up with her. We're drinking to cheer her up."

Lexi steadied the clubber, who was tilting at an alarming angle. "And how's that working out for you?"

"It's awful!" The clubber leaned closer, exhaling alcohol and exuding perfume. "She's really upset, and we don't know what to do!"

"Who are we talking about here?"

"Her! My friend!" The clubber pointed to a dazed young woman wearing a yellow party hat. It had slipped to her forehead, giving her the appearance of a mournful unicorn. "I promised to cheer her up, but it's not working. We bought her so many drinks, yet she just sits there."

It was unlikely Lexi had ever met this unsteady, babbling person, but it didn't matter. She thrived on this kind of spontaneous entertainment.

"I'll take care of it." She patted the woman on the shoulder. "Leave her to me."

With one glance, Lexi identified the heartbroken girl's first problem. Far from commiserating, her friends were making the most of their night out, drinking and giggling while the girl watched them in a resentful stupor. Lexi's augmented senses picked up the emotions spilling from her—traces of grief, anger, and envy, diluted by the effect of the alcohol.

"Hey, girls." Lexi reclined against the bar and rested a heel on the wood-textured plastic. "Having fun?"

"Hi, Lexi," said one of the women. Her shy voice was familiar, but as usual, Lexi had long discarded the name. "Can I buy you a drink?"

Lexi grinned. *Can I buy you a drink?* was the second-most-common phrase directed at her, just behind, *Don't stop.* But she had to stay focused. She was here to perform a good deed.

"You should be saving your drinks for your friend here." She placed a hand on the girl's bare forearm. "I heard you had a bad day."

The girl seemed lost for words, unable to do anything more than stare.

"It's hard to believe anyone could be so stupid," said Lexi, meeting her disoriented eyes. "Breaking up with a girl as beautiful as you."

There it was—the first blush of the night. "Um." The girl averted her eyes. "Uh." The first stammer, too. No surprise. They usually came as a package.

"You shouldn't sit here and just get drunk." Lexi shifted the girl's hat to the top of her head. "You'll just feel worse."

"I do feel worse," said the girl. "I wish I'd never come." There was a murmur of reproach from her friends, none of it convincing.

"Put the glass down and come dance with me. That'll make it better." Lexi extended her other hand. "Up you get."

The girl grasped Lexi's hand and allowed herself to be helped upright. By some miracle, she remained on her feet unassisted. She was attractive, albeit bleary, with a round, trusting face darkened by her petulant mood. If the evening went well, it was possible Lexi might even ask for her name.

They found their way to an open space at a safe distance from the booming speakers. The music had a sexy current to it, a sly, dirty rhythm buried beneath layers of dreamy fuzz. Just right.

Lexi took the girl by the waist and drew her in. "Oh," the girl said, her eyes widening. "You want to dance close."

It was cute when they were naïve. "I only ever dance close." Lexi moved with the music, and the girl followed her lead, even resting a tentative hand on Lexi's hip. "You have bad taste in friends, so I imagine your boyfriend was a loser too."

The girl gave a nervous laugh. "I guess so." She had become a dim shape illuminated by infrequent splashes of color, but her face, upturned and wondering, was visible enough in the ambient light.

The music suggested they dance slower and a little closer. Lexi obeyed. The grip at her hip tightened as the girl's breath came more quickly.

"You're really good-looking," the girl said. "My boyfriend was handsome, but not nearly as handsome as you. You're like pretty-handsome, you know?"

Lexi smiled, and the girl blushed again. "Yes, I know."

"Um." The girl's other hand finally made contact, resting upon Lexi's shoulder. "I've never done this before."

"You've never danced before? Then your boyfriend really was a loser."

"No." The girl giggled. "I mean, I've never danced like this with…" She sucked her lower lip into her mouth and looked away.

Lexi placed her mouth by the girl's ear. "Maybe it's a night for trying new things."

The quick breath that followed was all the confirmation Lexi needed. She caressed the girl's waist and hips, traveling a body hidden beneath tight fabric, and the girl slid her own hands to take hold of Lexi's behind. They pressed close, the girl's eyes bright beneath her lowered lashes, and followed the alluring rhythm.

As she danced, Lexi contemplated the girl's lips, which glistened with crimson lipstick. Not yet, but soon enough.

"Alexis? Alexis Vale?"

Lexi ignored the voice, too busy with the warm mouth moving against her own. She pushed the girl further into the booth, still kissing, and stroked her thigh. The girl broke the kiss, gave Lexi a look of glazed satisfaction and returned to kissing again.

"Alexis." It was a young woman's voice, steady and insistent. "Please. I need to talk to you."

Who the hell was this, and why didn't she have the sense to wait her turn? Lexi pulled away from the embrace, leaving her companion to pout in the corner of the booth. "I'm a little busy here," she said as she turned.

Her irritation immediately gave way to curiosity. The arrival wore a blue, gold-buttoned overall. Either she was a shut-in or, for whatever kinky reason, had chosen to dress like one. Her black hair had been swept into long bangs concealing the left side of her face, which was quite pretty—slender features, golden skin, mono-lidded eyes and a serious expression betrayed by the nervous twitching of her lips and the blush burning all the way to her neck.

"I'm sorry to interrupt." The shut-in studied the glossy tips of her boots. "But your life is in danger."

"Go away," said the girl huddled in the booth. "She's mine."

The shut-in took a deep breath and raised her head again. Despite her obvious anxiety, her clear green eyes were resolute. "My name is Mineko. I'm not leaving until I've spoken to you."

Lexi was having a good time, and it was well on the way to being upgraded to excellent. But a shut-in in a place like this? Too unusual to ignore.

"Give us ten minutes," said Lexi, touching her companion on the wrist.

"But Lexi…" The girl's eyes glistened. "Are you going to run off on me?"

"Of course not." Lexi took the girl's hand and kissed her fingertips, prompting an anxious smile. "Ten minutes, sweetie."

The girl gave Mineko a dirty look before sliding out of the booth, smoothing down her skirt and staggering in the direction of the bar. Lexi shifted across the couch and patted the cushion. After a second of hesitation, Mineko seated herself on the other end.

"Okay," said Lexi. "You have my attention. But if this is just a ploy to steal me away, forget it. I make a point of not ditching my girls."

"No. Nothing like that. I'm here about Project Sky."

"What is that, a cocktail? You want me to buy it for you?"

Mineko frowned. Seemed she was a typical shut-in, no sense of humor. "It was a failed Codist cybernetics project. They wanted to find a way to read people's minds."

Ah, fuck. So that's what this was about. Lexi took a cautious look around. Everyone nearby seemed too occupied with drinking and dancing to be prying. "No wonder it failed. I mean, mind-reading. That's some superhero bullshit, right?"

"The prototype chip found its way into the districts." Mineko seemed to have lost her nervousness, and she held Lexi's gaze. "People knew it was lethal, that everyone implanted had died. But every now and then, somebody would take the risk. And they'd die too."

That was hardly news to Lexi, and she certainly wasn't going to grieve over it now. "Tragic. Your point is?"

"There are rumors about a working implant. Just one. A unique cyborg."

Unease squirmed in Lexi's stomach. She laced her fingers behind her head and feigned a smile. "Fun story."

"Alexis, the project has been re-opened. My people know you exist, and they're looking for you in order to understand why their first attempt failed. If I can find you, so can they."

"First, call me Lexi. Second, how can you know any of this? You're just a kid. How old are you, anyway?"

"Twenty-two. But that's not relevant. I know for a fact your life is in danger." Mineko slid nearer. "Does it really work?"

As much as Lexi preferred to keep her advantage secret, it was hard to imagine a more harmless creature than this earnest, anxious shut-in kid. Besides, it seemed she already knew more than Lexi did. "Sure, it works. But I don't advertise it. It'd be bad for business."

"Do you have other augmentations? Or just this one?"

The kid's awed tone was endearing, and Lexi smiled. "Reflex and vision. One in the brain, one in the spine."

"Can you tell me how Project Sky works? How you do it?"

"Depends on the person. I find looking somebody in the eyes is the best way to focus. Sometimes I have to get close, even touch them. Other times I can pick things up from a distance. Everyone's different."

"Can you tell what I'm thinking now?"

This little thing was so sincere, it was impossible not to want to play with her. "If you give me permission."

Mineko nodded, and Lexi looked into her attractive green irises. "I don't feel anything from you yet."

Worry drew a crease on Mineko's forehead. "Is that good or bad?"

"From your point of view, good. It means you're harder to read." Still staring into Mineko's eyes, Lexi drifted deeper. Shadows clouded her peripheral vision as the first elusive traces of feeling appeared before her. Doubt, anxiety... The strands slipped from her grasp, and her drifting stopped.

"Damn," she said. "You're tough."

Mineko gave a quick series of blinks. "Did I do something wrong?"

"It's not your fault. Let me touch your face." Lexi placed a fingertip on Mineko's cool forehead and focused again on her eyes. Mineko's thoughts hummed around her, threads of interconnected memory permeated by varying heat and uncertain motion. The inarticulate canvas of a mind.

Lexi skimmed across its volatile surface. "You're afraid," she said as she touched upon a cold emotion gnawing at its neighbors. Another emotion jittered by, and she latched onto it. "And excited, too. You didn't really think this would be possible."

A warm, vibrant emotion hid behind the others—buried purposefully, it seemed. Lexi leaned in, and the sensation burned brighter. She chuckled. "And you're a little turned on."

The emotion heated further. "You couldn't be more mistaken."

Mineko's thoughts were becoming scattered, and Lexi frowned. "Relax. You're throwing me off."

Mineko took a deep breath, and her agitation settled. Lexi moved through stray ideas, idle impulses, and discarded memories while she hunted for the freshest thoughts, the ones most polished by a day's mental wandering. Impressions washed over her. Tapping through a digital tablet in search of notes, the calm voice of someone lecturing. *The first principle of Codism is…*

"You're a student at the shut-in University." Faces in motion, smiling and laughing. Cutting across a lawn to avoid a group of chattering young women. Eating alone. "You're a loner. Because…"

Lexi focused. Deferent visitors, an immense house behind gates, people staring, whispering. *That's her. That's the Tamura girl.*

"Your parents are important, powerful. That makes you different. The other students fear you—"

"That's enough, please. I believe you."

Lexi let the stolen thoughts collapse and returned to the reassuring world of a single mind. "You're going to get into trouble for this."

"Perhaps. But if you don't go into hiding, we're all in trouble."

Indignation pulsed hot in Lexi's chest. "Go into hiding? Are you serious? My life is damn good right now."

Mineko glanced over her shoulder. "For your sake and mine, you have to take me seriously. I can't sit here all night and try to convince you. It'll be noticed if I stay out any longer."

"Then get moving." Lexi reclined into the couch and yawned. Mineko's mind had been exhausting, full of tense repression. "I'll take your warning under consideration."

Mineko rose to her feet with obvious reluctance. "Please."

Lexi waved her hand dismissively. "Like I said. Under consideration."

"They know where you live. They know the clubs you frequent—that's how I found you. For all I know, there may be agents closing in."

"Consider me scared, okay?" This was getting too weird, and it was beginning to test Lexi's composure. She needed to get away from this paranoid shut-in and back to the life she understood. "Hurry home now."

Looking miserable, Mineko vanished into the crowded club. Lexi sagged on the couch and exhaled a long, tired breath. Now she was the one in need of cheering up, and no number of party hats would do the trick.

The jilted girl's name turned out to be Katrina, and after thirty minutes in Lexi's lap, the girl's bad mood had well and truly left her. As had most of her lipstick.

She chattered as they walked toward the depleted bar, and Lexi nodded despite being unable to hear a word. Kat—she had insisted on being called Kat—seemed a little quirky, but quirky was something Lexi could handle.

Kat's friends had abandoned the bar, leaving only the woman who had first approached Lexi. She sat surrounded by empty glasses while turning a blue party hat in her hands.

"Put it on," said Lexi. "It's your color."

"There you are!" The woman pointed the party hat in their direction. "You abandoned us!"

"I was being cheered up," said Kat. "Isn't that what you wanted?"

"Yes, but we didn't expect you to run away and become a lesbian. How are we supposed to hang out now?"

Lexi settled on a stool and kept an arm around Kat as she perched on its neighbor. "You have something against lesbians?"

"It's not like that." Every slurred word came accompanied by a drunken, forceful hand gesture. "I love lesbians. It's just that I didn't think you'd go and turn my best friend into one."

"I'm not your best friend," said Kat sternly. "And I'm not a lesbian, either."

The woman attempted to put on the party hat but found herself unable to navigate the elastic. "I know what this is. You're experimenting on the rebound, that's what this is."

Somebody swore nearby. A familiar unattractive figure forced his way across the dance floor, pushing through the spinning, thrusting people in his path. The Cobra—no, the Viper, that was it—brushed aside a final dancer and stopped before the bar.

"What's wrong?" Lexi exaggerated a sympathetic pout. "Girlfriend ditched you?"

"The boss really wants to see you," said the Viper. "Like, tonight. Not tomorrow, not next week, but tonight."

Lexi's amusement gave way to irritation. The Zookeeper didn't get to order her around. "So he can come out here and drink with me. He's not usually a snob."

"He wants to see you in his office, Lexi. He ain't coming out."

"But she has." The blue-hatted woman indicated Kat. "She's a lesbian now."

The Viper stared at her for several bewildered seconds, shook his head, and returned his attention to Lexi. "It's no big deal, nothing personal. He just has a headache tonight, doesn't want the noise."

Complying, though inconvenient, would at least be better than having this dumbass on her case all night. "Sure." Lexi released Kat and dropped from the stool. "I have to see the Zookeeper, sweetie. I'll be back."

She followed the Viper to a stairwell recessed in the corner. With each step nearer the dark opening, doubt nagged at her. She was on good terms with this gang, which was one of the cleaner ones in the district, a tough operation that specialized in moving recreational drugs—no prostitution, no extortion, just happy pills and powders. She shouldn't be worrying. Yet there was something weird about this. What if that shut-in had been right about her life being in danger?

"Hey, Viper," said Lexi as they reached the bottom step. "You sure I can't put this off until tomorrow? I don't want that girl to walk out on me."

The Viper gave an amused snort. "Sure. Like any woman ever walked out on you." He climbed several steps, stopped, and looked back. "C'mon, don't keep him—"

Lexi gripped him by the jaw, sinking her fingers into his flesh, and he grunted. She looked into his eyes and drove straight into his thoughts, tearing and scattering anything in her path. There it was: the boss himself, seated behind his desk, tapping his fingers in a patient rhythm. *Go fetch her.* In the corner, two shut-ins wearing black overalls. The Viper didn't know what the fuck they were doing there. Sure as hell wasn't going to ask. Not his problem, and besides, maybe Lexi had it coming. The queer bitch was so fucking full of herself...

She let go, and he stumbled back, rubbing his chin. "What the fuck!"

"He's sold me out." Lexi flexed her fingers. "You really are a snake, aren't you?"

The Viper stared at her. "How the hell did you..."

He was afraid, and that gave Lexi her opportunity. She lunged, caught him again, and focused. The fear expanded, a black, trembling cloud that swallowed up every other thought and feeling. The Viper moaned and sagged, held upright only by Lexi's grip.

"Don't move from this spot," Lexi said. "Or you die." She released him, and he sank to his knees. "I'm serious."

He closed his eyes and whimpered. Gratifying, but the effect wouldn't last long. Lexi hurried back to the bar, where Kat was helping her friend straighten the blue party hat.

"You know, this place is boring me," said Lexi, smiling to conceal her anxiety. Her heart was pounding, but otherwise she was holding it together. Not even a trace of sweat. "Tell me, have you got a nice TV?"

"Sure, I have a nice TV." A bright smile animated Kat's face. "Are you saying you'd like to see it?"

"That's what I'm saying. Maybe we could watch a movie together."

"That would be cool. I have a nice couch, too." Kat gave Lexi a shy look. "You could sleep on it if you wanted to stay the night."

Despite her agitation, Lexi couldn't resist a knowing smirk. Yeah, like she was really going to end up on some couch. "Could do."

"Hey!" The friend wobbled to her feet, slipped, and landed back on the stool. "You can't ditch us. We came here to cheer you up. Lexi, tell her."

No time for being nice. "Get a fucking clue," said Lexi. "You loved that she was upset, enjoyed every heartbroken second. You weren't here to cheer her up. You were feeding off her misfortune to make yourself feel good."

The woman stared at Lexi, mute and bug-eyed.

"Come on." Lexi took Kat's hand. "Before your so-called friends make you pay for all those drinks."

They hurried to the entrance hall. "I can't believe you spoke to her like that," said Kat, disbelieving, as they walked down the poster-lined corridor. "She's always been nice to me."

"Trust me. I'm good at figuring people out."

The exit neared, and Lexi braced herself. Her escape depended on whether the bouncer had been clued in on the double-cross. It didn't look good for a gang to be caught working with the shut-ins, so it was possible not every goon had been informed.

The bouncer was lounging against a wall, arms folded across his massive chest. He gave Lexi and Kat a curt nod. Lexi relaxed—seemed she was in the clear—and took the stairs at a casual pace while Kat trudged beside her.

The street was lit from end to end by mingled, multicolored neon lights. "You live far from here?" said Lexi.

"On the east side. I'm only a few minutes away from a station."

Lexi put an arm around Kat's shoulders and steered her down the street. It couldn't have been much later than eleven, and the entertainment strip was still doing plenty of business——nightclubs concealed beneath colorful frontages, movie theaters displaying animated marquees, brothels with hazily-lit windows, small eateries exuding the aroma of deep-fried food. A fun section of the city. Too bad, really. If the reigning gang had turned on Lexi, she wouldn't be seeing it again any time soon.

"The east side, huh," said Lexi. "You must be doing something right."

"I'm a nurse at one of Contessa's drug clinics."

Not a bad gig. Foundation's crime lords poured a lot of money into private clinics for treating those enforcers who got a little too close to the product. It was expensive, but nobody wanted to rely on thugs so doped up they couldn't even fart without freaking out and shooting each other.

"They say you're the best broker in the city," said Kat. "That you have all the connections."

"I bet that's not all they say about me." A bit of deadpan comedy, wasted on this wasted girl.

Kat shot Lexi a sidelong look. "Why are you leaving with me? You could have anyone you want. I'm nothing special. Do you just feel sorry for me?"

Lexi squeezed Kat's shoulder. "That's the kind of thinking that'll end up with you depressed, lonely, and wearing a stupid hat. This is your chance to sort your life out. Don't waste it."

"Yeah, maybe." Kat stared at the pavement as she tottered across it. "You think I should try dating girls? Maybe you'd like to…I mean, if you're available…"

It was adorable when they started crushing. And it had to be shut down as soon as possible. "No, I'm not. Just enjoy this while it lasts, and it'll be the best fun you've ever had." Lexi kissed Kat on the ear. "Now hurry up. The shut-ins are hunting me for the top-secret, mind-reading cybernetic implant I have embedded deep within my brain."

Kat rested her cheek on Lexi's shoulder. "You're funny."

CHAPTER 2

Judging by the gray glow passing through the branches of the tree outside, it was a little after dawn. Tempting though it was to fall asleep again, it was Tuesday, and Mineko's Social Ethics lecture started at seven.

She pulled back the warm sheets, stripped off her underwear, and washed under the heated spray of her little shower cubicle. As steam rose around her, the tension in her muscles eased, and memories of the past night returned. Foremost among them was Lexi Vale, the louche goddess who had lounged at the heart of that frenzied bedlam of colors and sounds.

This morning, Mineko's regulation uniform looked duller than ever: a navy-blue, one-piece overall with five golden buttons concealing a zipper. She hooked each button through its loop and smoothed down the sleeves.

Her modesty regained, she stood by the window. From here, the great walls that protected the University from the untamed city were obscured, though not concealed, by the trees in the ornamental garden below.

Several students had gathered on the benches to eat breakfast and read notes. Loneliness stirred, and Mineko looked away. They were also the children of privileged families, but she was a Tamura. No matter how modestly she might present herself in public, everyone knew the power her parents wielded. She was as far removed from the young men and women below as she was from the people living in Foundation's districts.

It was time to move, yet her body didn't want to respond—it felt too heavy with dread, sadness, and the knowledge of her own betrayal. Hard to believe that the night before, she'd dared walk the streets of Foundation, leaving for the first time the sanctioned boundaries of an enclave to enter an alien world where the Code didn't apply.

For now.

Five minutes before the start of the lecture, Mineko dashed through the theater doors and across the top tier of seats to her usual place in the corner. Most seats were filled, nobody being brave enough to risk a late arrival, and the heads below were attentively turned to the stage.

Mineko set her tablet in front of her, scrolled through last week's notes and checked the message bank. It was filled with messages from Kaori, who sent family updates daily, behaving as though her daughter were on the far side of the planet rather than a half-hour train ride away.

The ethics lecturer stalked onto the stage and took his place behind the podium. As always, he was exactly one minute early, and he spent that minute inspecting each chair while the students sat in tense anticipation.

"Nobody is late," he said. "Good."

He clipped a microphone to the collar of his blue-gray uniform and fell into his hypnotic, pacing stride. That constant motion across the stage was the only visual distraction available to a bored student. Social Ethics lectures took place without slides, video recordings or any opportunity for questions. Not that anyone would have dared pose any. This was a secular sermon to an audience who had no choice but to believe.

"Today is our second lecture on the Ethics of Social Cohesion." The lecturer waved a finger in the air. "Remember, what you learn today will be relevant in the coming exam."

The dreaded word hovered in the air, and the students seemed to shrink before its presence. *Today's material in exam,* Mineko typed.

The lecturer resumed pacing. "Remember the basics. The Third Moral Code is premised upon the total destruction of social atomization by adopting a moral form of hierarchical collectivism. Previous attempts at collectivism have foundered due to their flawed foundations—a basis in religion, for example, or nationalism, economic doctrine, and so on. The Code prospers because it collectivizes on the basis of moral human endeavor. We have learned from the basic error of libertarianism, the horrifying consequences of the free market, the facile naïvety of socialism. We have seen the destruction of our planet's environment due to industrial interests coercing states into willful ignorance. We have outlived partisan wars of ideology and religion."

Mineko straightened in her chair as she held back a yawn. Falling asleep in class was an ethical breach. Even coughing was a breach if it interrupted the lecturer during a passage he was especially proud of.

"Most human ideology is anarchy masquerading as harmony. Our founding premise is a biological model instead. In nature, every part both constitutes and organically defines the whole. We cannot function as single organisms any more than an organ of the body can survive apart from its greater structure. Thus, moral law is the law of biological survival. Overly permissive and fatally deluded societies have ignored this law, leading to chaos. Codism is right because it exists as the antidote to these failures. It is the healing doctrine for a dying Earth."

The lecturer rubbed his hands together, which meant he was about to delve deep into the pious, ethical drudgery he so reveled in.

"In the pursuit of social cohesion, the Code has twice been revised to account for the inability of a single person to recognize their actions have consequences for the greater body. As a rule, we hold that no body ought to destroy a part of itself when it might instead preserve it. Therefore, the solution to the destructive individual is re-education. The challenge is that not every psychology is amenable to gentle means."

So that was today's subject. Mineko pushed her tablet away and propped her head in her hands. It would be better to fail this question on the exam than sicken herself with the pretense of conviction.

"The Third Moral Code approved a neural procedure you will have heard referred to as 'wiping.' This term is pejorative, and I suggest you not use it. The entire procedure, which includes both medical and pedagogical components, is properly known as Reintegration. Refer to it otherwise, and you will jeopardize your final grade."

The lecturer stared into the distance. Mineko took the opportunity to glare at him—only for a second, but it was liberating nonetheless.

"The ethics of this process were debated. That debate is now over, settled by the fact that what is moral serves the whole. The so-called 'rights of the individual' inevitably lead to the fragmentation of society. Reintegration maintains perfect cohesion by salvaging an individual who might in more brutal times have been imprisoned or even executed. No ethical objection can in the end stand against it. The alternative is to endorse a flawed society primed for self-annihilation..."

The end of the lecture brought with it a sense of relief that lasted only until Mineko stepped through the theater doors. A black-uniformed man waited in the hallway, standing against the wall to avoid the departing throng of students. He was lean, dark-skinned, and expressionless, and his features, though handsome in their chiseled symmetry, were as hard as his eyes.

As students filed into the hall, they whispered while glancing at Mineko. After all, who else would a Code Intel agent be here to see? The man beckoned, confirming the universal suspicion, and Mineko's heart jolted. She couldn't run, of course, but she certainly couldn't ignore him.

"Ms. Tamura," said the agent. "I'd like a word."

"Yes." The numb, one-word reply was all she could manage.

Mineko followed the agent down the corridor, keeping her head low so as not to meet the eyes of the students milling around her. He stopped before an unoccupied classroom and tested the handle.

"This'll do," he said, and he ushered her inside.

The agent shut the door behind them, and Mineko took a deep breath. She could always lie, force him to prove his accusations. Her father would never let her be punished without considerable evidence.

"Relax." The agent walked between a row of desks to stand before the window at the classroom's far end. It overlooked the wall of a neighboring building; not the most scenic of views. After a moment contemplating the masonry, he turned back to face her. "I'm not a Codist. I only wore this uniform so people wouldn't be suspicious of me talking to you."

The revelation did nothing for Mineko's nerves. "What are you saying? Why would you admit that to me?"

"Because I don't think you're likely to tell anyone. My name's Kade August. I'm a journalist."

"Trespassing is forbidden." Sweat clung beneath Mineko's collar, and her palms had grown damp as well. "As is wearing a uniform you're not entitled to."

Kade seated himself on the broad ledge of the window sill and gave her a thin smile. "The Code doesn't apply to non-Codists."

"Civil Obedience Law is enforced wherever and whenever the integrity of Codist territory is threatened. They'd wipe you for being here."

"I'm not inclined to care what District Affairs thinks." Kade plucked the front of his stolen uniform. "To you, this is a symbolic, near-sacred garment. To me, it's just so much ugly black cotton."

Mineko glanced through the door's single pane. The corridor remained empty. "Why would you take a risk like this? You know who my father is."

"I certainly do. Tell me, what happened last night? What business did you have with Lexi Vale?"

Panic slammed the air from Mineko's lungs. So somebody had seen her. Now what? It seemed pointless to lie. If they had evidence, Code Intel wouldn't be playing games—they didn't care about confessions. No, Mineko had to steel herself for the truth.

"I wanted to see her, that's all." Mineko squared her shoulders and looked Kade in the eye. "I'm now guilty of associating with an intruder, and I had no shortage of problems already. You owe it to me to explain yourself."

"As I said, I'm a journalist. An investigative reporter for the *Revolutionary People's Gazette*. We speak the truth of the oppressive inequality the Codists perpetuate upon Foundation."

Nothing he'd said made any sense. "But why are you here?"

"Because Codists raided Lexi's apartment last night. Don't worry, she wasn't there. Seemed to have been warned in advance."

Mineko's head swum. She leaned on a study desk for support. "So she did listen to me."

Kade nodded. "What did you tell her?"

"I told her to go into hiding, that's all. They've gathered plenty of intelligence on her, and they've just been biding their time."

Kade's grim face was impossible to read. "I assume this is related to that aug of hers, the one we call the suicide chip. I'd heard rumors your people invented it. Is that true?"

It was one thing to steal secrets and act on her own initiative. Another entirely to confide in a mysterious revolutionary. Mineko stared out the window. Dark clouds had gathered to sap the morning light. Despite the gloom, the sound of laughter and striking leather suggested that a group of students was playing football on the lawn. Football was an approved activity, but only so long as it was non-competitive.

"Well, that's not important right now." Kade's tone remained measured. "What matters is conveying to Lexi that this isn't a game. She's shrewd, but she's arrogant too. She loves to take risks."

"Can't you explain all this to her?"

"Wouldn't work. She doesn't listen to me." Kade ran his fingers through his untidy black hair. "To be honest, I'm hoping you can do it. After last night, you might have earned yourself a little respect with her, and that puts you in a rare category of people. She may take you seriously."

Surely Mineko's bedside alarm would soon go off, rescuing her from an increasingly absurd dream. "Are you asking me to leave campus today? But it's dangerous, and I have classes…"

"You don't have another lecture until four, and I'm sure you can sacrifice a little study time. Tell me, how did you get in and out last night?"

It wasn't fair he should know so much while remaining an enigma, but sulking would get Mineko no closer to an explanation. "I used a service entrance. I stole the access code from my father's computer."

"Good. So there's nothing stopping you."

This man was infuriatingly persistent. "If Lexi doesn't trust you, why should I? Surely someone who can read minds is a good judge of character."

"I said she didn't listen to me, not that she didn't trust me. If she were here, she'd vouch for my honesty."

That made little sense, but Mineko was hardly an expert on human behavior. Besides, if Kade was trying to deceive her, his agenda was entirely inscrutable— why risk his life in a stolen uniform if not in the service of the truth? And Project Sky was such a terrible truth…

"Where can I find her?"

"There's a diner on the south side of the district, The Tofu Palace. I had a friend of mine arrange a meeting under the pretext of making a drug deal. In reality, the only person showing up is you."

"How am I supposed to get there?"

"I'll show you the way, but I won't hang around. If she spots me with you, she'll suspect a set-up."

Mineko blinked. The strange man was still there, fixing her with the stern look that suited his stolen uniform so well. There was nothing to do now but relent and hope this madness would come to a gentle conclusion. "I'll do it, but I hope you understand how terrible the risks are for me."

"Oh, I understand. I'm taking those risks too, remember. But Lexi isn't going to take care of herself. Like it or not, we're going to have do it for her."

"I have to say, she sounds like a very unreasonable woman."

Kade gave a wry smile. "She'll listen when it counts. You just have to make her realize that time is now."

It had been intimidating to walk the streets of the district by night, through colored lights and suggestive shadows, but at least the darkness had offered anonymity. By day, there was no chance of Mineko's overalls being mistaken for anything but a Codist uniform.

And strangely enough, nobody seemed to care.

"People see the uniform, they look away," Kade said. "And while that's useful right now, I wish it were otherwise."

Mineko stared around her. On either side, apartment buildings rose as high as eight stories, though most of their windows were boarded. Run-down stores squeezed between the apartments, their windows advertising everything from computer parts to freeze-dried food.

"Why aren't they resentful?" said Mineko. "Our enclaves are so rich."

"Misdirection." Now that he was outside, Kade seemed ill-at-ease in his stolen uniform, frequently tugging at the collar as if he wanted to remove it. "Despite being the real power in Foundation, the Codists let the gangs appear to rule. Thus, when things go badly, people blame the crime lords. Of course, when things go well, people simply credit themselves."

"I know the reasoning, but it's hard to believe it actually works."

"Political consciousness is a luxury most don't have. They're too busy trying to survive day-to-day. I write articles, but people have to actively choose to read me. It's not enough to start a revolution."

They neared an intersection flanked by a pair of inert traffic lights. A supermarket operated on one corner. White paint peeled from its walls and several of its windows were boarded, but the animated sign above the doors was lively enough—a many-hued jumble of letters that declared the odd site to be *The Conveni-Mart.*

A figure emerged from the supermarket trundling a trolley piled high with cardboard boxes. "What do people use for money?" said Mineko.

"Most people barter, but your currency has value on the streets. In fact, it provides the nearest thing there is to an economy. The gangs do deals with the Codists, they get paid, and the money circulates the districts. Even we revolutionaries end up using it."

Curiosity was beginning to eclipse Mineko's nerves, and she couldn't resist another question. "Are there many revolutionaries?"

"You're the daughter of Gaspar Tamura. You tell me."

Mineko bowed her head. Out here, it was all the more embarrassing to be reminded of her status. "I've overheard that our enemies number in the several hundreds. But my father and his people don't take you seriously. They say you should all be left to District Affairs to deal with."

"So they still underestimate us. That's good to hear."

"I suspect you don't have hundreds working on your newsletter, though."

The sound of Kade's laughter was unexpected—it was a pleasant, relaxed sound, nowhere near as grim as its owner. "No, you're quite right."

They reached the traffic lights, and Mineko thumped the 'walk' button, purely for the fun of it. After waiting for a pair of bicycles to fly past, she and Kade crossed the road to resume traveling on the far side. More apartment towers loomed about them, some with railed upper balconies. A man was standing on one such balcony while flicking out a towel. He had to be seven stories up—what would the view be like from there?

"You look at everything," said Kade. "I'd forgotten how novel all this must be for you."

"There's one thing I still don't understand. Why are you trusting me? I'm a Codist, and worse, I'm one of the elite."

"Late last night, I learned that Lexi had attacked a gang member at one of her usual clubs. That seemed strange, as she and that gang, the Menagerie, are tight. So I hurried over to investigate."

"And that's how you found out about me?"

"Exactly right. I questioned people at the club, asking if they'd seen anything unusual. They remembered that a Codist had been asking for Lexi. An Asian girl, they told me, early twenties, roughly five foot four, her face partially obscured by black hair."

A nervous jitter moved in Mineko's chest. If Kade hadn't been the only one asking questions… "So how did you identify that girl as me?"

"I've seen you in photographs of your family. The description was right, and I couldn't imagine who else would have that kind of knowledge."

Ominous. "Why do you have photos of my family? Do you use them for dartboards?"

"Know thy enemy." Kade pointed. "You know what's this way? South?"

"The Rail District."

"The very same. It used to be called Bare Hill, and you'll still find a few locals ancient enough to remember the name. I grew up around there. It's not as bleak as some, but it's not pretty." Kade gestured to the decaying apartment towers. "You probably think this looks like hell on earth. In reality, this is one of the nicest districts in town."

Once more, Mineko stared at the street around her, taking in the broken windows, the crumbling masonry, the cracked, pockmarked pavements. It was shameful, yet inspiring too. "I don't want to hide from the truth of what I am. What my family represents. I'd like to visit Bare Hill someday."

"You mean the Rail District."

"No. I mean Bare Hill." Mineko met Kade's eyes, which had by now lost much of their intimidating coldness, though it was still difficult to interpret what he might be thinking. "I'm sorry for being your enemy."

Kade smiled. "Which suggests you may well be my friend."

The diner turned out to be a cheerless, white-brick cube wedged between an accounting business and a closed-down pharmacy. The street outside was filthy, its gutters choked with bloated, putrefying garbage, and the only venue garnering any kind of attention was a rancid dive on the corner. Neon letters above the door gave its name merely as *BAR*. Perhaps it had a longer name that was only available on request.

"I'll wait inside the bar for ten minutes or so," said Kade. "If you don't come looking for me, I'll assume it's all gone well, and I'll head home to get out of this uniform."

Mineko eyed the windows of the diner. Even from the street opposite, there was no mistaking the slim, white-haired figure sprawled in one of the window booths. "Is white her natural hair color?"

"What? No." Kade chuckled. "Save the questions for her. She loves talking about herself."

"Okay. But won't you get into trouble in the bar, dressed like that?"

"They know me there." Kade gave her a thumbs-up. "Try to relax. You'll be in her good books now. She'll treat you like a princess."

Mineko could have done without the royal metaphor, but she nodded. She crossed the road, stepping carefully over the reeking gutters, and approached the diner with her head lowered. No, no, that was all wrong—she needed to be assertive. As she pushed open the door, setting bells tinkling above, she inhaled deep and held her head high.

The Tofu Palace couldn't have been less palatial. Its vinyl tile flooring had numerous sections peeled away, and a painted row of dancing soybeans decorated the counter. They looked like deformed green babies. Overhead, the interior lights buzzed as they saturated the room with excessive heat.

Lexi was the only customer. She sat in a booth that comprised two long seats facing one another over a thin strip of plastic. Each seat could have fit three people, but Lexi had chosen to laze on hers as if it were a couch, stretching her long legs and resting her back against the window. She lifted her hand in a nonchalant gesture of welcome.

"Good morning," said Mineko.

"Mineko, right?" There was something about the sly angle of Lexi's smile that made it difficult to hold eye contact. "I don't always remember names, but yours stuck."

"Yes." Mineko forced herself not to look away. The scandalous memory of Lexi kissing a woman the night before—that was her problem. That sort of thing definitely didn't happen on Mineko's side of the wall. "I'm sorry, but the person you thought you'd meet here isn't coming."

"That's okay. I wasn't really in the mood to take a job anyway." Lexi nodded at the opposite chair, and Mineko took a place at the table. "Edamame?"

Mineko blinked. "I'm sorry?"

Lexi pushed a small bowl across the counter. It contained a handful of green, fuzzy soybean pods. "Go on. I've stuffed myself already."

"I've never tried eating these before." Mineko took a pod and frowned at it. "It seemed too messy."

Lexi moved her fingers to her lips and mimed shelling a bean. "Like this. Pop it into your mouth and eat it. Don't toy with the poor thing."

"Um." Mineko fumbled with the pod, ejected a slippery occupant and crunched into its salty interior. "They don't taste how I expected."

Lexi grinned while stretching her legs further, giving the impression of a luxuriating cat in the sun—not a domestic cat, not with that smirk and those knowing eyes, but rather an alpha predator in her hunting grounds. "There's all kinds of new tastes to discover out here, believe me."

Had that been a veiled sexual innuendo? It seemed like there was an indecent suggestion in every movement Lexi made, each word she spoke. Mineko took a second edamame pod and gave it her full attention.

"I can tell I make you uncomfortable," said Lexi. "Want to talk about it?"

"I'm not uncomfortable." Mineko struggled with the stubborn pod. "I want to talk about the raid on your apartment."

Lexi rested her cheek on her palm, squishing it. "There's nothing much to say. You were right, and I'm sorry I blew you off. Now let's talk about why you're uncomfortable."

Perhaps it would be a relief to speak about it. "It's just... The Code is full of distortions, lies, and bigotries, but all the same, I was raised with it. I know that what I'm feeling right now isn't fair."

"I don't think you have the first idea what you're feeling." Despite the scathing sentiment, Lexi's tone was unexpectedly kind. "What's your Code say, exactly?"

"The first Codists, the Codifiers, idealized reproductive family units. 'Family is our first lesson in collectivism.' So the Code created many prescriptions around sexual activity. A woman kissing another woman, the way you were last night, that's something it strictly forbids."

Lexi pursed her lips. "Sounds like fancy prejudice to me."

"I know it's fancy prejudice. But my parents share it, and I learned so much from them..."

It sounded so cowardly. Mineko closed her eyes for a moment in order to settle her thoughts. To hell with the Code. She was going to think for herself. "I'm ignorant, Lexi. Educated in nothing but falsehood. Please excuse me for it. I intend to learn better."

Lexi twirled an edamame in her fingers as she gazed at Mineko. "You'll find bigots everywhere. Not so often someone who'll admit to being one. Who are you, exactly?"

"My father is the head of Code Security, Surveillance and Intelligence. Code Intel for short. My mother is a general in our military. I understood very early in my life that something was wrong with Codism, yet I've never had any way to protest, let alone fight back. But when my father began talking about Project Sky, I had no choice but to act."

"I don't know anything about it. Just that it's in my head."

"Your implant was intended as a tool for observation and punishment. The purpose of the Project was to create cyborgs who could pass through Codist society and discern who was truly loyal. But the ambition went further. Several high-ranking Codists harbored hopes that these cyborgs might also enter into

Foundation, re-educating the districts with perfect subtlety. Codism would spread like a popular movement."

Lexi arched an eyebrow. "Huh. So why make it an implant? Don't you guys have big nasty machines that can fuck with our brains?"

"I don't know the details. My father and his cronies aren't interested in the science. Just the practical applications." Mineko tried to shape her voice into something serious, even stern. "Lexi, they see you as the key to restarting Project Sky, which in their mind is the first step toward a unified Codist society. You possess the ability to share feelings, examine thoughts and erase minds, so you must recognize better than anyone what would happen if the Codists secured it for themselves."

"You're too serious for someone so young." Lexi sat upright, leaving her leisurely position by the window. "I don't really understand why you're here. What's in this for you?"

"The freedom to have my own views, even if I must always keep them hidden. And my own existence. Yes, they can Reintegrate me and take my doubts away. But then I won't be me." Mineko spoke the words with cold conviction. She had thought too many times about what it would mean to lie on that table, her head squeezed by clamps and her hands secured to her sides.

"Reintegration. That's where they wipe your memories, right?"

"Yes. And I'm sure there are others who secretly reject the Code. With my family connections, I may be the only one who can protect them."

Lexi nodded. If nothing else, Mineko had wiped the smirk from her face, leaving her handsome features solemn. "What do you need me to do?"

"They'll hunt down everyone involved in your implantation. Those people, you included, need to go into hiding."

"The guy who installed the aug." Lexi lowered her voice. "I guess they'll be looking for him too?"

"If they learn his identity, they'll be as eager to capture him as they are to capture you. We should warn him."

Silence. Mineko waited, her tension rising, while Lexi fixed the street outside with a brooding look. Finally, she exhaled a long sigh.

"Okay. His name's Zeke, and he's an interesting guy. You'll like him." She tilted the edamame bowl forward. "One for the road?"

CHAPTER 3

Lexi hadn't planned on seeing Zeke any time soon, not after his last stunt, but the kid was probably right. And cute, too. She stared like a bewildered tourist at the most mundane things: a dog chasing a boy on a bicycle, a woman asleep on the road, a store with a lurid window display of sex toys, two men loitering in an alley with switchblades in their hands...

"Careful." Lexi nudged her. "Not everyone likes being gawked at as much as I do."

Mineko bent her head and dropped her gaze, a chastened little pup. "Sorry. I just want see as much as I can before I go back."

"When we get to Zeke's, stare all you like. That's what they live for."

After twenty minutes of trudging through streets, fielding Mineko's countless questions—did Lexi know how to ride a bicycle? When did she learn? Were there many homeless people in the district? What was a *Hot Massage?* Did prostitutes object to being prostitutes? Why was that man vomiting?—Lexi stopped them outside an alleyway between a bar and a strip club. "Down there."

"I see." Mineko stared in the direction of Lexi's finger. "Do you know if he'll be there today?"

"He's always there. Come on."

The graffitied alley was just wide enough to allow Lexi and Mineko to walk it side-by-side. At its end, a neon-lit stairwell descended beneath a sign reading *Zeke's Lounge.*

"What sort of place is this?" said Mineko.

"You're just about to find out. Do you ever run out of questions?"

"Sorry. You must think I'm childish."

Lexi ruffled Mineko's hair. The kid didn't squirm away, but a hint of irritation broke through her grave expression. "Nah. You're fun."

"In truth, I do feel something of a child. I've been sheltered my entire life."

Lexi peeked into Mineko's eyes. Impenetrable. "You're handling this pretty well, then."

"Because of my parentage. I've been exposed to things other Codists aren't even aware of. I've seen forbidden material and I've heard restricted information. But there's still so much I don't know."

That was worth a grin. This sheltered kid was in for a shock and then some. "I can promise you've never seen anything like Zeke's crowd. But don't be intimidated. They're all show, and besides, I'm with you. Nobody messes with my girl."

"I'm not your girl."

Laughing, Lexi ruffled the kid's hair again and descended the stairs. Two parallel strips of electric red light guided them to the bottom, where a steel door was recessed into a cement wall.

Lexi pushed the buzzer, and a panel in the door shot open.

"Yeah?" said a voice like somebody gargling through a throat infection.

Lexi situated her face before the open panel. "It's me."

After a series of rattles, the door was pulled open by a hairy hand. One of Zeke's bouncers, an enormous mass of hair and muscle with teeth sharpened into needles, emerged and flashed a terrifying grin.

"Lexi. Haven't seen you for a long while." He peered at Mineko, who had taken a step back. "And you've brought me a snack."

"Keep your fangs to yourself, wolf-boy. I need to see your boss."

"Zeke's at work, but you can sit your butch ass in the waiting room." The bouncer withdrew, and Lexi and Mineko followed him into the lounge.

Illuminated by purple light, their modified bodies draped over couches and reclined against gritty cement walls, the modders were a showcase of human transformation: muscle freaks with spikes jutting from their bodies, naked tattoo addicts decorated from head to toe, and cyborgs with visible augs—steel scalps, metal hands, glowing eyes—sizing each other up. There was even a man with four eyes, all of them blinking out of time.

A scale-covered woman shot out a forked tongue as Lexi sauntered by, and she made a mental note to come back later and secure what could only be the world's freakiest oral sex. "How's Zeke anyway?" she said to the bouncer waddling ahead of them. "Still an asshole?"

"Oh, yeah." The bouncer gave a shark-like grin, and Mineko sidled closer to Lexi. "And he's missing you real bad. Always saying, 'Where's Lex? Why don't she do errands for me no more?' And I say to him, 'Zeke, honey, you're a fucking asshole. That's why.'"

Zeke's waiting room was small, sterile, and furnished by a single couch upholstered in decayed synthetic leather. In concession to human boredom, a television had been mounted on one of the walls. It played an old horror movie featuring lizard people chasing unwitting victims through caves. The lounge had been scarier.

Mineko perched on the couch while Lexi sprawled across what space was left. Even the way Mineko sat was suggestive of her personality—back rigid, knees together, hands folded. Taking up as little room as possible.

"I'm guessing you shut-ins don't do much body modding," said Lexi.

"Not like that." Mineko watched the scaled monsters flitting through the underground half-light. "'Individuation leads to social fragmentation.'"

"Catchy. But what about your haircut? Looks pretty individual to me."

Mineko brushed her bangs away from her face. "We're allowed a limited degree of self-expression. Codism admits that total visual conformity is a purely superficial form of collectivism. The stress of having no identity, none whatsoever, ultimately breaks people." She frowned as the lizardmen descended upon another helpless victim. "This is very gruesome."

"I think it's appropriate."

"I suppose the monsters are computer-generated. Do people still make movies out here?"

"Sure they do." Lexi winked. "I even acted in one once."

"Really?" Every time Mineko became intrigued by something, she perked up like a pet promised a treat. "What was the movie?"

"*Queer Girls Pool Party.* I played Girl Performing Cunnilingus. I'd hoped for a speaking part, but hey, at least I still got to use my mouth."

Mineko blushed and returned to staring at the lizard monsters. "Oh. Um. I see. You meant pornographic movies."

"I needed the money. They wanted me back for the sequel, but they refused to guarantee I wouldn't have to take it in the ass."

"What does that mean?"

Lexi laughed until her stomach hurt. "You are so cute."

"I'm not sure what was so funny about—"

The surgery door opened, and a man emerged with his upper arm wrapped in bandages. "You keep those on for a week or so," said a rapid voice behind him. "And drink plenty of water just in case. Like, ten liters a day. If you aren't pissing every five minutes, you aren't drinking enough."

The patient stumbled out into the lounge. A second later, Zeke walked into the waiting room, stopped short, and threw up his arms. "Holy shit, look who it is!"

Lexi slithered to her feet and stood with a hand on her hip, giving Zeke the scornful look he deserved. He didn't have an imposing build, a little shorter than Lexi and wiry rather than muscular, but the stubby, half-inch spikes embedded on his brow and over his bald head added a misleading touch of menace. He wore a surgical gown, and his arms were bared to reveal red, skull-headed dragons tattooed on both biceps.

"Haven't rusted yet?" said Lexi.

Zeke tapped one of the spikes over his left eye. "It's titanium, baby. You'll never guess what I just did to that guy."

"Won't I?" Lexi looked into Zeke's cool blue eyes. Pushing aside the emotions on the surface—confusion, genuine pleasure, a touch of apprehension—she reached the freshest memories, the ones still quivering from their recent imprint. Fiddling with surgical tools, making an incision here, rearranging tissue there…a row of slashes along a muscle, their edges moving like they were alive.

"Gills. You put gills in his arm." Lexi raised an eyebrow. "That's weird."

"Fuck!" Zeke covered his eyes with his hands. His long, jet-black nails seemed inappropriate for a surgeon, but then again, everything down here was a little inappropriate. "Don't pull that shit on me."

Did she laugh at Zeke's chagrin or keep being pissed off at him? Easy question. "I should have pulled that shit much earlier, you lying son of a bitch."

"It wasn't a lie. Just an omission." Zeke took off his gown. Underneath was a studded leather vest, which exposed the upper section of his chest and the complex tattoo adorning it. "They were painkillers, like I said."

She'd forgotten what it was like trying to squeeze honesty out of this little bullshit man. "Which you sold to street addicts. I don't deal hard drugs. You know that."

"Alcohol is a hard drug, and you deal that shit. Besides, everyone involved in that deal, from junkie to flunky, was happy. Except you." Zeke nodded at Mineko. "Who's the shut-in? University uniform, am I right?"

"I'm Mineko." Mineko's tranquil voice was a welcome change from Zeke's high-speed chatter. "You're correct, I'm a student. I've come to warn you that you're in danger. Are you aware of Project Sky?"

Zeke's expression remained blank.

"It's the aug," said Lexi. "My aug."

"Oh, the suicide chip." Zeke shrugged. "Okay, so?"

"It was a Codist invention," said Mineko. "But they never achieved a successful implant. Now they know about Lexi, they'll be determined to find out how you did it."

"This is a joke, right?" Zeke gave an uncertain chuckle. "Lex getting revenge for the painkillers?"

Lexi offered him her sweetest smile. "No joke. Time to kiss your brain goodbye, assuming you can find it."

"Huh. Excuse me while I go shit myself." Zeke sank into the couch and pressed his palm to his forehead. He hissed as he drew his hand away. "Ah! Fucking spikes!"

"I'm sorry," said Mineko, staring at her feet. "I know it's distressing."

"It ain't your fault, kid. But I wish I'd known earlier. I'd be hiding in a sewer pipe somewhere, drinking my own piss until this all blew over." Zeke sighed. "Stupid thing is, I don't even know how I did it. It just worked. I expected to have to wheel out a good-looking corpse. Instead, Lex opened her eyes, looked me in the face and said, 'You dirty motherfucker.'"

Despite herself, Lexi laughed, and even Mineko smiled. "We need to get off the street," Lexi said. "Just for a little. Is there anyone you trust?"

"Shit, I don't know. Anyone'd sell me out. My own mother would sell me out. I don't have friends. I have people who are just biding their time for a chance to kick me in the balls."

"Sure. I feel like I'm going to get my opportunity real soon."

"Yeah, well, maybe you'll forgive me now we're floating down a river of shit together. I did feel bad about the deal later. Missed seeing you around, too. You gave this place some class." Zeke glanced at the rampaging lizard people, and his frown returned. "What is this crap?"

"I think it's interesting," said Mineko. "We're forbidden to watch this kind of movie."

"No horror movies, no drugs, no sex. What do you all do for fun, sniff each other's assholes?" Zeke made a plaintive gesture. "Lex, you're the one with all the big friends. Pull some strings. Somebody you know must have a safe house."

"Maybe," said Lexi. "But it's hard to know who to trust. The Menagerie sold me out, and I thought we were close."

"Yeah, I heard the gossip. Bunch of try-hards anyway, all them animal names. Trying to be cool, picking all the toughest ones. The Jackal. The Tarantula." Zeke scrunched up his face in theatrical contempt. "Me, if I had to choose, I'd be the Alpaca. I saw a picture of one once. Woolly as all fuck."

"Zeke." Lexi raised her hand, and Zeke subsided. "Focus."

"Sure, sure." Zeke tapped along the spikes fixed to his brows, his usual thinking habit. "Hey, did you warn Callie?"

Shit. She'd forgotten about Callie. "Not yet."

"Who's Callie?" said Mineko, turning away from the movie.

"She's the one who sold me the thing," said Zeke. "Clever kid. Smuggler, mechanic, driver, a real all-rounder."

"How did she get hold of Project Sky?"

"She don't talk specifics. But over the years, she's supplied me with some serious black market shit. I didn't even ask for this, uh, Project Sky thing. She just rocks up with it in her hand, says 'Zeke, how rich are you today?' Turned out I was rich enough. And stupid enough."

"What did you do with my money, anyway?" said Lexi.

"Your cash picked up your bad habits. I blew it myself a few months later." Zeke took an electronic cigarette from his vest and touched it to his lips. The end of the cylinder glowed a pale blue. "Fucking shut-ins. I might as well douse my cock with kerosene and light a fucking match."

"You do that, and we'll go warn Callie. She still out west?"

"Oh, yeah. Same shitty little place. She's still pissed off at you, by the way." Zeke grinned at Mineko. "If you're gonna hang around Lex, you need to know she's like a roller coaster." With one hand, he mimed a roller coaster motion. "There's ups, there's downs, there's loop-the-loops. A real thrill ride. Some walk away grinning. Some walk away ready to puke."

"I don't know what a roller coaster is." Mineko didn't look at him as she spoke, captivated as she was by the movie. A lizardman pounced out of the shadows, fangs dripping, and she started. "Oh!"

"Quit watching that." Lexi prodded Mineko's shoulder. "It's bad for you."

"You guys go tell Callie the bad news, and I'll wait here," said Zeke. "In this nice safe bunker of freaks. Don't forget about me, okay?"

"We'll see." Lexi prodded Mineko a second time, and she finally followed, still casting backward looks at the television as they made their way into the lounge.

During their absence, the light had shifted to a vivid green. A few curious eyes turned Lexi's way, but most of the inhabitants ignored the arrivals in favor of admiring their own reflections in the lounge's many full-length mirrors. Lexi could relate.

Halfway across the room, Lexi paused. "Just a sec."

Ignoring Mineko's sound of alarm, she walked to where the scaled woman was reclining against a cement support. The woman looked up, and her lizard-like eyes narrowed.

"Hey, snake-girl," said Lexi.

"Hi, normal." The snake woman wore a white blouse and slacks, not exactly serpent attire, and it was hard to know how much of her body those scales really covered. Lexi hated to be left wondering. "You like my look?"

"Oh, I do." Lexi produced her seductive smile, the one that never failed, and the snake woman's expression became coy. "You know, I could heat that cold blood of yours."

The woman gave a nervous laugh, reddening beneath her scales. "I wouldn't think a vanilla like you would be into someone like me."

"I like my girls dangerous. Hiss your number for me, beautiful."

After a nervous glance left and right, the woman recited her number. Lexi took out her phone and added the digits to her enormous contact list of willing women. *Snake Girl*, she typed before saving the number. Hard to forget that.

"I have to slither along now," said Lexi. "But I'll be handling you soon enough. I'm impatient to feel those fangs."

She turned before the flustered woman could reply and rejoined the unhappy Mineko. "All done."

"What did you need from her?"

Lexi smirked. "I'll tell you when you're older."

―――――――――

Callie lived on the industrial fringe, far west of the University, and that meant a trip on the subway. The nearest station was only two streets away, and Mineko spent the short walk asking enthusiastic questions about body modding.

"Are tattoos permanent?"

"Yep. I have one myself."

Ahead, a ramp led into the underground station. The signpost above it read *METR*, the *O* long having parted ways.

"Really?" Mineko said. "Where is it?"

"That's a secret. If you want to see it, you'll have to get me naked first."

"Or find a copy of *Queer Girls Pool Party*."

It was a deadpan worthy of Lexi herself, and she laughed. "You're okay."

They descended into a fluorescent-lit, garbage-filled tunnel. Every surface had been tagged by gangs or decorated by graffiti artists, and as Mineko trudged along, she admired a vivid artwork on the ceiling. If she weren't more careful, the kid was bound to face-plant in something nasty.

"Never been in a subway, huh," said Lexi.

"We have a transit system of our own. It connects all the enclaves." Mineko marveled at her spray-painted surroundings. "But nobody's allowed to draw on the walls."

They arrived at the first subway platform. Wind hissed through the open tunnel, and droplets plinked from the ceiling onto the rails. A few people were waiting for the train, among them a leather clad trio—a lanky guy, a tall girl covered in scars, and a haggard, wild-haired woman. They loitered with the self-satisfied swagger of gangsters.

"Stay near me," said Lexi, and Mineko shuffled closer to her side.

The sound of her voice must have carried, as the haggard woman looked their way. "Hey!" she said. "Check out the queer!" She strutted toward them, and her companions trailed with less enthusiasm.

It took much more than this to intimidate Lexi. "Hi," she said. "Go ahead and admire me, but no touching."

"That's an ugly fucking haircut." The gangster's own straggly hair looked as if animals had died in it, but it probably wasn't wise to say so. "I don't even know what I'm looking at here. You a dyke or a faggot?"

"Are those my only choices?"

"Don't be a fucking smartass. You got a dick down there or not?"

Lexi summoned her most sultry smirk. "Treat me to dinner and maybe you'll find out."

"I told you not to be a smartass." The gangster sneered at Mineko. "And what about the shut-in? You this queer's little sex toy?"

Well, that escalated things. Lexi moved in front of Mineko. "Leave her out of this."

"The shut-in bitch should know better than to come outside. I suppose she wants to fuck you so bad, she can't help herself."

"C'mon, drop it," said the lanky gangster. "I just wanna go home."

"We're waiting for the train, aren't we? Plenty of time to mess with this…this whatever-the-fuck-it-is."

Lexi stared into the woman's glassy eyes. The contents of her mind poured over Lexi like oil, slippery and tacky. Emotions flaring and fading in seconds, thoughts arguing, a cracked temper reigning supreme. Lexi grasped a memory: waking in the dark, head throbbing, a moment of clarity. *I need to stop doing this shit.* Groping in the dark, wanting water. Touching a rat. Feeling its hair and gristly tail. Screaming. Rats. She hated rats.

Time to fuck this woman up. "You don't want to catch this train," Lexi said.

The gangster sneered, exposing damaged teeth, but confusion rose to join her anger. "What are you talking about?"

"Let me tell you about the last time I caught this train." As Lexi spoke, she kept a grip on that fragmented mind. "I sat at the back next to this real quiet guy. Halfway through the trip, I heard this sound like meat ripping. I looked across, and his chest was moving. All these lumps, pushing up his skin, moving in different directions."

She magnified the images that had emerged into the bitch's brain: naked tails, glittering eyes, the fear of being bitten, rabies, fat bodies swarming over her as she slept. "Then his chest burst open. He was dead, he'd been dead all that time, full of rats. They ran all over the train car, they ran all over everyone…"

"Bullshit," said the scarred member of the trio. Lexi's target, however, had taken a trembling step back.

"This whole subway is filled with the fuckers. You can't turn and not catch one watching you, can't put your hand out without something hissing and taking a bite." Lexi gave a final push, intensifying the woman's panic and disgust. "Someday you'll be waiting for a train, and the tunnel will flood with rats. They'll wash over you screeching and tearing—"

"We gotta get out of here! We gotta fucking go!" The gangster was hyperventilating, her rapid breaths accompanied by a wild twitching in her face. "We gotta go, we gotta go!"

With another shriek, she hurtled toward the entrance, followed by her shouting friends. None of the other waiting passengers had even looked up—why get involved, just another druggie, right?

Lexi gave Mineko an apologetic smile. The kid was still staring in the direction the gangsters had fled.

"You used Project Sky on her," Mineko said. "Why rats?"

"She had a fear of them, so I took it and made it worse. A lot worse."

A distant hum gained volume as a pair of lights illuminated the tunnel. The train hissed to a halt beside the platform, and Lexi and Mineko boarded the first car.

Most of the seats were rotted down to their frames, and the intact ones were covered in a mysterious residue. Fortunately, there were handles on the ceiling, only a few of which were repulsively sticky. The train accelerated, and Mineko shifted to avoid a rolling beer can.

"I guess your trains are nicer than this," said Lexi, swaying as the train took a rapid corner.

"Considerably." The windows rattled. "Does anyone maintain these?"

"Best not to wonder." The train gained speed, setting its windows shuddering even more violently. "If you're scared, you can hold my hand."

Mineko watched the white panels flickering hypnotically on the tunnel walls. "Thank you for offering."

Lexi smiled. What a funny kid.

Narrow chimneys topped by black plumes of smoke filled the skyline. Mineko wrinkled her nose. "Those can't be healthy."

"You think?" Lexi kicked a cardboard box rude enough to be in her path, and it landed in the middle of the street. The road markings had faded, making the potholed lanes indistinct, but it hardly mattered: the only vehicles that made any use of the western highway were the shut-in trucks sent to collect the bounty of the factories.

"Zeke said that Callie is angry with you. Do you mind if I ask why?"

Lexi sent a second piece of debris flying. It landed in a pothole. Let the kid think she'd done that on purpose. "Callie's just riled up over nothing."

"How long has she been riled for?"

"Uh…three years, I guess." Lexi shoved her hands into her pockets and picked up her pace. Easier not to think about that incident, at least not until she had no other choice. "She's a loner. A little strange."

They passed a construction yard busy with activity. In the shadow of an immense shed, sparks flashed from welding torches while workers carried steel beams toward a scaffold, constructing the skeleton of something as yet undeterminable. A group of people were sharing their lunch behind the fence. Several gaunt children sat with them, squabbling over scraps. Mineko gawked at them with obvious dismay.

Bad as it all looked, it smelled worse, and Lexi tried to breathe as little as she could. The shut-ins sometimes distributed medicines to the factory workers, but most of the drugs ended up on the black market. When that happened, gangs sold them right back to the sick workers who needed them. One of those social ironies and not a very funny one.

Callie's place was at the end of a ribbon of pavement that snaked around the edge of an abandoned factory lot. A junkyard behind a mesh fence neighbored the garage that doubled as Callie's home and workshop. Lexi strode across the cracked pavement—straggly weeds had pushed their way through it, not realizing the air up here was even worse—and toward the open garage door. Mineko trotted in expectant pursuit.

Inside, the garage was a mess of benches, tools, and scrap. The scent of rust and oil lingered in the air. Callie's van was parked amid the disarray, its white surface streaked with grime. Callie herself stood at a workbench, a tool in hand. She set it down and gave Lexi a mistrustful look.

In the intervening years, it seemed she had gained a little weight, but not enough to lose her athletic appearance. She had full hips and a curvy ass—captivating under a tiny pair of khaki shorts—but her waist was trim, and her arms and legs toned. Her black tank offered little coverage, and her tanned skin was streaked with grease. Another oily dab marked one of her round cheeks. Typical Callie.

"Lexi?" Callie brushed aside her auburn hair, which provided an untidy frame for her heart-shaped face. One look into her expressive eyes—her prettiest feature: lustrous brown irises accentuated by dark lashes—made clear nothing had been forgotten. "What are you doing here?"

"Sorry." Lexi resisted the urge to slink away. "I know you're probably not thrilled to see me."

"Understatement." Callie's attention shifted to a point behind Lexi's shoulder, and her lips parted in a shy smile. "Hey."

"Hello," said Mineko. "I'm sorry we interrupted your work."

"It's okay. I can work and talk at the same time." Callie took a wedge-shaped tool and set to prying at some stupid gadget. "Come in."

Lexi slouched into the garage—the last thing she needed right now was a guilt trip. Mineko strode past, staring at everything around her.

"What are you working on?" she said.

"An auto part I scrounged up. It's broken, but I'm hoping I can fix it."

"May I watch? I've never seen anyone fix an auto part."

Callie's smile widened, bringing out the dimples on her cheeks. "Sure." She levered the top of the gadget away, lifting a trailing set of wires with it. "It's a converter. It makes energy use more efficient."

"Does your van run on electricity, then?"

"Yup. I used to have a gas-powered one, but there's nothing left to fuel those but vapor." Callie pointed into the device. "You see this?"

Mineko leaned forward, fascinated. "Oh, it's melted."

"Right. Acid damage, maybe. I was hoping it'd just be a loose wire."

"Can you fix it? Or is it too melted?"

Callie laughed—not a sound Lexi had expected to hear today—and shook her head. "Any melted is too melted."

After several more seconds of close inspection, Mineko looked up, her face bright. "I've never seen anything like it. You must be very clever to work with this old technology."

An attractive shade of pink suffused Callie's face, and Lexi grinned. A few more appreciative remarks like that, and Mineko would have a friend for life. An insecure, clingy friend who played with scrap metal and never seemed to wash her hands.

"It's not so hard." Callie glanced at Mineko's uniform. "Are you a student?"

"Yes. My name's Mineko."

"I'm Callie, though I guess you already knew that." Callie gave Lexi an uncertain look. "I'm not going to lie, I'm kinda confused."

"The Codists are tracking down people connected to Lexi's implant. I'm afraid you may be in danger."

Callie put a hand on her hip, a cocky little adventuress. "That's okay. I'm used to danger."

"Not danger like this. Trust me. My father is the head of Code Intel."

Callie stared open-mouthed at Lexi, who nodded. "They raided my apartment last night," Lexi said. "It's serious."

"May I ask where you found it?" said Mineko. "The implant?"

"The shut-ins keep vaults in the desert," said Callie. "Whenever I stumble onto one, I break the electronic locks and take a look. A few years ago, I found a few chips in a box marked *Project Sky*. I'd heard old smugglers talking about it, so I knew what they were. Suicide chips."

"Do you know their purpose?"

"The story is they'll make you live forever if you can survive the implant. Which is probably bullshit, but people chance it. The thought of selling them made me sick to my guts. I considered leaving them there, but I needed the cash, so I took one, just one, and sold it to Zeke. I guess I should have left that one too."

"Focus on the present," said Lexi. "You're always stealing from the shut-ins. You must have experience getting them off your back."

Callie frowned at her grease-stained palms. "You and me need to sort something out first. Can we go outside?"

Lexi laughed. "Are you challenging me to a fight?"

"I'm serious. Mineko, we won't be long. You can look around if you like, but be careful. Some of this stuff is sharp."

Lexi followed Callie out of the garage and over a stretch of dry, hard dirt. Behind the junkyard fence, ungainly piles of scrap glittered under the midday light. Callie linked her fingers through the mesh and stared into the distance.

"So, did you bring me out here to show me your junk?" said Lexi.

"You know what this is about. You fucked up my life."

Lexi scoured her soul. Nope. Sympathy not found. "Yeah, well, fucking is what I'm best at."

Callie slumped against the fence. "You aren't even a bit sorry, are you?"

"I don't give a shit. I tried, okay? I looked deep within my soul for shits, but there were none. No shits to give." Lexi sighed. "You take everything too personally. It wasn't as if I went after her. She came to me."

"Don't remind me."

God, this melodramatic fucking kid. "You're the one who seems to want to talk about it."

Clouds drifted above, slow and tinged with pollution. In the distance, a dog bayed. Lexi waited. They'd never really been good friends, and while that was mostly Lexi's fault—Callie was the emotional type, and Lexi kept those at a distance—it made her easier to shut out now.

Callie gazed at the sky. "Mineko seems really nice."

"Sure. She's a good kid."

"Don't call her a kid. It's patronizing. If she's at the University, it means she's at least nineteen."

"Right. A kid. Like you." Lexi laughed as Callie grew even more sullen. Still too easy to tease. "Don't take it personally. I was a kid once too."

"You're only thirty, for fuck's sake." Callie gnawed at her thumbnail while frowning at the clouds. "I guess we could drive to one of the old bunkers out west. Take a bit of tinned food, stay under for a little while. You and Zeke will be bouncing off the walls after an hour, but it beats getting wiped, doesn't it?"

Buried underground with two ex-friends, eating century-old food from a tin and creeping out into the desert to take a piss? Why, it sounded like paradise. "Let's call that Plan B and keep thinking up a Plan A."

"If you say so. Do you think Mineko's going to get into trouble for this?"

Lexi shrugged. "She doesn't seem to care much about that. It's been fun dragging her around. She looks at everything like it's just fallen from the sky."

"You have any idea why she's helping us?"

"Says she doesn't believe their bullshit anymore. Thinks she's fucked if they get this chip working and they use it on her."

"Makes sense." Callie pushed back from the fence. "Let's go. I don't want her to step on something and get tetanus."

They found Mineko contemplating a rack of tools. "What's caught your eye?" said Callie. Too cool to care, Lexi lounged against a workbench.

"This old baton." Mineko tapped a long steel stick. "Is it for self-defense?"

"I use it to break windows, that's all. I pack something a little more serious for protection." Callie retrieved an ugly single-barreled shotgun from under a workbench. "And there's a pistol in the glovebox."

"Oh." Mineko took a nervous step back.

Lexi snickered—the kid looked like a frightened animal—but Callie gave a sympathetic smile. "Don't worry, I won't point it anywhere near you." She returned the shotgun to its hiding place. "Would you like a drink? You must have walked a while to get here."

"Sure," said Lexi. "I'll have a rum and—"

"Not you." Callie opened a bar fridge and searched through its glowing interior. "What do you like, Mineko? Carbonated juice? This one says raspberry, so it's probably water, red dye, and a bunch of chemicals." She showed the bottle to Mineko. "You might recognize the brand. I nabbed a crate from a shut-in truck."

"Yes! I love this!" Mineko popped the lid. "Would you like the first taste?"

"Sure." Callie sipped the drink before handing it back to Mineko. "Fizzy."

Mineko beamed. It was surprisingly touching to see that serious face so transformed. "And you have a whole crate of these?"

"Sure do. Drink until you pop."

Mineko took a sip while Callie watched her with a thoughtful smile. "May I ask how long you've been a smuggler?" Mineko said.

"Since I was thirteen. Eleven years. How long you been a student?"

"Three years. I'm twenty-two." Mineko passed the bottle to Callie, who swigged from it. "Do you really not want to give Lexi a drink?"

"Don't worry about me," said Lexi. "I came out here specifically to die of thirst."

Incredibly, Callie laughed. "Okay. If she helps me pack the van, I'll let her have a drink."

Mineko nodded. "I'm glad. By the way, what's this here?" She indicated a jumble of little widgets scattered on a bench. "I couldn't figure it out."

"Oh, that's an old pocket watch. I took it apart to see how it worked."

"Will it tell time again if you put it back together?"

Enthusiasm lit Callie's round face. "If I do it right. Want to see? It should only take a few minutes."

"Uh," said Lexi. "Do we really have time for this? No pun intended."

Mineko shot her a reproachful look. "She did say it would only take a few minutes. I'd like to see the watch."

"And you will!" Callie took a pair of tweezers from the workbench. "Now, this bit here is the main plate…"

As the kids huddled together, Lexi stared out at the wasteland of cement, steel, and stacks. It was no surprise Callie was weird: living out here with nobody for company but hungry dogs, sleeping to the distant rumble of machinery, waking to an oppressive horizon always vomiting smoke.

Three years. It was a long time to hold a grudge, maybe, but Lexi was in no position to talk. She watched the chimneys, her gaze unfocusing, until she could scarcely distinguish between the smog and the sky.

CHAPTER 4

Mineko admired the watch ticking in her palm. Each cog had been tiny, an intricate little marvel, and it was thrilling to imagine them working behind the face. She clicked the cover shut and traced its embossed design. A hunter-case watch, Callie had called it. She'd even shown Mineko how to wind it with a tiny key.

With much thumping and grumbling, Lexi and Callie packed the van full of crates and boxes. Lexi moved with her usual languor, while Callie bounded about the garage with enthusiasm, only ever pausing to shift the artless tangle of reddish-brown hair from her eyes.

"What's this one?" Lexi hefted a yellow plastic crate. "It's way lighter than it looks."

"Tubes of nutrient-rich paste. You know, peanut butter and stuff."

"Sounds like a romantic dinner." Lexi tossed the crate into the van. "Are we done yet?"

"Pretty much!" Callie clapped her hands. "Let's go. In the back, Lexi."

Lexi stuck out a sulky lip. "The back? Why do I get the back?"

"Because I said so." Callie nodded to Mineko. "You get the passenger seat. Jump in."

The passenger seat! Why was that so exciting? But first—

Mineko held out the watch. "Where should I leave this?"

Callie curled Mineko's fingers shut. "You keep it."

Mineko's delight competed with her politeness, and politeness won. "No, I couldn't."

"You helped me fix it. Please take it."

It seemed wrong, a gift to a wealthy person from someone who had little. Yet Mineko loved the watch. It was a relic of another world, a piece of this wonderful workshop. "Thank you. And call me Min, if you like."

Callie dimpled. "And you can keep calling me Callie."

"Cute," said Lexi. "Meanwhile, Zeke is being dragged away, weeping and wondering why we never came back for him."

Mineko clambered into the passenger seat. The van's front cabin was worn but still comfortable, providing plenty of room to stretch her legs, and the dashboard looked pristine. A mesh partition separated the cabin from a rear cargo area with a single seat. Lexi's smirk seemed to occupy the entire space.

Callie hopped into her seat and slammed the door shut behind her. She snatched a flat-topped cap from the dashboard, grinned at Mineko from under its brim, and started the ignition. With a quiet growl, the engine awoke and settled into a low vibration.

"Have you been driven often?" Callie said.

"No, never. I only use our transit system."

"You're in for a treat." Callie drove the van out of the garage and braked just outside. She tapped a button on the dashboard, and the garage door clattered down. "Remember to buckle up."

After studying the unfamiliar seatbelt mechanism, Mineko took the obvious approach and pushed the thin bit into the open bit. A satisfying snap suggested she'd done well. "How long will it take to drive back?"

"We need to detour to avoid the main road, so about half an hour."

The van rolled onto the blasted asphalt and gained speed. Empty lots flew by, punctuated by broken buildings. A flicker of excitement moved in Mineko's chest. This was definitely something new.

"Check in the glovebox," said Callie. "There's some sweets in there."

Mineko opened the glovebox. There was the gun Callie had alluded to, a terrifying gray pistol with a black grip. Being careful not to touch it, she fished out a plastic bag filled with colored jelly balls. "You mean these?"

"Yep, those. Put them between us and we'll share. And, of course, we need some music."

Callie prodded a button, and a monstrous tune ripped through the speakers and pulsed at their feet. It was like no music Mineko had ever heard, an energetic interplay of massive percussion and fuzzy rhythm. An androgynous voice screeched through the nightmare.

Lexi sighed. "I'd forgotten about your shitty taste."

"And I'd forgotten I need to drown you out." Callie turned a dial, and the music amplified. As if spurred on by the clamor, the van rocketed, swerved around a pothole and screamed toward the remote cityscape. Mineko gripped the fabric of her uniform. So this was how she was going to die.

"Don't look so worried. I know what I'm doing." Callie twirled the wheel, and the van spun into a side-road. Impossibly, it began to pick up even more speed as it cruised toward a horizon of jagged mountains, dusty desert, and clear, pale sky. "Try one of the sweets, it'll calm you down."

Mineko took a vibrant yellow sweet. It was sugar-dusted and chewy, and the moment she swallowed it, an immediate craving for another followed.

The music gained in pace and fury, and Callie tapped her wheel to the hammering rhythm. A chorus erupted as the van skidded around another corner, and she joined in:

"There's a long night coming with a knife in its hand
And a cold dawn rising to bring life to the damned..."

Lexi groaned from the back. "Come on, Roux."

"Sorry." Callie glanced at Mineko. "I usually drive alone, so..."

"Don't stop," said Mineko. "I like hearing you sing."

Callie blushed, and Mineko's excitement surged. That blush suggested Callie might be shy, and that meant they had something in common.

The van sped on, filled with furious sound. The distant city—a fractured line of towers beneath clouded blue, edged by abandoned suburbia—crept closer. Mineko reached for the sweets. Her hand bumped against Callie's.

"You're going to eat them all." Callie swatted Mineko's wrist. "I think you've already finished all the yellow ones."

"I can't help it. They're addictive."

"Well, if you have to pick up a habit while you're out here, yellow gummy addiction is probably the safest." Callie popped a green cube into her mouth. "You know, I could go faster."

"Let's not," said Lexi, her voice tense.

"It's an open road, and it's in good shape. Min, what do you think?"

Mineko smiled. "Let's go faster."

The speedometer needle, already wavering near its rightmost point, jumped several notches. The road blurred as wind howled by the windows, audible even through the music. Everything about their sole ownership of this once-great road was both frightening and intoxicating, and an overwhelming sense of liberation took hold of Mineko. For the first time in her life, it felt as if she were free.

The chorus returned, and on an impulse, Mineko joined in: "There's a long night coming..."

Callie gave her a delighted look. "Hey, you've got it!"

To hide her embarrassment, Mineko stuffed another sweet into her mouth and watched Foundation hurtling toward them. Her parents were somewhere beyond those splintered towers, unaware that their daughter was zooming across the desert, immersed in forbidden music.

A slow smile moved on Mineko's lips. She had never been more certain that the Code was a lie, yet in that moment she couldn't have been happier.

Driving through the University District proved a different experience altogether. Callie was forced to creep the van forward, often having to stop for pedestrians who stared into the windows as they passed. Some seemed curious, others resentful, and many wore little expression at all.

"Now I remember why I never come here." Callie frowned at a woman shuffling across the street. "It's like they're trying to slow me down."

"You need to learn to share the road," said the sarcastic presence in the back of the van. "How you doing up there, Minnie?"

"I'm okay." Mineko hunched in her seat as a pedestrian glared directly at her. "I shouldn't have eaten so many sweets, though. My stomach hurts."

An opening appeared in the crowd, and Callie directed the van toward it. "So what's the story with these parents of yours?"

Hopefully Mineko could be honest without alienating her new friend. "My father is Head of Code Intel and is on the Committee. My mother is a general in the Codist military. She's in charge of enclave defense."

Callie honked at a drunk man spinning in circles on the road. He shambled off, the ragged hems of his trousers trailing behind him. "So they're important people. No wonder you're clued in."

They drove down a familiar street—Mineko recognized a movie theatre by its damaged marquee, which scrolled nothing but gibberish—and through an empty intersection.

"My parents trust me," Mineko said. "It's painful to have to betray them. But what they're doing is wrong. Sometimes I suspect they know it too."

"Well, I think you're doing a noble thing. And in this city, that makes you pretty special."

Mineko lowered her head, trying to conceal her smile. "What about your parents?"

"My mom was a drug dealer and my dad some guy who sprung on her in an alley. She's dead, and I hope he is too." Callie raised a hand as Mineko opened her mouth. "No need for sympathy, okay? On this side of your wall, you'll hear plenty more stories like it."

The van zipped by the subway station, sending rubbish scattering, only to brake to a sudden halt. A crowd of people had filled the street outside Zeke's lounge. A sleek black car was parked nearby. Mineko's breath caught. "That's one of ours."

"Seems your guys like black," said Lexi. "That's okay. I like black too."

Callie inched the van closer to the mob. It proved to be a mixture of curious onlookers and the inhabitants of Zeke's lounge, whose adorned bodies added a touch of color to the gathering.

"Can we get him out of there?" said Callie. "Or is it too late?"

"Like hell we're going in," said Lexi. "You think he'd risk his skin for us?"

Mineko's stomach twisted. "You can't leave him."

"No, what we can't do is help him. Leaving him is easy."

There was a sharp rap on the passenger-side window, and Mineko gasped. Kade stood on the street, his knuckles still resting against the glass and his expression serious. He'd swapped the stolen uniform for a high-collared, knee-length brown trench coat.

Callie rolled down the window, and an excited hum of human conversation poured in. "Afternoon, Callie," said Kade. "Let me guess, Lexi's your cargo."

"Well done," said Lexi dryly. "You get full marks and my permission to fuck off."

Callie glared at her. "Shut up. Kade, what's going on?"

"Three agents entered about ten minutes ago. I suppose Zeke tried to barricade himself in, but they'll get him out eventually."

"You can't let them take him," said Mineko. "They'll torture him."

"We can't do anything about that now. You and Lexi need to get away from here."

An excited whispering rose from the crowd. Two agents in black uniforms, a man and a woman, emerged from the alley with a struggling Zeke between them. A third agent walked ahead, waving his baton to disperse the crowd. No firearms were visible: presumably they hadn't been issued with them, given it was crucial they took Lexi alive.

"Go." Kade stepped back. "Drive, Callie."

How could Mineko make them see? The torment, the brutality, the whimpers Zeke would cough up amid sprays of gore…and it didn't have to happen, not if they showed courage. They outnumbered the agents, who were only flesh and blood. Didn't they realize these people were only human beneath their uniforms?

Mineko undid her seatbelt, opened the glovebox and grabbed the pistol. Lexi sat bolt upright. "Min, don't you dare—"

Mineko jumped out of the van and ran through the scattering crowd, clutching the lethal object in her right hand. The trio of agents stopped, and she pointed the pistol at their leading member.

"Ms. Tamura!" The agent's dour face twitched. "What are you…where did you get…"

"Let him go." The way Mineko's hand was shaking, there was no way to predict who she might shoot if she pulled the trigger. Yet even if they did surrender, she could hardly let them go. They'd seen her now, and of course they'd recognized her instantly. What agent wouldn't?

"Hey, kid!" Still wriggling in the grip of the agents holding him, Zeke gave her a frightened grin. "Turns out you weren't joking."

"Be quiet." An agent twisted Zeke's arm, and he yelped. "Ms. Tamura, put that weapon down and explain yourself."

The air seemed to have suddenly grown thin—either that, or Mineko's lungs had forgotten how to function. Her hands trembled, and her palms had become so slick it seemed possible the gun might soon slip from her grasp. She tried to reply, but without oxygen, no words were possible.

"She's going to hurt herself," said the female agent. "We'll subdue her and bring her back with us."

The lead agent winced. "You really want to be responsible for that?"

"Better than the alternative, isn't it?" The agent glared at Mineko. "Last chance, Ms. Tamura."

A tremendous blast rang out in answer. Callie Roux stood on the sidewalk, her shotgun pointed at the sky. She opened the barrel, rammed another shell in and snapped the gun shut. "Get the hell away from her."

The crowd of spectators surged in panic, cutting Callie from view. Mineko was jostled from her feet by a colliding elbow, and the gun flew from her grip. She flailed at the open space beneath her. Cement struck her palms. Pain shot up her arms.

Taking advantage of the confusion, Zeke broke free and ran. The lead agent whirled, baton raised, only for Lexi to step from the crowd and block his path.

"Hey, shut-in," she said. The agent lunged, and Lexi danced away with her usual lazy grace. "Better get up, Minnie."

Panic and pain almost stopped Mineko's breath, but she found a reserve of strength. "Lexi, they know me…"

Lexi winked. "I'll take care of it."

Two of the agents closed in with their batons, jabbing and striking. Even against two opponents, Lexi effortlessly weaved away from every strike, though her uncanny agility seemed to have its limits. Each time she tried to close in for an attack of her own, an incoming blow forced her to jump back.

The remaining agent took a tentative step toward the fight, hesitated, and stepped back again. "I'm going to look for the prisoner. Be careful subduing Vale, you don't want to damage her impla——"

Kade dashed across the pavement, his trench coat streaming behind him, and tackled the agent to the ground. The man grunted as his body met the cement, and he and Kade fell to violent wrestling.

In the same moment, Callie aimed her shotgun at the female agent. The woman froze, her attention darting between Lexi and the barrel pointed at her chest.

Faced with only a single adversary, Lexi pressed her assault. She slipped under a wild thrust and caught the agent's head in both hands. His face went slack, his irises dulled and he slithered to the ground.

"Min, get out of here," said Callie. "Run to the van."

Good advice, but moving was impossible. Mineko could only stare, take in the scene, follow every motion. She was pinned in place. Her legs, her hands, even her voice——none of it responded to her will.

A soft hand took her own and squeezed it. Too numb to be startled, she looked up. Zeke.

"I got you." He ushered her away from the fight, putting an arm around her waist once it became clear her own feet had failed.

Behind them, Callie held the female agent at gunpoint while Lexi placed a hand upon the woman's head. With her crown of white hair and haughty stance, Lexi looked like some high priestess offering a blessing. When a second later the agent crumpled to the ground, it became clear her gift had been nothing so divine.

"She's blasting their brains." Zeke spoke in an excited babble. "So they don't remember us. It's the scariest shit she can do."

He guided Mineko to the back of the van, aided her inside and seated her on the chair. "You okay? You look a little out of it."

"I'm not sure." Mineko stared at her bloodied palms. "I hurt myself."

"Let's see what Callie's got here." Zeke detached a box from the van's inner wall, undid its latch and peered inside. "Paracetamol might help. Put this in your mouth and let it dissolve, okay?"

Zeke pressed a small orange pill into her hand. Mineko attempted a thankful smile before placing it on her tongue.

"Kid, I don't know what to say." Zeke's face wrinkled up as he smiled. "Ten minutes ago, I'd never have believed a single person on this planet would stand up for my ass."

The front doors opened, and Lexi and Callie jumped into the cabin. A moment later, Kade climbed into the back of the van. He pulled the doors shut and set the bolt. "We want to move quickly. When those three don't call in, their bosses will sit up and take notice."

"On it," said Callie. Mineko's stomach lurched as the van performed a sharp U-turn. It soon became clear why Lexi had resented being put in the back— everything shuddered with the van's noisy motion.

Callie glanced back. "You okay, Min?"

"I'm okay. But the agents will tell my father."

"They won't." Lexi sounded uncharacteristically grim. "Those poor bastards have less brain function than Zeke right now."

"You wiped them? Project Sky can do that?"

Lexi peered at her fingernails. "Yeah." She looked up at Kade, and her eyes narrowed. "What the hell are you doing here, anyway? Don't you think I have enough shit to deal with?"

"It don't matter, Lex, come on," said Zeke. "We gotta get somewhere safe, figure out what to do."

"I know what to do," Kade said. "Callie, take us to the Open Hand shelter in Urban District Four."

"What's Open Hand?" Every time the van shifted, Mineko's stomach lurched with it. "Why will they help us?"

"They're do-gooders," said Lexi. "Charitable types. Weirdos."

A thud sounded beneath them, and the van bounced. "Rock," said Callie. "Sorry."

Kade grimaced and steadied himself. "Open Hand is organized and sympathetic. They'll shelter you while we figure out what to do next. And you can finally clue me in on what's happening here."

There was no way Mineko could risk going somewhere as remote and forbidden as Urban District Four. Much as it hurt to acknowledge it, her adventure was over. "Callie, can you let me off near the University?"

The van jerked to a sudden halt, and Callie twisted in her seat. "You aren't coming with us?"

For all that this hurt, Mineko managed to keep her voice level. "It's time for me to go home. I've done all I can on the outside."

"You serious?" Zeke clutched her sleeve. "Your folks will wipe you."

"I'm sorry to say it, but she's right," said Kade. "Every Codist agency would hunt for her if she left. Lexi's got enough heat as it is."

"So? Nobody says they have to hide together." Callie thumped Lexi on the shoulder. "Lexi, for Christ's sake, say something. Tell her to stay."

Lexi gave Mineko a thoughtful look. "You sure about this, Minnie?"

"I don't have any choice. The enclaves are my home."

"I'm not doing it," said Callie, her voice tight with fury. "I'm not driving you there. You'll be safer with us. We'll look after you."

"She already made up her mind," said Lexi. "Take her back."

"They'll fucking wipe her!"

Mineko met Callie's stricken gaze. "I have to take the risk. I'm grateful for your support, but I'm sorry. This is as far as I go."

Callie bowed her head, took a breath and set the van in motion again. "If you change your mind, say so."

The journey resumed in silence. Callie brooded over the wheel, Zeke rocked on his heels, Kade seemed lost in thought, and Lexi slouched against the passenger window with her cheek cupped in her hand. Mineko shut her eyes and focused on the subtle motions of the vehicle. Humming, turning, shaking…

The van gave a final jolt before settling.

"We're just a street away," said Callie in a monotone. "So I guess this is it."

"Thank you." Mineko rose and waited for Kade to open the van doors. Outside was a narrow lane, unoccupied. The high wall of the University was visible at its end.

They assembled in the street, except for Kade. He remained standing inside the van's open rear doors, his expression inscrutable.

"Take care." Zeke patted Mineko on the back. "You did good."

"Yeah, she did." Callie gazed at Mineko, a hint of moisture in her eyes, before looking away. "Shit, Min."

"I'm sorry." It felt as if there were a hand around Mineko's throat and a boot on her rib cage. "Thank you for helping me."

"Is there any chance we'll see each other again?"

"I wish we could. But I can't see how it's possible."

"Well, just in case..." Callie took the tiny key from her pocket. "Keep it wound, okay?"

"Careful with that," said Lexi as the key exchanged hands. "It's the key to her heart."

Her round cheeks crimson, Callie scowled at Lexi. "Shut up."

Mineko contemplated each face in turn. Zeke appeared miserable, his glittering eyebrows scrunched together. Lexi had regained her ironic smile. Kade still betrayed no emotion. And Callie—she was looking at Mineko with such intensity, such palpable regret, that the pressure on Mineko's throat and chest became unbearable.

"Maintain a level head in there," Kade said. "If suspicion falls on you, keep denying. In a society like yours, truth is subordinate to power. You have powerful parents and that makes you powerful too. Never forget it."

"What he said." Lexi rested a hand on Mineko's shoulder. Her smile eased into something more affectionate than teasing, and an unexpected warmth flooded Mineko's face and chest. "I owe you, Minnie-Min. See you around."

Every second she lingered would only make it more painful. "Goodbye." Mineko turned and hurried down the sidewalk. No point looking back. It would only intensify the storm of dismay and apprehension building inside her.

Today's crimes were considerable. She had assaulted her father's agents, handled a firearm, spent a day out of boundaries and revealed confidential information. There was only one possible outcome if she were caught. Though her parents loved her, the Code was clear. And unmerciful.

CHAPTER 5

Lexi ranked Urban District Four as one of the most depressing districts in the city, a neighborhood of ruined residential blocks, towers reduced to defiant steel bones and hollowed-out warehouses fronting silent streets. Not a single decent nightclub anywhere to be found.

Amid the district's copious graffiti appeared a recurring symbol, an open palm sprayed in vivid purple, which always came accompanied by an arrow. Directions to the Open Hand soup kitchen.

Callie stopped the van. The street ahead was blocked by people waiting outside a large warehouse. A steady procession shuffled into an open door and exited by another, the ones escaping looking less miserable than the others. Most of the crowd wore little more than street grime, but quite a few were well-dressed. Misfortune spared nobody, and even the richest could find themselves ruined overnight. It was simply too easy to lose it all.

"Well, here we are," said Callie. "What now?"

"I'll call them." Kade prodded his phone. "Hey. It's Kade. Yes, I've heard already. I have Lexi Vale with me and some other friends. We're in a van out on the street… Yes, I know the one. We'll be there in a minute." He returned the phone to his pocket. "There's a garage around the back of the warehouse. They're waiting to let us in."

Callie turned the van, and they cruised into a narrow alley that cut behind the warehouse. They drove until they reached a garage door rattling upward.

Callie directed the van through the door and down the ramp, and they plunged into a large, well-lit underground garage. "Check out the wheels," said Callie, perking up. "Looks like heaven."

Lexi had never seen so many intact vehicles in once place: trucks, vans, jeeps, even a trio of jet-black motorcycles, their sleek carapaces gleaming beneath the overhead lamps. A staircase in one corner ascended to the first floor of the warehouse—assuming, of course, that the building obeyed the usual laws of time and space.

As Lexi undid her seatbelt, two people marched into the garage. A man and a woman. They wore black leather trench coats buttoned to the collar, complementing their military bearing.

"Be nice to those two," said Kade with wry self-awareness. "They're my friends."

"Thanks for the warning," Lexi said, no less droll. "I'll try not to hold it against them."

The group exited the van. "Good afternoon, comrades," the man said. A mop of ginger hair flourished on his gaunt, freckled head, and his lips formed a skewed grin. "You must be Alexis Vale."

Now there was a name that didn't see a lot of mileage. "It's Lexi. Nobody calls me Alexis."

"But I rather like the name Alexis. It has a regality to it, don't you think?" The man looked her up and down, and his smile widened. "Let me say two words to you: Project Sky."

Pompous bastard. "Here's two more for you: so what?"

"I'm correct though, aren't I? That's your augmentation."

"Before you start prying, why not introduce yourself? You don't look like you're here to give me soup and a blanket."

"Rest assured, we're caretakers of the poor. But charity comes from a heart of indignation. I'm Nikolas, and this is Bunker One. Above, the poor are fed and treated. Below, plans are made to fight for their futures."

Lexi shifted her attention to the woman, a stern blonde with a high forehead, downturned lips, tanned skin, severe blue-green eyes and, in complete contrast with her other features, an adorable button nose. "Who's your friend?"

"My name's Amity." Amity spoke with clipped impatience. "I'm second-in-command here. I hope you appreciate that secrecy is important to us."

"So I won't be allowed to invite girls over?"

"Be quiet for once," said Callie. "This is serious."

"Ah!" Nikolas directed his enormous grin toward Callie. "Calandre Roux, the smuggling prodigy. A pleasure to make your acquaintance. And you…" he pointed at Zeke "…are unknown to me. What's your profession, sir?"

"Uh." Zeke shifted from foot to foot. "I'm a surgeon."

"He's a body modder and tattooist," said Kade. "Surgeon is pushing it."

"Hey, I do more than mods, jackoff. I do some pretty fucking delicate work. I mean, I put that aug right in Lexi's brain." Zeke tapped his skull for emphasis, though Lexi was yet to be convinced an actual brain was inside. "That's brain surgery, motherfucker. You think you can just walk into any tattoo parlor and get that shit done?"

Nikolas chuckled. "Well, I'm convinced. A doctor you are, and your surgical talents will certainly be useful. We'll protect you from the Codists, and in return, you may use your talents to treat the sick. What do you say?"

"Not much of a choice." Zeke scratched behind one of his piercing-laden ears. "Yeah, sure. Heal the sick. I'll be a regular angel of mercy, just watch."

"Very good." Nikolas rubbed his long, knobbly hands—strangler's hands. Of course, Lexi was too enlightened to judge someone just for having big, creepy strangler's hands. "Alexis, you are in grave danger. You must allow us to provide you refuge."

A little too pushy for Lexi's tastes. "Must? Don't I have a say in this?"

"Why would you say no?" said Amity, her eyes narrowing. "You're just a common drug dealer. There's nothing you can do against the Codists."

"I'm not a drug dealer. I'm a broker. Totally different things. Who told you I was a dealer?" Lexi adopted an exaggeratedly outraged stance, both hands on her hips. "Was it Kade? I bet it was Kade. I'll kick his ass—"

"I apologize," said Nikolas. "My lieutenant has a habit for bluntness, even when her facts are not yet in order." Amity's scowl deepened. "And the inestimable Ms. Roux, would you accept our assistance as well?"

Callie gave him a suspicious look. "What's the cost?"

"Your presence alone enriches us, be assured. Are you three hungry?"

"Uh, yeah." Lexi touched her empty stomach. "Now that you mention it."

"Allow us to feed you, then. The kitchens are upstairs—you can't miss them. Kade, if you don't mind, we'd appreciate you stay behind so that we might share information."

"Yeah, yeah," said Zeke. "Revolutionary business, sure, don't want people like us getting in the way. C'mon, guys."

After a short journey across the garage floor, Lexi, Callie, and Zeke reached the stairs and began climbing. The stairwell contained multiple landings, allowing the steps to wrap around all four walls of the shaft. On the third landing, Zeke stopped and peeked over his shoulder.

"I gotta say, those people weirded me the hell out. Did you read anything from them, Lex? You know, with your magic."

"I didn't try," said Lexi. "That guy talks too much, though. And the woman looked like she wanted to eat my spleen, shit it out, and bury it."

Zeke rapidly bobbed his goofy little head. "Yeah, that military attitude. Like kids playing soldiers. I don't want to be caught up in some suicide pact shit."

"Calm down," said Callie. "If Kade trusts them, they can't be too bad. It's Min we should be worrying about."

Zeke nodded. "You think she'll be okay?"

"I don't know. I hope so. Lexi, did you see her expression when she walked into my garage?"

"Sure," said Lexi. "I imagine it's the way I look when I walk into a bar full of horny women."

"Everyone thinks I'm weird for collecting old things. Like that hunter-case watch. It was sealed up in a bunker along with some ammo, tinned food, the stuff people pay for." Callie gave a wistful smile. "But for that watch, even though it was the most beautiful thing I'd seen in weeks, nobody would offer more than a couple of bucks. Nobody looked at it the way I did. I'll never forget how her eyes lit up when she saw it working."

"She loved that fucking monster movie, I'll tell you that," said Zeke. "Jumped right out of her skin."

Cute stories. Kinda touching. But not a subject that Lexi cared to dwell upon. "She was a sweetheart, but we can't do anything about it. Let's go eat our slop."

Lexi pushed the double doors open with both hands, never one to do things by halves, and a wave of heat met her. The kitchen was stuffed with industrial cooking equipment, the source of the warmth. A group of Open Hand lackeys stirred and seasoned immense pots of soup that were ladled into bowls then passed through windows into waiting hands beyond. Animated conversation, bubbling food, ventilation fans, and the chattering of the hungry queue combined to make an overwhelming din.

Callie nudged Lexi. "Check her out."

Lexi checked. Standing over one of the pots, churning the soup with a long metal spoon, was a thin, olive-complexioned woman sporting a strawberry-pink Mohawk. Numerous gold sleepers and studs decorated her face, and her tight black jeans and crop top accentuated her narrow frame while showing off her stomach. Very intriguing.

"Wait here," said Lexi. "I'm going to get you two some soup."

"You don't want any?" said Zeke.

Lexi grinned. "I'm going straight for dessert."

She sauntered toward the woman, who remained focused on her work, so far oblivious to the queer divinity coming her way. She was maybe an inch shorter than Lexi, and her facial features mixed strength with delicacy—sensual lips and high cheekbones, a defined jaw and an aquiline nose. Despite her height and squared shoulders, her skinny build, slender neck and shaved scalp gave her an air of fragility.

"Hi there." Lexi stood with a hand on her hip and lowered her lashes to complement what she intended to be a sultry smile. "I'm Lexi."

The woman lifted her eyes—a melancholy blue-gray. "Pleased to meet you." Her voice was husky, melodious. "I'm Riva Latour."

As she gazed into Riva's eyes, Lexi found something reaching back. So Riva was one of those. Every now and then, Lexi met someone who was easily read, an emotional bleeder. Riva's mind felt like gossamer, beautiful but vulnerable, streaked through with doubt, resolve, pride, loneliness...

"Are you okay?" Riva rested her spoon against the pot. "You have the oddest look on your face."

Lexi blinked as the stolen impressions faded. It was as if she'd just immersed her mind in a pool of warm water. "Sorry. I was distracted by your eyes. They're the most beautiful I've ever seen."

Riva gave a quiet, nervous laugh—the uncertain sound of someone who suspected a joke at their expense. "If you're hungry, you only have to ask. There's no need to charm me first."

"I can't turn the charm off. It just happens."

"In that case, I no longer feel special. May I ask why you're here?"

"I'm a fugitive cyborg." Lexi laughed as Riva's expression became incredulous. "No, really. I'm a dangerous and wanted individual."

"And your friends?" Riva glanced at Callie and Zeke, who still loitered in the doorway. "Are they fugitive cyborgs as well?"

"Just boring regular fugitives. Would you mind if we have some bowls of, uh... stuff?"

Riva ladled a cream-colored liquid into three metal bowls. "This is a cauliflower soup with added soy protein. We play around with seasoning to improve the taste, but it's warm and filling, and that's what matters."

Lexi peered into a steaming bowl. "Looks hot. But I can handle it."

"I'm sure you can." Their eyes met again, and Riva's subtle smile confirmed what Lexi already knew. All that Lexi had to do now was give this girl her opportunity.

"Do you have a break coming up?" Lexi said. "Maybe you can join us."

The smile faded. "Sorry. It doesn't stir itself."

Lexi waited a moment longer, but it appeared Riva wasn't shifting. Lexi placed the bowls on a tray, added some spoons, and headed to a small table in the corner.

Zeke and Callie seated themselves as Lexi laid out the feast. "Enjoy," she said. "It's cauliflowers."

"You mean cauliflower." Callie puffed on a spoonful before tasting it. "It's not bad. Better than the stolen military rations I live on."

Lexi tried the soup. It really wasn't bad at all——warm, just as Riva had promised, with a thick texture and a hint of savory flavor beneath its rich saltiness.

"So, did you get the girl?" said Zeke.

"Not yet." Lexi licked her lips. "If I'd known a babe like her was working for Open Hand, I'd have been queuing here every day."

Callie took a slurp from her soup—no manners, that kid. "Do you ever think about anything but sex?"

"Nope. You got me. I'm just a drooling libido."

"I'm serious, though. Is it even possible for you to talk about a woman without being sleazy about it?"

"Sure. I talk about you in non-sleazy ways all the time. Mostly to warn people that you're a serious pain in the ass."

"I used to think you were so cool. That way you act like you're doing the world a favor just by being in it. But it's getting old, Lexi. Maybe it's time to grow up a little."

It was hard to decide whether this was pathetic or amusing. "You're the one wasting your life pining for your bitch of an ex-girlfriend. I mean, what's the deal there? Are you really so insecure you don't think you can land anyone else?"

Indignation simmered to the surface of Callie's thoughts. "Go to hell."

"I'm already there. You, Zeke, and Kade. It's like a race to see which of you will be first to make me fall into a pit of existential despair. You've taken the lead, by the way."

"Jesus, Lex," said Zeke. "Go easy on her."

"Shut up and eat your soup." Lexi took an angry sip of her own. Fucking Callie Roux, carrying her heartbreak like a trophy. Even that goddamn streak of grease on her cheek was beginning to piss Lexi off.

She swept her bowl aside. "I'm going for a walk."

"A walk?" Zeke raised his spiked brows. "We don't even know where we're allowed to go."

"'Allowed?' Grow a spine."

Lexi pushed through the kitchen doors and set off down the corridor at a leisurely pace. She turned aimlessly at each intersection, moving deeper into the featureless halls. They were tight passages of industrial cement lit by recessed overhead lights, and before long she had lost any sense of direction.

After some time wandering, she found a white door. From behind came the sound of low murmuring, electronic beeping and someone groaning. A sadistic torture chamber? Only one way to find out.

She walked into what seemed a treatment room of some kind, filled with rows of beds accompanied by medical equipment. Several of the beds were occupied by blanketed patients, most unmoving but a few stirring and twitching. A pair of nurses attended to them.

One of the nurses, a man with a surgical mask pulled low to reveal his puzzled face, looked up as Lexi entered. "Are you meant to be here?"

"Probably not. These people are here by choice, right?"

The nurse shot her a disapproving frown. "Of course they are."

An immense patient strapped to his bed gave a desperate grunt, and the bed rocked as he shook the restraints. His eyes were glassy, and saliva flecked his lips. He groaned and tossed the bed again. The second nurse hurried to his side and put a hand on his shoulder.

"Why is he tied up?" said Lexi. "Here by choice, you said."

"The restraints are for his protection. He's suffering from addiction to a popular street drug, and we're giving him a course of treatments that will prevent these episodes from occurring."

"That's nice. And who pays?"

"Society, if we do nothing," said Riva from the doorway. She entered with a tray of food and began to place bowls at the bedsides.

Lexi leaned on a medical monitor as she watched Riva at work. A regular angel of mercy. Usually Lexi was cynical about that sort of thing, but she could make an exception here. "So, do you feel like playing doctor with me?"

"Very funny. Nikolas and Amity wouldn't be happy with you wandering around like this. Amity especially."

"I'll keep that in mind. Wandering around is more fun when I know people disapprove."

One of the nurses coughed, and Riva took Lexi by the arm. "Let's talk outside."

Lexi allowed herself to be steered out the door, and she and Riva faced each other beneath the heated glow of the hallway lights. A septic scent lingered in the air, one Lexi hadn't noticed before, mingled with the fading aroma of soup.

"Do you want to talk about it?" said Riva. "Whatever's troubling you."

Damn it. So much for Lexi's carefully managed nonchalance. "Shit." Lexi brushed her hair back with her fingers, a gesture hopefully sexy enough to be face-saving. "I guess I'm not coming off as cool as I mean to be."

"You just seem a little tense."

"I've had a rough day, that's all. The shut-ins raided my apartment, and then I had to hurt some people."

Riva took a step back. "You hurt people?"

If only Riva knew. There was nothing worse than wiping a mind, probing through its discordant haze and excising it in a frantic instant. Each memory dissolved into white light. Obliterated. "I didn't have a choice. I wasn't happy about it."

"As a pacifist, I understand how you feel."

Well, that was adorable. "Are your friends downstairs pacifists too?"

A hint of injury flashed into Riva's eyes. "I can tell you're cynical. But Nikolas and Amity do genuinely care about the people of Foundation. They're the very last hope for many."

"I don't trust them. But I think I trust you."

Riva's shy smile returned. "Were you joking about being a cyborg?"

"No joke. I have an aug that's never worked in anyone else. Now the shut-ins want to put me under a microscope to find out why I'm different."

"That's horrific." Riva radiated warm, gentle sympathy. "I hope you'll be safe with us."

The sound of footsteps marked the arrival of that son of a bitch Kade. He strolled down the hall, looking rumpled but purposeful in his weathered trench coat. "Lexi. Nikolas wants you back downstairs."

"I'll leave you to it," said Riva. "Take care." She gave Kade a nervous look and hurried away, the tray clutched to her chest.

"Hey." Lexi glared into Kade's grim, unapologetic face. "You asshole, you scared her away."

"I'm sure she'll come back," said the asshole. "You don't really have time to flirt right now, anyway."

"What's with those two downstairs? They act like they're part of some whackjob paramilitary outfit. I mean, 'Bunker One'?"

"Open Hand take themselves seriously, and so they should. The issues they face here are real."

Lexi tried to penetrate his dark eyes, but Kade was impervious to quick scrutiny. "How much do they know about me?"

"It's your call how much you divulge. If you're skeptical about their motives, read them."

Kade turned to leave, and Lexi followed without enthusiasm. Fucking revolutionaries. All they did was get people killed, even those who never wanted to be involved in the first place. Misguided martyrs stockpiling guns and waiting for some suicidal day of judgment.

But that wasn't her problem. Her problem was Kade and the memories he brought with him—memories of tarnished steel tracks, sunsets like blood suffusing a flame, two shadows stretched alongside her own. Days of love and regret. Days she didn't want to remember. Couldn't afford to even if she did.

———

Amity had called it the 'strategy room', a pretty grand title for what proved to be an old storage area. Even the cabinets fixed to the walls were marked as containing cleaning supplies. A flimsy table—no doubt they called it the strategy table—stood in the center of the cramped space.

Nikolas and Amity sat side by side, their serious faces illuminated by the soft light of the room's single bulb. Amity boasted perfect posture, while Nikolas slouched with his fingers pressed together, looking like a tousle-haired villain.

Glancing into his pale green eyes, Lexi discerned nothing more than a hint of caution. Amity's eyes betrayed nothing.

The four visitors arranged themselves around the table. Zeke seemed bored, Callie sulky, Kade guarded.

Nikolas gave them a crooked smile. "Much as I would love you all to stay with us indefinitely, I'm afraid you do pose something of a risk."

"So I won't get to live in this bunker forever?" said Zeke. "I'm heartbroken."

"Right now, this much is clear." Nikolas separated his hands in an expansive gesture. "The Codists will eventually reach you here. Staying isn't an option even if I could allow it."

"So we'll go south," said Callie. "If we make it to Port Venn, we're golden."

"That's what Amity and I were thinking. Though I don't approve entirely of the regime there, it will at least provide protection from the Codists."

"Uh." Zeke raised his hand. "Isn't that just going from one bad thing to another? I mean, it's just a different bunch of crazies in charge."

Nikolas nodded. "I'll grant it's a dangerous city, but there are no true refuges in the world."

Lexi set her feet on the table, to Amity's obvious displeasure. "Maybe I don't want to go to Port Venn. I'm a nobody there. Foundation is where my reputation is."

"I appreciate the inconvenience, but what else do you propose? You live, as I understand it, a very conspicuous lifestyle. You can hardly expect to continue it and not be captured."

"I'd have thought you'd like it there," Callie said. "Plenty of rich people for you to take advantage of."

"And what about you?" said Lexi. "You ready to abandon your little garage, all that precious junk of yours?"

"Well, it's not forever, is it? Just until the trail grows cold."

This freaking kid. This wasn't about her, so why did she keep pushing in with her opinion? "Easy for you. It's not your brain they're looking for."

"On which note, tell us about Project Sky," said Amity. "The legend is that it provides immortality. Which is absurd. What does it really do?"

"Sorcery." Lexi wiggled her fingers beside her head. "I can read minds."

"I don't have time for your foolishness. What is Project Sky?"

"She's not kidding," said Zeke. "I know it's some wild shit, but it's true."

Nikolas glanced at Kade, who nodded. Nikolas's shaggy ginger eyebrows shot upward. "Can you read our thoughts right now?"

"It depends on the person," said Lexi. "From this distance, I probably couldn't get much from either of you. But if I got close enough, sure, I could read your thoughts."

"And if they had more cyborgs like you at their disposal…" Nikolas frowned. "Yes, I see it now. But what I don't understand is how you knew they were coming for you."

"None of your business," said Callie. "And if you're smart, you won't ask that question again."

"Callie, it's okay." Kade put a hand on Callie's shoulder. "We can't tell you their identity, but we have an insider. A sympathetic person with access to high-security Codist channels."

"You can't identify them?" said Amity. "Not even to us?"

"You know I won't name a source, Amity. Not even to you. And I won't tell the *Gazette* either, not when exposing the truth would put people's lives at risk. If the Codists achieve their aim here, we'll lose the refuge even of our minds, and we'll be trained to love our servitude."

Lexi gave a theatrical yawn. "Scary stuff."

"We can talk about this later," said Callie. "Right now, we have to do something to help our insider. They're completely cut off. Can you help me get in touch with them?"

"That depends on many things," said Nikolas. "Allude a little."

"They're inside an enclave. A big one. It's risky for them to leave."

"I see. In that case, they would be exposed very rapidly if they attempted to use the cellular network." Nikolas raised a finger. "However, we do have an encrypted radio channel. Depending on which enclave your friend is in, they may be able to communicate on it."

Amity drew in a sharp breath. "You can't just give one of our radio phones to an unknown Codist. Are you mad?"

Nikolas pursed his lips. "Kade, do you vouch for this person?"

"I do," said Kade.

"It's not a matter of faith," Amity said. "It's a matter of risk."

"I apologize," said Nikolas. "It seems my second and I will need to have a discussion first. I'll be certain to have a response for you tomorrow. For now,

I suggest you relax for the remainder of the evening. We have films in our recreational room."

"You got snacks?" said Lexi. "I can't really enjoy a film without snacks."

Amity gave her an incredulous look. "What is wrong with you?"

If Lexi kept pushing, was it possible Amity would murder her right here and now? "Hey, I just like snacks. Don't you? Or did someone you love choke to death on a piece of popcorn?"

Nikolas leapt to his feet, almost upending the table, and grasped the seething Amity by the shoulder. "Meeting adjourned, I think."

CHAPTER 6

A row of white-blossomed trees lined the path to the elite dormitory. Mineko inhaled their delicate scent as she walked under the pale boughs.

Students loitered on the path, engaged in nervous discussion. Exam talk. Mineko could sympathize, though in truth, she didn't have to worry. A word from her parents and Student Administration would find that a processing error had lowered her grade average. It had happened before.

After passing through the dormitory's sliding glass doors, Mineko crossed the marble tiles of the lobby and entered the stairwell. She paused on the first landing to glare at the immense oil painting hanging there. It depicted an ancient dean clutching a book and offering a bemused, placid smile to the viewer. As a First Codist, he wore no uniform; the Second Code had introduced the hated jumpsuits.

Mineko hurried to the door of her room and swiped her keycard. A low buzzing note played, and the lock clicked open. She took in her lonely refuge—the narrow bed with its rumpled sheets, the tree outside the window, the desk at which she spent evenings staring through branches toward the stars—and her chest began to ache again.

What a cruel taste of freedom that had been.

Would she ever see them again? She would have liked to talk more to Kade, who had seemed so clever. Despite his profane prattle, Zeke had been nice too. He'd given her a painkiller. Lexi had been intimidating but exciting as well. And then there was Callie.

Mineko took the watch from her pocket and flipped it open. Twenty past four. The second hand performed a full circuit, coaxing the minute hand to creep onward, and her ache intensified. She'd always wanted a friend to join in her private jokes and observations, someone to keep her company and share her secrets. In other circumstances, maybe Callie could have been that friend.

As if to taunt her, footsteps pounded down the corridor, accompanied by the sound of laughter. Even if another student did share Mineko's doubts, they too would hide them, meekly growing into their future roles, concealing their anxieties and crying in private. The way she was crying now. Wanting for comfort, helpless without it...

She closed her eyes and held the watch tight. For a minute she listened to its gentle ticking, letting that sound occupy the entirety of her thoughts.

But no—she couldn't sulk like this. She might be able to help the others.

She retrieved her study tablet and tapped its screen, awakening it. After navigating to her message bank, she typed a quick message to Kaori: *Missing you both. May I come for dinner tonight?* Her index finger sent the message on its way, and she flopped back to the bed.

Missing you both.

It hadn't even been a lie. At home, she didn't have to hide her disdain from her lecturers, didn't have to endure all this solitude, didn't have to wonder—in moments so bleak she seemed tiny and still, like something unborn—whether she'd ever sleep beside the warmth of another body. At home, she could watch confiscated movies with her father. She could sit in front of the fireplace and fall asleep, warm and drowsy, while her parents talked freely about matters she was forbidden to know.

She could feel loved.

The tablet chirped. Kaori was always quick to reply; she never seemed to be far from her phone. Mineko tapped the message open.

That would be lovely! Your father is in a foul mood today, but if anyone can cheer him up, it's you. We're serving at half past six. Would you like to stay the night?

Mineko prodded out a response: *I'll be there in about thirty minutes. Not sure if I can stay.* There was no chance she'd stay. It was simpler to wake here, in this solitary emptiness, and pretend that nothing else existed.

———————————

The Codist underground loop connected each enclave and avoided Foundation's district transport system entirely, ensuring that no Codist would ever have to witness the reality of the world's decay. Each train featured gleaming steel exteriors, plush interiors, and cabins containing no more than four seats. The lighting was steady, the cushions luxurious. Graffiti was unimaginable.

Mineko took an empty cabin, as was her preference. Comfortably settled on soft upholstery, she focused on the humming sound of the train in motion. No matter how hard she tried to blank her thoughts, Callie's music still repeated itself in her head. The rhythm she recalled clearly, but the lyrics were vague. Had it been a cold night coming? Or a long night?

A calm, genderless voice murmured overhead. "Ten minutes until arrival at Urban Enclave One."

She needed to stop thinking about Callie. And Lexi. The memory of that languid, white-haired libertine was far too dangerous. The way she'd kissed that girl at the nightclub...

Mineko had been taught that such things were wrong, but it hadn't looked wrong to her eyes. Quite the opposite. And—mortifyingly—Lexi had read her thoughts and seen her guilty fascination.

"Now arriving at Urban Enclave One."

Mineko exited the train, followed the platform, and waited on the escalator as it rose toward a square of gray light above. The dark steps terminated, and she stepped into the open air.

Urban Enclave One was a natural park and a residential haven. The industrious First Codists had shifted immense mounds of dirt to form small hills and valleys, the sides of which were decorated with colorful foliage. Trees lined paths winding through grassy terrain, their branches brandishing translucent leaves, and a melody of running water and lively birdsong played through the air.

Little wonder Kade held the Codists in such contempt.

Mineko turned to the path leading home, and her heart beat harder. Kaori was sitting on a bench, smiling in Mineko's direction.

"How long have you been waiting here, Mother?"

"Not too long." Kaori left the bench and met Mineko halfway down the path. "And I wish you wouldn't call me 'mother.'"

"It's important to show respect to one's parents. They're the foundation of the family unit."

Kaori laughed and squeezed Mineko's shoulder. "They're teaching you too well over there."

Mineko was unable to hide her pleasure any longer, and Kaori smiled back, her eyes warming. "There you are," she said. "I knew my daughter was hiding somewhere inside that sulky young woman."

They looked alike, or so people said. In reality, Kaori was several inches taller, graceful, and far more beautiful—at least in Mineko's estimation. Her navy overall was embellished with gleaming awards and insignia, and her black hair was cropped short, adding to her look of impishness. Her lips never seemed far from a smile. It was hard to believe she had killed people.

"We really need to talk about this haircut of yours." Kaori brushed Mineko's bangs aside. "Are you trying to disguise how pretty you are? I'm still waiting for you to bring a young man to meet us."

Not this again. "You'll be waiting a long time. I don't want somebody getting in the way of my career."

"Your career in Neuroethics." Kaori raised an eyebrow. "We need to talk about that too."

"It's an interesting field."

"But it's so theoretical. You're a practical person, just like your parents. Are you so sure you wouldn't serve the Code better elsewhere?"

Mineko scrunched her nose, and Kaori chuckled. "Never mind. I'll berate you over dinner. Come on, let's walk."

They followed the path through the shade of a high bank. Branches above filtered the early evening light, dappling the stone trail with bright streaks and gentle shadows. The clamor of ducks rose from Mineko's left, and as she strolled, she admired the birds gliding across the water.

"Remember when you used to feed them?" said Kaori.

"I remember. A big one nearly took my fingers."

Kaori began to hum a simple tune, a few bars repeated, and Mineko fought against her rising sense of happiness. It wasn't right to find solace in this false paradise, and though her parents weren't monsters, they were still responsible for atrocities. She couldn't let herself forget that, even if she did love the sight of her mother humming in the evening light, her face lifted to the sky.

"You said Dad wasn't in a good mood," Mineko said. "What happened?"

"Oh, it's work-related." The smile left Kaori's lips. "Some of his operatives were assaulted in the city today. Naturally, he's upset."

"Assaulted?" Mineko's stomach wriggled. "That sounds serious."

"It's very serious, but don't let his mood bring you down, too. You're here to cheer him up, remember."

The path reached a moderate incline, and Mineko focused on pushing her way up it. Kaori, the show-off, marched upward without any visible effort. At the crest, Mineko drew in a welcome lungful of air.

The family mansion sat atop the next hill. It was among the largest structures in the enclave, and the high fence around it emphasized their family's status while lending a touch of the paranoid. A walled house within a walled neighborhood— what were they trying to keep out, ducks?

"It's our anniversary coming up," said Kaori as they traversed the path curving toward the front gate. "Twenty years."

"Are you planning to celebrate?"

It was a silly question—of course they were. Her parents seemed to enjoy the ideal relationship: harmonious, respectful, and genuine. It made them especially obnoxious when discussing any subject related to romance.

"We'll be having a party," said Kaori. "You'll have to come. You can bring some friends."

"I don't have any friends to invite."

"Still? Well, don't worry. It's only a matter of time."

They paused inside the front hall to remove their boots. Mineko crouched to unlace hers, while Kaori stood one-legged as she unbuckled her left.

"How is work?" said Mineko.

"Stressful. I spend most of my day shouting at people, and then I come home completely hoarse. Everyone seems to have lost their heads lately."

"Should I worry about you?"

Kaori smiled as she tugged off her other boot. "Not just yet."

They continued down the hall, their feet silent on the carpet, and into the wide foyer connecting the two wings of the mansion. An impressive staircase ascended to the second floor.

"Is anyone else going to be at dinner?" Mineko said.

"Yes, I think so." Kaori placed a foot on the first step and beckoned. "He's in the study. Let's go distract him."

They thumped up the stairs and arrived at the solid wooden door of her father's study. The door was ajar, and Kaori nudged it open further. "Dearest, I've brought you a visitor."

A familiar groan issued from inside. "Not another one."

"Don't worry. This is our favorite visitor."

Kaori took Mineko by the shoulders and pushed her inside. Gaspar was sitting behind his desk, his back to a window overlooking the reddening sky. The weariness cleared from his face, and he leapt to his feet.

"Min!" Gaspar grabbed her hands. "What a surprise! Are you here for dinner? To stay?"

As Mineko tried to free herself from his enthusiastic grip, a deep relief stole over her, tinged with guilt. So neither of them knew about her misbehavior. "I'm here for dinner."

"Well, that's wonderful, but won't you stay? Your room is all made up."

Mineko returned his smile without enthusiasm. He was tall, fair-skinned and gangly, and his gaunt face inspired terror in his subordinates. For Mineko and Kaori, however, he only ever demonstrated indulgent affection. His famous temper was reserved for spectacular dressing-downs of house staff and security personnel.

"I can't," said Mineko, managing finally to rescue her hands. "If I do, I'll miss my morning classes."

Gaspar's smile broadened. "And nothing could be more fatal to your education than missing a lecture on Social Ethics. What have you learned lately? What's on these exams of yours?"

"My last class was on Social Cohesion. We're learning what holds a society together."

"I'll tell you what holds it together," said Kaori. "Steamy sex, that's what."

Mineko's parents were shockingly irreverent when it came to the Code, despite both of them being tasked with its enforcement and preservation. Mineko had learned much of her cynicism from them, just as she had discovered there were limits. Levity was acceptable, but not open disapproval.

Gaspar winked at Kaori. "Marriage is the bedrock, isn't it?"

"The bedrock for a good bedroom." Kaori fluttered her lashes, and Gaspar laughed. They were disgusting, both of them. "I was just asking Mineko when she was going to bring us back a young man."

"Let's talk about dinner instead," said Mineko. "What will we be having?"

"Imitation squid. And a chocolate cake for dessert, served with brandy. I think it'll start around six."

"Yes, around then." Gaspar glanced at his watch. "Which is only thirty minutes away. In the meantime, you'll have to entertain us with stories, Mineko." He sat on the corner of his desk—his long legs touched the ground even seated—and gave her an expectant look. "Have you made any friends yet?"

Mineko fidgeted beneath her parents' combined attention. "Not yet."

"That's such a pity. Is there a reason?"

"People get nervous when they find out who my father is."

Gaspar winced. "I suppose they would. Well, it's their loss, isn't it? Perhaps you should try taking up a hobby. The University has art classes…"

A tall shadow cut across the carpet. Agent Lachlan Reed loomed in the doorway, his posture deferential but his mouth fixed in an insolent half-smile. He had a wide face with full lips, pallid skin, and large brown eyes that glittered with sarcasm. His dark hair was slicked back to accentuate his widow's peak. To Mineko's disbelief, she'd once overheard the maids whispering about his handsomeness.

"Good evening, ma'am." Lachlan nodded to Kaori. "And you too, Mineko. Do you have a minute, sir?"

"Damn you, Reed. Can't you see I'm enjoying a moment with my daughter?"

"I can see it, sir." Lachlan ran a hand back across his scalp, a habitual gesture that surely left him with a disgustingly greasy palm. "Should we postpone our discussion of recent matters?"

"Hardly. It does Mineko good to see how our business is conducted."

"I'm quite conscious of that. I was more concerned that a woman of her intelligence would be bored by our tedious affairs."

"Spare me your drollness." Gaspar growled as he pressed his fingers to his temples. "Look, dinner's not far away. Go down and wait in the parlor, have somebody pour you a drink. Is Dr. Wren here yet?"

"Admiring your front garden, sir."

"Make sure she has a drink too. Is she allergic to anything, do you know?"

"Well, there's nothing listed on her file. Are you implying I ought to inquire personally?"

"Don't be cheeky, Agent Reed." Gaspar's lips twitched, and the humor returned to his eyes. "Yes, ask her. The last thing I need is to kill the poor woman with mock squid and brandy."

"Of course." Lachlan retreated, pulling the door shut behind him. Good riddance.

Gaspar released another long sigh. "Sorry, sorry." He gave Mineko a distracted look. "Business. Now, let's talk about your grades…"

The dining room was modest—at least, relative to the size of the mansion—and every seat but one had been filled. Mineko sat beside Kaori, Gaspar took the head, and their two guests were seated opposite.

The first guest was Lachlan, looking wolfish as always at the prospect of a fancy Tamura meal. Beside him sat a skinny, pale woman wearing a neat black bob, a white scientist's coverall, and a look of acute terror.

"Introductions are in order," said Gaspar. "Dr. Wren, this is my wife, Kaori, and my daughter, Mineko. Wife and daughter, this is Dr. Valerie Wren. She's working for me now."

Kaori laughed. "Thank you, husband. Dr. Wren, it's a pleasure."

"Valerie is fine." Valerie seemed incapable of holding eye contact for more than a few seconds. "Thank you. It's a pleasure."

"Hello," said Mineko, not wanting to be left out, and Valerie gave her a nervous smile. "What are you a doctor of?"

"I'm a neuroscientist. Your father has just assigned me to a new project. It's very…" Valerie swallowed. "Very exciting."

Servants emerged to deliver food on platters, and Gaspar rubbed his hands as his meal was placed before him. "Feast away. Don't hold back. There's always more."

An aromatic plate of pale chunks immersed in dark sauce settled before Mineko. She stabbed a piece of imitation squid and placed the salty, chewy morsel in her mouth. Washing it down with a sip of red wine, she earned a puzzled look from Valerie. Alcohol was forbidden to students, but her parents delighted in flouting the little laws.

Gaspar nodded at Lachlan. "Now's your chance to talk my ear off."

"Yes, sir." Lachlan returned an untouched piece of squid to his plate. "After questioning bystanders, we've identified four of the five assailants."

Mineko stopped chewing.

"I have photos on file for three." Lachlan propped a tablet in front of him. It displayed an image of Lexi standing in a shadowed room, her handsome face inclined away from the photographer. She wore a high-collared black jacket and thick eyeliner, which contrasted with her pale face and white hair to give her a spectral appearance.

Mineko took another sip of wine. Hopefully the alcohol flush would conceal her blushing.

Kaori spoke first. "Quite a distinctive person. Is it a woman?"

"People seem to think so. Her name is Alexis Vale. Or Lexi, as she prefers. A notorious character in the districts. She has close ties to the top gangs, enough so that some of their leaders were very reluctant to provide us with information. But they all cooperated eventually."

"Have a good look, Dr. Wren," said Gaspar. "This is your prize specimen right here."

"How remarkable," said Valerie in a distracted murmur.

Kaori reached for her wine. "And should we feel sorry for her?"

"That depends on your view, ma'am," said Lachlan. "She works as a 'broker'— someone who facilitates deals between gangs. Selling drugs, ending wars, and cementing alliances, that sort of thing."

"I'm sure the implant helped her build that career," said Gaspar. "Not quite what your predecessor had in mind for his invention, Dr. Wren."

Valerie glanced up from the food she was prodding. "I'm sure."

Her predecessor? Mineko looked at Valerie with new interest. Then this was the head of Project Sky, and, in theory, Mineko's greatest enemy. Though it was hard to be afraid of a timid woman struggling with a piece of imitation squid.

"So what do you have on her?" said Gaspar. "How substantial is the file?"

"I'm adding to it every day, sir," said Lachlan. "In addition to talking to the gangs, I've learned a great deal from the many women she's had intimate relations with. She left more than a few of them bearing grudges."

"She's a homosexual?" Kaori scowled. "Then we certainly shouldn't feel sorry for her."

Lachlan gave a cold smile. "It's a different world out there, ma'am."

He took a quick bite of squid, dabbed his lips, and swiped the screen again. This time, the image was of Kade. He was stepping from a doorway, his eyes narrowed in the direction of the photographer. A sympathetic impulse jabbed at Mineko's chest. Did Kade know that he was being followed? How much danger was he really in?

"I know this one very well," said Lachlan. "Kade August. He writes for the *Revolutionary People's Gazette*."

"If you know him very well, why is he on the loose?" said Kaori.

"Because I'm a dedicated subscriber. His work is very entertaining. After all, why silence the mouthpiece of dissent when we can learn from it instead?"

"Your usual Machiavellian nonsense. If it were my decision, I'd round up all these people in a single night."

"And on we go." Lachlan tapped the screen and summoned a covert shot of Zeke drinking at a bar, his spiked head shining beneath red-tinted light. Despite the ambience of the shot, nothing could make that odd little face seem menacing. "This is Zeke Lukas. Surgeon, body artist, club owner."

"Ouch!" Kaori laughed. "Do you think he did that to himself?"

"Quite possibly." Lachlan turned the screen toward Valerie. "Believe it or not, Dr. Wren, this odd individual achieved what a team of Codist scientists was unable to do."

"I see." Valerie didn't meet his gaze, instead jabbing at another squid chunk. "How embarrassing for us."

Lachlan chuckled before setting his tablet aside. "The fourth was an experienced smuggler, Calandre Roux. She's better known as Callie. I don't have an image of her on file, and we're not certain why she was involved. However, she's a known supplier for Lukas, and I believe she and Kade are acquainted."

Cold remorse snaked its fingers around Mineko's insides. So they hadn't even known about Callie. It was Mineko who had dragged her into this nightmare, destroying the quiet, constructive life Callie had built for herself on the edge of civilization. Mineko filled her glass — water this time — with a shaking hand. What had she done?

"A smuggler," said Kaori. "The less of those around, the better. They seem to think anything we leave in the open belongs to them."

"Some compassion might be warranted. Roux was orphaned young and entered her shadowy trade at the mere age of thirteen. She's twenty-four now. Five foot six, average build, reddish-brown hair, brown eyes, and a fair but tanned complexion. She owns a white van, which was noted at the scene. I have operatives out looking for it."

"And you mentioned something about a fifth?" said Gaspar.

Mineko's terror became complete. She sat still, clutching her glass but powerless to lift it. How could the onlookers not have remembered her?

"There was a confused statement about someone in a dark overall. But there was panic immediately afterward, what with the gunfire, and nobody could give a clear account of who this individual may have been."

Mineko downed her water with a grateful gulp. Impossible as it seemed, she remained safe.

"Interesting, interesting." Gaspar looked toward Valerie, who gave him a terrified smile. "You had the chance to observe the victims, I believe."

"Yes, yes. They had definitely been...well, wiped." Valerie's left hand moved in a fluttering, agitated motion. "To varying degrees, but all of them will require substantial re-education. It's the most frightening thing I can imagine, the technology being deployed as a weapon—"

"So it's Project Sky," said Lachlan.

"Yes. Project Sky. It succeeded, but…not under our watch."

Lachlan smirked. "Well, it's your watch now."

"I…I, yes. Yes." Valerie lowered her wretched gaze. "Yes, it is."

Kaori glared at Lachlan before leaning over the table. "Tell me, Valerie, how do you like your meal?"

"Oh, it's very…" Valerie's nervous smile expanded into a frightened rictus. "It's very nice. Have you ever, uh, have you ever had real squid?"

"Once, but I don't remember how it tasted." Kaori impaled another portion. "My grandfather despised our soy-based diet, these imitation meats. He wanted, as he put it, the 'real thing'. He never quite wrapped his head around the fact that the real thing no longer exists. Not in any quantity."

"They're very intelligent, squid. I couldn't imagine eating one." Valerie's attention darted around the room, lingered for a moment on Mineko and finally rested at a point somewhere above Kaori's head. "I usually forget to eat at work, I'm so busy. Sometimes I think I might—"

"So about these people," said Gaspar, and Valerie fell into meek silence. "You think they'll have gone underground?"

Lachlan nodded. "I think it likely, sir. In any event, I'll take care of this personally from now on." He speared a piece of squid and inspected it. "I haven't gone hunting for quite some time, but I'm sure I still have the predator instinct."

"Oh? Back into the field, then?"

"Well, let's be candid. I'm still the best agent you have, and we need to capture this cyborg promptly and cleanly. And then Dr. Wren will demonstrate the progress we all expect."

Valerie took a hurried sip of water. "I think so, yes. By the way, I was wondering…well, my predecessor. Would it be possible for me to meet him? To exchange notes?"

"I'm afraid your predecessor's career came to an abrupt end. It was thirty years ago, and several members of the Committee at that time were prone to overreacting." Lachlan shrugged. "You know how it is."

The dinner table fell silent. Gaspar and Kaori picked through their meals, while Lachlan continued to subject the trembling Valerie to that repugnant smile of his. It was shameful to know the threat of murder and retribution hung over her family's dinner table, and Mineko laid down her fork and knife with a sudden clatter that turned every head toward her.

"Dr. Wren," she said. "Valerie. You seem very pale. Would you like me to show you around the back garden? There should be a little light left."

"Yes, that would be…" Valerie's voice shook as she set down her cutlery. "That would be very kind, Mineko, yes. Um, I just… I'll just drink this water first." Her face averted from the others, she finished her glass and sighed. "If we may be excused…"

"Of course," said Gaspar. "We'll postpone dessert a little so that you don't miss out. It'll be very good. Some kind of cake, I think."

Lachlan continued to smile at Valerie as she fumbled with her napkin and rose to her feet. "I hope the fresh air revives you, doctor. You look a little pale." He glanced at Mineko. It was impossible to read whatever message gleamed in his eyes. "As do you, Mineko."

Mineko matched his stare until he looked away. "I'm ready," said Valerie. "Which way?"

In the evening gloom, the back garden seemed a sinister gathering of strange silhouettes. Nocturnal sounds filled the air: the croaking conversation of frogs, an insect whine and, in the distance, running water.

Valerie stood within a wedge of interior light and stared at the first pinpricks in the night sky. Mineko waited, tasting with each breath the crispness of the air. Though Mineko knew nothing about her new companion, it was a relief to finally be free of the tension of the dining room.

"Thank you for taking me outside." Valerie's twitching seemed to have subsided. "I wasn't feeling very well, as you noticed. I ate too quickly."

"I'm sorry Lachlan frightened you. He's a fixture around here. They joke that I should call him Uncle Lachlan, but I don't see the funny side."

"I think it was just… I think I must have misunderstood what he meant." Valerie held an electronic cigarette to her lips, and its blue glow tinted the shadows. "Do you mind me asking what it is you study?"

Was she genuinely interested, or just making small talk? "My major is Neuroethics."

"Oh, how exciting, what a wonderful choice. Of course, I'm a neuroscientist, so I would think that. What led you to choose it?"

"When I was seven, my tutor was wiped. He'd been inventing his own stories to entertain me instead of telling ones approved by Education. Another of the house staff overhead him. Because of who I am, they gave him the maximum punishment." Mineko stared at the tip of Valerie's cigarette as it faded to black. "When I next saw him, he didn't know who I was," she said. "I begged for a story, and he gave me a blank look. 'I don't know any stories,' he said."

Valerie inclined her face into the darkness, concealing her expression. "You think what they did to him was wrong."

There was a hint of sympathy in her voice, and Mineko was tired of lying. "I know it. The Committee once knew it. And even though they're teaching us now that it's right, I still know the truth."

"You're a very brave girl." Valerie's voice was soft and distant, almost a whisper. "You aren't alone, you know. According to the few notes I inherited, my predecessor ended Project Sky because he believed it was unethical. The test subjects kept dying, you see. They were all volunteers, but still he thought...all those young men and women, those promising lives, what was the point?"

"Why were they dying?"

"The implant simply seemed to, um, I guess...overload the nervous system, I suppose you'd say. Some survived with severe brain damage, but most just..." Valerie gave an uncertain laugh. "Certainly the invention is exciting. Imagine being able to read, even manipulate, thoughts, emotions, and memories. But the cost has been terrible."

"Can't we do that already? Read memories?"

"No, not quite. There isn't a computer yet invented that can encode such information for our viewing. But there is one device in nature that has that function built-in." Valerie tapped her temple. "Project Sky was supposed to transmit data from one brain to another. Not as a digital representation of consciousness, but as an experiential one. One that we could understand on our intuitive human terms."

This was headache-inducing stuff. "How could you possibly transmit from one brain to another?"

"Neural activity is accompanied by a kind of short-distance radiation, which exists on a spectrum we weren't able to detect until recently. Its behavior is still unknown to us, very much a question for the physicists, but it does offer a suggestive basis for the many anecdotal tales of interaction between minds." Valerie chuckled as she drew on her cigarette again. "It was a very controversial discovery, that one. They had to rewrite a few things, and the parapsychologists gloated for years."

"But if what you're saying is true, Project Sky didn't actually work. Not in our experiments."

"Perhaps it did." As Valerie warmed to her subject, she accompanied her words with enthusiastic gestures. "Perhaps that's why the subjects died—their brain couldn't handle their new faculty. Or perhaps we had it all wrong from the beginning. We can't know, because no one survived or remained lucid to describe what had happened to them. All the records show is that their neurons lit up in a brilliant display, and then...nothing."

As horrifying as it sounded, Mineko couldn't afford to betray too much emotion. She made an appropriately thoughtful sound. "I see. But this woman from the districts, she has a working implant?"

"Yes, it's incredible. I don't know, um, what you know...I mean, I don't know what's appropriate, but, uh..." Valerie hesitated, perhaps struck by the realization she was talking to a mere student.

"It's fine. My parents like me to be informed. Why else would they talk around me at dinner?"

Valerie's tongue darted across her lips, and she gave a quick nod. "Of course. Yes, today we saw proof that her implant is working. To some extent, anyway. At the very least, in its most destructive capacity."

Perhaps now the conversation was getting somewhere productive. "Why do you think that is?"

"An obvious theory presents itself. We only tested on people who grew up here." Valerie indicated the garden walls. "The Codist movement is five generations old. Thanks to our wealth and isolation, we've enjoyed superior conditions—fresh food, access to medicine, protection from radiation and heavy metals. The gene pool is different, the environment is different..."

It was clear where this was going, but it seemed wiser to play dumb. "Why does that matter?"

"Foundation's greater population may contain mutations and variations that simply aren't represented among us. This Alexis may have a genetic feature we lack. Or she may lack one that we have and which prevents the aug from working." Valerie frowned. "Of course, there are rumors the operation was tried several times in the districts without success, so whatever this distinctive quality is, it's not necessarily widespread."

In other words, Lexi might be a mutant. Mineko couldn't wait to break the good news. "Are they very different to us, the people outside?"

"Bless you, no. They're *Homo sapiens* in all their diversity. I mean, uh… ethically speaking, of course, they're tremendously different." Valerie took a quick glance over her shoulder. "But biologically, they're us. Even if another hundred generations passed and they became mutated beyond recognition, they would still be human. A species can accommodate many variations."

It was hard not to like this gawky scientist with her tremulous voice and agitated mannerisms. Harder still to believe she was the one who might become responsible for the end of all free thought.

Mineko took a cautious breath and arranged her words carefully. "As a neuroethicist, I'm interested in the idea of a person reading another's thoughts. It seems problematic to me."

"Well, some would say so, certainly. But it could also ensure greater safety, and, uh…" Valerie lowered her eyes. "Uniformity. Which, as you know, is what we all aspire to."

"But a species can accommodate many variations. You just said so."

There was a long silence. Mineko's heart thumped painfully against her ribs. Had she been too audacious?

Valerie touched the cigarette to her lips again, and the blue light flared. "I'm afraid they'll kill me. Or wipe me. My only chance is to find this woman and study her, and what if she's a freak and we have no way of repeating the miracle?" She moved the cigarette away and sighed. "When I applied for this position, they asked if I had family or close friends. I said no, and seeing the satisfaction on their faces, I knew I'd made a terrible mistake. But it was already too late."

Mineko remained quiet. How could she wish Valerie luck when she hoped so fervently that Project Sky would fail?

If only life were as simple as the horror movie in Zeke's lounge. When hideous monsters were pitted against a good, resilient humankind, the sides were clear. But in this world, the enemy was her own family, and she herself wore the uniform of oppression.

"Let's go back inside," she said. "We'll miss dessert."

Valerie nodded, but neither of them moved. Instead they gazed into the shadows, both silent, as night consumed the last of the day.

CHAPTER 7

Lexi opened her eyes. A cement ceiling, springs jabbing her through an unfamiliar mattress, thin sheets drawn over her body...

Oh, yeah. Now she remembered.

Pulling off the sheets, which seemed for several frantic seconds to be fighting back, she escaped the bed and stretched her limbs. Another night on that mattress, and there wouldn't be an unknotted muscle in her body.

Callie lay sprawled on the opposite bunk, her tangled sheets tossed away from her body. She'd slept in nothing but her tank top and panties, yet sweat beaded her bare skin. Strange. It hadn't been a warm night.

Lexi watched her, guilt stirring. In sleep, Callie looked cherubic, her lips parted and her long lashes fluttering. Was it possible Lexi had been too hard on her? The kid hadn't really done anything wrong.

Well, no time to worry about that now.

Lexi picked up her crumpled shirt and sniffed it. Not terrible. Not great either. She dressed as quietly as she could, slipped on her boots, left the room and headed down the hall. If she remembered right, the kitchen wasn't far away.

As she walked, the grated floor clanked beneath her feet, and the rusted pipes around her produced disturbing thumps. As a place to live, this bunker didn't really do anything for her, but as the set for a horror movie, it would be perfect. She could see it now, Nikolas and Amity as a pair of serial killers...

She sauntered into the kitchen. Even at this hour, it was full of people cooking up soup. Seeing Riva's pink mohawk in the crowd, Lexi grinned. No better way to start the day.

With extra swagger, she crossed the room and leaned on Riva's bench. "Tell me, how do you look this gorgeous first thing in the morning?"

Riva smiled without looking up. "Hey, Lexi."

Lexi smiled back. Neither *beautiful* nor *handsome* did this woman justice—she inhabited that captivating world in-between. "You ever get any trouble in this place, looking as queer as you do?"

"Not in the bunker. People keep their opinions to themselves. Outside, yes, I get trouble."

"Yet you're still feeding these assholes."

"I like to think the hate stops with me."

"How noble. I have the sudden urge to kiss you on the mouth."

Riva glanced at Lexi's lips, blushed, and looked down again. "Maybe you could help me in the kitchen instead." She tapped a tall pot beside her. It was full of goop, but the hotplate beneath was unlit.

"Are you asking me to spoon with you?"

Riva laughed, startling a passing volunteer. "That's exactly what I'm asking." She twisted a nearby knob, and a dull red glow spread across the hotplate. "There's a spoon on the counter. All you have to do is keep it from burning, add seasoning, and ladle it out when servers come by."

It sounded like pure tedium, yet anything was worth it to keep this cutie's attention. "I've never done anything like this before. Either people cook food for me, or I buy it prepackaged and hope it doesn't explode in the microwave."

"Don't worry. I'll be here to make sure you don't hurt yourself."

They exchanged amused looks, and Lexi took the chance to admire her face again. That striking nose, those pensive eyes and exquisite lips... Yes, this was going to lead to a happy ending. Maybe even several.

***

As Lexi churned her spoon through the soup, trying to move it fast enough to create a whirlpool, the kitchen doors flew open. Callie strode in, looking tough yet adorable in her cap and a battered biker jacket. Seeing Lexi, she stopped short. "You're kidding."

"Callie Roux." Lexi waved her dripping spoon. "You hungry?"

"What are you doing? Are you... Are you helping?"

"She's very obliging," said Riva. "So your last name is Roux? Were your ancestors French refugees?"

"Probably." Callie treated Riva to a dimpled grin. "I don't speak a word of French, though. My mom barely even spoke English."

"My grandmother spoke French, but my parents never learned. My name's Riva Latour. It's a pleasure to meet you."

"Likewise. So, how the hell did you get her to work in the kitchen?"

"She whispered romantic French poetry in my ear." Lexi whacked her spoon against the pot, jettisoning several clinging droplets. "Something about caressing my silken thighs. And in a passionate frenzy, I cried out, '*Oui! Oui!* I will stir with you!'"

Callie giggled, which was immediate cause to become suspicious. "What's with you?" Lexi said. "You're in a good mood."

"Nikolas gave me that radio phone." Callie patted the bulging pocket of her jacket. "I'm going to deliver it to Min."

"But she's inside an enclave. Isn't that going to be dangerous?"

"Sure, but I'm a smuggler. This is what I do. You're just pampered."

She was a cheeky little creature who deserved a withering comeback, but it was important to keep things cool in front of Riva. The soup hissed. Lexi gave it a frantic stir. Shit, this was difficult work.

"Here." Riva ladled soup into a bowl. "Eat before you head out."

Callie dipped her finger into the soup and sucked it clean. "Tomato!"

"Can you do that again?" said Lexi. "With your finger."

Callie laughed. "Eat me." She took a big spoonful of soup and licked her lips. "This tastes so good. Sure beats my usual breakfast of tinned beans."

"So how are you getting to the University? You can't take the van. They'll be looking for it."

"Nikolas said I can borrow one of those big Harleys downstairs. I'm so excited. I haven't been on a hog in years."

"You ride a bike on the city streets?" said Riva. "You must be brave."

Callie beamed. "I trust my reflexes. Never met a pothole I couldn't swerve around. If you need proof, maybe I could take you for a ride."

Callie was trying to cut in on the action. Unacceptable. "Better get moving," Lexi said. "Your soup's going cold on you."

"Hint taken." Callie gave the spoon a final lick. "Thanks for the soup, Riva. Keep your eyes on that Lexi. She seems nice when she wants to be, but she's trouble."

Lexi watched Callie strut from the room. The girl might have been annoying, but it was still fun to imagine her astride one of those mean-looking bikes, bare legs against black steel...

"You seem distracted," said Riva. "I assume you're thinking about something inappropriate."

"Always a safe guess. So, do you think she's right? Am I trouble?"

"I'm certain of it. By the way, do you have any spare clothing?"

"Nope." Lexi mimed sniffing her armpits. "Why, am I fragrant?"

"Not yet. But if you keep stirring at that pace, you're bound to work up a sweat."

"I'm not worried. My body odor is an aphrodisiac."

"I believe it. Even so, maybe you'd like to borrow one of my shirts. We're about the same build."

It was a convenient excuse to check out Riva's body again, though the amused arch of her eyebrow suggested the ruse had failed. "You're right, we look pretty close," said Lexi. "There's even less of you, though."

"I have no idea why. I eat plenty of soup."

Too easy. "If you're in the mood to eat something else…"

Riva blushed. "Are you always so brazen, or have you decided I'm easy?"

"Nothing like that. I'm just a chronic flirter." Maybe it was time to dial down. "It's supposed to make you laugh, but if it creeps you out, be sure to tell me."

Smiling, Riva adjusted the heat on her burner. "No, keep misbehaving. I think I like it. Meanwhile, your soup is burning."

"Shit!" Lexi swirled the soup. "By the way, don't think inappropriate flirting is all I can do. I'm a very intelligent conversationalist."

"So engage me in an intelligent conversation until my break, and then we'll go get that shirt."

Lexi scrunched her forehead, feigning deep thought. "Uh, to be honest, it's pretty early by my standards. My brain's a little sleepy. Maybe you can kick things off."

"Then tell me about your friends. I've seen that spiky-headed man walking around the bunker. What's the story there?"

"Oh man, that guy. That fucking Zeke. Let me tell you about Zeke…"

Riva's room was slightly larger than the one Lexi shared with Callie, and its overhead light cast a steadier glow. The sheets on the small bunk had been smoothed, and clothes were piled at its foot. A little table in the far corner supported a basin of water under a mirror. Tattered posters adorned the walls—pictures of long-dead rock musicians, spindly and genderless, plus a few arty-looking movie posters.

"Nice place." Lexi ran her fingers along a bare stretch of metal shelving. "No television, though."

"I watch movies in the rec room. I can't afford my own TV."

Lexi wandered the room, driven by genuine curiosity. She'd visited more women's bedrooms than she could count, but she rarely had the opportunity to inspect their contents. There was usually too much sex going on.

"Would it disgust you to learn that I'm rich?" she said.

Riva narrowed her eyes. "Yes. Leave my room immediately."

"If it makes any difference, I've probably just lost it all."

"Because of these people hunting you?"

"It's looking that way." Lexi stared at a poster of a willowy musician attacking an electric guitar. "You should show Callie this. She enjoys the heavy stuff."

Pleasure beamed in Riva's eyes. "She seemed really nice. And she's very cute."

"Sure. But I think you're better suited to someone sophisticated."

"Why rule yourself out so soon?"

Lexi laughed, but her amusement subsided as she reached the basin. Medication blister packs were strewn around it, a small ocean of foil. She reached for a pack, and Riva stopped her hand.

"Don't," Riva said, her tone too gentle to be a reprimand.

Lexi chewed on her lower lip. "Are you sick?" That might explain some of the anxious vibes she'd sensed.

"No." As Riva stared at the blister packs, Lexi picked up more traces of intense emotion: apprehension, alarm, dismay. And above all, the urge to run and hide. It was a terrible imperative, so primal that every other feeling quailed before it. Lexi had brushed against such knots of inner torment before. They were like chasms in the psyche, rifts in the soul. Some real fucked up shit.

"Are you okay?" said Riva. "You've gone very quiet."

"It's my implant, that's all. I get these dizzy moments."

It didn't seem to alleviate her concern. "If you don't mind me asking, what does this implant of yours do?"

This didn't seem like the right time to confide. "Well, as it happens, I'm augmented in a few ways. Reflexes, vision. I'm a real killing machine."

"As a pacifist, I'm not sure I can share my clothing with a killing machine."

"I promise I won't kill anyone while wearing it." Lexi shrugged off her jacket. "So, let's take a look at this shirt."

"I have some clean tops here. Nothing fancy." While Riva rifled through the clothes at the foot of her bed, Lexi undid her shirt and bared herself to the cold air. Riva looked up and reddened. "Oh, I'm sorry…"

"Should I have warned you? I've never really felt the need for a bra. I can barely fill an A-cup."

Despite her blush, Riva continued to stare. "I can relate."

Being admired was a definite thrill. Lexi angled herself to give Riva a better view, balled her shirt and tossed it to the bed. "I don't mind being flat. I love boobs, but I don't really like them on me, you know?"

"I think I understand." Riva handed a plain black tee to Lexi. "There's body spray over there."

Lexi took the canister and inspected the label. "Exotic scents. What do you think that means?"

"No idea. It smells like a rainforest growing inside a chemical plant."

The canister rattled as Lexi shook it. She depressed the nozzle, emitting a hiss and a pungent cloud, and directed the spray across her body. An aroma like chocolate, vanilla, and hazardous gases. "Where did you get this?"

"A friend. For all I know, it's insecticide with the label swapped."

Now freshly scented, Lexi pulled the replacement shirt over her head. A nice tight fit. She put on her jacket and gave it a quick, two-handed tug before turning to the mirror and shifting her white spikes from one messy position to another.

Satisfied, she gave Riva her most alluring smile. "What do you think?"

Riva laughed nervously. Her blush hadn't diminished one bit, despite Lexi's breasts being once more covered. Maybe she was wondering how to make the first move.

Well, Lexi could take care of that.

She placed a hand on Riva's shoulder, took her by the waist and pulled her close. A frantic tangle of emotions swarmed behind Riva's eyes, a buzz of contradictions—desire and dread, excitement and horror, pleasure and grief. Not good.

Lexi loosened her hold on Riva's now-rigid body. "Riva?"

"I can't." Her eyes glistening, Riva retreated out of Lexi's reach. "I wanted this, but I can't..."

A tear slipped down Riva's cheek, and Lexi's stomach convulsed. Shit, what had she done?

"I didn't mean to scare you." Hell, Lexi had scared herself. "I only meant to kiss you. If I'd known it would scare you, I'd never..."

"It's me, not you. I'd hoped I'd be brave enough, but I'm not."

"Brave enough? Are you a virgin, is that it? Because that doesn't…" Lexi broke off. That wasn't it. The real answer lay behind those tearful eyes, somewhere in the darkness Lexi had sensed before. "I just wanted to make out with you, that's all. I wanted to be assertive, sexy. I messed up."

"I told you, it's not your fault." Riva turned to the basin and splashed her face. "I must look ridiculous."

"No. I think you've been hurt in a big way, and you're scarred up inside. But it'll get better." Hell, Lexi was no good at this. She'd become so good at manipulating people that she'd forgotten how to console them. "Just tell me we're still cool."

Her face dripping with water, Riva stared into the mirror. She didn't seem to be looking at her reflection. She didn't seem to be looking at anything. "Yes. We're cool."

It still felt wrong, terribly wrong. "Listen, we can have boundaries. I can stop the flirting, the innuendo. The last thing I want is to make you uncomfortable."

"Please don't change a thing. It's been a long time since anyone made me laugh, let alone feel attractive."

"But right now, you need me to go?"

"Yes. Just for now."

"Okay. Sure." Lexi managed a smile, but she didn't have to look in the mirror to know it was a shitty effort. "Thanks for the shirt."

Before she stepped through the doorway, she glanced back. Riva still stood over the basin, staring at—or maybe through—her own reflection.

With as little sound as she could manage, Lexi closed the door. She'd fucked *that* up.

The door to Lexi's room was ajar. She approached it cautiously—could Callie be back already?—and peeked through the opening. "Oh, it's you."

"Where have you been?" Standing at the foot of Lexi's bed, her arms folded, Amity looked every bit as unfriendly as she had the day before. "I've been looking for you. Get in here and close the door."

Was this an unexpected sexual advance? Hopefully not. For once, Lexi wasn't in the mood. She trudged into the room and shut the door.

"You said you could read any mind you wanted to," said Amity.

So it was an inquisition. Not much better. "Sure. To my knowledge."

"Prove it. Tell me what number I'm thinking of."

"Uh, sure." Lexi peered into Amity's eyes. Easier to read a wall. "I'm going to have touch you, okay? On the face is best."

"Fine." Amity squared her shoulders. "Do whatever you want to."

"I'm sure you don't really mean that." Lexi touched Amity's high forehead and felt for her mind. It reached back, a whispering, weaving mass. Apprehension: a trembling feeling that disturbed the emotions around it. Determination: hard, cool, vying to hold everything in place. Behind those…anger, deep anger, a molten core of fury.

"Why are you so angry?" said Lexi, retreating from the scalding heat.

"I'm not angry. What number?"

It was easy to find, a free-floating thought above that seething bedrock. "Eighteen."

Amity breathed out slowly. "What color?"

A flash of crimson. "Red."

"Tell me why I've come to you."

"That'll take me deep. I might see things you don't want me to."

"I have nothing to hide."

Everyone had secrets, whether they knew it or not, but Lexi pressed on. The deeper she went, the more confused the impressions became. Voices—shouting, murmuring, a man screaming her name—and images, too many to pick apart without time and care. Abandoned streets. Gunfire. Contorted faces. A knife. Pain. A man lying in a pool of blood. Her hands shaking. *You son of a bitch.*

Too deep. Lexi retraced her steps and explored the surface. Now here was something fresh, a vibrant memory no more than an hour old. An argument with Nikolas. He was cautioning her, patronizing her. *These decisions are outside the scope of your responsibilities…*

"You and Nikolas fought. You didn't want to give up the radio phone."

"That's right." Amity's face remained calm, but her voice betrayed her astonishment. "I can feel you in my head. It's like a cold finger brushing down my spine."

"You can feel it?" Surprised, Lexi lost her thread, and Amity's thoughts slipped away. "Nobody's ever said that to me before. Is it uncomfortable?"

"No. Just cold. Keep going."

Lexi withdrew her hand. "Your mind's frightening. Just tell me."

Amity still hadn't changed demeanor. "I want you to use your power to help us. Nikolas thinks your implant is immoral, but we don't have the luxury to moralize. We need to act while we're the only ones with this weapon."

A dangerous line of thinking. "Don't bring me into your revolution. Smarter people than you have tried and failed."

"What have you ever done to justify your comfortable existence, Vale? You've lived like a coward, a willing accomplice to the world's end."

Lexi tried a winning grin. "Not going to lie, your flattery needs a lot of work."

No luck cracking that stern façade. "I don't flatter. Nikolas told you that there was no cost for our protection, but he was wrong. There's always a cost. I need you to help me."

Having felt the violent contours of Amity's mind, Lexi didn't need to ask what the consequences of refusal might be. "Help you do what?"

"I suspect one of my people has been working for the Codists. I'm keeping him in a safe house several blocks away. He won't talk, and Nikolas is too soft to let us interrogate him thoroughly."

"So you want me to take a peek in his head, is that it?"

"I need to know what the traitor has revealed. I need to know if we're still safe here. If this base were raided, everyone would be wiped. Or killed."

Everyone. That would mean... Lexi sighed. "Keep talking."

"Nikolas vetoed my idea. He believes your implant is evil, that a person's mind is sacred. But the alternative is death—death for us and for this traitor too. Come with me tonight to the safe house and we'll end the farce."

This wasn't Lexi's scene. Dealing with gangs was easy, just a matter of stroking egos and ensuring a steady cash flow. This driven bitch was something else altogether. "And that's all?"

"That's all. I'll tell Nikolas the traitor caved in to guilt."

"What if he finds out?"

Amity compressed her lips to a hard, resolute line. "That's not your concern. I can deal with him."

If it meant keeping Riva safe—not to mention preserving Lexi's only hiding place—it seemed justifiable enough. "All right. I'll do it."

"Good. I don't expect I'll enjoy working with you, so let's try to have as little contact with each other as we can."

"Your loss." Lexi took another quick look into Amity's eyes. Nothing now but that defiant mental wall. "By the way, you might want to do something about that anger of yours. It can't be good for you."

Amity left without answering, though the force with which she slammed the door made her sentiments very clear.

Lexi flopped onto her bunk and closed her eyes. If there was ever a time she needed to relax...

She unzipped her jeans, slipped a hand inside and cupped her vulva, feeling its cleft shape through her panties. Just twenty minutes ago, she'd been horny as fuck for Riva. Now all she could think of was how badly she'd upset her. And then there was Amity's threat... With all this going on, how the hell was Lexi supposed to get off?

For as long as she could remember, sex had been her escape of choice, though she only went for women. Something about men left her cold. Almost every night, she tried to squeeze some action in, even if it was only minor: quick fingering in an alley behind a club, some furtive oral sex in a darkened corner, romantic shit like that. And she always masturbated before sleeping. Even the night before, with Callie in the other bunk. Subtly, silently.

Zeke had once suggested that her sex drive was caused by screwy hormones. Had even proposed she get tested, find out if she had too much testosterone. *Too much,* like a little extra would be a bad thing.

Maybe that was Riva's appeal. She had all the physical characteristics that Lexi had learned to love in herself—wide shoulders, absent hips, flat chest, angular facial features. But obviously Riva wasn't at peace with her looks. She needed confidence. And Lexi had fucked up her chance to help.

She tried an experimental grind against her palm. Nope. Nothing. For once, her libido was elsewhere.

Sighing, she drew up her zipper. Maybe next time.

CHAPTER 8

The bell chimed, and every student in the lecture theater seemed to exhale at once. "It seems we're out of time," said the despised lecturer whose subject, History of Codified Society, made even Social Ethics seem like a good time. "Don't forget what you need for the exam." She scowled at the class as they fled their seats.

Mineko escaped through a side door to the recreational lawn, which stretched beneath a clear morning sky. Most of the students on the grass seemed to be studying, though one pair was engaged in a desultory game of catch. She cut across the lawn, passed an ornamental pond swarming with orange fish, hurried over a flagstone section and reached the long row of white-blossomed trees.

Several students loitered on the path, the brats of lesser dignitaries. They frowned as she hurried past them. They envied her the advantage of her family name, and why shouldn't they? The highest strata of elite society, those departmental heads who formed the all-powerful Committee, was impermeable by any means other than birth.

Avoiding eye contact, Mineko made her way into the dorm building and up to her room. She really needed to stop dashing everywhere with her head down—she looked guilty even when she wasn't misbehaving.

She swiped her card, opened the door and stared. Callie sat on the edge of Mineko's bed, dressed in a gray maintenance uniform. Beneath the brim of her cap, her face was bright with mischief.

"Hurry up and come inside!" she said. "Somebody might walk past."

Her heart hammering, Mineko entered the room and shut the door. "How did you get in here? Callie, this is so dangerous…"

Callie took off her cap and shook out her hair. It fell in wild disorder, and she flicked a strand from her forehead. "Kade set me up with this uniform and a handy entrance code. As for your room, I kinda broke in. It's the sort of thing I'm good at."

"You weren't seen?"

"Sure I was seen, but nobody looked twice. I even fixed a few light bulbs just to keep in character. I also opened up your air conditioner panel to see how it works, but I put it back together afterward, don't worry."

Gripped by meekness, Mineko found herself incapable of taking a single step closer. "Did the others make it to safety?"

"Sure did. Lexi's found herself a hottie to play with, and I'm pretty sure Zeke's sleeping off a few bottles. How about you? Are you holding up?"

Mineko closed her eyes, and dizziness swept through her. She had to tell the truth, even though it would ruin everything. "No. I've done something terrible."

"What do you mean?"

"They didn't know about you. Not until the fight outside Zeke's. It's my fault you're involved." Mineko opened her eyes. Callie's face expressed worried compassion, no anger at all. Another guilty lurch rolled through Min's core. How could this woman be so understanding? "You've lost everything, and it's my fault. I'm sorry."

"It's not your fault."

"But it is. I'm such an idiot." Mineko's vision blurred and her throat tightened. "All I wanted to do was help, and I got it wrong. I'm hopeless…"

"Min, no. Shit, come here." Callie leapt to her feet, put an arm around Mineko and led them both back to the edge of the bed. Mineko fought not to sob, instead drawing and releasing shivering breaths. She lost the struggle, and to her horror and shame, she began crying.

"It's okay, it's okay." Callie squeezed Mineko close, and the spasms began to subside. "You did the right thing."

Mineko rested her cheek against Callie's shoulder. Each breath brought in Callie's scent: the sharp smell of oil, the fragrance of her hair and the light aroma of her sweat. "It gets worse. Lachlan Reed is hunting you."

"What's a Lachlan Reed?"

"He's my father's second-in-command. The only Codist cyborg."

"Lexi's a cyborg too. She'll kick his ass."

"He's six foot six, Callie."

Callie chuckled. "So I'll help her do it. Relax. I'm not worried."

"But I've destroyed your life."

"I'm in trouble, sure, but it's trouble that makes me come alive. All you did was break me out of a quiet spell."

Mineko pressed herself closer against Callie's side. She was so warm, so solid. "But your home, all those wonderful things you own…"

"Forget about that. It's just junk. I'm way more worried about you. Does anyone suspect anything?"

"I don't think so. But last night, I had dinner with my family. They talked about you, and Lexi, and Project Sky. And the whole time I was thinking..." Mineko's voice wavered. "I'm betraying my own parents. They'll hate me if they find out, yet I don't have a choice. I'm stuck."

She was rambling, but she'd never before had a chance to express her fears, let alone with a comforting arm around her. "I love them, but I hate the life they'll force on me. I want to be free, but I don't dare leave. I don't belong anywhere."

"That's not true." Callie's smile brought out the full force of her dimples, and Mineko's eyes blurred again. "Hey, you know how I got here? A big Harley-Davidson."

"A what?"

"A motorbike. Motorcycle. You know, two wheels, vroom-vroom?" Callie turned an invisible throttle in the air, and Mineko laughed, finally diverted from her inner tremors. "Yeah, you get it! It was a beautiful ride. Tearing down the streets, leaning into the corners, the engine snarling beneath me. Someday I'm going to take you for a ride. You'll love it."

"But I don't know how."

"It's easy. You just sit behind me and hold on." Callie's smile became wistful. "We'll cruise down to Bappy's in the Rail District, where they serve the best spicy tempeh burgers you'll ever taste. The cinema across the road does 3D screenings on Saturdays. It's not much fun alone, but when you've got someone with you..."

The ache was back. "You know I'll never be able to do any of those things."

"Sure you will. And afterward, we'll cut across the desert and head up the mesa, and I'll show you how the sun looks when it sets over the basin. It melts into the horizon, and the stars that come out afterward are brighter than any you've ever seen. I'll teach you how to spot the constellations."

Mineko blinked back more tears. It was beautiful, but it was torture. "Do you know many constellations?"

"Pretty much all of them. I spend a lot of time out there just stargazing. Thinking about all the wrong things."

Mineko attempted to smile, but she only managed to make her lips tremble. "I'm sorry about crying on your shoulder."

Callie gave a soft laugh. "Don't be. I cry most days." She moved her arm away, and Mineko sat upright. "I brought you something." Callie plucked a chunky phone from her breast pocket. "This is a radio phone that uses an encrypted channel. Apparently, it goes to a receiver in the Open Hand base. They gave you a codename to identify yourself: Blue."

A codename? That was exciting. "Why Blue?"

"They only know you as the Project Sky informant, so blue skies, maybe. It suits you, though." Callie glanced at the door. "I wish I could stay longer, but Kade's waiting for me, and I'm worried about him."

She was leaving already? Mineko gripped Callie's sleeve as she searched for some excuse. "Tell me about Kade. Do you know him very well?"

"We aren't regular buddies or anything, but I trust him. And I don't say that about many people." Callie touched Mineko's hand. "I'll be honest. My hope is you're going to agree to escape with me right now. We can do it, I swear. We can walk right out of here."

How did Callie not understand that being exiled to the hellscape of Foundation was as terrifying as the threat of being Reintegrated? At least in the enclave, Mineko had her parents. She had the power of her family name. Out there, she was nothing.

"I can't," she said. "And you can't come back here again."

"But what if they catch you?"

"It's a risk I've chosen to take, just as you chose to take a risk coming here. As it stands, I think I managed to get away with it. Nobody identified me, and I could well be safe. But out there, the danger is certain, isn't it?"

Callie frowned. "I guess."

"Don't think it isn't a hard decision to make. It's the hardest I've ever faced in my life. I want to be free. I don't want to live under the Code. But I don't want to be dead or alone, either."

"You won't be alone. I'll watch out for…" Callie trailed off. "God, I'm dumb. If I were in your position, I wouldn't listen to me, either. You don't know me from anyone."

"I believe you're kind and sincere. But it's a huge thing you're promising. I don't know how anyone, even the best of people, could guarantee it."

"Yeah." Callie patted Mineko's wrist before standing. "Okay, I'll go. For now. But you better keep winding that watch."

It was so unfair that they had to part already, while the warmth of Callie's body was still imprinted on her own. "I still don't understand why you gave me such a beautiful present. I don't feel like I deserve it. I don't feel like I deserve anything."

"I often think that way too, even though I know better. You have to stop listening to that voice. Trust what other people think of you." Callie walked to the door, averted her eyes—had those been tears?—and reached for the handle. "If you ask me, a girl like you deserves the world."

The door opened and closed, and she was gone.

CHAPTER 9

The alleyway stank, but it beat being caught in the open air. Kade waited beside the big bike while trying not to breathe through his nostrils. There wasn't much risk Callie would be detected—she was a professional, after all—but he couldn't help but be nervous.

Footsteps echoed at the far end of the alley. There she was, thank God, apparently unharmed, though her face was grave.

"She didn't want to come," Callie said. "I begged, but she still said no. I fucking hate the Code."

Kade looked away as Callie unzipped her uniform. She was dressed underneath, but that didn't make it right to watch. "Hold on to that anger, and you might become a revolutionary yet."

Callie stashed the uniform in the bike's storage compartment. "Not if it means taking orders."

"You think I take orders?"

"You have an editor, right?"

Kade laughed. "That's not really the same thing."

"If you say so." Callie ran a hand over the bike's polished chassis. "I wish I could keep this."

"You'd just end up pulling it to pieces to see how it works."

Callie gave him an impish grin. "I already know how it works."

"Well, if you're in the mood for another joyride, I could use a lift back to the *Gazette*."

"Sure. Any excuse to keep it a little longer." Callie swung a leg over the bike. "Hop on."

Kade sat on the back seat and held Callie by the waist. As much as he trusted her, the tickle of anxiety in his chest just wouldn't subside. "You won't get me killed, will you?"

"Not if you don't let go." The engine started with a roar that vibrated through Kade's chest. "And no hugging. That's for girlfriends only."

Callie knocked back the kickstand and twisted the throttle. The bike tore through litter as it punched out of the far end of the alley. Callie leaned, bringing the bike into a sharp turn away from the University walls, and they rocketed out of the turn and blasted down the street. The wind built to a screech, and Kade tensed as Callie kicked up another gear.

The street ahead was mostly empty, a long strip of battered asphalt between residential buildings and food stores. The same street Kade had walked Mineko down, as it happened. As much as he wanted to ask Callie more questions about her, it was impossible to speak over the sound of the wind. Easier just to wait for the ride to be over.

Two intersections flickered by, and Callie swerved to avoid a pothole. She might have been young, but the sureness with which she directed the bike hinted at the seasoned expert she was.

As she slowed to weave around some kids playing ball on the road, Kade took the chance to speak. "Did Mineko tell you anything?"

"She said there's some guy named Lachlan Reed hunting us."

Lachlan? Hell. That was going to make a difficult situation a whole lot worse. If anyone could outwit and overpower Lexi, it would be Lachlan—or Commanding Agent Reed, as he was called these days. "I see."

"The *Gazette* is under the ice cream place, right?"

"The very same."

"Does it actually serve ice cream?"

"That it does."

Callie punched the air. "Hell yes!"

The bike released a furious growl and shot forward with enough speed to set Kade's teeth buzzing. The road became a high-paced smear, and he clutched Callie's waist, not caring anymore about whether he was holding too tightly. Smugglers were a daredevil breed, and Callie Roux was one of the wildest. Still, she knew what she was doing.

A bicycle flew out of an intersection ahead, and Callie jinked, almost clipping its back wheel as she passed. She laughed. "That was close!"

That did it. Kade closed his eyes.

The *Revolutionary People's Gazette*, being something of a clandestine operation, was concealed in a basement beneath the cheerful front of Smiletime

Soy Ice Cream. Callie secured the bike in the shop's fenced back lot, and she and Kade entered via the rear door.

Tubs of colored ice cream crowded the shop floor. "Help yourself," said Kade, and Callie grabbed a cone and stacked four rainbow scoops atop it.

Kade descended the narrow stairs to the basement, followed by the busy, messy sound of Callie enjoying her treat. She had plenty of talents, but eating pretty wasn't one of them.

As he left the final step, Kade fumbled for the light switch. The lonely overhead flicked on.

"Ritzy," Callie said.

"It's not so bad." In truth, the room still looked like a grotty basement, with the addition of a few tables and chairs, some desktop computers and, lurking in one corner, an immense multi-function printer. "Looks like everyone's still in bed."

"Or the *Gazette* is only you. Admit it. You invented the other contributors."

"You got me. It's all an excuse to eat ice cream."

Kade ducked into the kitchen. Now that he was giving a guest tour, it looked a little shabbier than he'd remembered. Sad microwave, sadder fridge, tiles that seemed ready to pick themselves off the floor and crawl away. "We do clean in here, just so you know."

"Is that one of your cleaners?" Callie pointed to a cockroach. It waved its antennas at her before fleeing beneath a cabinet. "Or is that your editor?"

"You've got something against editors, haven't you?" Kade opened the fridge, and its low hum intensified. "You want a beer?"

"No thanks. I've got ice cream." Callie slurped some bright goop off her cone. "So, what's the latest in revolutionary news?"

Kade retrieved a can and ripped back the tab. He took a sip of the bitter brew before returning his attention to Callie. She had ice cream on her chin, but she'd find it herself sooner or later. "The most important development right now is Project Sky. But I can't report on it until Lexi is safely in Port Venn."

Callie licked ice cream from her lips, completely missing the blob below her mouth. "She really hates you, doesn't she? I can't understand why. You're, like, the least hateable guy I know."

Now there was a subject best avoided. "She has her reasons."

"I'm sure they're stupid ones." Callie bit off the end of her cone and sucked out the remaining ice cream. Her eyes widened. "Ah, fuck! Brain freeze!" She groaned as she crunched into the cone again. "I can't stop. It's too tasty. But it hurts so much."

Kade chuckled. He'd first met her a decade ago, back when she'd been an incongruous teenager working the smuggler routes alongside hardened men and women. He'd taken a photo, too, and still had it somewhere—same messy auburn hair, same dimpled grin. But despite the smile, there'd been a deep sadness in her eyes. That hadn't changed, either.

"She's so arrogant." Callie wiped her mouth with the back of her hand. "She doesn't care about anything or anyone."

"Lexi's arrogant, but she's not uncaring. Just the opposite." The subject twisted Kade up, as always, and he took a deep breath. "Anyway, let's get off that topic. I want to know what Mineko told you."

"Just let me wash the sticky off." Callie twisted the sink faucet, which gave an alarming groan and issued a splurt of tin-scented water. She splashed the water on her hands and rubbed them together. "I changed my mind about wanting a drink. I'm thirsty now."

"Help yourself."

Callie rummaged through the fridge and took out a bottle of fizzing soda. "My mom never let me drink this stuff. As soon as I could crawl, she wanted me to drink whisky. Such a goddamn drunk. Never stopped swearing. Her last word, honest to God, was 'cocksucker.'"

"Epileptic seizure, wasn't it?"

"Yeah. There was a dog barking outside, and she looked out the window and screamed, 'Quiet the fuck down, you mangy little cocksucker!' The dog barked again, like it was daring her to do something, and bam. Down she went." Callie took a quick gulp from the bottle. "It was almost funny, you know? She'd survived through so much shit, and in the end what did her in was calling a dog a cocksucker."

"We need to get you writing for us. You could have your own column."

"The lonely hearts column." Callie picked at the bottle's colorful label. "You know anything about a Riva Latour? She's Lexi's latest victim. Pink Mohawk, super skinny. Pretty face, husky voice. Seems really gentle."

"I don't know this Latour, but I laid eyes on her briefly yesterday. I don't have much contact with anyone at Open Hand but Nikolas and Amity."

Callie wrinkled her nose. "What's the deal with Nikolas, anyway? He's weird."

"He's a good man. Over-cautious, but for the right reasons."

"What do you mean, over-cautious?"

There was no way to get into this too deeply now, so Kade would just have to simplify it. "I mean he doesn't want to hurt anybody. I understand his position, but we're going to have to spill some blood to establish a fairer society. There's no getting around it."

Callie frowned. "And the woman? Amy, wasn't it?"

"Amity. No, she's not over-cautious. Not by any measure." Kade drank the last of the beer, crushed the can and tossed it into the bin. "To be blunt, she's ruthless. And I hate to say it, but we need people like her."

"I don't know. Maybe we ought to be better than that."

"Don't try to quote Nietzsche at me. It's already been done."

"I don't even know what that is. All I'm saying is, if you try to out-asshole an asshole, you'll end up an even bigger asshole."

Kade smiled. "That's a good paraphrase, actually. Albeit a little rectal for my readership."

"I know, I'm stupid. I guess if I were smarter, I'd see the sense in hurting people just for wearing ugly overalls."

She was teasing, but even so, Kade gave her a serious look. "Trust me, violence is the least preferable option. But at present, it's our only option."

"Why? Shut-ins aren't necessarily bad people. I mean, look at Min."

Min. Already using nicknames. "I'm curious to know what you think about her."

"She's brave, but she's got no chance. Even though it wasn't easy for me growing up, at least I got to fight back. When people pushed me around, I told them to get fucked. Sometimes I even got away with it. But when you're a shut-in, pushing back just gets you wiped. You can't struggle, you can't resist, you can't escape. There's no future."

"Being a Codist of her status is a tremendous privilege," said Kade. "She's never had to worry about homelessness, hunger or sickness. But that being said, there's such a thing as sickness of the soul."

"The way she looked at me, it broke my heart. She was so grateful I'd visited, but even more surprised, like she'd never imagined anyone could care that much about her. You know how people cry when they lose somebody they love, how violent and desperate that is? Like their body is trying to rid itself of all that pain?"

"Yes. I know it." Better than he knew anything else.

"She cried like that on my arm. Not for something she'd lost, but for something she was never going to have. We can't let her go on like that."

Brave and sensitive as always. Classic Callie Roux. "It's funny. I remember a dirty-faced girl who looked me in the eye and told me she was going to be the richest smuggler in history. Back then, I wouldn't have placed bets on you being alive in another year. Yet here you are, bolder than ever."

"I've not been so bold. Not lately." Despite the regret in her voice, Callie's smile had returned, faint and thoughtful. "It's so stupid. Back then, all I wanted was money. Now all I can think about is how I wish I were loved."

Which was worse? To be like Callie, waiting for the love who wouldn't hurt her, or to be like him—having known and lost a love so rich that everything in his life had seemed to branch from that one source?

"There's nothing stupid about it," he said. "And I have no doubt you'll find what you're looking for."

"Maybe. For all we know, Port Venn's packed with sweet-natured women who can't resist a rugged charmer like me. I just have to hope Lexi doesn't get to them first."

Back on *that* topic again. It was going to be a tough week. "When it comes to Lexi, give her a little time. She does tend to give respect where it's due. Once she knows you better, you might be surprised."

"If she can't even get along with you, what the hell hope do I have?"

On that point, Kade didn't have any answers. Just a sudden need for a second beer.

Something heavy scampered down the stairwell, a storm of padding paws. The *Gazette*'s other investigative reporter, Mahesh, entered with Goldie, his big German Shepherd, galloping by his side. Mahesh unclipped Goldie's leash, and the dog bounded toward Kade and sniffed his boot.

"Hey, comrade." Kade ruffled Goldie's flank. "Behaving yourself?"

In response, Goldie placed a paw on Kade's knee.

"Someone has been down here." Mahesh hung his coat by the door. "Goldie was sniffing around the steps, whining."

"It was Callie Roux. She's gone now."

Kade scratched Goldie's snout while Mahesh vanished into the kitchen and clattered through its contents. The microwave chirped, and Mahesh returned with a small, steaming plastic pot of...whatever it was. "That stuff looks disgusting, man."

"It's good protein." Mahesh twirled his plastic fork through the stringy contents of the pot. "Roux. The smuggler girl, right? Sexy, redheaded lesbian?"

"The one and only." As the only other investigative reporter on the *Gazette*, Mahesh was technically Kade's rival, but they shared information when it mattered. "Heard anything about Open Hand lately?"

Mahesh deposited a mass of noodles in his mouth. "Why?"

"Don't interview me. Just indulge. And swallow those before answering."

"Just the usual. Tension between your buds Nikolas and Amity. I think it's going to boil over soon."

Talk about bad timing. "You think Amity might start a splinter movement?"

Mahesh shrugged. He always shrugged, even when he had an answer. "They can't fight like this forever. Right now, they have a mole, and they've been squabbling over how to interrogate him. It's not a good look."

Kade gave Goldie a final pat, and the dog ambled away. "I suppose Nikolas doesn't want to torture him. It's the right call."

"But doing nothing makes him look weak. Fact is, they're going to have to make up their minds whether they're a charity or a resistance cell. They can hand out food and blankets, or they can bring down the Codists. They can't do both."

"I hope you're wrong about that." Kade glanced at his screen. The latest article wasn't coming together, mostly because his heart wasn't in it. The state of Foundation's transport system? That didn't need an exposé. You only had to catch a train to see it yourself.

"Go talk to Amity, then. You're the only person alive who's not scared of her." A noodle dropped from Mahesh's fork to his shirtfront, and he grunted. "What's the deal with Roux? She used to be one of the best smugglers out there, but I haven't heard anything about her for a couple of years."

A contented snort came from the corner of the room, where Goldie had settled himself into his bed and begun snoozing with his paws over his nose. As far as guard dogs went, not exactly terrifying.

"She's been under the radar," said Kade. "Now she's working on something with me, but I have to keep it close to my chest."

"If that's how you want it." Mahesh plucked the noodle from his shirt and flicked it in Goldie's direction. Showing good taste, the dog didn't even look up. "So, why were you asking about Open Hand?"

"They're looking after a friend of mine."

"Lexi Vale, you mean."

Damn it. "It doesn't give me comfort to know you've learned that already."

"The street's buzzing with talk about her and the Menagerie. This has the potential to turn into a major gang war if Vassago or Contessa get protective. A good broker is hard to find, let alone a prodigy like Vale. She's going to be irreplaceable to them."

"Reed's involved. They're not going to put their necks out."

Mahesh gave his lunch a particularly vicious jab. "Fucking Reed."

Kade returned to his feet. Goldie raised his head, sniffed, and buried his snout in the blankets again. "I'm headed out. Hold the fort."

"You're just avoiding that crappy story about the subway." Mahesh peered at his own screen, and his expression turned gloomy. "At least you aren't writing about restaurant hygiene standards. You think the people are going to rise up because their tofu got chopped on dirty plastic?"

"It's all for the cause." Kade raised a fist. "Fighting back, one paragraph at a time."

"Can't it be one sentence at a time? I'd feel like I'm making progress that way." Mahesh cracked his knuckles, placed his fingers above the keys, and inhaled. "Here we go. Winning the war."

He typed with wild gusto, his fingers springing over the keys and thumping hard at the end of every line. "Oh, and be careful out there, okay? When you get secretive like this, it usually means you're in trouble."

"I'll be careful. For a start, I won't eat at the restaurants in your article." Kade saluted the room. "So long, brothers."

"Solidarity, comrade."

Goldie gave a drowsy snort. A true hero of the revolution.

The grim apartment tower bordered the blighted Rail District, keeping company with shattered buildings and streets filled with debris. Six stories of drab cement.

Nobody would believe that Foundation's most glamorous and successful broker had chosen to live here.

Kade pressed the buzzer, producing a long, unbroken shrilling sound. The intercom crackled. "What?"

"I want to talk to the building manager."

"That's me. And I repeat: what?"

"I want to visit Lexi's apartment."

"You can't do that. She said nobody was to go in."

So far, just as Kade had expected. "I understand. Can I bribe you and get this over with?"

"Bribe me? What do you think I am?" The door opened, and a large man with a stomach gently swelling over his pants appeared. "Do come in."

The foyer smelled like sour milk and dead cats. Kade waited by the chipped counter as the manager waddled around it. He squinted at Kade through puffy eyes.

"You aren't a shut-in, are you?" the manager said. "They made a big enough mess last time. And they scared the shit out of my residents."

A plastic bag in the corner rustled. Mice maybe, or perhaps the bag itself had come to life, animated by whatever strange odor haunted this room.

"I'm an old friend," Kade said.

"Lexi doesn't have friends. Just girls and business associates. If you're not lying, you better have a way to prove it."

"I thought you were going to take a bribe."

The manager scratched his impressive chins. "Maybe, but I have to know how much to gouge you for. If you're actually a friend, we can settle for something more reasonable."

"Okay." Kade bowed his head. At least the floor tiles seemed clean—in fact, they were cleaner than the counter. How the hell had that happened? "I know she can afford to rent anywhere in this district, but she chose this place, even though it's like living in the devil's armpit. Why? Because it puts her near to something important. A grave."

"Yeah, the graveyard on the corner. She goes out there every few days. You haven't been spying on her, have you?"

"No. I go there too, but on different days. We have an arrangement not to run into each other."

The manager nodded slowly. "So you knew that dead girl. Ash."

"Right. The three of us grew up not far from here, a couple of blocks over in the Rail District. When we chose the grave, we wanted to make sure Ash ended somewhere further from where she'd started. I've always felt there's something depressing about being buried where you were born."

The manager's pudgy face drooped. "I get you. You know Lexi from way back, is that what you're saying? Real old friends?"

"As old as it gets. I've known her since we were just children." Kade lowered his voice. "The agents who tossed her room aren't done hunting for her. She needs my help."

The manager unhooked a key and pushed it across the counter. "I don't need your bribe. Room Nine. Don't make a mess or move anything, okay?"

Kade smiled. "I appreciate it."

The elevator seemed a dubious prospect, so he took the stairs. The door to the fourth floor opened with an unhappy squeak and refused to close afterward. Kade gave it a final futile push before following the threadbare carpet to the door of Room Nine.

Discounting the overturned mattress spilling its stuffing and the drawers hanging loose, the apartment was nicer than its external surroundings might suggest. The carpet was plush and vibrant, and the walls had been repainted. Not much furniture, though: a wardrobe and some drawers, a couch, and a television. And a queen-sized bed, naturally.

Kade peered through an archway and discovered a kitchen. Its spotless surfaces suggested it had never been used. Beyond was a small door that presumably led to a bathroom. Not how most people would expect the elegant, fashionable occupant to live, but then she didn't really live here. Just inhabited the place now and then.

The wardrobe had been left open, revealing a row of stylish jackets in disarray. Kade flicked through them and smiled. There it was, her first jacket: a black bomber they'd found forgotten in a bar. It had been a loose fit for a thirteen-year-old, especially one as skinny as Lexi, but she'd worn it with pride, swaggering the neighborhood with her blonde hair slicked back and picking fights with anyone who laughed.

Lexi had spent a lot of her childhood fighting. Any label people stuck to her, she took as an insult. She'd brood over it for hours.

I'm not like you, she'd said to him once as they'd sat by the old railroad lines. *I don't want to be a boy. I don't want to be anything.*

Kade neatened the jackets, shut the wardrobe, and took a step back. It had to be around here, so where was it? The agents had already split the mattress, taken apart the pillow…where else?

He stopped by the full-length mirror beside Lexi's bed. He was looking a little rough these days, bristling with stubble, his forehead creased by lines. His hair had been doing its own thing for months—he was shaggier than Goldie. But it was still reassuring to see that tired man reflected in the glass. Especially with the memories this room was stirring.

Where would she put it? Kade turned in a circle. She would've hidden it somewhere she wouldn't find it by chance. Maybe with something else from the past, an object connected in some way. Maybe…

He opened the wardrobe and rifled to the bomber jacket. It had a single pocket, buttoned. Tensed for disappointment, Kade popped it open.

And there it was.

It was Ash who had found the bomber jacket. Kade had wanted it, had fought with Lexi for it, but Ash had laid down the law as she always did. It would fit Lexi better, she'd told them, and Kade had backed down. He would have done anything to win Ash's approval. To make her smile.

Later that night, Lexi had relented and let Kade try the jacket. In a murky pane of glass, he'd seen the spectacle Ash had been protecting him from: a scrawny kid in a jacket tailored for the body he could only dream of having. He'd given the jacket back to Lexi, tears in his eyes, and she'd hugged him.

You looked badass, she'd said. *You just need to grow a little more, that's all. Then I'll let you wear it. I promise.*

He stared at the photo in his hand. Ash. The frozen dead. Maybe this would remind Lexi, and she'd listen to him the way she once had. Or maybe—the thing he feared most—she'd never forgotten.

If so, there was nothing Kade could do.

CHAPTER 10

"This sucks," said Zeke. "Lexi's reading my mind." He cleared his throat. "I mean that as a joke, obviously."

Riva peered at him over her cards. "Well, obviously. Nobody here really believes in mindreading, do they?"

"Zeke might." Lexi glared at the loudmouth idiot. "He's big on psychics, angels, all that stuff. Crystals. Orbs."

Zeke gave her an apologetic look. "Oh, yeah. I'm fucking wild about it. Check my aura like three times a day, keep in touch with the fucking Martians… So, how about my shitty luck, huh?"

It was poker night, Callie's idea, but none of them had wanted to play for money. They'd found a box of screws to gamble with instead. After an hour, Zeke barely had enough left to assemble a miniature bookshelf. To be fair, it wasn't just his shitty luck—he'd been right about Lexi reading his mind.

"This'll comfort you." Callie handed Zeke the whisky flask. She owned a healthy pile of screws, though it was nothing next to Lexi's silver mountain. "Show us your hand, Riva. I know you've got something good."

Riva smiled. "I'm not sure I remember all the combinations."

"You're doing okay, though," said Zeke, the flask hovering near his lips. "How'd you end up working for a bunch of Open Hand stiffs, anyway? You seem too cool for that shit."

"Isn't it obvious? For the money."

Callie broke into giggles. "This one's funny. Let's keep her."

"She's cute," said Lexi. "But can she play poker?"

Riva tossed a few screws into the pot. "I call. Let's see your bluff."

"No bluff, babe." Lexi spread her cards on the table. "Hurts, doesn't it?"

"Full house," said Zeke with approval. "Kings full of jacks. Fucking glad I folded now."

"I should've joined you." Callie showed her hand. Three of a kind. "What have you got, Riva?"

Riva placed her cards on the table. Four tens and the Three of Hearts.

"Yes! You beat her!" Callie raised a hand, and Riva returned the high-five. "How's that feel, Lexi?"

Lexi grinned. She'd been genuinely blindsided—reading emotions didn't help much when her opponent didn't know the value of the cards she was holding. Still, the round couldn't have gone better had she planned it. It was Riva's affection she intended to win back, not a bunch of stupid screws.

She had to give Callie credit: the poker night had been the highlight of an otherwise shitty day. Callie had spent the afternoon in her van, dismantling junk and cleaning gadgets. Zeke had helped the medics perform a round of vaccinations. Left to herself, Lexi had watched television and sulked, wondering why the hell Nikolas was taking so long to get things moving.

This, though, this was good. Relaxing. It was even nice watching Callie jostle Riva in her seat, the sulky smuggler now as playful as a kitten. Flirting hard, in fact, but Lexi could hardly blame her.

Zeke collected the cards. "Let's get this started!"

Before he could start shuffling, there was a sharp rap at the door. "It's Amity," said a voice from outside, and the door opened, proving Amity to be an honest woman. "I see you're all busy wasting time."

"Don't judge," said Riva. "I'm off-duty."

"You can remain that way. I only need to borrow Alexis."

"Lexi," said Lexi. "Enough with this Alexis crap."

They stared each other down. "Lexi," said Amity in the bitter tones of a general conceding her most valuable territory. "Do you remember our earlier discussion? Well, the moment is now."

"Seriously? Can't you see I'm bonding?"

"I said that it's time. Come with me."

As much as Lexi wanted to tell her to fuck off, Amity didn't seem like the kind of woman it was wise to argue with. "Sorry, guys."

Callie frowned. "Is everything all right?"

"I'm good. Don't stop playing just because of me." Lexi laid a hand on Riva's shoulder. "We'll do this again tomorrow, okay?"

Riva nodded, but she didn't seem convinced.

Lexi joined Amity in the corridor and gave the group an apologetic wave before closing the door. "Thanks for ruining a lovely evening."

Amity shrugged. "Follow me. No dithering."

"What's the rush? It's half past eleven."

"Don't try my patience." Amity peered down an adjoining hallway. "We have to exit by a back way, or else we might be seen."

The back way in question opened into an alley choked with refuse and bordered by jagged steel fencing. The air stank, the night was moonless and the graffiti— well, it was some nasty shit, definitely not the refined graffiti Lexi was used to. She looked wistfully behind her as Amity shut the door.

"Don't make that face," said Amity. "I've no sympathy for you."

"Can't we go back and play poker? You'd be amazing at it."

"I'm even better at destroying people who test my patience. Hurry up."

No arguing with that. They plunged into the darkened alley. "The gangs around here," said Lexi as she stepped over a puddle of sludge. "They're pretty rough, right?"

"Very rough." Amity strode several meters ahead, her broad-shouldered physique intimidating in the gloom. "And they have little love for Open Hand."

In the shadows, a complex form shifted beneath an old blanket. Could have been a sleeping person. Could have been a pack of rats mating. Lexi picked up her pace. "So what stops them messing with you?"

"Me." Something rattled in the dark. Amity glanced in its direction, frowned, and continued walking. "Are you able to defend yourself?"

"If I'm not up against an eight-foot roid freak with a great white shark strapped to each arm, sure. Next question. Why are we going through the seediest alleys imaginable?"

"Efficiency. Anyone who causes trouble on these streets eventually answers to me. With a little luck, we'll find them first."

"So you're a vigilante hero and I'm your sidekick? A dream come true."

A street lamp towered above the chipped cement, its glow scattering the shadows. Abandoned houses lined the street beyond it. Most looked uninhabitable— collapsed roofs, open windows, missing doors—while a few had been demolished, leaving open lots strewn with bricks.

"We're not far," said Amity. "Two more blocks. But first I need to clarify something."

"Clarify away."

"You've been spending time with Comrade Latour."

A snake of apprehension slithered into Lexi's bowels. Seemed like a sketchy line of inquiry. "Sure. She's cool."

"Well, I'm ordering you to leave her alone. We need her focused upon her tasks, not distracted by you."

The fuck was this? "I'm not one of your volunteers. You don't get to order me around, and you sure as hell don't decide who I get to spend time with."

With the speed and force of a Rottweiler launched from a catapult, Amity grabbed Lexi by her shirt and shoved her against the fencing. It proved to be just as sharp and uncomfortable as it looked.

"I don't need some arrogant dyke interfering with my operation and my people," Amity said. "You're a drug-dealing piece of refuse, and I won't let you drag her down to your level. Stay away from her, or I'll show you why the gangs fear me."

Shit. Despite the pressure on her chest and the cold fencing at her back, Lexi couldn't help but laugh. "You are one mean fucker."

Amity released her. "I'm not going to warn you a second time."

"Good. The first time was boring enough." Lexi straightened her jacket and flicked back her hair. "Handle me like that again, and you can interrogate this guy yourself."

The remainder of the journey was undertaken in silence. Their route took them through increasingly sinister alleys, each one perfect for an ambush, and by the time Amity stopped them outside a door at the back of a two-story brick building, even the sound of Lexi's own footsteps had begun making her nervous.

A flight of stairs took them into a basement, a damp, grotty hollow in the earth, livened only by a television blaring in front of the world's least attractive couch. Four surly revolutionaries rose to salute Amity. Lexi gave them a cheery salute of her own.

"Comrades," said Amity. "Nothing new?"

"Nope," said one of the sentries, whose only distinctive feature was a collection of sad, wispy strands on his chin. "Nothing."

Lexi ambled closer to the television. "Hey, I know this movie. At the end, it turns out that——"

"Shut up!" said a revolutionary sprawling on the couch. "I haven't seen it." She gave Amity a plaintive look. "Who is this?"

"An interrogator," said Amity. "Take us to the prisoner."

One of the guards drew the bolt on a battered door. The cell behind it held a pale, emaciated man crouched on some rags, twitching beneath his thin clothes. Lexi's stomach turned. It didn't look like he'd been having a great time.

"Amity," said the prisoner. "You've made a mistake. Please let me go."

Amity shoved Lexi into the room. "Do it." The revolutionaries exchanged glances, and one murmured into another's ear. Amity frowned at them. "Be silent."

"Do what?" said the prisoner. "What are you going to do to me?"

Lexi knelt by the man's side. "A favor, by the looks of it." She peered into his glazed eyes. Nothing returned to her but the incoherent fragments of a frightened mind. Poor bastard. "I'm going to touch your face, okay? It won't hurt."

The prisoner tensed. "Please let me go. I told Amity everything."

"Just trust me. I'm not like the people who've been hurting you." Lexi began to reach forward, slowly. "May I?"

"Why are you asking him?" said Amity. "Just get it done."

"Unless I have a good reason, I prefer to ask first. And you being an impatient bitch isn't a good reason." Lexi returned her attention to the bewildered prisoner. "Is it okay?"

He nodded, and she placed two fingers lightly against his left temple. As their eyes met, Lexi moved in, sweeping through the traumatic impressions of his long imprisonment to the memories concealed beneath.

They'd really done a number on the guy. His body ached, especially his teeth, jaw and lower back, and the light beyond the door stung his eyes. The sound of the door being unbolted had been ingrained into his fear reflex. Fear and pain— no shortage of that here. He was afraid of the shapes that loomed over him, just shadows, faces he'd once known...

Talk, you asshole. Pain. *Hit him again.* Fear. *Amity said we're not supposed to hurt him.* Confusion. *Just do it. It's what she really wants, anyway.*

Deeper now. The darkest memories fluttered by, unraveling, and she arrived at a place of greater lucidity—his life before the endless hours in the cell. There'd been midnight meetings, a man on a street corner. A big guy. Huge. He wore a black uniform. Always seemed to be smiling...

Telling them anything, everything. Shame so intense he could taste it, a nauseating presence in his guts and throat. He longed to tell Nikolas. But what if the shut-ins really could bring her back?

"Your daughter," said Lexi, and the prisoner's eyes filled with tears. "You thought she'd run off. Then a man got in contact with you. A shut-in, an agent. Told you that he knew where she was."

"I wanted her home." The prisoner spoke in a cracked whisper. "I didn't want her hurt."

"I don't care why he's a traitor," said Amity. "Just tell me what he knows."

Lexi focused. One recent memory was especially potent, as if it had seared itself with great force into the man's mind. She coaxed it toward her and immersed herself in the moment.

Being woken…a rough shake of his shoulder, a face obscured by the gloom. Eyes hovering in the dark. *Keep quiet.* One of his captors—one of the women. *Say anything, and we kill your girl. You say one word to that crazy cunt…* The door closing again, the bolt sliding shut.

Lexi returned to the clarity of one mind. As she stood, she cast a casual glance toward the revolutionaries by the door. The woman on Amity's right seemed on edge, and her hand had slipped beneath her jacket. Not hard to put the pieces together. Deadly, jagged pieces.

"Well?" said Amity. "Has he told them about Bunker One?"

Lexi moved first. As the revolutionary drew a pistol, Lexi caught her wrist and pushed it upward, and the first shot—an intense splitting pop, deafening in this small space—hit the ceiling. A second shot rang outside, followed by the sound of something hitting the floor.

Another revolutionary filled the doorway, a pistol in his hand. He turned it on the startled man standing to Amity's left and fired.

Before the shooter could act again, Amity slammed her palm against his face, crushing his nose and smearing his face with blood. As he reeled, she drove her fist into his throat. Blood sprayed from his mouth.

The moment of carnage distracted Lexi from the woman struggling in her grip, who took the chance to lunge with her free hand. Lexi moved just in time to avoid being struck. She wasn't strong enough to restrain the woman any longer, and that gun was still between them. Time to act.

"About that movie." Lexi touched the woman's forehead. "The guy was dead all along. Hell of a twist, right?"

She looked into the woman's eyes and tore into her exposed mind, shredding its contents as she flew. Lexi concentrated harder, and the woman's mind erupted into white flame. The woman's slack body hit the floor grotesquely, a thing both heavy and empty.

Queasy to the point of dizziness, Lexi took a deep breath. There was a reason she rarely did this.

"What have you done to her?" Amity was standing over the wreckage of her assailant. Blood splattered her hands and coat. It didn't look like any of it was hers. "God, look at her eyes…"

"She'll live. But somebody's going to have to remind her how to tie her shoelaces." Lexi pointed to the man at Amity's feet. "Is he dead?"

Amity wiped her hands on her trench coat. "I hope so."

"You did that with your bare hands?"

"I didn't have time to reach for my knife." Amity squatted beside the revolutionary who had been shot. He'd fallen to his knees, and his breath came in ragged gasps. "Is it serious?"

The man shook his head. His face glistened with sweat. "I don't think so. Grazed a rib. But it hurts like hell."

Amity looked through the doorway and exhaled a dismayed breath. "Bess is dead." Her mental wall had cracked, exposing writhing, gnawing dismay. "I don't understand what just happened."

"Those two were working for the shut-ins. They'd been screwing with your interrogation by pressuring your prisoner to keep quiet."

"But that doesn't make sense. They could have simply killed the traitor to silence him." Amity stared at the prisoner, who had retreated to the corner and was sitting there, hunched. "I see. They were prolonging this man's suffering in order to cause me and Nikolas to feud. Thus damaging the unity of Open Hand."

"What kind of sick fucks would come up with a plan like that?"

"Sicker fucks than you know. Did this man ever meet his contact?"

"He only met the guy at night, but I could tell he was tall. Heavy build."

"Lachlan Reed." Amity bared her teeth. "I'll look into the matter of the traitor's daughter, but I suspect she's a red herring. This particular agent is an opportunist, not a kidnapper."

The man who'd been shot groaned. "Amity…"

Amity nodded. "We have to get you medical help."

"I know a guy who's pretty good with a scalpel." Lexi said. "By the way, your jailbird here was tortured. He's pretty fucked up."

"That's not true. I gave orders for him not to be harmed."

Another smart person made stupid by arrogance. "How many numbers do I have to guess before you get the point? I don't know who tortured him, but somebody did."

"But I trusted these people. I chose them myself."

"Let me guess, you chose them because they could fight. I've seen it before. Some idiot crime lord surrounds himself with killers, thinking it'll make him the toughest guy around. Truth is, anyone who can kill without hesitation isn't the kind of person you want at your back. Or your front. Or anywhere within one hundred meters of you." Lexi snapped her fingers. "Come on. You don't have time to stand here wondering how you fucked up so bad. Someone's been shot, remember?"

"Of course." Amity stared at her blood-smeared hands. "I'm sure I can explain this to Nikolas. He'll understand."

"Two of my people are dead." Nikolas paced the floor of the strategy room, his fingers working in frantic agitation through his hair. "One appears to be comatose. The other is wounded. To add to the debacle, you yourself, Amity, are responsible for one of these deaths."

"It was self-defense. Are you questioning my right to protect myself?"

"I'm questioning your judgment!" For a guy who'd seemed so mellow before, Nikolas sure had a hell of a temper. His rubbery features stretched into angry contortions, and his eyebrows jumped with every shouted emphasis. "You used Project Sky, that terrible device created to subdue and control free minds, and this madness is the direct consequence!"

If his fury had any effect on Amity, she gave no indication. "Traitors were exposed. This may have saved us from an even greater disaster."

"You have no authority to make such decisions by yourself. I insisted that Alexis not be used in this fashion. No, I commanded it." Nikolas glared at Lexi, the only other occupant of the so-called strategy room, before looking back to Amity. "And you tell me the man was tortured?"

"Yes." Amity closed her eyes. "But I didn't order anyone to do so."

"I took you under my wing when the others warned me not to. You were too dangerous, they told me." A note of reproach entered Nikolas's voice. "Perhaps I should have listened to them."

"Their object is to divide us. Don't play into their hands."

"You're the one dividing us!" Nikolas returned to his fervid pacing and agitated hair-pulling. "Even traitors must stand before me and be held accountable, not be simply killed or wiped. Wiped!"

He shook his head at Lexi. "The technique of our enemy, used in our name. I don't blame you, as I know you were coerced, backed into a corner... But Amity, you should have known what it would mean to turn her loose. To give her no choice."

Amity matched his furious stare with a cold look of her own. "You act as if I had a choice myself."

"You did have a choice. Everything that transpired was a consequence of the choice you made. Your judgement of late has been poor, you have proven yourself unable to adhere to even the most basic—"

This pompous rant was starting to grate on the nerves. "Get over yourself," said Lexi. Nikolas gaped at her. "She's right, and you're being an asshole. You stuck that guy underground and forgot about him. If you think that gives you the moral high ground, you're delusional."

Nikolas grimaced. "Please stay out of this, won't you? You're only making it more difficult."

"I'm sure I am. It's much tougher to talk shit when someone's calling you out on it." Lexi inspected her neatly-trimmed nails. "Amity didn't force me, either. I chose to go. I chose to read that guy's mind. I chose to turn that woman into mindless jelly. So don't blame Amity. Blame me."

"Don't lie on my behalf," said Amity. "I pressured you into this."

"You give yourself too much credit." Lexi gave Nikolas an insolent smile. "What are you going to do now, Nicky-boy?"

Nikolas pointed to the door. "Amity, please leave us. You may keep your rank, but this is your last warning. No more incidents."

"As you wish." Amity glanced sidelong at Lexi, who winked. Amity averted her eyes and hurried from the room.

After the door had closed, Nikolas sighed. "What are you doing, Vale?"

"Whatever I want to. It's my method. Time to get used to it."

Nikolas resumed pacing, hands clasped behind him. "May I tell you something about Amity? It may help you to understand her unique character."

"So long as she wouldn't mind my knowing."

"It's common knowledge. She joined Open Hand after having killed a prominent gang member in one of the neighboring districts. A number of his friends were eager to exact vengeance. She had a reputation for viciousness and lethality, and much of our leadership at that time wanted nothing to do with her. They saw her as a blood-soaked executioner. I alone saw the fallen angel."

"I've met some killers in the business, and I can tell you, she's the real thing. She ripped that guy apart."

"Indeed. We wish to reach out with an open hand, but at times we must reluctantly use a fist. Amity is that fist. The local gangs live in terror of her, and our own recruits are almost as intimidated. Her self-control is often impeccable, yet at all times it feels that there is a savage beast within her, waiting to be unchained."

"You have the weirdest way of talking, you know that? Fallen angels, savage beasts…"

"We revolutionaries tend to adopt the rhetorical patterns peculiar to those texts that inspire us. For me, that means the inestimable works of Angelo Abramo. A man with a colorful, one might even say fantastic, turn of phrase. A writer of magical allegory turned to revolution." Nikolas arched an eyebrow. "Your friend Kade, on the other hand, is fond of blunter writers. I believe he has a particular liking for Orwell."

Way to pivot to an unwelcome subject. "He's not my friend."

"You may not be his friend, but he most certainly is yours." Nikolas reached into his pocket. "This afternoon, he brought me this."

Lexi accepted the photo with an unsteady hand. She stared at the image— seeing that frozen smile never got any easier—before flipping the photo to read the swirl of blue ink on the back. *Love you, cuz. A.* Both photo and message might be scanned, reprinted, or looked at endlessly on her phone. But nothing could replicate the feeling of holding the original. It still bore Ash's fingerprints, the ink from her pen…

"I still mourn for her," said Nikolas. "As I imagine you must."

Damned if she'd tear up in front of this asshole. Lexi put the photo away and tried to find her composure again. It wasn't the reminder that shook her most— she knew Ash was dead, and looking at the photo didn't change a thing. No, what stung her was that she had forgotten this keepsake even existed.

But Kade had remembered.

Nikolas's elastic face had grown subdued, as if the anger he had unleashed on Amity had tired him. "Loss scars our soul. Some become so scarred, little recognizable is left. Amity is one such walking wound."

"Then be compassionate instead of treating her like she's a child who just fucked up."

"I've tried. If you think you have the talent to reach her, be my guest."

"I never asked to be part of this. I was happy the way things were."

Nikolas smiled without warmth. "Were you?"

"I'm finished, okay? I'm done with your weird ass." Lexi stalked to the door and seized the handle. He didn't say a word, just let her leave, and that was the most frustrating thing of all.

Lexi tapped twice. No answer. She tapped again, this time more insistently, and the door shifted a crack. Amity scowled through the opening. Seeing Lexi, she softened the scowl to a frown. "What?"

"Can I come in?"

Amity withdrew, leaving the door ajar. Her room was a little smaller than Riva's, with some of the space stolen by a thick pipe running up one wall. A narrow bed had been pushed into a corner, an old chest of drawers sat at the bed's foot and temporary shelving had been arranged around the room. No wall decorations beyond a simple mirror.

"Huh," said Lexi, closing the door while Amity moved barefoot across the room and sat on the edge of her bed. "I expected something bigger."

"I don't see why you would."

"Pretty wild night we just had." Lexi drifted around the room, inspecting the shelves. A few old belt buckles, some flasks, a pocket knife—nothing exciting. "I guess you're still upset."

"I don't get upset." Amity sat as erect as if she were being graded for posture. "I'm only sorry you had to witness that farcical scene between Nikolas and me."

"Fuck him." Lexi took a pair of reading glasses from a shelf. "These yours?"

"Not everyone can afford vision augmentation. Or even eye surgery."

"Talk to Zeke. He'll fix you up." Lexi put the glasses on, marveled at the blurry world they revealed and returned them to the shelf. "By the way, is he going to pull through? The guy who got shot?"

"Yes, he's fine." Amity spoke softly, an unexpected change from the clipped, cool delivery Lexi had become used to. "Why did you stand up for me? I've done nothing but insult and exploit you."

"A whim." Lexi paused before the mirror and stroked her scalp's shaved section. Growing back fast. Hopefully Callie had some clippers in her van.

"I'm sure you didn't come here to ogle yourself."

Lexi pursed her lips, admiring her pout, before turning away from her reflection. "What you said before about Riva. I want to clear that up."

Amity lowered her head. "I see."

"I'm only here temporarily, so what does it hurt if I spend some time with her? I mean, she likes me. Are you homophobic or something?"

"Not in the least. You're simply a bad influence, and I don't want to see her hurt. I have a duty to everyone in Open Hand."

"What makes you think I'd hurt her?"

"Fine. Do as you please. I'll just trust she has enough sense and taste to keep you at a tactful distance."

It didn't feel like much of a victory. "Don't misunderstand me. I don't need your permission, and I'm not looking for it. I just don't want any drama."

"Well, you came to the wrong revolutionary bunker, didn't you?"

A slow smile curved Lexi's lips. So Amity did have something resembling a sense of humor. "Where'd you learn to fight like that?"

"Necessity."

"You ever killed anyone before tonight?"

"You know very well that I have."

That clipped, cool attitude was starting to get a little sexy. "Am I still an arrogant dyke?"

"I apologize for that unseemly remark. Though I did mean what I said about you being gang trash. Your gangster friends share responsibility with the Codists for the desecration of Foundation and its people. They're traitors to humanity."

Ouch. Low blow. "I'm not actually in a gang, okay? I just do work for them. Anyone who wants to survive out there has to work with the gangs at some point."

"Fine. You're just ordinary trash, not gang trash."

Lexi laughed. "I promise, there's nothing ordinary about me. How much longer are you going to let Nikolas push you around, anyway?"

"I don't want conflict between us." As if suddenly wearied, Amity cupped her head in her hands and slouched forward. "But he shouldn't have given that contact of yours a radio phone. He shouldn't have waved my objections aside."

"He was right about the phone, but you were right to be cautious. You're right about my aug too. It's dangerous, but there are times to use it. Tonight wasn't such a bad idea. It wasn't your fault it all went so wrong."

"You could abuse your power in so many ways, yet you don't seem to be tempted to. I'm not sure I could be so disciplined."

"Good thing you aren't the Chosen One, then."

They appraised each other in silence. Amity wasn't attractive by the standards of preening clubbers, but Lexi had her own tastes, and Amity satisfied them just fine. A stern, athletic older woman who seemed to be perpetually brooding over some perceived insult, took no shit from anyone and could kill on a whim—definite appeal.

"It can't be easy," Lexi said. "Dealing with his crap."

"Sometimes I can't stand the sight of him, yet I need him. I don't have his charisma or his knack for leadership. But I shouldn't be telling you this. There's nothing you can do."

Forget the threats, the murder, the politics. This woman needed a lengthy distraction, and so did Lexi. She gave her a crooked smile. "I could take the edge off."

"With your implant?"

"No." Lexi knelt before Amity, laid both hands on her knees and looked up into her widening eyes. "With my mouth."

Amity blushed. "You can't be serious."

"Why not? All you have to do is sit back and relax."

"That's ridiculous." Despite her protests, Amity made no attempt to remove Lexi's hands from her knees. "Even putting aside that I have no interest in you, just hours ago, you were flirting with Riva."

"And now I'm flirting with you. You don't have to touch me, you don't even have to look at me. Just let me do what I do best, comrade. You can imagine I'm Lenin for all I care."

A long silence ensued. Neither broke eye contact. Finally, Amity turned her head away. "If you tell anyone…"

"Not a word."

Lexi reached into Amity's lap, popped the button of her trousers and drew down the zipper. She eased off the trousers and took a moment to admire Amity's bare, unshaven legs. Impressive calf muscles. "Nod once if you're still with me."

Amity gave a barely perceptible nod. Lexi stroked her fingertip up the inside of Amity's thigh and over the crotch of her panties, and Amity inhaled a quick breath. Encouraged, Lexi hooked a finger around the panties and coaxed them over Amity's hips.

"Another chance," Lexi said. "If you don't want this, say so now."

Amity opened her mouth, bit her lip and looked away again. Lexi pushed apart Amity's knees and leaned in.

Amity smelled good and tasted better—the distinctive, aromatic flavor of an active woman who infrequently bathed and never trimmed. When it came to eating pussy, Lexi was an enthusiast for the entire experience: that hint of iron inside the vagina, the tang of sweat outside it, the coarse texture of labia majora sucked between her lips, the smooth skin of a clitoral hood sliding under the tip of her tongue…

Breathing rapidly, Amity held Lexi's head and forced her deeper. Lexi obliged, pushing the tip of her tongue further inside, and Amity began to move her hips while issuing soft moans. Lexi glanced up and caught Amity staring back, her eyes dull and her face flushed.

Amity looked away, but it was too late—her mental wall had fallen, exposing the shivering contents of her mind. Lust, excitement, a hint of delicious disbelief. And a consuming desire to fuck the gorgeous face trapped between her legs.

Amity's grinding motions became forceful, as if she were desperate for the pressure of Lexi's mouth. Lexi gripped Amity's hips and licked her clit hard. Amity climaxed with a full-body spasm, releasing a startled gasp and twisting her fingers through Lexi's hair.

"Oh, God." Amity stared at the ceiling. "Don't tell anyone. Promise me."

"I promise."

"Good. Now go away. I…" Amity closed her eyes and took in a deep breath. "Goodnight."

Smirking, Lexi returned to her feet and took in the sight of Amity sitting dazed and blushing, her pussy still wet and parted. "Thank you, comrade."

Amity put her hands between her legs. "You're welcome. Get out."

CHAPTER 11

The children of the elite enjoyed a breakfast menu so extravagant it seemed almost satirical. While the students in the main dormitories feasted on prosaic meals of textured soy protein and legumes, the buffet before Mineko contained such steaming luxuries as *Pan-Fried Faux Pork with Cashew* and *Miniature Leek in Black Bean Sauce.* Why a miniature leek? Did it taste any better for being smaller?

Mineko took a container of edamame, and the kitchen hand gave her a curious look. "I've never seen you take the beans before, Ms. Tamura."

"I'm trying new things." Mineko ladled rice onto her plate and covered it with a helping of the mock pork and sauce. With the bowl in one hand and the plate held precariously in the other, she made her way to a little table in the corner.

Beyond the nearest window, the morning sky was clear, and the blossom trees were still. She chewed on a soft piece of mock pork while skimming through her study notes. Nothing occupied her thoughts, however, but the cherubic face of Callie Roux.

A throat cleared, and Mineko looked up. Lachlan stood before her, his face made even more unpleasant by its broad smile.

"Good morning, Mineko," he said. "Enjoying your breakfast?"

Mineko forced herself to swallow. Lachlan never came to campus. Was she in trouble? "My breakfast is fine."

"Mind if I sit down?"

"Not at all," she said while trying to wish him out of existence.

Lachlan drew out the opposite chair. "How's the exam preparation?"

"Fine. Why are you here?"

"Last night, you and Wren spoke privately." Lachlan reclined in the chair, and it gave an unhappy creak. It clearly hadn't been designed with his imposing build in mind. "Did she say anything I ought to know about?"

"I'm unaware of what you ought to know about, Lachlan."

Lachlan took an edamame pod and frowned at it. "These don't look very appealing."

"Please don't play with my food."

Students drifted by, laughing and chatting. Lachlan gave them a quick, suspicious look, as if there might be revolutionaries concealed among them. "You and Dr. Wren," he said. "Would you say that you got along well?"

Before answering, Mineko took a quick mouthful of food—no point letting it get cold—and swallowed. "We have similar interests. She's a neuroscientist, and I study Neuroethics. So we had plenty to talk about."

"I'm certain you did. I escorted her home after dinner, and during her nervous conversation, she mentioned how impressed she was with you. 'A remarkable young woman.' That was her estimation." Lachlan popped one of the beans into his mouth. "These are very salty, aren't they?"

"I couldn't say. You interrupted me before I could try any."

Lachlan smiled and split another pod between his fingers. "As you're in a blunt mood this morning, I'll treat you in kind. I want you to spy on Valerie Wren for us."

Mineko stared at him, fork still raised. Of all the reasons Lachlan might have been here, that was one she had never anticipated. "Spy on her?"

"I was going to sugarcoat it by suggesting you befriend her, but I can see you're an adult now and deserve adult explanations." Lachlan leaned closer. "She's a reclusive woman with no friends or immediate family. That means we have no straightforward way of evaluating her moods and behavior. But perhaps you, with your disarming demeanor, can find a way to uncover her private side."

The thought of exploiting Valerie's friendliness soured the previously pleasant taste in Mineko's mouth. "I'm not a spy. Is my father aware you're asking this of me?"

"He tells me, again and again, that you're destined to the business and should be involved. I can't see why he would object."

Lachlan's close proximity was putting Mineko off her food, and she poked her breakfast one last time before putting down her fork. "It's unethical. You're asking me to betray her confidence."

"That's an odd comment from an ethics student. I'm asking you to help me support a fellow Codist's well-being. That kind of solidarity is essential to the functioning of our ordered society. Trust me, you don't want to get that one wrong on the exam."

There was no way out—Lachlan had her comprehensively trapped. If she refused his offer, she would seem disloyal, and the last thing she needed was to raise any suspicions.

"I just meant that I'd feel bad about it," Mineko said. "Dr. Wren seems very nice."

"Understandable. But you'd be making your parents proud, and you'd be serving the Code. Think of that instead."

Easier to think of throttling him. "What exactly would you have me to do?"

Lachlan took a data drive from his pocket and placed it beside her plate. "Dr. Wren's security file is on this drive. Look it over and then establish contact. Find a way to secure her confidence, at least to some small extent. I fully expect her to be loyal and dedicated, but she's leading a very important project. It's a stressful position. We need to think of her long-term welfare."

As she pondered, Mineko chewed on a mouthful of cold rice. This might give her a chance to learn more about Project Sky, and she could choose herself what information to leak to Lachlan. Besides, if he hadn't picked her, he would have selected someone else. At least this way, she had a chance to protect Valerie if protection were needed.

She finished her rice. "Thank you, Lachlan, for trusting me with this responsibility. I'll do what I can."W

"Good day, Mineko. And don't worry if this cuts into your study time." Lachlan winked. "Exam results can be quite flexible."

He departed the dining room while the students around them fixed their eyes on their food. Every Codist, no matter how honest or devoted, knew better than to look too long at someone in a black uniform.

As she scooped up more rice with her fork, Mineko glanced at her blue sleeve. How long until she too was forced to wear that sinister black?

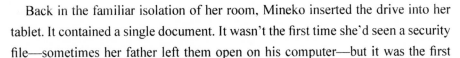

Back in the familiar isolation of her room, Mineko inserted the drive into her tablet. It contained a single document. It wasn't the first time she'd seen a security file—sometimes her father left them open on his computer—but it was the first time she'd known the person in question.

The attached photo showed Valerie frowning at the camera from beneath blunt bangs, looking every bit as nervous as she had at dinner. She was forty-three years old, had been born in Foundation Hospital Three and her parents had both been scientists. One a physicist, one a biochemist. That was to be expected. Codist children usually followed the career paths of their parents, graduating with the same degrees and working in the same departments. A fact Mineko was acutely aware of.

The file listed every detail of Valerie's career and education, including her grades, which put Mineko's to shame. Intriguingly, Valerie had worked in Reintegration for two years as a chief technical advisor; the job had ended with her resignation, after which she had moved to a less-prestigious position as a scientific advisor for Hospital Two's neurosurgery ward.

Project Sky appeared as the final note on her career timeline, accompanied by the title of her new role: *Project Supervisor*. Mineko prodded for further details, and a message flashed.

Subject offered position due to excellent qualifications, deep knowledge of relevant field and lack of close social ties.

Lack of social ties? A reference to the secret nature of the Project? Or, as Valerie had feared, had she been selected because her isolation made it easier to eliminate her if necessary?

The final section, *Security Concerns*, was blank. Of course. Nobody with a questionable history would have been assigned to a project of such importance. No, Code Intel would endorse someone like Valerie Wren: a brilliant scientist with a clean record, no close friends and a career that, until now, had been less impressive than her credentials, save for a brief stint in Reintegration.

Mineko gave her nose a thoughtful rub. How was she supposed to find enough common ground to befriend a reclusive woman twice her age? Even though she and Valerie had spoken candidly the night before, Mineko was Gaspar Tamura's daughter.

Still, there was no harm in trying.

The file included Valerie's personal number. Mineko navigated to her comm client and added Valerie as a new contact, prodding each digit in. Two more quick taps began the dialing process. It was probably the wrong time to call, but if she didn't do it now, it would be on her mind all day.

As the sixth beep chimed, it occurred to Mineko that she hadn't prepared anything to say. Maybe it wasn't too late to—

Click. "Hello?"

"Um, hello, Dr. Wren. It's Mineko Tamura. I hope I'm not disturbing you."

"Oh! Mineko! I'm just on the train now, going to work... I, uh, how did you find my number?" Her skittishness was still endearing.

"It's in the directory. Do you mind me calling you?"

"No, not at all. Is there something I can help you with?"

"Well, it's exam time…"

"Oh, is it? You poor thing. I remember how much stress I went through with my exams." Valerie gave a brittle laugh. "Of course, that was me. You're a very clever girl, and I'm sure you're quite confident."

"Actually, I'm a little apprehensive. There's a section on Reintegration in the exam, and I don't feel ready for it."

"Oh, Reintegration. I remember you and I talked about that briefly. As it happens, I know quite a bit about it."

Mineko shook her head silently. This woman was so leadable. "I hoped that might be the case. I was wondering if you'd help me study. If I could just discuss the material with you, I'm sure I'd learn a lot."

"Oh, absolutely, I'd be—"

The calm voice of the train interrupted her: "Five minutes until arrival at Laboratory Two."

"Sorry," said Valerie, followed by a breathless, nervous giggle. "I'm almost there. No, I'd be happy to. Would you like to talk by message or in person?"

This had been too easy. Maybe Mineko really was destined for Code Intel. "I find it easier talking face-to-face."

"In that case, you could come over for dinner. Whenever you like. It won't be fancy, and my place is a little messy, but…" Valerie gave another of her odd, skittish laughs. "Well, there's a nice view from the balcony."

"Is tonight okay? The exam is next week."

"Yes, yes, tonight would be fine. I'm quite looking forward to it. It's nice to be remembered. Um." Valerie cleared her throat. "Well, I have to disembark soon, so I'd better say goodbye. But how lovely to hear from you."

Mineko smiled. It really was sweet how hopeless Valerie proved to be. "I need your address, remember. And a time would be good."

"Oh! Of course! I live in Urban Enclave Eight. It's a tower residence, Tower Three. I have the fourteenth level. And, uh, six PM?"

"Thank you, that sounds good. I'll see you there at six."

"Oh, good. Um. Goodbye for now. The door is opening, you see, I have to rush…" There was a tremendous clattering sound. "Oh, I dropped my phone! It's not broken, thankfully, but I gave myself quite a fright…"

"I'm glad it wasn't damaged. I'll see you tonight." Mineko tapped the disconnect button, and the tablet became silent.

Well, how about that—a private dinner with the head of Project Sky, approved by Lachlan Reed. It was hard to imagine a greater stroke of luck. The next time she spoke to Lexi, Mineko would be able to explain everything about her implant, and everyone would be impressed. Kade would marvel at how clever she was, Callie would be proud of her…

The prospect of helping the others had reversed Mineko's mood entirely, and now evening couldn't come soon enough. It helped that Valerie wasn't a daunting personality. Perhaps she too felt alienated from Codist society. Despite the age difference, it wasn't implausible they might have things in common after all. And Mineko had liked her worried eyes, her apprehensive smile.

Was this sufficient justification to use the radio phone Callie had given her? Surely they'd be interested in hearing her news. And she was so very desperate to know if they were still safe.

Mineko hopped off the bed, opened her wardrobe and stood on her toes. Running her hand along the top shelf, she bumped her fingers against the radio phone. It only had two buttons, one a sliding switch marked *Receive*, the other a depressible button marked *Transmit*. Simple enough.

Mineko slid the switch, and static hissed. Her heart trembling, she held down the transmission button. "This is Blue calling…"

Several agonizing seconds passed. The phone produced nothing but ominous dead noise. "This is Blue. Is anyone—"

The static cleared. "This is Bunker One. Please re-identify yourself." The voice was unfamiliar, but whoever he was, he sounded serious.

"My codename is Blue. I was told I could use this line."

"Acknowledged, Blue. What do you have to transmit?"

How likely was it that someone could intercept this radio transmission? Callie had said the channel was encrypted, but could these revolutionaries be sure that Lachlan's team hadn't already cracked it?

Yet Mineko had to take the risk. "Is Callie Roux there?"

"Please hold for a moment."

The static returned, and Mineko clutched the phone tight. Why was it taking so long? Had something happened to them? Why had she even done this stupid thing? She should have waited until she had a better reason.

The line became clear again, and a new voice—mellow, male—spoke. "Good morning, Blue. I'm Nikolas Reinhold, Commander of Open Hand."

"Oh. Hello. Aren't you apprehensive about talking to a Codist?"

"You came with excellent character references. Though I must say, you sound younger than I expected. But youth is no impediment to greatness, isn't that so?"

So, revolutionaries were a little strange. It was to be expected, perhaps. "Are they all right? My friends?"

"They are very well, but I'm afraid you can't speak to them. They're being relocated to another bunker. We had a security incident last night."

"An incident?" Mineko swallowed hard. "What happened?"

"Nothing that should concern you. The chief outcome was to convince me Alexis is better suited to a remote location." Nikolas made a thoughtful humming noise. "I'll see if I can arrange a way for you to contact them later today, but at the moment, I have other preoccupations. I trust you have nothing urgent to share?"

Mineko sank onto her bed, flattened by disappointment. She hadn't realized until now how badly she wanted to hear their voices, Callie's most of all. "No. Nothing urgent."

Another hum, this time sympathetic. "Do keep yourself safe, my young comrade. Those who liberate themselves are the bravest of us all."

The static returned, and Mineko flicked the switch. So much for that.

CHAPTER 12

Kade jumped his bike to the curb, sped past the glittering asphalt and bounced back to the road. Good thing he'd spotted the glass in time—this wasn't the kind of neighborhood a smart person walked through. In the inner districts, the gangs focused their violence on each other, wary of drawing the attention of the Codists. Out here, though, a different rule prevailed: live by the switchblade, die by the switchblade.

Callie had parked her van outside a ramshackle office building. Nobody was visible but Zeke, who sat between the van's open rear doors. It was hard to admire the profane body modder, who had become a big figure in Lexi's life right about the time she'd started to grow distant from Kade, but there was no reason not to give him a chance. Kade called out his name.

Zeke raised his head, and morning light glittered off his piercings. "Nice bike."

Kade dismounted. "Where's everyone else?"

"Callie's around back trying to get the power working. The others are just inside. Apparently, it's a shithole in there."

"Nikolas told me what happened last night. How's everyone doing?"

"We're okay. Keeping it together." Zeke grinned. "Fucking Lex, though. She's already picked up some girl, Riva, and brought her along. Cute wisp with a Mohawk. Callie seems keen on her too. It's all a big, queer-lady love-in."

"And you're doing what now, exactly?"

"Me? Just keeping my head down. I mean, we can't all be fucking cyborgs or smugglers or crazy guerilla fighters." Zeke indicated the door with a tilt of his head. "Your scary friend is in there."

"I assume you mean Amity. Thanks."

"Sure thing. Tell her to lighten up a little, huh?"

Not much hope of *that*. Kade entered the building via its front door. Sunlight illuminated a filthy reception room. A front desk lay in two splintered halves, and every window pane was shattered, with the shards still strewn across the floor. Amity stood at the far side of the room, wrestling with a doorknob.

She turned. "What are you doing here?"

It was, from Amity, tantamount to a warm welcome. "Investigative journalism. You don't have the key for this door?"

"I thought I did, but it doesn't fit. I'm going to have to get that smuggler to open it." Amity thumped the door with her palm. "This place scarcely qualifies as a bunker anymore. It's been abandoned for years."

"I heard about the events of last night. Why did you do it?"

"Because she's an asset. And to my endless surprise, she has potential."

Now that was unexpected. According to Nikolas, Amity had expressed nothing but animosity toward Lexi from the moment she'd arrived. "I guess you've finally seen her in action," Kade said.

For no obvious reason, Amity reddened. "I need to get this door open, if you don't mind. And it's about time these lights came on—"

The sound of lively chattering interrupted her. Lexi entered the room accompanied by a skinny, olive-complexioned woman wearing a black tank top, tight jeans, and tall, buckled boots. Her exquisite face, haunting blue-gray eyes, and vibrant pink Mohawk made her seem more than a match for the handsome hedonist beside her. Riva, surely.

"Shit," said Lexi. "This place does have rats." Carefully measured syllables of contempt.

"Lexi." Kade made eye contact without fear—he had nothing to hide from her. "Did Nikolas give you the photo?"

The hostility left Lexi's face, replaced by a sheepish expression. "Yeah."

And with that, the tension seemed to break. "I'm Kade August." Kade extended his hand to Riva. "*Revolutionary People's Gazette.*"

Riva allowed her hand to be shaken. "Riva Latour. I love your writing, comrade. It's an honor."

"You're very kind." Kade admired her again. Pretty enough to make him wish he'd shaved.

Lexi sauntered over to Amity. "You still struggling with this door, sweet thing? I'd have thought a badass like you would just kick it down."

"I'm going to find the smuggler," said Amity, her voice strained, and hurried from the room. Lexi watched her leave, grinning like a satisfied feline. Something was going on there. Eventually Kade would get to the bottom of it. For now, however, he was more interested in Riva.

"I heard that you came here from Bunker One," he said.

"Nikolas wanted a volunteer to make our guests comfortable." Riva said. "I'll be cooking, cleaning, and, if this morning is any indication, continually swatting Lexi's hand away from my ass."

Kade raised an eyebrow. "Don't give Lexi a free pass to be a pig."

"I just figure our friendship has developed to that stage." Lexi draped an arm over Riva's shoulders. "I like this girl, August. She had me cooking, can you believe it?"

"Not until I see it for myself." It was strange—nostalgic—to be talking to Lexi this way. A temporary truce, no doubt, facilitated by Riva's presence and the odd circumstances.

"You might not get the chance. In a few days, I'm off to Port Venn, according to Nicky-boy. Mind you, Callie's going to kick up a fuss if we leave without her precious Minnie-Min."

"So she's still determined to rescue her?"

"Yup. She's been mooning about all morning. Though as I remember, that's standard practice for our Callie Roux. At least she's still getting shit done. Which reminds me…" Lexi slunk to the door. "Hey, Zeke, you lazy fuck! Come help us clear this junk out of the corridor!"

An indignant shout returned: "I got delicate hands. You know that!"

"Riva's got delicate hands too, you asshole, and she's working her ass off."

"I gotta be able to hold a scalpel! I can't do no fucking lifting or whatever!"

"You're a pathetic piece of shit, you know that?" Lexi stepped back from the door. "Someone help me drag the bastard inside."

"He's a surgeon." Riva's laughter was charming: husky, soft, and warmed by wry amusement. "I think we can excuse him this once."

"I'll help you," said Kade. "What's in the way?"

"Heavy boxes stacked on each other. I can't say I'm sure why. They're in the hallway to the basement where the bunker facilities are."

"Odd. And there's still no light?"

"Not until Callie fixes the wires," said Lexi. "Lucky her van is full of tools. Not least of them Zeke."

Riva laughed again, and Lexi gave Kade a smug look. He knew that expression very well—*check out how great I am.* He'd not missed that one so much.

"Come on," she said. "I want to see what's behind those boxes."

Lexi and Riva struggled to shift the smaller boxes while Kade applied himself to moving the largest. The most formidable was an immense white crate that Kade pushed aside with both hands, grunting with each shove.

"That must be a heavy sucker," said Lexi. "What's in it?"

"Printer cartridges," said Riva. "It says so on the side." Hands on her hips, she surveyed their work. They'd almost cleared a path to the stairwell at the far end of the hall. "Powerful cyborg that you are, Lexi, I don't suppose you'd like to move the last one?"

Lexi knelt before the final box, slipped her fingers beneath it and groaned as she stood. "Hell, this is hard. Why do I have to do it?"

"To impress me, maybe?"

"I assumed you were interested in my personality, not my physique."

"Yes, but now that I've experienced your personality, your physique is your last hope."

Unexpectedly brutal. Kade chuckled, and Lexi gave him an unexpected grin. "Don't take sides, journalist. Remain objective." A light bulb flickered into life above them. "All praise the goddess Roux. Let's take a look."

An Open Hand sigil had been sprayed above the stairwell that descended into the clammy air of an underground passage. Kade took several quick steps to get ahead. If there was trouble ahead, he'd prefer it came to him before the women. Of course, if he admitted that sentiment out loud, Lexi would punch him in the mouth.

As they advanced into the gloom, Lexi's eyes shone with white luminescence. Riva drew a startled breath. "Lexi, your eyes."

"It's my vision aug." Lexi turned the spectral glow on Riva. "Sexy, isn't it?"

"Does that mean you can see down here?"

"A little, but not much. Kade, find a switch, won't you?"

Kade fumbled against the wall and brushed a knob of plastic. With an erratic flicker, several fluorescent tubes activated overhead. It seemed they were standing in an old galley. Charred kitchen equipment took up one corner, and several dining tables occupied another.

Another light tube glowed, and something moved in the shadows of an adjacent room. A thrill crawled down Kade's neck. "Stay back." They wouldn't listen, but it was the kind of thing a tough guy like him had to say. "I'll check it out."

"Like hell." Lexi headed toward the source of the sound, and Kade hastened to keep up. They entered the next room. Lexi hit the switch.

An unkempt man was pressed against a cement wall, his chest heaving with exertion. Matted hair concealed his face. "Get out," he said in a broken rasp. He drew a switchblade from his ragged jacket and ejected it. "Don't come near me."

Kade stayed in the doorway, his eyes on the blade and his pulse quickening. The man may have been a wreck, but the edge on his knife seemed plenty sharp. "This bunker belongs to Open Hand."

"Nothing belongs to fucking nobody."

"It's okay." Riva advanced a few steps into the room. "We can share. There's plenty of space for everyone."

"Don't go near him," said Kade. "He's dangerous."

"We don't know that." Riva took another step forward, her palms raised. "Nobody means you harm. We're looking for shelter too."

The squatter brandished the switchblade. "Get your own place."

"Riva, come back." Lexi's voice held no trace of its usual cockiness—she was anxious, and nakedly so. "Let me handle this."

"Don't worry." Riva arrived at the middle of the room, and the man tensed. "I'm Riva. Some friends of mine usually look after this shelter, but they'd be happy to let you stay. And we'd like to take refuge with you."

The man's hands began to shake, and he gave a racking cough. "I told you to get out. It's my place."

This was dicey, but what could Kade do? Clearly, Riva was one of Open Hand's true believers, a genuine adherent to its charitable teachings. If she were anywhere near as stubborn as Nikolas, nothing would sway her. Good old Comrade Reinhold tended to raise stubborn acolytes.

"It's our place," Riva said. "Not yours, not mine, but ours. Didn't you just say so yourself? Nothing belongs to anyone."

The switchblade lowered an inch. "Right. I said that."

"So it can't be your place. Only our place." Riva held out her hand. "We have food, water, and blankets. We've started up the generator. You can be warm and fed tonight. Please let us share what we have."

"Them two back there." With the tip of his blade, the man pointed to Kade and Lexi. "They want to kick me out. They don't want to share nothing."

"They're cautious. Scared. Same as you." Still that gentle, understanding tone.

"Well, I ain't giving you my fucking flick knife."

"I'm not asking for your knife. I'm only asking for your hand."

Someone clattered down the stairwell behind them. Callie's cheerful voice rang out. "Hey, anyone down here?"

"Fucking liar!" The man lunged, and Riva screamed. Panic erupted—Riva stumbling, Lexi dashing, the man raising his knife again...

A moment of clarity lit the chaos. Kade rushed the man and drove him hard against the wall. Pinned the squirming, emaciated body to the bricks. Raised his fist.

"No!" From her limp position in Lexi's arms, Riva held out her bleeding palm. "Don't hurt him. He didn't mean it."

"What's going on?" Callie sounded breathless as she jogged into the room. "I heard a scream. Riva, are you okay? Did this guy hurt you?"

"Not as much as we'll hurt him if we put him back on the street." Riva closed her eyes. "I'm a little dizzy."

Kade lowered his fist and backed down. The man stood subdued and shivering with his head lowered. "Do you understand what just happened here?" Kade said.

The man staggered to the furthest corner of the room and crouched there, a huddle of dirty limbs, torn clothing, and unwashed hair. "I didn't want to hurt her. But this is my place."

"Don't tell Amity." Riva's face glistened with sweat. "Just say I cut myself."

"Let's get you fixed up," said Lexi. "Come on." She guided Riva from the room with an arm around her waist.

Callie fidgeted, as if anxious to follow. "The poor thing. Do you think she's okay?"

"Let's hope so," said Kade. "Where's Amity?"

"Tearing into Zeke. She was pissed that he was lazing about in the van." Callie hunkered down in front of the trembling man. "Hey, guy. You can't just sit there forever, you know."

The man slowly turned his head toward her. His shaking eased, and he blinked several times as if coming to consciousness. "You're pretty."

"And you're filthy. When's the last time you had a bath?"

"Bath's a waste of water." The man produced a cough that might, from a different set of lungs, have been a chuckle. "Hope I didn't cut her bad."

"Me too. She's a friend of mine. But you gotta worry about yourself as well, and we have a doc. He might be able to take a look at you."

"The girl told me food. Blankets."

"Sure. Food, blankets. That's what this place was meant for. Looking after people." Callie peered up at Kade. "Are you going to do something, or do you just like to watch?"

It was a fair point. A reporter's habit, maybe, hoping to memorize each detail so that he could reproduce it later in print. "Get up," Kade said. With obvious trepidation, the man placed his gnarled claw in Kade's palm. Kade hauled him to his feet. "You have a name?"

"Isaac Landon Hill. That's what it is."

"You don't seem too steady on your feet, Isaac."

"Been down too long in the dark." Isaac expelled another frightening cough. "Getting real hard to move them boxes I put up. Was resting, getting my strength back, when you came by."

"Why would you need to hide in the dark?"

"I crossed some people. The kind you don't cross."

"That makes sense," said Callie. "The gangs out this way can be seriously unhinged. We're talking cutting up people and nailing them to things, like whoever can be the most fucked-up wins a prize."

Isaac gave her a mournful look. "They'd have seen you come in."

"That's fine," said Kade. "We're not scared of your gangs. There's only one real terror in this district, and you're about to meet her." He released Isaac's hand, and the man remained on his feet. "Come on, Callie. Let's go think up some lie to tell Amity."

Noon arrived, bringing with it dark clouds and a strong breeze that rattled the antennas atop the street's crumbling buildings. In the back of the van, Zeke tended to Riva's injured hand while Lexi knelt beside her, holding the undamaged one. Callie sat by the road, her arms around her knees and her face turned to the sky. Watching her, Kade was touched by a sense of solidarity. He'd been there.

"And it's just you here," Amity said to the unfortunate Isaac Landon Hill, who after five seconds in her presence had become a timid diminution of his already wretched self. "Nobody else?"

"Just me, ma'am." Isaac plucked at the frayed edge of his sleeve. "You leave your van there, somebody's gonna take it."

"You let us worry about that." Amity beckoned to Kade. "Come with me."

Kade followed her into the building, which was now illuminated by a powerful overhead light in addition to the noonday glow streaming through the windows. Amity directed them through the door she'd been struggling with and into an office left relatively untouched by time.

"Wonder if this works." Kade brushed dust from a computer tower. "It's fascinating what you can dig up from old hard-drives."

"Investigate later."

Floorboards creaked as Amity advanced on a wall safe. She twirled the dial, and after three spins—each producing a satisfying click—she opened the safe door. Inside were a pair of black pistols and several boxes of ammunition.

Amity offered a pistol to Kade, and he glanced at the safety as he took it. She concealed the other pistol inside her trench coat. "I trust you still have the nerve to pull a trigger."

"Yes. And Callie's packing too. I saw a shotgun in the back of that van."

"I understand you know her. Is she reliable?"

"I'd vouch for her any day. Brave, tough, and loyal to a fault. In a pinch, I couldn't ask for anyone better beside me."

"Interesting. Most smugglers are self-serving mercenaries. I suppose we're lucky to have her, seeing as we'd have no power otherwise." Amity slammed the safe shut. "It was Reed, by the way, who orchestrated the prisoner farce."

"He's in charge of the hunt for Lexi as well. It seems he's shaking off the cobwebs."

"You know his mind better than anyone. Why didn't he take Lexi by force as soon as she was identified? Why involve some ridiculous gang?"

"Because Lachlan revels in making the gangs do the work of the Codists. His signature style is coercion, unwitting proxies, deception. That's how he plays the game."

Amity sneered. "Like a coward?"

How to explain to Amity that Lachlan, for all his faults, was still a mind to be respected? "Like a strategist. If a high-powered gang broker like Lexi vanished into a vehicle escorted by agents, it would put the Codists in the spotlight. They don't like that. So Lachlan tried to make it seem like a gang affair. He wanted people to assume she'd crossed somebody in a deal, that she was getting what she deserved."

"And you won't divulge the identity of your informant? Not even to me?"

"Not even to you." Remaining silent was the best Kade could do for Mineko, for whom there could be no escape route, no safe house. It was all too easy to imagine her sitting in the dark, waiting for a fateful knock at the door, her clever eyes filled with tears.

For a moment, Amity pursed her lips, her green eyes livid with offense—but then her scowl softened slightly, as it sometimes did for a special few. "You look troubled. May I help in some way?"

"I'm fine. It's just been a hard couple of days."

"I understand. Did Riva really cut her hand while moving debris?"

Kade shrugged. "That's what she told me."

"I don't like having that Isaac around. Something about him puts my hackles up."

"Amity, I've never seen you with your hackles down."

She treated him to a rare smile. "True enough."

A floorboard squeaked. Lexi stood in the doorway. "A rendezvous, huh? Secret revolutionary business?"

Amity blushed and studied her own hands as if they were the most interesting things in the world. Odd.

"Something like that," said Kade, breaking the tense silence. "Mostly we were hoping for a conversation without any wisecracks."

"I don't like being left out." Lexi entered the room in that languid way of hers. She'd always been the coolest one in their childhood trio, capable of confounding street bullies with nothing but a sardonic grin. Kade had for months been tongue-tied in her presence. Then she'd opened up to him, the first of many times to come, and he'd discovered she was almost as frightened as he was. Just much better at hiding it.

"We'll write you an invite next time," said Amity. "Now stop pouting."

"Mr. Landon Hill is a mess, if you're wondering. A junkie. He's strung out, his head's all confused." Lexi spun her index finger beside her left ear. "All blurry up here."

"But not a threat? Just a harmless addict?"

"Right now, he's a threat mostly to my nasal passages." Her smile teasing, Lexi closed in on Amity and brushed a strand of hair from her forehead. "You staying here with me tonight, beautiful?"

So that was it. Lexi was trying to seduce Amity, and it was making her uncomfortable. Hard to resist the old urge to pull Lexi aside and give her a lecture on respecting women. She had always thought of herself as uniquely desirable—it was unfathomable that her attentions might be unwelcome. One of Lexi's least pleasant attributes.

Amity took a quick step back. "Don't touch me like that. And yes, I'm staying. As punishment for my apparent misdeeds, Nikolas expects me to devote all my time to your protection."

"Mmm. Fun." Lexi frowned at Kade. "And what about the revolutionary journalist? How long until you leave me the hell alone?"

"I'm not going anywhere just yet," said Kade. "An extra body might be useful around here. At least while you settle in."

Lexi shot him a contemptuous look from beneath her lashes. "A body? Sure, I can arrange that."

"Watch your tongue," said Amity. "You and the smuggler may be capable enough, but we have three people here who can't defend themselves. I have no intention of seeing Riva harmed, and I'd prefer that idiotic body modder and the vagrant remain intact as well. I'll take any strong, reliable ally I can. Especially one as capable as Kade."

"Uh-huh. Me. I think we can take the risk. This place stinks enough without adding an extra asshole."

Kade had long given up defending himself. The fierce compassion inside her, the depth of sentiment he had relied upon in childhood, that was closed to him now. But she still cared about others. He'd seen the way she'd looked at the injured Riva, recognized the tenderness in those eyes that only he could read. He could at least exploit that, no matter how much it hurt him to do so.

"Consider what will happen if Isaac is right about these gangs," he said. "Imagine them running wild on Zeke or Riva. Me being here might make all the difference."

"Exactly," said Amity. "I've lost good people because I didn't have another pair of eyes and ears. With lives at stake, Lexi, your petty grudges couldn't be more irrelevant."

Kade tensed—if there was one thing Lexi especially hated, it was being scolded, especially by multiple people.

"Fine." Lexi stalked from the room and slammed the door.

Amity winced. "I don't know how you remain so calm when she talks about you that way."

"Growing up, she was always there for me and Ash. Whenever there was trouble, she handled it. Right now, she needs more help than she realizes, and the way she's chosen to live, she doesn't have anyone left who cares about her the way I do."

Amity stared at the footprints Lexi had left in the dust. "I suppose if she's related to Ash, there must be some good in her."

"We should take Isaac's ramblings seriously. I saw a lot of gang tags out there, and I wouldn't be surprised if we get paid a visit."

Amity placed her hand on her trench coat, just above the pocket where she'd concealed her gun. "Good."

CHAPTER 13

On the paved square beneath Residential Tower Three, four tall lamps held the evening at bay. Several Codists occupied the square's benches, watching the sky as it darkened.

Mineko strode through the tower's sliding glass doors. The lobby was circular, pristine, and lemon-scented, and sedate music was piped in from a speaker overhead. An elderly man in a red engineering uniform sat on a couch, while a child knelt in the middle of the tiled floor playing with blocks. She was four, maybe.

Mineko took a careful detour around the girl's construction work and pressed the elevator call button. The doors opened immediately, and she entered a spacious elevator that smelled, once again, like lemon. A pleasant odor, yes, but this seemed excessive.

She poked the button for the fourteenth level. The elevator sealed itself before beginning its quiet ascent. It arrived at its destination with a delighted chime.

Mineko followed a corridor to a plain blue door and prodded the buzzer. After a brief delay, Valerie opened the door and gave Mineko a startled look. Had she forgotten their arrangement?

"Mineko, hello!" she said. "Right on time."

No, that was just her regular look—Mineko had nearly forgotten. "Hello, Valerie. I hope you're well."

"Oh, yes. Very well. I hope the same is true for you."

"It is. Thank you."

Valerie smiled. She had unbuttoned the collar of her science uniform, the only off-duty concession Codists were allowed, and she seemed less apprehensive than she'd been at dinner.

"I'm glad you didn't get lost," she said. "I mean, not that you would! But I'm glad you didn't, all the same."

"This is for you." Mineko held out a box of chocolates.

"Oh, for me?" Valerie peered at the box. "Gracious. This is quite a gift."

It was indeed, a brand of dark liqueur chocolates made unavailable on the regular Codist market for no other reason than to enhance their decadence and thus their appeal to the elite. Mineko had been given the box on her last birthday but never gotten around to opening it.

"I'm grateful you've let me visit on such short notice," she said.

"No, no, it's…" Valerie continued to marvel at the chocolates. "I've never been given chocolates. Or anything." A flighty laugh escaped her, almost as if by accident. "I'm so very touched. Please, come inside."

Valerie ushered Mineko into a modest living area. A small couch faced a television, and a little dining table was accompanied by two chairs. The room connected with a bathroom, a kitchen, a bedroom, and a balcony, each of which Valerie identified while pointing to the appropriate exit.

"It seems like a nice apartment," said Mineko, after Valerie had ceased pointlessly naming the rooms.

"It's not so bad." Valerie fumbled with the air conditioner. "I'm sorry, I've set this far too high."

"I thought the temperature was fine."

Valerie flashed a frantic smile. "I hope you'll like dinner. I've never dined with company at home. The meal, I'm afraid it's not fancy. Actually, I microwaved it inside a box." She placed the chocolates on the table and admired them. "I'm sure you're used to much nicer things."

"Please don't be worried. I'm not fussy."

Judging from the surrounding shelves, it seemed Valerie collected statuettes. Though essential items like food, clothing and medicine were dispensed without cost, Codist workers still received a salary scaled to their position and qualifications, and overpriced objects like these little figurines were produced purely as a way to recover that money. Lachlan had once commented over dinner on the absurdity of it, while noting that it was one of those psychological touches that made Codism work.

Each statuette depicted a man or woman bearing some prop appropriate to their station. A tiny man in an orange uniform had a shovel over his shoulder; a woman in a gray uniform carried a box of tools; and there was a student, dark blue, with a reader in her hands. Mineko picked up the little student and inspected her from various angles.

"I suppose you think I'm silly," said Valerie. "Spending my money on those things."

"Not at all." Mineko replaced the figurine, which tapped against the shelf with a hollow sound suggestive of its cheapness. "It's not as though there's anything more interesting to spend money on."

"Well, there are books. I buy a lot of books."

Mineko looked her in the eye. Reassuringly, Valerie was her height. Codists were taller on average than Foundation's general population, and so despite being five four, Mineko was always looking up at people.

"They're not real books," she said. "They're propaganda."

Valerie blushed. "Um. How blunt."

"It's not a controversial opinion. We're not allowed access to non-Codist literature, which means by definition that what we do read is propaganda." A statement unlikely to get Mineko in any trouble, given that any idiot could see it. It would be different, of course, to take the sentiment further and suggest there might be some virtue in having access to the vast repository of banned books. Now that was the kind of reasoning that got a person wiped.

"If you say so." Valerie placed a hand on her hip, frowned, and dropped it again, clearly uncertain what to do with her hands. "Shall we talk before dinner? Or are you hungry?"

"Let's talk as we eat." In the Tamura household, discussion over dinner was a sacred tradition. "What are you microwaving?"

"It's, um…it's in a sauce." Valerie darted into the kitchen, from which soon came the sound of frantic rustling and the beeping of a microwave.

While waiting for Valerie to return, Mineko stood before the door to the balcony and contemplated the shadowed enclave below. Valerie held only a modest position in the Codist hierarchy, having authority over a research team and nothing more, and everything about this enclave suggested its other inhabitants were similarly unremarkable. The parks were small, the towers stacked high. Certainly no mansions. Of course, even the lowest Codists—maintenance workers, drivers, cleaners—lived in absurd comfort compared to the people beyond the walls.

"Do you like the view?" Valerie had returned with a plastic tray and a worried expression. "I'm nearly on the top floor. Um, this is yours." She placed the tray on the table, set a fork beside it, and stepped back. "Oh dear. It looks very sad."

The meal was impossible to identify. Several off-gray lumps lurked in a bubbling sauce of a similar color. Its savory aroma invaded Mineko's nostrils and refused to leave. "How interesting."

Valerie bit her lower lip. "It looks just awful, Mineko. I'm so sorry."

"It looks delicious." Mineko sat at the table. "I'll wait for you."

"Perhaps I should adjust the lighting." Valerie tinkered with the room's lighting controls. The overhead bulb dimmed and took on a subtle flicker, illuminating the table in soft, shifting tones. Dancing shadows deepened around the room. "Is that nicer?"

It made it harder to see the dinner, so the answer could only be yes. "It was fine before, but yes, this is nice."

"Oh, good. I realize I'm terrible at this, but I'm trying very hard. I have some wine. I'll bring that out too. I know you're not allowed, but you drank it at dinner before, so I thought…"

"I'm different, yes. My father isn't likely to surrender me for Reintegration just because I've tasted a little alcohol."

The microwave pinged, and Valerie rushed back into the kitchen. Mineko gave the meal a cautious poke with her fork. It didn't poke back—a good sign.

As she contemplated the food's bubbling surface, Valerie made two return trips from the kitchen, first with a bottle of wine and two glasses, next with an identical tray of her own.

"The box doesn't even say what it is," she said as she settled into place. "It just says *Soy Protein in a Sauce*. That's all it says. *A Sauce*."

"To be fair, that's the closest I could come to describing it."

"Yes, it's quite indescribable." Valerie stabbed one of the lumps, put it in her mouth and chewed. "It tastes fine, though. Or so I think."

It tasted like squishy nothingness submerged in sodium, but that was no problem. Mineko disposed of several lumps and took a sip of wine. Valerie ate at her own pecking, erratic pace, often pausing to give Mineko an apprehensive glance. There was something alluring about her, viewed through the soft radiance, and the shape of her lips—sad but sweet—was reminiscent of Callie's. Or maybe that was the wine at work.

"I suppose you'd like to talk about the exam," Valerie said. "I shouldn't waste your time."

"There's no hurry. I'm curious to know more about you."

"Me?" Valerie dabbed quickly at her lips with a napkin. "Oh, but there's nothing to say."

"You told me you didn't have any close family or friends. Why is that?"

Valerie stared at her plate. "You ask such direct questions."

"I'm sorry. I don't mean to offend."

"No, I'm not... I mean, you have such a lovely way of speaking, and you seem so genuine. I could hardly take offense." Valerie scowled as one of the lumps refused to stay on her fork. "I don't see my parents, and I don't have any siblings. As for friends, well... It's difficult for me. I don't relax around people very easily." She gave Mineko a serious look. "You see, I'm not good at being sociable. You may not have noticed, but I get nervous."

To avoid revealing her amusement, Mineko slowly chewed on another piece of soy protein.

"Yes, it's difficult," said Valerie, peering at her meal. "My work keeps me busy, and I don't socialize with my co-workers because it seems far too complicated. Fortunately, it hardly troubles me at all."

The sadness in her voice gave emphasis to the lie. "I expect I'll be like you," said Mineko, "when I'm your age. I don't have any friends now, not a single one."

"Surely not. You're such wonderfully engaging company."

From anyone else, that would have been sarcasm. From Valerie, it was enchantingly sincere. "I'm actually very shy."

"But you must at least have young men interested in you. I mean, you're such a beautiful...um, I mean..." Valerie cleared her throat. "Well, you're very pretty, is what I meant to say. When I was your age, I was very plain, so nobody was interested at all." She stared into her wine glass. "I say was, but of course, it's even more true now that I'm an old woman."

A strange, exciting atmosphere had settled over the table. With it was an impulse to flatter Valerie, to help her see her own attractiveness. "Forty-three isn't old."

"Well, I feel it talking to you. After all, I'm old enough to be your—" Valerie blinked, and a deep wrinkle joined the faint lines on her forehead. "How did you know my age?"

Whoops. Having let herself become immersed in the conversation, Mineko had forgotten there were some things she wasn't supposed to know. "I asked my father how old you were."

"Oh, did you? Whatever for?"

"I suppose I'm like him in some ways. I always want to learn all there is to know about everything." Perhaps more flattery would help smooth over the mistake. "I was very surprised when he told me your age. I thought you were at least ten years younger than that."

Valerie blushed, and a bewildered smile dissolved her worried expression. "Listen to you. What a thing to say."

She resumed eating, still wearing the silly grin, and Mineko's tension eased. To keep things that way, she proceeded to drink half a glass of wine.

"So, your exams are troubling you." Valerie took a tentative sip from her own glass. "Do you enjoy your classes?"

"No." A pleasant fuzz had settled in Mineko's head. "Would you enjoy listening to hypocrites talk about how wonderful Reintegration is?"

Another crease indented Valerie's brow. "You must realize the frank way you talk about these things is…well, it's dangerous."

Dangerous, yes. But in this strangely lit moment with her nervous companion, to test the limits of speech and thought no longer seemed so fearful. What if it really could end somewhere, the tyranny and injustice of the Codist elite? What if it could end with her?

"It's only dangerous if the wrong people hear it," said Mineko. "I don't think you're the wrong people." She pushed her glass out of temptation's reach. "What do you think of Reintegration?"

"It's…a humane form of punishment. The alternatives would be worse."

"What does it say about us as a society that we need such a solution?"

Valerie seemed to draw inward, her wine glass pressed to her lips and her eyes desperate. "You must know I can't answer that."

Once again, fear had created a chasm between them. Perhaps Mineko could try the same approach Kade had used to lead her across it—speaking firmly and pressing the point, but always with patience. "My father said you worked in Reintegration."

"I did." Valerie slumped against her palm, her bangs pushed askew by her fingers. "It's like you said before. People come out oblivious of the last five years, the last decade, sometimes even a lifetime. They don't remember what they said to you going in or even why they're there." Her eyes glistened. "I didn't have the stomach for it."

"How is work going on Project Sky?" Mineko had asked the question gently, but Valerie still twitched as if startled. "If you don't mind."

"We're trying to understand the research notes that were left. I don't want to experiment until we have Alexis Vale. It's not worth killing for."

"I feel very sorry for this woman."

"I'm certain you do. You're a very gentle person. But you heard what they said. She's drug dealer, and...um, and a sexual pervert."

A flash of indignation cut through Mineko's alcohol-relaxed thoughts. Lexi deserved better than that. "A sexual pervert?"

"They said she was...you know." Valerie couldn't have appeared more wretched. "A homosexual."

"I don't see anything wrong with that. It's certainly no justification for using a human being as a scientific experiment." Mineko was going too far now—not even the wine could conceal that—but she was angry. Angry at Lachlan for drawing her into his machinations, angry at Valerie for being so meek and, most of all, angry at herself for being complicit in all this cruelty and cowardice. "In any case, the Code doesn't apply to the inhabitants of the districts, so it's ridiculous to expect them to conform to our standards."

"I don't disagree. It's natural for people to be attracted to...to all kinds of other people. Um." Valerie looked away. "I truly don't understand how these prejudices have taken hold in our society. There're so many rational aspects to the Code, but there are other things which are just senseless. And if someone did feel...if they did have an inclination in some way...well, they can't do anything about it, no matter how many years they spend wishing it would change, that they could be... be normal. They can't even be Reintegrated."

Mineko's anger winked out. Now all she felt was a surge of compassion, and a deep, instinctive desire to hug Valerie close. "Have you ever felt such an inclination?"

After several seconds of silence, Valerie gave one of her characteristically agitated laughs. "You do ask such novel questions." She opened the box of chocolates. "Let's try these, and then we'll talk about your exam."

Inclination. Such a passionless word for the intoxicating thing Mineko had wrestled with for years. She'd made eye contact with girls in lecture theaters only to be left with her face warm and her chest tight. She'd lingered to admire a girl on the campus lawn or had looked back, body aching, to watch one walk away. But until she'd seen the leonine way Lexi carried herself through the world, so proud of her appetites, Mineko had never realized those feelings didn't need to be shameful.

Valerie reached for a chocolate. Mineko took one as well, and as she did she deliberately brushed Valerie's fingers with her own.

Valerie blushed and dropped the chocolate in her haste to withdraw. Mineko gazed into her eyes until the nervous scientist finally looked away, exhaled and poured another glass of wine with a shaking hand.

It all made sense now. The flustered fumbling, the uncertain speech, the nervous blinking—traits of an anxious person, yes, but this went further.

Valerie Wren was attracted to her.

"Let's go to the balcony," Mineko said. "I want to see the view."

As she stood with her hands on the railing, the night air cleared Mineko's head and made her earlier verdict seem less sure. In fact, nothing seemed so certain out here. Two days ago, she'd been a brave woman, defying her own society to help Lexi and the others. That was who she always wanted to be. But such bravado was frightening and so hard to sustain...

Below her, lamps and lit windows blazed in a black basin from which issued the rattling, creaking sounds of nocturnal insects. Above, the stars were clear.

"Mineko," said Valerie. "The things you've said tonight would get you in terrible trouble. Please be more careful."

"I trust you, though."

"You shouldn't. And I shouldn't trust you, but for some reason I do. It's silly, really. I ought to be terrified of you." There was just enough light cast from the living room to see Valerie's shy smile. "But you speak with so much sincerity and courage."

"I'm not as brave as I wish I was."

"I'm glad you aren't. You'd only get yourself hurt. Please promise me you'll hide these thoughts of yours."

The stars above were strewn in what seemed to be senseless disarray. Callie had claimed to know their patterns, their hidden constellations, and that meant there was order amid the confusion.

But Mineko needed someone to help her see it. And she was alone.

"I'm allowed to think," she said. "We're not forbidden our thoughts."

"Once we complete Project Sky, things will be otherwise. We have to train ourselves to think appropriately. It's the only way."

"Do you think life is better over the wall?"

"I imagine it's far worse, but then I'm much older than you. When you're young, it's easy to think there must be some solution, some way out. This place takes many things from you, and hope is one of them. I've given up dreaming, Mineko."

Mineko gripped the railing, pressing her palms into the cold steel. "I can't endure this loneliness. I couldn't do it for another twenty years. I don't think I can even do it for one more day. I have so much to say, but I'll never have anyone to say it to. I'll never laugh. I'll never be loved."

A hoarse frog call joined the whine of the insects. A deeper sound hummed behind it, a low rumble in the distance. A convoy of trucks, maybe, passing out west. Valerie remained silent.

"My exams don't matter," said Mineko. "I don't think they intend to let me become a neuroethicist in any case. They're waiting for me to change my mind. When I don't, they'll force me. Code Intel is my future."

"Then why come to see me? If the exams don't matter, why are you here?"

"Would you rather I hadn't?"

"I don't know. Perhaps. Certainly if I'd known tonight would be so…well, so very odd, I wouldn't have said yes."

Out in the sobering night air, it was harder to believe in the erotic connection Mineko had sensed before. Yet her desire for intimacy had only been intensified by the thought of growing old, and now the idea of doing something audacious took hold of her, leaving her both queasy and excited. In Codist society, it was proper to marry young and produce a family. Anything else was unseemly. For a young woman to throw herself at a middle-aged woman—that would be a true rebellion. The kind of rebellion even Lexi might agree with.

"I asked whether you'd had forbidden inclinations," said Mineko. How calm she sounded, as if these weren't the most terrifying words she'd ever spoken. "I asked because I've had them myself."

Valerie's eyes widened, two ghostly white circles in the half-light. "You mustn't ever admit that."

"You've had them too. You're having them right now."

"Please." Valerie's whispered plea was barely audible. "You need to stop. If you don't, I won't be able to resist, and I have to…"

Mineko took Valerie's hand and pressed it to her cheek. Valerie's fingers were both hot and cool on her skin, and Mineko gripped them tighter. "Please."

Valerie closed her eyes. "I can't."

"I have to know. You may be the only person who can help me find out."

Trembling, Valerie ran her fingertips across Mineko's lips. The ache in Mineko's chest crept to lower parts of her body. "I don't understand how this can be happening. You're too beautiful for me…"

How was she going to do this? Mineko had never given much thought to kissing—not until Lexi had demonstrated its attractions. Well, she could imitate what she'd seen and hope for the best.

She cupped Valerie's face and leaned in close. Valerie's lashes fluttered, and her lips parted as Mineko pressed their mouths together. At first, it seemed she'd made a mistake—were they supposed to stand here, just squashing each other's lips?—but then Valerie tilted her head, her mouth opened wider and something warm brushed against Mineko's tongue. Everything inside her jolted at once.

As they kissed, Valerie stroked the side of Mineko's neck, and Mineko placed a hand upon Valerie's breast. Even under the thick material of a science uniform, nothing had ever been as thrilling as the soft weight in her palm. A surge of triumph joined the emotions running riot through her. Lachlan had thought to manipulate her, but now here she was, defying him and her parents in the most potent way she could. Neither her body nor her mind belonged to the Code tonight. They were hers to surrender to this woman, who so deserved the comfort they could bring.

"Mineko." Valerie gasped the name as she broke from the kiss. Her eyes were dazed, her blush complete. "We'll be caught. They'll say I seduced you, even though it was you who…"

"Do you not want this?"

"I want it so badly that I'm letting myself make a terrible mistake." Valerie took a deep breath before pushing Mineko away. "I can't let you make that mistake as well. You should go home."

"But…" But what would she do with this tumult inside her? "I'm telling you, nobody will ever know."

"That was my first kiss. I imagine yours as well. And now it's all I can do to keep from crying, because I'm even more conscious of what I'll never have." Valerie looked to the sky, which had darkened further. "I'm not as bold as you. Maybe if I were young again."

"I didn't mean to make you cry." Mineko touched Valerie's shoulder. "At least let me comfort you."

"You're too special to risk yourself for somebody like me. You'll go on to do wonderful things. I'm certain of it. Whereas history will remember me for my role in this terrible project, because I'm too afraid to act otherwise."

The pleasant feelings were subsiding, leaving only the nausea. "I'd still like to see you again. We should be friends."

"Yes. But we must meet in public next time. This was..." Valerie glanced into the softly-lit room. "A bad idea. I suppose part of me was fantasizing it. I just never expected it might actually transpire." She laughed. Mineko had never heard another sound quite so sad. "I suppose I should be flattered."

"Have you been attracted to many women before?"

"Yes, though I find men attractive too. But I can't just marry one and forget about it. I know that if someone is around me often enough, they'll figure me out. They'll see it in my eyes."

Mineko's stomach was settling now, and a weary kind of composure reasserted itself. "After Project Sky, they may quite literally do so."

"Yes." Valerie gazed at the stars. "I truly hope we never catch her."

CHAPTER 14

The blanket looked like a burial shroud that had been passed down ten generations without ever being washed. "I'm not touching it," said Lexi.

"Shit, Lex, come on." Zeke wrung his hands. "There could be rats under it. Or worse. Like a giant spider, all mutated and shit."

"That's why I'm not touching it." Or anything else in this room, if she could help it. Sludge had congealed in the corners, and the pipes on the ceiling had rusted straight through. The overhead light had claw marks on its cover—how the fuck had anything reached that high?—and the sink…well, best not to even think about the sink. "Go on. Do it."

"Give me one good reason."

"Because you're an asshole, and nobody will mourn you if you die."

"Ah, shit." Zeke flung back the blanket, exposing a mattress that couldn't have been more stained if somebody had wiped their ass with it before vomiting over any clean sections left. "Jesus. I'm sleeping on this?"

"You could give it to Isaac. Probably smells better than he does."

"We oughta burn it. Hell, stake it first, just in case it comes back."

"C'mon. You must have slept on worse."

"I don't think there is worse. I think God made this thing to punish mankind." Zeke groaned and rubbed his temples. "Fuck. Why does Amity get to decide who sleeps where? I don't want to share with that junkie. Kade gets his own room. He's a fucking man of the people, right? If anyone should be rooming with junkies, it's him."

Satisfying as griping about Kade might be, Lexi didn't feel much like humoring Zeke. "Amity likes him. She doesn't like you. You work it out."

"She's a mean bitch, huh? At least that Riva is nice. I tell you what, before that shit went down last night, I was having one hell of a good time. She cuts through the tension, you know? Keeps you and Callie from fighting."

Now that was a subject Lexi could warm to. "Sure. Riva's fun."

"You told her about yourself yet? Come clean?"

"Come clean about what?"

"Give me a break, man. You know what."

Lexi would have preferred to lick the soiled mattress than have this conversation now. "There's no point. A few more days and she's gone."

"Why not? You're always complaining that the girls you hook up with are vanilla. Now, as far as I'm any judge, that girl ain't no vanilla. She ain't even fucking Neapolitan."

All those drunken, confidential conversations with Zeke were coming back to haunt her. "I told you, a few days and she's gone. New topic, okay? I want to know how much cash you salvaged."

Zeke leered. "I was wondering when you'd bring that up."

"I didn't want to raise it in front of the do-gooders. I have a couple of thousand in my wallet—"

"You what? Jesus, don't you worry somebody's going to pick your pocket?"

"This is me we're talking about. Anyone picks my pocket, the next thing they're picking is their teeth from the gutter."

Zeke sniggered. "Well, I got some money, yeah. Before they dragged me out, I wadded up the cash in my safe and stuffed some in every pocket I had. I'd have started on my orifices if I had time."

God, it was hard forcing this dumbass to get to the point. "How much?"

"Just a little over ten thousand. Less once we trade down in Port Venn."

"I hope it's enough to get started. I'm not going to be poor again."

"With that implant of yours, you'll clean up wherever you go." Zeke eyed the mattress. "You think this thing looks better on the other side?"

"Good question. I'll leave you to find out."

"Aww, c'mon, Lex, give me a hand with this. Don't be a bitch…"

Lexi left him to his frantic muttering. The corridor outside ran from the galley to an infested chamber that Riva had called, without irony, the bathroom. Along the hall's length, doors opened into various sleeping quarters.

As she passed by, Lexi glanced into each room. In the one to her left, Kade stood shaking out a blanket. In the room opposite, Amity stared at a deluge of black water as it *glooped* out of an old faucet. She gave Lexi an miserable look, and Lexi responded with a cheery thumbs-up.

Upon nearing the galley, heavy music became audible, a sound like a dinosaur caught in a trash compactor. Amid the din, it was possible to hear Callie and Riva in conversation. Lexi stopped just shy of the entrance and listened.

"I prefer their first album," said Callie. "Way heavier than the later stuff."

"They matured, that's all." Riva's soft voice was harder to make out through the atrocious noise. "If you don't like *From Death to Daybreak*, I don't think we can be friends."

"Gotta admit, I do love the title track. When I play it loud enough, wild dogs start howling."

"You're lucky. Back at Bunker One, I'm forbidden to turn the volume up high. Apparently, the music travels through the pipes."

Callie laughed. "Well, now's your chance."

"Where do you live, anyway? You said you travel a lot, but you never mentioned if you have a home."

"I keep a little garage and junkyard out past the factories. Not far from where the city turns into sand."

"Is it dangerous?"

"Nah. There's no real gangs out my way, and the local workers rely on me to fix the old machines whenever they break down. I hope they'll keep an eye on my place while I'm gone."

An intense barrage of drums interrupted the conversation. When Callie next spoke, her tone was different—apprehensive. "I don't mean to be a bitch, but I need to warn you about Lexi."

Lexi tensed, her breath catching.

"What do you mean?" said Riva, sounding puzzled; not alarmed yet.

"Remember when Zeke was bandaging your hand and she put on that big concern act? Stroking your forehead, murmuring nice things? Don't be fooled. She doesn't care about you. She's a sociopath. She just wants to get laid, and then she'll be on her way like you never existed."

Now this was definitely not good PR. Lexi sidled closer and strained to hear over the howling electric guitars.

"She's made clear she's not interested in a relationship," said Riva. "And she's leaving for Port Venn soon. I think she's been honest with me."

"Maybe. But girls fall in love with her, whether they intend to or not, and then they get hurt. I don't want to see that happen to you."

"Is there a story behind this? Something between you and her?"

Time to interrupt. Lexi strolled into the kitchen, and the girls looked up from their work. Callie had her hands in the depths of an oven, while Riva was scrubbing the dark crust from a stove fixture.

"Aren't you two cute," said Lexi. "Having a good time?"

"Sure are." Callie looked as smug as a cat hooked to an intravenous drip of milk. "We're also getting a lot of work done. Unlike you."

"Hey, I can do work. Watch this." Lexi took a sponge and scrubbed at a discolored scab of grease. It refused to shift, and she tossed the sponge aside. "Okay, forget that. Truth is, I'm here to keep up team morale. I'm a natural leader."

"There's nothing down here more full of shit than you. And the toilet at the other end of that hall is literally full of shit."

Riva laughed, and Lexi gave her a sorrowful look. "Take a break, Latour. You got a nasty cut. You shouldn't be working."

Riva frowned at the bandage encircling her left hand. "Are you sure?"

"I'm sure. Get some fresh air. Grab a snack from the van."

"If you insist, thanks for catching me, by the way." Riva set down her brush, walked up to Lexi and placed a light kiss on her cheek.

A pleasant tremor left Lexi momentarily dizzy, not to mention speechless. It was hard to think of anything witty after that fleeting contact with Riva's warm lips. "Um. Yeah. And, uh, thanks for landing on me so gently." Damn. Not her best.

As Riva exited the galley, Lexi admired the alluring motion of her butt. Never had black denim looked so good. Maybe it wasn't too late to convince Amity to reconsider the bedroom arrangements.

Lexi's ass-induced trance was broken by the sound of giggling. "You are so smitten," said Callie. "It's adorable."

"Smitten? Me? Did that music finally knock out your frontal lobe?"

"You should've seen the look on your face when she kissed you. Staring into the distance, your mouth open like you were trying to catch flies."

"I did not look like that." Lexi gave the counter a savage rub with the nearest damp sponge. "She startled me, that's all."

"Sure, sure." A screw popped loose from the hotplate and skittered across the counter. Callie stopped it with her palm. "Got you, you little bastard."

Lexi dipped the sponge into water for a second attempt. "By the way, I'd appreciate it if you didn't talk me down behind my back. Let me earn my own bad reputation."

"So you were eavesdropping. I thought you walked in at a very convenient time." Callie twirled the screw between her fingers, her face thoughtful. "I'm trying to watch out for her, that's all. You told me yourself that you don't care about the women you sleep with. It was how you justified what you did to me, remember?"

Decent comeback. Lexi flicked soapy water, and Callie yelped and ducked away. "But I'm not sleeping with her, am I?"

"You're working on it, though."

"And you aren't?"

Callie blushed and began working at another screw. "I'm just being friendly. She's really sweet."

Never had a girl more badly disguised her feelings. But Lexi wasn't in the mood to tease any more. "Yeah, she is. And believe me, I could use a friend around here."

"You have friends. You just treat them like shit. Maybe all some of them need is to hear you say sorry."

Callie's tone was pleading, and vulnerability trembled on the surface of her beautiful brown eyes. "Trust me, I know," said Lexi, plunging the sponge back into the water.

When trouble finally arrived, it did so around four o'clock, wearing a blonde mullet and a leather jacket with *Motherfucker* stitched across the back. "Nice van," it said while picking its nose. "Got much mileage on it?"

"Hell if I know," said Lexi, who had only just surfaced to catch a little fresh air. Driven by a stupid desire to impress, she'd cleaned the entire kitchen. It was now spotless, but Lexi's arms felt like they'd been chewed by gorillas. "I don't even know what mileage is."

"You have some friends in there." The gangster looked like something that might have crawled out of the mattress in Zeke's room. His head was a mass of scarred flesh, lank hair, and broken teeth, and somebody had cut lines into his biceps and let them scar, forming an ugly fucking tattoo. "Am I right about that?"

"Why, are you in charge of planning dinner invites?"

The gangster spat. Why was it that people like him always went around spitting on things? "I'm trying to figure out if you're a man or a woman. You sound like a woman, but I'm not one hundred percent certain."

Lexi had met some intimidating guys in her time, but this jerkoff wasn't one of them. "Maybe I'm neither. That thought confuse you, Motherfucker?"

The gangster swaggered toward her, ape-like and sneering, and stopped just inches away. "Whatever the fuck you are, you're in deep shit. This block is part of our territory."

Lexi made a show of surveying the street. On one corner, a pharmacy had caved in, its ceiling peeled away like a festering sore. The gas station beside it was nothing but rubble atop a stretch of cracked, scorched cement. Opposite, several houses stood windowless amid an ocean of wiry weeds. "It's a real catch."

"Go inside and tell your friends this is Rusalka's territory. You can stay here, maybe, but you've got to talk to the lady in charge first."

This walking piece of gristle answered to a woman? Well, that was a pleasant surprise. "What happens if we don't?"

"For starters, we take the van. Then we mess you up." The gangster shrugged his bulky shoulders. "Don't see why you'd want the hassle. We're just watching our turf."

If they'd sent this guy to negotiate, he was probably the nicest and most articulate of the bunch. A disturbing thought. "Okay, sure. I'll go talk to my friends, and you get the silverware ready."

"Uh-huh." The gangster returned to appreciating the van, and Lexi retreated into the bunker and descended to the galley.

Callie and Riva were sitting at a freshly-polished table, still listening to the noise they had the audacity to call music, while Isaac sat on a bench and gnawed at a protein bar.

"Where's Amity?" said Lexi, and like something from a horror movie, they all swiveled to look at her. "Hey, don't turn at once. It's creepy."

Riva turned the volume down. "What's up?"

"We have a visitor outside. A messenger from someone called Rusalka."

Isaac spat out a piece of his protein bar. "Rusalka?"

"Thanks for the echo. That name mean something to you?"

"She runs the toughest gang in the district. One crazy bitch."

Curious how male crime lords were treated with awed respect, while the women were always labeled crazy bitches. "And I suppose you're acquainted personally?"

"She wants me dead as shit."

"I have no idea how dead shit is, so I'll just take that as an emphatic yes." Lexi flapped a hand at Callie and Riva. "One of you two fetch Amity for me. Even if this Rusalka eats live babies and bathes in blood, she can't be anywhere near as frightening as our big bad blonde."

"That may be unwise," said Riva. "Amity doesn't negotiate with gangsters."

"If she prefers to rip out Rusalka's spine and stab her through the heart with it, I'm fine with that, too. I just don't want to front up to some local queenpin without muscle to back my play."

"I'd rather it didn't come to that. Let me talk to her first."

Riva left the room, and Isaac returned to nervously tearing at his protein bar. Lexi sidled up to him. "Why do they want you dead, Landon Hill?"

Looking into his eyes was like staring down an empty well. He expelled another guttural cough. "Not your business."

"While we're looking after you, it's plenty of my business."

"There's no need to intimidate him." Callie was sprawled in her seat, her boots on the table in front of her, but she looked worried rather than relaxed. "Zac, we need to know."

Isaac licked his cracked lips. "I took something wasn't meant for me."

"Drugs?"

"Maybe." Isaac averted his bloodshot eyes. "I didn't hurt nobody."

No surer way to piss off a gang than to touch their stash. "I wouldn't say nobody," said Lexi. "I mean, you fucked yourself over pretty good." She plucked at his thoughts, testing a greasy strand. He was telling the truth, and she didn't want to go any deeper than that. "How does Rusalka operate? She have a code?"

"Yeah, she got rules. Like, no pimping. And she kills rapists with her own hands, hangs them up in the street. But that don't make her nice. They did seven kids a few months back. Made the mistake of starting their own gang. She had them cut to bits, strung 'em along the street. Dangling off the electric wires." Isaac picked at the foil of his protein bar. "I was cleaner then, so I saw it. Remembered it. Wish I'd been doped up instead."

"You aren't bullshitting me, are you?"

"I believe it," said Callie. "Foundation used to be the home of over ten million souls. It's a big city. And the farther out you get, the more desperate life becomes, until there's no easy way to tell men from dogs. Inner city types like you tend to forget that."

"Open Hand hasn't forgotten." Amity stood in the doorway, flanked by Riva and Kade. "We'll be accepting this invitation. Roux, bring your shotgun."

The gangster didn't speak as he led the group through the abandoned streets. In the silence, a persistent breeze rattled loose awnings while bearing a dust that tasted bitter whenever Lexi breathed it in.

Zeke had stayed back with Isaac, but everyone else had insisted on tagging along. Amity and Kade kept close to their gang escort, while Lexi, Callie, and Riva trailed behind. Lexi wasn't crazy about Riva accompanying them, but she would at least be well-protected.

They walked onto a street that looked like the target of an air bombing. Every second house had been demolished, and the sidewalk was coated in gray soot. A recurring tag appeared amid the graffiti, a prominent, incomprehensible red scrawl that presumably was Rusalka's sign.

"We're almost there," said the gangster. "Just down the end of the street, see?" He pointed to the open gates of a scrapyard some meters distant.

"They live in a scrapyard?" said Lexi. "Callie, you'll fit right in."

Callie smirked. She was toting her shotgun, but the gangster hadn't cared. If anything, it probably made him take her more seriously. Only an idiot would attend a gang meeting unarmed.

A peeling sign above the yard's gate declared it to be *Cozy's Junkyard*. Presumably, Cozy was so much scrap himself nowadays. A path of packed earth wound between piles of junk—shattered televisions, rusted bicycle frames, fridges bristling with mold. After a few minutes of walking, the group arrived at a large area enclosed by layers of crushed cars, each one a mangled slab of steel and aluminum. A group of gangsters waited at the far end of the clearing, most of them rough enough to seem ready for recycling themselves.

A towering, leather-clad woman stood in the group's center. She had a white scar on her cheek, a colossal mane of knotted black hair and an imperious look in her narrowed eyes. Frighteningly, she was taller than any of her companions by a full head and shoulders—roughly seven feet by Lexi's estimation.

"Five of you." Even her voice was terrifying, the kind of deep, muscular tone best suited to growling threats in dark alleys. "Who's in charge?"

"I'll talk for us," said Riva. "I'm Riva Latour."

The fuck? Lexi glanced at Amity, but she seemed calm, her demeanor as steely as ever. Shit. These two had planned this behind Lexi's back. A flash of irritation heated Lexi's blood. Fucking Open Hand amateurs.

Rusalka stared at Riva's Mohawk. "You dress tough, but you're built like a stick, girl. If that wind gets up any more, we'll lose you." The gangsters around her snickered, as stupid lackeys were inclined to do.

"I'm from Open Hand. Does that mean anything to you?"

"City gang, maybe." Rusalka shrugged. "No. It doesn't."

"We aren't a gang. We help anyone who needs us. Right now, we're harboring some friends who are being hunted by the Codists."

"The fuck is a Codists?"

"The ones you call shut-ins."

Lexi tried not to groan. Riva was open, sincere, and earnest. All the wrong traits for negotiating with a hardened devourer-of-men like Rusalka.

"So you're more scared of shut-ins than you are of me," Rusalka said. "Is that right?"

"Not more scared. But we trust you more. People like you and I struggle every day to eat, to be sheltered, to stay healthy. Codists don't know what that's like." Riva stood with her head high, exuding confident sincerity. Admirable spirit, even if she was about to get a nasty lesson in gangster psychology. "The building we've occupied was once an Open Hand safe house. We're willing to ask your permission to stay in it."

Amity frowned—maybe Riva had invented that concession herself—but Rusalka nodded. "You're respectful. That's good. But why are you hiding from the shut-ins? I don't want them in my district."

"They have no idea we're here. It's only a precaution."

"Don't bullshit me." Rusalka took a menacing step closer, and Lexi tensed. "Those motherfuckers know everything. They only leave us alone because we aren't even human to them. Just so many rats. And I want to keep it that way."

"I promise you, they won't come here."

"But it's a risk, isn't it?" Rusalka touched the handle of a knife sheathed at her hip. "And if you're telling the truth, the longer you hang around, the bigger that risk gets."

Amity's cold voice rang out. "Get your hand off that knife, or I'll gut you before your next breath."

Lexi swallowed hard, trying to keep cool through her alarm, while the gangsters shifted into aggressive poses, their hands moving to their various weapons. But Rusalka only laughed. "I knew straightaway you were the leader of the pack. So why aren't you the one talking to me?"

"Because you disgust me."

"Now there's an attitude that'll get you buried."

Amity curled her upper lip. "You have no right to dictate to me and threaten my people. Be glad I've even condescended to accept your invitation."

This was going well. "Hey," said Lexi. "Maybe we should—"

Rusalka drew the knife and flipped it. To Lexi's disappointment, she caught it with style. Whenever some gangster tried that little flourish, Lexi always prayed for them to fuck it up, just for the comic value.

"Here's my offer," said Rusalka. "If you can cut my other cheek, I'll let you do whatever you please."

"Cut your cheek?" Amity took a vicious-looking hunting knife from the depths of her trench coat. "I'd rather slit your throat."

Kade winced, and Riva caught Amity by the arm. "Am, please," she said. "Don't make this worse. Just apologize."

"It's too late for that." Rusalka gestured to the gangsters behind her. Lexi braced herself for a swarm of scarred, bad-smelling thugs, but instead the gang withdrew several paces. "I have to say, you're one crazy bitch."

Lexi sighed. Not that again. "Okay, that's enough. Time out, you naughty girls." She sauntered across the clearing and stood before Rusalka. "You are really fucking tall, did you know that?"

Rusalka frowned down at Lexi. "Who the hell are you?"

"I'm the one hiding from the shut-ins." The knife in Rusalka's hand looked even sharper up close, but Lexi wasn't fazed—she had a talent for negotiating with peculiarly violent people. "We aren't staying long, so let's make a deal. We'll keep out of your way and you keep out of ours."

"She just promised to slit my throat!"

"Nobody ever said we'd be friends. Just that we'd have an arrangement."

"And what's in it for me? You have nothing I want, pretty boy."

It was cute when they made that mistake. "You're wrong twice. I do have something you want, and I'm not a boy. Though I'll give you this, I am very fucking pretty."

Rusalka chuckled. "Boy or not, you have balls."

"I have some info you'd appreciate too. Does the name Isaac Landon Hill mean anything to you?"

"Lexi!" Riva's shocked cry echoed through the scrapyard. "Don't!"

Rusalka's smile exposed her canine teeth. "Go on."

"Stinky bastard about this high, right? Face like a puckered dog's ass?"

"Now you I can deal with." Rusalka shot a contemptuous look at Amity and sheathed her knife. "Let's talk."

"Lexi, you can't do this," said Callie, clueless as ever. "It's wrong."

"Forget these guys." Lexi pointed backward with her thumb. "They flatter you, they insult you, they don't know what the fuck they're doing. Me, I know how this works. A fair trade, that's what we need here."

A quick probe of Rusalka's mind confirmed that her suspicion had faded, replaced by enthusiasm for her coming revenge. "A fair trade," Rusalka said. "Is that what you're proposing?"

"A deal from which we both come out richer. Of course, I'm assuming you're the kind of gang boss that has her shit together and will negotiate with a broker like the leader of any serious fucking group would."

Rusalka glowered, but it was clear the point had been made. "All right. Give us Isaac and you can stay."

Now for the twist. "I don't think so. He's worth more than that, given all the shit he stole."

"Well, what? What else do you want?"

"You have anywhere we can sit down and talk? More private, maybe?"

Rusalka glanced at her gang. "Sure. You can bring one person."

Considering the rough crowd assembled, that was a no-brainer. "Come on," said Lexi, gesturing to Riva. No response, just a reproving look.

"Go with her." Amity pushed Riva forward, and Riva stumbled before falling into a reluctant walk. "Don't take too long, Lexi."

"I'll take as long as I please."

"We'll go to the gang shelter," said Rusalka. "It's on the other side of the yard." With her index finger, she began to single out individuals from the gang. "You five. Stay here and watch these people. You, come with me. The rest of you disperse." The gang slouched off, minus the five lucky sentries and a burly woman with a face coarser than sandpaper. She joined Rusalka and treated Lexi to a perfectly charming death stare.

Lexi smiled back. "Lead on, beautiful."

The gang shelter turned out to be an ugly shed nestled between mounds of junk. Inside was a makeshift bar with unsteady-looking furniture built from scrap. Unlabeled bottles were arranged behind the counter. Most likely, their contents had been brewed in a barrel by some enterprising thug.

"Odd choice for a bodyguard," said Rusalka. "Injured already."

"That's how you know she's lethal," said Lexi. "Only one good hand, and I'd still trust her with my life." The joke did nothing to shift the reproachful look from Riva's face. "Hey, mind if me and her have a moment?"

Rusalka swiped a bottle from behind the bar. "If you have to. We'll be in the other room." With her hulking counterpart close behind her, she strode into the adjoining room and shut the door.

Lexi faced Riva, whose expression was still accusing. Eventually, she'd be able to explain everything, but it still hurt to be misunderstood in the interim. "Babe, listen—"

"Callie warned me about you," said Riva. "And she was right. You don't care about other people."

Fine. Lexi would take care of this now. "I'm not handing Isaac over, okay? It's just the only card I have to play right now. Once I get Rusalka to myself, everything changes."

"How? How does everything change? What can you possibly do in here that you couldn't out there?"

"You'll see for yourself. And you have to admit, Amity wasn't helping."

Riva blushed. "I didn't help much either. I asked her to let me start the negotiations, and look at what happened."

"It was a good speech wasted on dumb thugs. You impressed me, and that's what matters."

In the brief silence that followed, the wind hissed overhead, rattling the corrugated-metal ceiling.

Riva bowed her head. "Why did you bring me? I'm not any use to you."

"Because I want you close." Lexi squeezed Riva's shoulder. "We're all going to come out of this fine. Isaac included. Trust me."

"Okay, Lexi." A touching warmth softened Riva's smile. "I trust you."

It seemed she meant it too, though God only knew why. "Let's go, huh?"

The shelter's other room was a lounge furnished with busted couches sprouting rusty springs and pale stuffing. Rusalka reclined on a three-person sofa while her big friend stood sentry by the door.

"Sit." Rusalka gestured to the couch opposite her.

Lexi obeyed and winced as a spring prodded her back. Riva sat down beside her.

Rusalka swigged from her bottle, studied Lexi, and nodded. "Talk."

"There's no rush." Lexi sank back, only to be jabbed by another spring. It was a goddamned bed of nails. "You ever heard of Prince Vassago?"

"I may rule over the back of nowhere, but I'm not ignorant."

"He's a close acquaintance of mine."

Admiration flashed. "Are you telling me you work for Prince Vassago?"

"He only works with the very best, and there's no broker better than me."

As Lexi spoke, she sifted through Rusalka's thoughts. Most of her recent memories were violent, bloody ones, but a few were more to Lexi's liking—the moaning, panting, licking, thrusting kind. It seemed Rusalka enjoyed a bit of vigorous fun with favored members of her gang. No preference as to gender. Helpful to know.

"You've got an intense stare on you, girl."

"So I'm told. Anyway, Vassago's real name is Samuel Brink. I call him Sammy. The occult thing he does, the blood and the skulls, it's all just for show. I mean, why would he make a pact with the Devil? Next to Sammy, the Devil is a fucking saint."

"I'm not stupid. I know there's no such thing as devils."

"But it works on plenty, doesn't it? Sammy's powerful enough that superstition begins to make sense. He didn't get the idea by himself, either. Takes a certain kind of mind to come up with that." Lexi shifted to a more relaxed position, her legs crossed below the knee. "See, your average gangster is just a violent reflex on legs. They need thinkers like me to fill that empty space. It's only because of us this city isn't in total anarchy."

"We aren't a fancy inner city gang. Nobody out here stops to chat. It's kill or be killed."

"I hear you." Lexi extended her hand, and Rusalka gave her the bottle. Lexi took a cautious swig. Strong enough to blast a hole in the bottom of her stomach if she weren't careful. "But it's a question of attitude. If you want to run this district, you need to behave like you're entitled to it. Disguise the fact you're a ragged bunch of meatheads hiding in a scrapyard, looking like something out of a Z-grade apocalypse. Take this Isaac business, for example."

Rusalka's anger flickered, but Lexi—who was still loosely entangled in the dark, slithering cloud of Rusalka's thoughts—soothed the emotion before it could take hold. "What about it?"

"Let's say someone like Isaac stole drugs from Vassago. Used them all, fried his brain and vanished. What do you think would happen?"

"Don't ask me trick questions. I haven't got time for that."

"To a kingpin like Sammy, a few drugs are nothing. A man like Isaac is worth even less. Say a cockroach nibbled at your dinner and then got away. If you were to hunt that cockroach, you'd seem pathetic. Like you were the kind of woman to lower yourself to seek vengeance on an insect."

"If someone crosses me, they have to pay the price. Otherwise nobody will respect me."

Lexi took another sip from the bottle. The alcohol stung her mouth. Hopefully, Zeke could hook her up with some new teeth afterward. For now, she needed to switch to a different kind of drug. "You have anything that doesn't taste like it was brewed in a dead dog's stomach? Maybe something small, about so…" With her thumb and forefinger, Lexi indicated a space the size of a tiny pill.

"Yeah." Rusalka took a pill bottle from her jacket and shook three orange tablets into her palm. Gold dust, judging by the shape and color. She popped a pill before handing the other two to Lexi and Riva. Lexi swallowed her pill, while Riva closed her palm around the other.

"If you aren't going to take it, just fucking give it back," said Rusalka, and Riva, looking sheepish, forfeited the drug.

Rusalka turned her attention back to Lexi. "What was your name again?"

"Lexi Vale." As was her habit, Lexi followed her name with a suggestive smile. "Just so you know, being on gold dust tends to make me horny."

Rusalka smiled as her gaze traveled down the full length of Lexi's body. "Is that right."

It had been a gamble—some drugs messed with her aug, though fortunately gold dust wasn't one of them—but it had paid off. Rusalka's mind was rapidly becoming a fuzzy, slightly aroused soup.

"Tell me," said Lexi. "Do you think you'd get respect by smashing a cockroach? That people would be impressed, be frightened of you?"

"Of course not."

"If you ask me, this whole Isaac thing makes you seem weak. Someone like Sammy, he'd just ignore it. He'd want everyone to see he's too rich to care about a few drugs, that he has better things to do than stomp bugs. After all, it's not like you can get your shit back, and a dead junkie is pretty lousy compensation."

"I hadn't thought of it that way. Out here, somebody steals from you, you need to send a message to the district."

"Let Isaac scurry off, and you are sending a message. You're telling the rabble you don't waste time on nobodies." Lexi grinned. "Did I mention you're really fucking tall?"

"In passing."

"I can't help but wonder what it'd be like to sit in your lap."

A slow smile parted Rusalka's lips. "I'm not stopping you."

With measured grace, Lexi relocated to Rusalka's lap. Rusalka put an arm around Lexi's waist, pressing their bodies together and bringing their faces close—very close.

"So you think I should forget about Isaac." At this distance, Rusalka's murmur was like sultry thunder. "That's your fancy broker advice."

"That's right." Lexi nuzzled Rusalka's neck. Her skin smelled of sweat and tasted like iron, and Lexi's appetite stirred. "But what would I know? I only work for Prince Vassago. Contessa. The Red Huntsman. The Menagerie."

"Impressive." Rusalka slid a hand up Lexi's inner thigh. "But if you aren't going to give me Isaac, what are you bringing to trade?"

Lexi smiled as Rusalka's hand reached her crotch. "For you? Anything."

The kiss was abrupt, intense and forceful enough to flatten Lexi against the couch. Rusalka weighed roughly two hundred tons, and her grip was so strong that it seemed suddenly plausible she herself had compacted all those cars outside. The second their mouths separated, Lexi drew in a much-needed breath.

"It's a tempting offer," said Rusalka, still looming over her. "But if the shut-ins do show up, what then?"

Lexi cupped Rusalka's face. As their gazes locked, she slipped deeper into Rusalka's mind. Not too deep, though—this wouldn't quite be a manipulation. More like a massage.

"Tell me who's in charge of this district," Lexi said.

"I am." A hint of offended pride stirred, and Lexi encouraged it to expand. "My gang might not look like much to you, but we've been on top for years. Everyone out here will tell you so."

"So you don't answer to anyone?"

"That's right." Rusalka kissed Lexi's neck while squeezing her thigh. "I'm second to nobody."

Lexi glanced at Riva, who stared back. It was impossible to resist dipping into her mind and sharing the view from her eyes: a snowy-haired, androgynous temptress pinned under a female titan. Lexi licked her teeth while holding Riva's gaze. Riva flushed, and a commanding sensation stirred between her legs.

With effort, Lexi returned her attention to Rusalka, who in her lustful stupor hadn't realized she was only a side attraction. "If you're second to nobody here," Lexi said, "you should be able to protect me from anyone."

Doubt rose, but Lexi flattened it, instead teasing out more of Rusalka's pride and hubris. "The shut-ins have a lot of firepower," Rusalka said.

"You don't rule a district unless you decide who lives and dies there. If you're scared of a few shut-ins, you don't deserve to lead a gang."

Indignation flared. Lexi extinguished it, leaving nothing but the shame of the insult. "Nothing scares me," said Rusalka. "Nothing. You better remember that."

"Big words, yet still no promises." The drug had given Lexi a light buzz, nothing too serious, and it was hard to keep from giggling. "I can't believe you thought I was going to let you fuck me. I don't fuck cowards."

"Watch your mouth," said the gangster standing guard. Steel scraped on leather as she drew her knife. "Or I'll cut another on your throat."

Rusalka averted her eyes. Lexi had conquered her mind, controlling each emotion as it came. "I told you, nothing scares me," Rusalka said. "If I say you're safe in this district, you're safe."

Lexi leaned in. Rusalka moved to complete the kiss, but before their mouths could meet, Lexi instead placed her lips against Rusalka's ear. "Then promise me I'm safe."

Rusalka shivered. "You're—"

A gunshot rang out.

CHAPTER 15

Tired of standing, Kade dragged a pair of plastic crates from the trash and flipped them. He seated himself on one and patted the other. "Take a seat."

Callie perched on the crate and rested her shotgun across her knees. "What about Amity?"

Kade squinted through the noon light. Amity remained in the middle of the junkyard clearing, her arms folded and her back erect. "No point offering. She'd only say that sitting is for the weak."

Most of the gangsters had grown bored with playing sentry and had, like Kade, started relaxing on requisitioned bits of scrap. One pair, however, had chosen to stay on their feet. They watched Amity with the wariness of rabbits eyeing a wolf.

Callie tugged down the brim of her cap, further shadowing her face. As usual, her eyes were thoughtful, two deep brown circles expressive of sensitivity and heartbreak. "Why is Amity so unfriendly?"

A big question and only time for a little answer. "She's suffered to the point she can't get any relief except for when she's hurting somebody else."

"So you feel sorry for her?"

"No. I admire her a great deal."

Wind rushed through the junkyard, whistling over open bottles and setting trash rattling down the scrap piles. Amity turned and stalked up to Kade, her shadow stretching long behind her. "You've lowered your guard," she said.

"Nobody here is eager to fight, except for you," Kade said. "What would you have done if Lexi hadn't stepped in?"

"I'd have taken care of it. In any case, she's handling Rusalka now."

"Yeah, by selling out poor Isaac," said Callie. "Someone should go back and warn him."

"It's a bluff," said Kade. "I can't imagine Lexi doing something so callous."

Amity bowed her head. Her hair shone golden in the sunlight, and had her face been less grim, the effect might have been beautiful. "Of course it's a bluff," she said. "She has *Project Sky*. She could make that monster obey any command she wanted."

"You sound like you have faith in her."

"I acknowledge she sees things we can't." With the tip of her boot, Amity pushed a small scrap of metal through the dust. Back and forth, a pensive gesture, scratching a line in the ground. "And she took Riva in order to protect her. That speaks well of her motivations."

"Poor Riva," said Callie. "She tried so hard to convince Rusalka."

"Riva means well, but she doesn't understand the gang mentality. Lexi does." Amity stopped toeing the dirt and met Kade's eyes. "If we had her, we could accomplish anything."

A troubling idea, and one that she definitely hadn't gotten from Nikolas. "Forget about it," said Kade. "Lexi's independent. And she's marked now."

Callie grinned. "You think she's going to end up screwing Rusalka?"

"Don't be preposterous," Amity said. "It's as if you assume she can have any woman she wants."

"But you can't deny she has sex appeal. Kade, be honest. Did you have a crush on her when you two were growing up?"

An idea amusing enough to make him smile. "I was in love with someone else," said Kade. "Lexi was always more like a sibling. Even now, it's hard to think of her as anything but family."

"Probably just as well, given she's not into guys. That's the one thing she and I have in common." Callie turned her cheeky smile on Amity. "Speaking of which, I notice she's been checking you out."

"I've no interest in hearing your smutty fantasies." Amity stormed off.

Kade laughed. "Thousands of years of human civilization, yet we still can't get over the fact we sometimes have sex with each other."

"When I told my mom I was gay," said Callie, "she chased me around our home with a broken bottle. Kept rambling about how I'd never give her a grandchild. I pointed out we could barely feed ourselves, let alone a grandchild. Apparently that was a 'pervert excuse.' Whatever that means."

"I never grow tired of stories about your mom. What was the context?"

"I was twelve at the time. Had a crush on the girl living above us. Kissed her that same summer, and it felt like I'd conquered the world." Callie gave Kade a bright, curious look. "You ever been with a guy?"

"I'm open-minded. I like to think that I see past gender. But it was a woman that I fell in love with."

"What happened? Did she leave you?"

Would it have been easier if she had? "No. She died."

Callie's face fell, and Kade smiled. That was what he liked most about her, that instinctive empathy. "Ever since," he said, "I'm attracted to people who remind me of her, often in ways I don't even register at first. They might resemble her, or it'll be something more subtle, like the way they laugh. I can't stop wishing for her."

"I'm sorry." Callie toyed with a flyaway strand of her hair. "I wonder what hurts more. Losing the person you loved because they died, or losing them because they betrayed you."

"Death. It reminds us that our time will come too. Once, we deluded ourselves with religious consolations, but that sort of thinking is gone now, peeled away like the soil, broken like the coral, dissolved like the glaciers. When we killed this planet, we proved there was no God but us."

"Are you quoting yourself, Mr. Writer?"

Kade gave a wry shrug. "Maybe."

"I just wish Lexi and I weren't always fighting. She thrives on it, but it only leaves me feeling sad and ugly. I don't know how to—"

Callie was interrupted by the sound of raised voices. Amity had begun arguing with two of the gangsters, her body language suggestive of a snake about to strike.

"Shit," Kade said. "Wait here." He hurried over, his hand moving to the gun in his trench coat.

"Five seconds," said one of the gangsters, a lean man with a scar crossing his lips. "If you're lucky."

"You're a pathetic junkyard dog," Amity said. "Do as your mistress commanded and slink back to your pack."

Kade sighed. Never bring a bloodthirsty guerrilla to a gang fight. "Someone want to tell me what this is about?"

The other gangster, a squat woman with a shaved head, gave Kade a menacing look. "We were just telling your girlfriend how lucky she is."

"Yeah," said the scarred man. "Saying how Rusalka would have sliced her up, left her open and stinking."

The poetry of the street. Kade nudged Amity in the ribs. "Let it go. Come sit with us."

"I'm content where I am," Amity said. "I'll be even happier when this scum leaves me alone."

The woman's jacket creaked as she folded her arms. "Easy for you to talk that way now, bitch, when Rusalka isn't here to put you in your place."

A thoughtful look settled across Amity's face. Kade braced himself.

"I'll give you one last opportunity to do something intelligent," she said. "Get away from me, or I'll put you down."

"You can't touch me. Rusalka would—"

Amity moved with a speed made all the more terrifying because she wasn't in any way augmented—it was pure anger that drove her, the blood rage of a woman with plenty of cause to want the world dead. One vicious grab and twist later, the gangster screamed, a sound accompanied by the snap of bone. Kade's stomach turned.

"My threats have consequences." Amity released the woman's broken arm and shoved her to the ground. "Remember that."

The other gang members returned to their feet, seeming more bewildered than outraged, while the scarred man licked his lips. Sprawled on the soil nearby, the crippled woman clutched her arm and whimpered.

"You can't just walk away from doing that," said the scarred man. "You can't just break her fucking arm and walk away."

"I'm not walking anywhere. You, on the other hand, would do well to make some distance." Amity turned her back on the hapless gangster. "I'm sick of looking at your face."

"Don't you turn away from me, you fucking whore."

"That's enough," said Kade. "Trust me, she can do much worse."

"Motherfucker." The injured gangster staggered to her feet, her ruined arm hanging. "You crazy fucking cunt, look what you did!"

"It's a clean break," said Amity. "You should be grateful."

The woman glared at her companion. "You fucking pussy. Are you just going to stand there and watch?" She touched her arm and hissed. "Christ. Shoot the bitch."

A nervous twitch animated the scarred man's lips. "Fuck it." He drew a snub-nosed revolver and leveled it at Amity's head. "Turn around." He clicked back the safety. "Turn the fuck around!"

Shit. Kade sucked in breath. It would be a miracle if the gangster had more than a few precious bullets to go with the gun, but it would only take one. "Amity, he's not bluffing about the gun."

"I'm aware of that," said Amity. "And if he has any sense, he'll put it away, go back to his friends and wait for his mother to return."

"Jesus. You're as childish as they are." Kade inched up to the gangster. "Listen to me. Rusalka isn't going to be happy if you pull that trigger. It's her that decides the punishments around here, not you."

The man sneered. "Shut your dumb black mouth."

"Hey, you racist son of a bitch." Callie marched across the dirt, furious, her shotgun raised. "Don't you dare talk to Kade that way. I'll blow a hole right through you."

A gang member sidled close, a knife in hand, while another reached for the strap of her rifle. Kade tried to focus through the dizzying panic constricting his lungs and speeding his blood. This was going south fast.

"You won't shoot," said the scarred man. "You're chickenshit. Fat-ass black-loving bitch. Look how your fucking hands are shaking."

The thug was right. Callie wasn't ready to pull the trigger, and anyone looking at her pale face could see it. "Take it easy," Kade said. "There's no reason this has to end with blood."

"He apologizes first," said Callie. "And then he backs the fuck down."

The man leered at Callie. "Yeah, right." He broke into jeering laughter. "Watch this. I'm gonna make her piss herself." He pointed his pistol at her face. "Bang, bitch…"

Kade lowered his revolver.

Her boots ringing against the ground, Lexi sprinted toward the body. Rusalka strode behind her, while Riva and the bodyguard jogged in pursuit. Lexi reached the corpse, covered her mouth and looked away.

"You shot my man," said Rusalka, toneless.

Lexi touched Rusalka's forearm. "Easy. He'd have a good reason."

The gangster lay at Callie's feet, the back of his skull reduced to a glistening mess. Callie stared down at him, her face drained of all color. Riva put an arm around her waist and murmured into her ear.

"He turned a gun on my friend," said Kade. "And I don't take chances with the lives of my friends, Rusalka."

"See? Asshole had it coming." Lexi gave Rusalka a meaningful look. "Can't have your thugs coming up with their own ideas."

Rusalka remained silent. Maybe Lexi could read her, but Kade saw no hint in that haughty face as to what the gang boss might be thinking.

"I'm sorry," said Amity. She hadn't flinched at the gunshot, but her eyes betrayed a horrified understanding. "It's my fault. They were looking for trouble, and I was eager to give it to them."

"She broke my arm," said the crippled gangster. "Rusalka, she—"

"Shut up, or I'll break the other," said Rusalka. The woman cringed. "I told you to watch. Not to stir up trouble. To watch." Rusalka gestured at the corpse. "Get this out of here."

One of the gang members took a tentative step forward. "But—"

"He had orders, and he ignored them." Rusalka glared at the gangster until he retreated, cowed. It was little wonder she'd risen to the top, with her lofty physique and the aura of command that came with it. "If things went down here as I expect they did, this man must be a quick shot."

"I have to be," said Kade. "Journalism's a dangerous profession."

Rusalka inspected Kade with obvious appreciation, and Lexi smirked. "You'll be happy to hear that Rusalka and I have come to an understanding," she said. "Isn't that right, boss?"

"It is," said Rusalka. "While you all show me proper respect, you have my protection in the district. As for Isaac, in my eyes he's dead already." She sneered at the body being dragged across the scrapyard. "If it weren't for the shitstains I have to work with, I could run this city."

"That's true." Lexi winked. "Vassago would have nothing on you."

Classic Lexi. Her streetwise braggadocio combined with a little outrageous flattery turned even the proudest gangsters into putty.

Rusalka stroked Lexi's hair before giving her a gentle shove away. "Get out of my sight. Put that van away too. There's a garage two blocks down from you, heading east along Waite Street. Blue frontage, sturdy door. Here's the key." She took a bunch of keys from her pocket and tossed one to Amity, who caught it. "I expect to get that back."

"You will," said Lexi, her voice lively with insinuation. "I wouldn't want to leave without saying goodbye."

Amity sighed. "For God's sake."

The trip back to the bunker proved surprisingly cheerful. Lexi strutted with her arms around Callie and Riva both, providing a steady flow of amusing chatter. Callie had regained her spirits enough to laugh along with Riva, who seemed happy in her newfound company.

Even Amity had mellowed. She walked beside Kade, a short distance behind the lively trio, with her hands in her pockets and a pensive look on her face. She took her role as the group's guardian seriously, and hopefully this was one shock that would get through to her.

For his part, Kade struggled to relax. Killing wasn't a habit for him, and he could still taste the nausea that came with taking a life. Nobody ever knew what a person might be capable of given another chance, and Kade was big on second chances.

Unfortunately, the way life played out, he was rarely in a position to offer them.

Lexi whispered in Callie's ear, and Callie giggled. "I thought those two were at war," said Amity. "Now look at them."

"Because of her." Kade nodded at Riva. The late evening light burnished her chiseled cheeks, warmed her olive skin and set her Mohawk blazing a brilliant pink. "The peacemaker in their midst."

"Nikolas predicted she would have a calming effect upon Lexi. I suppose insight like that is why he leads Open Hand."

The wistful note in Amity's voice was impossible to miss. "We all have our role to play. A talent to draw upon."

With a gleeful whoop, Lexi stole Callie's cap and placed it on her own head. Amity laughed. "It seems some have more talents than others."

Amazing. Kade could count on his fingers the number of times he remembered seeing Amity laugh. "Lexi's not what you assumed her to be, is she?"

"She's still a creature of the gang world. But she seems to have resisted the worst of its influences."

Their hideout came into sight, and Lexi cheered and raised the pilfered cap. Callie took the opportunity to grab it back, much to Riva's amusement. "It's a rarity to see Riva so relaxed," said Amity. "She's usually very shy."

"You wouldn't guess from the way she wears her hair."

"I suppose it's a form of defiance. In any case, nobody hassles her in Bunker One. I make sure of it." Amity scowled into the distance. "There's the coward we left behind."

Sure enough, Zeke was sitting on the sidewalk, instantly recognizable by the gleam of titanium across his scalp. The group approached him, and he bounced to his feet. "You guys made it back. That's cool."

"Worried for us, were you?" said Lexi. "Just as well you didn't come. Things got a little messy."

Zeke peered at the group, as if mentally counting each member. "Did anyone die?"

"Yeah. Amity. But she was such a stiff when she was alive, you can't even tell the difference." Lexi jostled him, and he grunted. "So why aren't you underground?"

"That Isaac dude was freaking me out. Mumbling to himself. So I waited out here in the mumbling-junkie-free zone."

"Oh, yeah, Isaac. I have good news for that stinky bastard. Let's go break it to him." Lexi draped an arm over Zeke's shoulders and directed him toward the door. "You should've seen Rusalka. She was seven feet tall."

"No, she wasn't," said Callie. "Maybe six foot seven."

"Either way, she was fun for a merciless savage. I sat in her lap. Most dangerous lap I've ever sat in."

Kade made to follow the other inside, but Amity stopped him. "Wait." She looked him in the eyes. "Do you intend to tell Nikolas about my mistake?"

"It's my job to report the truth. But my duty is to protect the people I care for. Duty comes first."

Gratitude softened Amity's features, suggesting the woman she might have otherwise been. "Thank you for saving Callie's life. I can't understand what I was thinking."

Kade took one of her callused hands and pressed it. "You weren't. That other part of you took over."

"You and Ash always treated me as a comrade, from the very beginning. Besides Nikolas, nobody else would even talk to me. I never dared ask why the two of you were different."

"Ash always saw the best in people. I always followed her lead." Kade released Amity's hands. "Let's see how Isaac reacts to the good news."

Isaac was hunched over a table in the galley, running his fingers over the scored marks in its surface. He looked up, and for a second confusion filled his eyes, as if he'd forgotten who they were. "Riva," he said. "Callie." They were the only names he seemed capable of remembering. "Rusalka let you go?"

"More than that," said Lexi. "She's not hunting you. Heat's off, big guy."

"That don't make sense. I crossed her."

"And I made her feel funny in her sexy parts, so now everything's smoothed over." Lexi walked past the burners, flicking them on and off, before grinning at nobody in particular. "Don't all rush to thank me."

"While you parade yourself in grotesque self-congratulation," said Amity, "I'm going to contact Nikolas. I'll tell him we've secured the bunker and will be here overnight." She returned up the staircase, her trench coat flapping at her heels.

"I still don't understand how you did it," said Riva. "Lexi, it was like you had her hypnotized. I know you're irresistible, but this was something else."

Lexi sat on the edge of a bench, crossed her legs, and stared at Riva. After a few seconds of silence, she smiled. "Okay, sure. That implant of mine the shut-ins are after? It's named Project Sky. Out here, we call it the 'suicide chip.' You ever heard of it?"

"No. But 'suicide chip' sounds terrible."

"Sure is. It's killed or left brain-dead anyone else who's had it installed. I'm the only success story." Lexi paused, presumably for dramatic effect. "It lets me read minds. Enter people's heads and play with what's in there. That's what I did to Rusalka."

"Is that a joke? Are you seriously saying you can read my mind?"

"More or less."

"But that's…" Riva looked to the others in the room, no doubt trying to determine whether this was a prank at her expense. "How do you do it? How much do you see?"

"Anything I want to. The trick is to look into somebody's eyes, though sometimes I need to—"

"Did you use it on me?" Riva's strained, shaking voice was shot through with panic. "Lexi, did you?"

"Of course not. I haven't read you, Riva. I'd never do that."

"She's telling the truth," said Kade, his throat tight. Something very bad was happening here. "You can trust her."

"You should have told me." Riva had begun to cry, and her words came with difficulty. "Why didn't you tell me?"

Lexi reached for Riva's arm. "Babe, I swear, I never—"

Riva took a hasty step backward, and Lexi touched nothing but air. "I need to be alone. Don't follow me." With the clumsy haste of somebody overwhelmed, she ran from the room.

Lexi remained where she was, her hand still extended. "What did I do?" It had been a long time since Kade had heard her sound so plaintive. "Kade, what did I do?"

It had been even longer since she'd turned to him for support. "She's scared," he said. "You would be too."

"We need to go talk to her," said Callie, whose eyes had already welled with sympathetic tears. "Come on, Zeke." She rushed from the room, and Zeke—after a guilty glance at Lexi—hurried after her.

"Shit." Lexi slouched against a bench and sighed. "I know she's hiding something, but I'd never invade her privacy. Never." She glared at Isaac, who had resumed his muttering. "Can you shut the fuck up?"

Looking terrified, Isaac shambled up the stairs. Now it was just the two of them.

"Do her feelings matter that much to you?" said Kade.

"Of course not." The bitterness in Lexi's voice suggested otherwise. "Yeah, I've used the chip on her. I can't help it, can't switch it off. Every time I look at her, it hits me straightaway how fucking unhappy she's been. When she smiles, Kade, you have no idea. I'd forgotten what it feels like to do that for somebody. It's like it was with you and me."

So she did remember. That fact alone was enough to keep any words from escaping Kade's throat.

"I'm fucked now. I had a job. A reputation. It's all gone." Lexi stared at her reflection in the polished bench top. "And now you're all getting hunted because of me. But it's not my fault, okay? Fuck all of you. It's not my fault." She fled up the stairwell, while Kade watched her leave, helpless and aching.

He found Riva in her quarters. She was cross-legged at the foot of her bunk, her cheeks smeared with tears and eyeliner. "Can I come in?"

Her subdued nod seemed acknowledgement enough. After considering his options, Kade crouched by the bed. It gave Riva the advantage of looking down at him, and when someone was this upset, every little thing helped.

"Callie and Zeke came to visit me too," said Riva, her voice thick. "But I sent them away."

"But you don't mind me being here?"

"I've wanted to talk to you since you arrived. Lexi treats you differently to everyone else. Every time she looks at you, she seems older. Tired."

"Yes." Kade touched Riva's wrist. "But we'll talk about me and her another day. For now, try to understand. For better or worse, the implant is part of her. She can't turn it off, and she can't help reading people. Right now, she's grieving for the pain she's caused you."

"I know. But I feel naked. You can't imagine what it's like to be this vulnerable."

If only she knew. But now wasn't the time. "Well, you can't imagine how much I envy you."

Riva blinked. "What do you mean?"

"You don't know how much I've missed..." Kade's voice cracked. Damn, this was hard. "Don't push Lexi away. She'll respect your secrets."

"This isn't just any secret. I don't want to hide it or be ashamed, but I also don't want her to look at me differently. If she finds out, she will." Riva wiped away a fresh tear. "I wanted this to be something good. It's been so long since I had anything good."

Even with her stained, glistening face, Riva remained beautiful. A defiant misfit who refused to be broken, even though this world so often seemed purely a tool for breaking. Little wonder Lexi was protective of her.

"You're probably confused why she had that augmentation installed," Kade said. "Given it should almost certainly have killed her."

"No. I've already guessed. She wanted to die."

Beautiful *and* perceptive. "We grew up together. Her, me, and her cousin, Ash. I was the runt, always getting in their way. Lexi was the brave one, the schemer, getting us into and out of trouble. Ash was our leader. She kept us on the straight and narrow. Planned for the future. Found ways for us to be clothed and fed. If it weren't for her, Lexi would've disappeared into some gang or other, and I'd be... God knows."

"What happened to Ash?" Riva spoke gently, as if she were the one who'd come here to give consolation. "Is she dead?"

"Yes, but I can't talk much about that right now. I'm raw enough as it is. What I can say is that Ash and I became lovers, and Lexi ended up on the outside. She became jealous, I suppose. Alienated. And when Ash was killed, she blamed it on me. I share her view."

"Was it really your fault, or are you just punishing yourself?"

"The way she died, how could I not want to punish—" Kade ran a hand across his face. The knot in his throat was suffocating. "Lexi couldn't cope. But true to form, instead of putting a gun in her mouth, she flipped a coin."

"Project Sky."

"She can see into my thoughts. That means she knows how heartbroken I am. How much I still love her. All my repentance, my grief, my loneliness, she can feel that with me. And she still won't forgive me." Kade exhaled in an attempt to break the knot, but it only cost him more precious air.

"Kade…"

"She never expected to live, understand? When the implant succeeded, she came back and lived like a ghost. You know how there are spirits in mythology who can't forgive the living because they envy them the warmth of their blood, the beating of their hearts? That's how Lexi sees me. She hates that I kept my faith, that I'm still fighting for the cause that Ash and I believed in. The cause that took both of us from her. And like every angry ghost, she can't roam far from the place she died."

"But she seems so confident."

"That's her glamor, her shield. She's always had it. As kids, we'd see her prowling the streets like she owned them, only to find her crying herself to sleep the very same night. Now we're not there to comfort her, I suspect she doesn't let herself cry that way anymore."

Riva closed her eyes. "What do I do?"

"Trust her. She'll help you bear this, no matter how heavy the burden. I know that to be true." Kade rose to his feet, a little unsteady. "Just because she's leaving for Port Venn, that doesn't mean you shouldn't enjoy what time with her you can. If I could have just one more day with Ash…"

It was suddenly too much, and he left while he could still see through the coming blur.

CHAPTER 16

A rush of cold air met Lexi outside, and she zipped up her jacket. The sun had sunk low. At night, Foundation's club districts were bathed in neon radiance and the enclaves glowed like beacons, but this far out on the fringe, there was nothing to stop the streets being enfolded by gloom: a kind of darkness Lexi hadn't really seen since her childhood.

Fortunately, her vision aug had kicked in, and she could see the street in shades of silver and gray. The trade-off was the pale white light that would now be shimmering across her irises. It tended to scare the shit out of people.

Isaac Landon Hill proved no exception.

"Fuck!" He fumbled for his pocket, apparently forgetting he'd handed his knife over to Amity, and pressed himself against Callie's van.

"Relax, Hill. It's just me and my sexy cybernetic eyes. What are you doing? I thought you were scared to be outside."

"You was all fighting." Isaac remained flattened against the van. "Didn't want to be around trouble."

Poor guy—his life had trained him to see danger in everything. Even two kittens quarreling in the street would probably have spooked him. "Don't worry. This won't affect you."

"Did you break up with your girl? Riva?"

For some reason, the question left Lexi unutterably sad. "Maybe."

"She looks at you all the time. Even when you don't notice."

No way to respond to that. Lexi joined Isaac beside the van, standing as near to him as his body odor permitted. "What's your next step?" she said. "Score another hit?"

Isaac stared at his feet. "Didn't think about that yet."

"You want my advice, don't skip out. They're good people."

"Skipping out is what you're doing now, though."

Perceptive for a junkie. "That's different. I don't need the help. Now get inside. If you're not quick, Amity might not let you back in."

"Which one's Amity?"

"The blonde who looks like she's digesting glass."

"Oh." Isaac shuffled to the door and looked back, his face half-concealed behind a lank curtain of hair. "She's looking at you all the time too."

He was gone before Lexi could think up a retort. She oriented herself, choosing as her landmark the fractured finger of a distant tower, and began walking. The pavement passed beneath her wandering feet as she fell into her stride.

Project Sky. It was nice to finally have a name. Calling it a suicide chip had always been too morbid, especially as touching another mind could often be an experience of overwhelming beauty. Those first few weeks, probing every person she met… God, what a trip it had been.

But it had become a burden too. Respect for privacy had been ingrained in her from childhood, and Lexi had soon decided not to abuse the chip. Outside of emergencies, she used it only against gangsters, who manipulated other people daily and fully deserved to be exploited in turn.

Still, sometimes people spilled, and she couldn't help but read them. Riva was right to be afraid. Yet Lexi wanted nothing more than to make her feel safe. To be a comforting presence.

The contradiction hurt.

Fuck, it was dark. And freezing. What was she doing out here? This city was dead, and she was just another insect scuttling through its guts…

As a teenager, she'd listened to Kade and Ash discussing history, politics, and philosophy. Only one topic had interested Lexi: the queer movement, a rights crusade brutally crushed in the twilight of the twenty-first century. Ash and Kade had shown her videos and articles. She'd watched footage of marches, riots, speeches. Camps. Purges.

Queer. A word with tarnished origins as a slur, but unlike so many slurs, it had a meaning that a victim might wear with pride. *Different. Strange.* In this fucked-up world, who wouldn't be proud to be either?

Ash had been obsessed with poverty, and Kade with eco-socialism, whatever the fuck that was. But as far as Lexi was concerned, the planet was already fucked, and its occupants had always been fucked. Humanity was taking its final ride on the blasted ball of rock it had screwed and wasted. What was there left to save?

Still, it would be better not to plunge into that abyss alone…

The shadows moved, and Lexi took a frantic swing. A hand caught her wrist. "Calm down," said Amity. "I've broken enough arms for one day."

"How did you know I was gone?"

With her imposing stance and physique, Amity was as intimidating on this abandoned road as any nocturnal thug might have been. "Isaac pointed me in the direction you'd fled. If he hadn't, I suppose I might not have caught you in time."

"The bastard sold me out."

"More likely he saved your life."

Their words, even spoken in murmurs, seemed far too loud in the hush of this shadowed street. Amity waited, her green eyes patient, while Lexi tried to regain control of her startled body. She took a deep breath. "Did he tell you what happened?"

"I know you're running from Riva. Maybe you think it's easier on her, but you're wrong. She feels safer with you there. We all do. Even me."

"You? I find that hard to believe."

"I take comfort knowing I'm not watching over them alone."

It suddenly seemed absurd to be standing enveloped in cold shadow, surrounded by streets as bleak and final as open graves. More absurd still to be away from their company. She missed Zeke's carefree crudity, Riva's shy demeanor and husky voice. She even missed Callie Roux, that frustrating creature of contradictions—sometimes a lively, dimpled imp, more often a pouting thing with dark, sorrowful eyes.

And Kade. That patient, articulate, forgiving son of a bitch.

"Take me back," said Lexi. "I'm not sure where I've wandered to."

"I can see that." Amity took Lexi's hand and squeezed it for a startling instant. "Don't let me lose you again."

Callie was sitting on her bunk, a pair of earbuds plugged into her head, a pillow held between her knees and chest. She looked up and plucked out an earbud, leaving it hanging. "You okay? I was wondering where you'd gotten to."

"Just went for a piss." Lexi kicked off her boots, flopped on her bunk and stared at the blotched ceiling. "Go back to your music."

"I'd like to talk about it, though. About you and Riva."

"You said it yourself. I don't give a shit about her."

"I was wrong then, and you're lying now. I saw the look on your face when she ran out. It was all I could do to keep from crying."

"Why do you care?" Lexi didn't mean the remark with any cruelty—it genuinely made no sense. "All I've ever done is make you miserable."

"Back at the junkyard, when she saw me trembling, the first thing she did was try to comfort me." Callie hugged the pillow closer. "She's so sweet and so lonely, and you were making her happy until now. That's why I care."

There was no way Lexi was going to let this feel-good moment punch through her darkness. "And I don't make her happy anymore, so it's up to you. Go visit her room, put on some bad music and grind on her for a while. I bet that'd cheer her right up."

"No chance of that. She wouldn't even let me talk to her. Told me she needed time. I felt so useless."

"So? You're a smuggler, not a therapist."

Callie twisted the wire of an earbud around her index finger. Fidgety kid, always playing with something. "You're really upset, aren't you?"

"No. I'm a pitiless cyborg. All I feel is an urge to destroy humans."

"She cooked me up some food earlier to test out the grill. It was amazing. The best meal of my life. And while I was eating, I caught her watching me, smiling, like she was so proud and happy to have fed me. It made me get this tight feeling right in the center of my chest. You feel that same way about her, admit it."

Lexi sighed. "Here's a little secret. I don't take disappointment well, and that's why I'm a colossal bitch. Not because I don't care, but because it hurts too much when I do. Now you know."

"We can still go talk to her. You and me. We can make it right."

There was a soft rap at the door. Both Lexi and Callie sat up. "Come in," said Lexi, her heartbeat gaining pace.

The door opened to reveal a subdued Riva. Streaks of mascara under her eyes suggested she'd been crying, and guilt washed over Lexi, leaving her insides unsettled and her mouth dry.

"Hey, guys," Riva said. "I wanted to say I'm sorry."

Callie's cheeks dimpled. "Oh, chickadee. There's nothing to say sorry for."

Lexi patted the empty space beside her. "C'mon, get over here. Close that door behind you."

As Riva crossed the room, Lexi looked into her eyes. Riva held her gaze. The relief that followed was as overwhelming as it was unexpected. Lexi hadn't realized how much she'd feared losing that small intimacy. Nor had she anticipated how much it meant to be trusted.

"Don't just stand there, Latour," she said. "There's plenty of room on this bed for that skinny body of yours."

Riva reclined on the mattress. Lexi put an arm around her thin shoulders and drew her closer. "I didn't mean to hurt you, babe."

"I know," said Riva. "But I was scared."

Callie flopped to her belly, still clutching the pillow, and began to kick her legs. "I hope you're feeling a little better now."

Riva's smile was forced—not even a flash of happiness in her pale eyes. For the second time, Lexi had put this woman through the wringer, and the thought of it sent a sharp pain through her throat and into her chest. "Callie," she said. "Put some music on."

"Music?" said Callie. "You mean the music you hate?"

"Yeah, put it on."

Callie switched on her little portable stereo. Music poured out, an ear-melting deluge of sound.

"Riva," said Lexi. "See that tin on the side-table?"

"Sure." Riva reached for it. "Candies."

"Callie found them down here. They're a hundred years out of date."

Riva laughed and unscrewed the lid. "Really?" She held a pastel-shaded sphere to the light. "Did either of you try one?"

"We weren't brave enough," Callie said. "It could mutate us."

"Might be worth it," said Lexi. "The things I could do with a third hand…"

Callie rolled to her back, becoming a dreamy sprawl of tanned limbs and auburn hair. "Then go ahead and try one of those nasty candies. Grow all the groping hands you need."

Lexi took the candy from Riva's fingers and placed it on the tip of her tongue. Completely tasteless. She sucked it into her mouth, rolled it over her teeth and spat it out again. "It's like sucking on wax. Gross."

"I can't believe you did that," said Riva. "That thing should be in a museum, not in a mouth."

Callie grinned. "To be fair, Lexi's mouth couldn't get any dirtier."

Lexi tossed the spit-soaked candy. Callie shrieked as it bounced against her cheek. "Lexi! That's disgusting."

"True," said Lexi. "But it was a fantastic shot."

Giggling, Riva laid her head upon Lexi's shoulder, and Lexi tightened her hold on Riva's waist. Their bodies fitted in such a way as to connect them shoulder, waist and hip, and the motion of Riva's breath and the warmth of her skin quickly became so sensual—so comforting—that to be parted from her was as horrifying an idea as pulling back a blanket on a winter's morning.

A guilty thought broke through Lexi's contentment, and she peeked at Callie. There was enough envy in those lonely brown eyes to rouse even Lexi's sympathy.

"I like this song," said Lexi. "What's it called?"

Callie perked up. *"Burned by Injustice.* The bass line is catchy, isn't it?"

"Oh, yeah. I can't make out what they're singing, though. All that growling and screaming. Are there any lyrics?"

"Of course there are." Callie deepened her voice to a ludicrous rasp. "Burned by injustice! You can't trust us!"

Lexi raised both eyebrows. "That's the chorus?"

"It's the entire song. Those two lines, repeated over and over."

Lexi laughed. There wasn't a trace of tension left in her, not one nervous knot, not one lump of remorse. What a great fucking feeling that was.

"You might enjoy the rest of the album." Callie sat cross-legged and beaming, her mood entirely transformed. "It's awesome. Right, Riva?"

Riva gave another of her endearingly self-conscious giggles. "Right."

"There's this one track at the very end. It's acoustic, which I usually don't get into, but it has this amazing riff." Callie strummed the air, humming what was presumably the amazing riff. "I'll play it next."

All it had taken to cheer Callie up was to bring her into the conversation. That was how friendless the poor kid felt. Living out on the edge of Foundation, staring at the badlands, believing she was forever alone...

"Tell us a story, Roux," said Lexi, and Callie's eyes lit up further. "What's the furthest you've ever gone in that van of yours?"

"I went way up the coast once. Took me two weeks. Every morning, I stopped to recharge the batteries. I didn't take the highway, just these old dirt roads cut through the rock. I'd look up each evening and see the silhouettes of coyotes on the cliffs."

"Was it frightening?" said Riva. "Being so far out by yourself?"

"No, it was peaceful. Sometimes I'd be driving in the shadow of some canyon, and time would seem to stop around me. So silent, you can't imagine it. There are places in Foundation where it's almost dead quiet, but you can still hear those shut-in trucks, or a distant generator, or the factories way off. And out in the desert, the old farmland, you've got the buzzing of insects and the wind sifting the sand. But down in the canyons, the air is totally still. I'd stop the van and sit a while on some boulder, listening to my own breath."

"Did you find any towns? Cities?"

"Lots, all swallowed up by dust. Sometimes I explore, but mostly I steer clear. You never know what you'll disturb." Callie twirled her hair, an absent mannerism that was quickly becoming familiar. "I thought the coast would be beautiful, but it wasn't. It's like a long, chalky graveyard."

"Don't get morbid," said Lexi. "You've got your whole life ahead of you. Tell me about all the cool shit you're going to do."

"I've always wanted to fly a plane. That way, the mountains won't stop me. Even the ocean won't stop me." Callie closed her eyes and smiled. "Everyone thinks I'm crazy for spending so much time in the wasteland. But until you've been out there, you've never seen the sky. Those ruined cities, they only make you think of death, but that sky…"

"Do you think you'll ever go back?" said Riva.

"I hope so. I'd love to hold a girl while stretched out under that sky. Listening to her breath and mine, nothing in the world but the two of us." Callie brushed her lashes—another familiar gesture. "I'm sorry. I'm such a baby sometimes."

Before anyone could reply, the door shuddered beneath an inimitable barrage of knocks. "Come in, Amity," said Lexi, and the door cracked open. "What's up?"

"I have a call for Callie." Amity opened the door wider, revealing the phone in her hand. "It's from Blue."

CHAPTER 17

Above her, a light panel emitted a steady electric buzz. Outside, insects thrummed in the night. Within her, each breath came slow and steady. As she meditated, memories rose and confronted her. The rubbish strewn over the street outside the Tofu Palace. The highway flying beneath a cloudless sky. Kade's brooding eyes and his wiry, unkempt hair. Lexi's slinky way of walking. Callie's winning smile.

Mineko opened her eyes. At this late hour, the study lounge was nearly abandoned. It was just her and a gangly young man who peered at his reader with studious intensity. That suited her fine. She needed solitude, but she wasn't ready yet for the grim familiarity of her room.

Though the lounge was quiet, it was irritating in its opulence, a reminder of Codist extravagance. A plush carpet spanned a floor of creaking oak, polished walls displayed gilt-framed portraits of Codifiers, a chandelier glittered on the ceiling and ornate water features trickled in the corners. A pair of sliding glass doors overlooked white trees clustered in a courtyard. Beautiful. In theory.

But there was no real beauty in Codism. Only ugliness beneath a veil, just as Kaori's puckish face concealed repellent bigotry. The Codifiers had insisted——Mineko often imagined them hissing their decrees with tongues purpled and swollen—that procreation was the organic aspiration of the species. Anything else was the aberrant invention of cultural anarchists who wanted to create chaos through complexity.

But Mineko knew better. She had ceased to believe from the moment her tutor had been wiped and Codism's cruelty had been laid bare to her. She had seen confiscated videos, read banned books. She knew that other societies existed beyond the decaying borders of this one.

And last night, she had kissed a woman.

The sliding doors opened. Of course it would be Lachlan Reed, as if summoned by the strength of her emotions to torment her. He crossed the carpet with his usual measured stride. His hair glistened beneath the lights, as did the teeth revealed by his insincere smile.

"So diligent," he said. "Studying at this hour."

As quietly as he'd been studying, the other student stole from the room. Lachlan chuckled. "Do you think he's afraid of me?"

"What do you want, Lachlan?"

"You're so brusque." Lachlan towered over her, but she met his gaze with no trace of fear—or so she hoped. "Have you seen Dr. Wren yet?"

"Yes. How did you know I would be here?"

"An intuition. Tell me, did anything interesting pass between you two? Something you might want to inform me about?"

Did his phrasing imply a hidden provocation, or was Mineko being paranoid? "She's fearful. She knows that failure would mean serious repercussions."

"The poor thing. But I can't imagine she'll fail us. She has a solid record."

Even that sounded like a threat, and Mineko's anger redoubled. No one person more represented the hypocrisy of Codism than did this hunter in black. He was the agent to whom the law only applied in daylight, the thug who bloodied his hands so that her father could attend government meetings without any stain on his own, the cyborg whose very existence was in clear contradiction of the Third Moral Code.

Perhaps it was the lingering exhilaration of her treacherous thoughts. Perhaps it was the rage smoldering in her gut. Perhaps it was the thought of Valerie Wren alone in her apartment, studying the night from her balcony. Or perhaps it was only Mineko's wish to see patterns in the stars as the sun melted over the mesa. Whatever the reason, defiance took hold of her, and it spoke through her without fear.

"Project Sky is wrong," she said. "It's immoral. It needs to be stopped."

Lachlan shrugged, his slight smirk still in place. "I suppose you're right."

Was he taunting her? "The Code makes clear that Codism is voluntary. To force it upon others is a betrayal of our values."

"The First and Second Moral Codes suggested as such, yes. The Third, however, clearly states that only a society adhering to the Code can be considered civilized." Lachlan spoke without any trace of reprimand. Just insubordinate amusement. "You'd almost think there's some agenda in all of this, wouldn't you?"

"I want Codism to succeed, just as you do." It wasn't true, but Mineko wasn't about to turn this into a confession—that would be like a sheep admitting to a wolf that they fantasized about being eaten. "But not some corrupt form of Codism that is only a reflection of our basest impulses."

"If you follow your father, you'll be on the Committee someday. Perhaps you'll help write the Fourth Moral Code. I'm sure you have many ideas. But I've known you a long time, Mineko. Why don't you just speak your mind?"

"I am speaking my mind."

Lachlan's smirk became a predatory grin. "I don't think you are. Why don't I just say it for you? The Code is a baseless, contradictory doctrine designed to control an unwitting populace. Say it. I won't bite."

It was as shocking as if Lachlan had removed a mask and revealed himself to be Lexi in disguise. An unformed reply trembled on Mineko's lips and died. What was she supposed to say to that?

Lachlan laughed. "Yes, it's quite scandalous. But we're the enlightened ones, you and me. Do you know what amuses me most? In moralistic works of literature, tyrannies are always so very seductively sinister. They consume free thought, they dominate the individual, they crush every last trace of will. People are reduced to spiritless organisms, to labor units, to entertainment. Yet what do we have? A bunch of miserable people in uniform eating regulation soy food. Not much of a brave new world, is it?"

"You don't believe in the Code?"

"Oh, I believe. I see it in operation every day. And I suppose wiping people's memories is fairly compelling as far as dictatorial evil goes. But still, we've a long way to go before we're pushing old people into grinders and using them for food."

It was surely a trap, a way to bait her into an admission. "You're talking nonsense, Lachlan."

"And you've been talking to my old friend Kade August."

The warmth drained from Mineko's face. "I don't know who you're talking about."

"Good-looking fellow. Five-ten, about one hundred and forty pounds. Dark skin, brown eyes, black hair. Tends to go about in an old trench coat. Seems serious at first but lightens up when you get to know him." Lachlan gave an ironic smile. "Sound familiar?"

As if conjured by survival instinct, the words came easily. "I think I know the man you mean. He told me he was with Code Intel, and I believed him. He took me aside and revealed he was a journalist seeking the truth about Project Sky. I told him I didn't know anything. When he insisted that I must, that my father would know everything, I told him I wasn't my father."

"And you never reported this encounter?"

"He threatened me. I was afraid that if I told anyone, he'd come back and hurt me. I know I should have mentioned, but…"

Lachlan gazed at her, his expression unreadable. "Angelo Abramo began a famous treatise with the following line: 'Breathing is our first act of defiance.' His daughter Beatrice later offered the following commentary upon that line: 'Breathing is involuntary; true resistance must be chosen.' A obscurer thinker, but rather sharper. Much less florid than her father."

Had she tricked him or not? What was he babbling about? "I don't understand."

"Don't you?" Lachlan's chuckle was so self-satisfied that Mineko's anger reached unendurable limits, enough to impel her to stand and draw to her full—if unimpressive—height. "Please, don't get up on my account."

She'd had enough of being meek. "Don't taunt me, you son of a bitch."

"Now that's language I don't usually hear from you."

"I'll speak to you as I please. I won't be your toy any longer. I've denied who I truly am to play the role of the puppet you all intend me to be…" Mineko had lost control, but it didn't matter—Lachlan's startled look was reward enough. "You leave Valerie the hell alone. She's frightened of you, the way we're all frightened of you, but I refuse to be scared anymore. You're my father's lackey, and when I tell you to heel, Lachlan Reed, you will heel."

"You see? Honesty's not so hard after all."

Mineko pointed to the glass doors. "Get out."

"Naturally. It's late, and you need rest. We'll talk soon."

As he strode from the room, Mineko contemplated picking up a vase and throwing it after him, but her anger ebbed as quickly as it had risen. What had she done? A lifetime of composure squandered in an instant of rebellion.

Exactly, perhaps, as Lachlan had intended.

Mineko sat on her bed and pressed her shaking hands together in her lap. He knew. It was the only explanation for his flippant, taunting heresy. Perhaps he even knew what had happened between her and Valerie. But if that was so, why didn't he turn her in? Was his love for scheming and plotting really such that he'd risk crossing her father?

Whatever his motives, there was no escape from this battle of wills between her and him. And he would win, of course. She didn't dare do anything that might draw the ire of her parents, and so he would continue to mock her as he had done today, using her as a piece on his board.

Mineko took the watch from her pocket, and the trembling in her hands eased. She closed her eyes and tried to remember the scent of Callie's hair, the warmth of her arm. They'd spoken together right here on this bed, in this lonely room…

Someday, I'm going to take you for a ride. You'll love it.

But I don't know how, she'd said, her heart squeezed tight.

It's easy. You just sit behind me and hold on.

It only took seconds to retrieve the radio phone from its hiding place. Mineko inhaled a deep breath before depressing the call button. "This is Blue. Is anyone there? This is Blue calling."

The static cleared. "Acknowledged, Blue. Please hold."

Silence again, ominous. The breeze moved through the branches of the tree outside, rustling its white blossoms, and Mineko watched as several petals fluttered loose. Had the petals been freed or had the blossoms been shredded? Did it make any difference?

"Good evening, Blue." She recognized the calm, reassuring voice, though the name took a second longer to come to mind—Nikolas. "Are you well?"

"I want to talk to my friends." Mineko's voice wavered. She took another breath. She hadn't realized how close she was to falling apart. "Please."

"Have no fear. As promised, I've arranged a way for you to contact them. I've merely been awaiting your call."

"I can talk to them now?"

"I believe so. It's a little complicated, but suffice to say I've established a relay. You will talk to the radio here, and the radio will transmit your call across our rudimentary cellular networks to the phone of a colleague of mine. There may be a slight delay, and it's not secure on our end, but it sounds to me as if you have an urgent need. Isn't that so?"

"Yes. Thank you."

"No need to thank me." There was a quiet click over the line. "I'm putting you through. All the best, my friend."

The phone dialed, and Mineko waited, tense, as it produced six beeps. The line clicked again.

"Amity," said the stern voice of an older woman.

"Um, this is Blue. Nikolas said I could—"

"Yes, fine. He's explained it to me. I assume you want to talk to Lexi."

Mineko eased her grip on the phone. If she wasn't careful, she'd break the precious thing. "Yes, but I want Callie first."

"If you insist. I have to walk down a corridor, so be patient." A series of noises ensued—footsteps, a door opening, the steps returning with a touch of echo. A series of thunderous knocks. "It's Amity." The sound of heavy music became audible. "I have a call for Callie. It's from Blue."

A voice replied, too distant to be made out. "She asked for her specifically," said Amity.

Lexi—it could only have been Lexi—blew a wolf-whistle. Somebody laughed, and a door swung shut.

"Min?" Callie sounded worried but hopeful. "You there?"

"I'm here. I'm—" Mineko's throat tightened, and she swallowed. "I'm sorry if this is a bad time."

"No such thing. We're just chilling out; me, Lexi, and Riva. You haven't met Riva yet, but you'd like her. She's really cool." Callie's voice softened. "I've missed you, Min. I worry about you all the time."

There it was again, that weight on her chest. "I've missed you too."

"Lexi, quit it!" Callie laughed. "She's making kissy-faces at me. Thinks she's funny. Riva, can you turn that music down? I can hardly hear the phone...sure, that's better."

Mineko steeled herself. She'd explain everything, and she wouldn't let herself cry. "I'm in trouble. Lachlan knows what I've done, and I think he's threatening me with exposure."

Callie drew in a sharp breath. "Then that's the end of the line. You've got to get out now, whether you like it or not."

"It's not so simple. Fleeing the enclave will mark me as a traitor to the Code, and I can't stand the thought of letting my parents down. I know it's ridiculous, but..." Mineko wiped her eyes, trying to keep her tears at bay. "I know I can't have both. I can't be their daughter and still be free. But I love them, Callie. I don't want them to hate me." A sob broke free, leaving her helpless and ashamed. She'd said she wouldn't cry, yet here she was. "I'm pitiful."

"Oh, Min. You've done enough, you hear me? We'll take you somewhere safe. Just let me come get you. I'll do it tonight. I'll leave right after this call."

"But I need to be here. I'll pass on information. I'll be useful. I've made friends with the head of Project Sky, and she thinks Lexi has a mutation."

"I don't give a shit about Project Sky. I want you out of there."

Could it be so simple? Could Mineko really step out a side door, jump into Callie's van and be driven into the night, rescued from this torment? She opened her mouth to form the reply she wanted most to give—but no, it couldn't be. Her parents would hunt Lexi forever if they thought she were connected to Mineko's disappearance. Whoever gave Mineko refuge would never know peace. And eventually, Code Intel would find her, and those who sheltered her would have their minds erased.

"I can't," said Mineko. "Like I said, it's too dangerous."

"I already told you, danger doesn't matter to me."

"Callie, don't. You're only making this harder. I didn't call to be rescued. I only wanted to hear your voice, that's all, because it's so lonely here, and so quiet…" Another tear welled, hot and prickling. "Would you describe where you are now, so I can imagine it?"

Callie sighed. "Sure. We're in a grotty basement bunker that feels like something out of a horror movie. It's a little cement cubicle with two bunks and a sink that looks like somebody bled to death in it."

"Is it cold?"

"A bit. I found a heating system, but the pipes are in such bad shape, I don't dare turn it on."

"You mentioned somebody named Riva. Will you describe her?"

"Oh, sure. She's about Lexi's height and super skinny. She's a real looker, a total babe, and she's got this amazing Mohawk. And now she's blushing, so imagine her bright red. Also, she just waved to you."

"Please wave back. Does she work for Nikolas? I spoke to him earlier."

Callie giggled. "You really never do run out of questions, do you?"

The sound of Callie's laughter, edged though it had been by concern, revived a little of Mineko's happiness—enough at least to get her smiling again. "I'm sorry. Do you have a plan yet?"

"We're leaving for Port Venn in the next few days. Please come with us."

Port Venn, where Codists were shot on sight… "I told you, I can't."

"What if I said I wouldn't leave Foundation without you?"

Heat burned across Mineko's face. "You couldn't possibly mean that."

"I can take you where your people would never think to look. Consider it, Min. And meanwhile, you stay out of trouble. Turn the key on that watch. Remember, they don't own you and they never will."

What could Mineko possibly say to that? She blinked away more tears. "I'll remember."

"I think Lexi wants a word with you. I should say goodnight, but we'll talk again soon, okay?"

"Okay." The words came out in a near-croak. "Goodnight, and thank you. I'm so grateful." She fumbled for some final remark, something to demonstrate how sincere she was. "I loved our trip together in the van. All that desert, the road stretching forever, how happy you looked. I'll remember that always. Or for as long as they let me keep the memory, anyway."

Had that been too much? The line had gone silent. "Callie?"

"Call me soon, Min. Please."

There was a distant exchange of chatter, and Callie's voice—was she crying?—receded.

"Hello, Minnie." Lexi's sultry tone provoked an incriminating flutter in Mineko's chest. "I don't know what you said to Callie, but Riva's handing her some tissues."

"Hello, Lexi. Are Kade and Zeke okay?"

"They're fine. Forget about them. Eavesdropping on you two, I got the impression you were in trouble."

"I was in trouble from the moment you met me."

"If you need help, say so. I'll give you the addresses of some places to stay."

"I appreciate that, but it's not possible."

"So what's your plan? Live your shut-in life, do whatever the hell it is shut-ins do? For that matter, what do you do?"

"We play non-competitive sports and read approved Codist romances."

"Approved Codist romances? A man in a uniform meets a woman in a uniform, and they marry and have a uniformed baby. Is that about right?"

"Yes. There's no sex in them whatsoever. You just turn the page and there's the baby."

"No wonder you're so straight-laced. You definitely need to come out." Lexi gave a sly chuckle. "From behind those walls, I mean."

Mineko had to end this. Talking to Lexi stirred too many dangerous thoughts. "I have to go. I'm sure being on this line is risky."

"Sure, real risky. You might get addicted to the sound of my voice. But before I let you go, I want to say something. There's nothing wrong with looking out for yourself, okay? Don't let them swallow you up. You're better than they are."

Mineko had never heard Lexi sound so serious, and for an instant she was speechless. She cleared her throat, and her voice returned. "Say goodnight to Callie again. And Riva. Goodbye."

She released the transmit button and dropped the phone. Her hands had resumed trembling, but some of the fog had lifted from her mind, making it possible once more to imagine waking to another day.

She lay back and gazed at the ceiling. Her fear had subsided, taking with it the memory of Lachlan's menace. It was time to undress, to shower and sleep, but she was too drained to move. Easier to lie here and think of Callie's gentle voice. To imagine being in her arms again. To dream of the freedom that meant.

Murmurs rose and faded in the corridor, a breeze swept leaves across the courtyard, petals produced papery whispers and pipes rattled overhead. It was as close as the dormitory ever came to silence. As near, for now, as she could find to peace.

***

The bar's lighting shifted like the beat of a failing heart—strobing at one moment, pulsing slow the next. Instead of the slinking, scattered drone Mineko remembered, the speakers were screaming the music Callie had given her, every note vibrating like a saw.

Kaori and Gaspar stood near the bar, sipping from wine glasses, while Valerie served the drinks. Mineko leaned over the counter and placed a kiss on Valerie's lips. Neither parent noticed. They were blind that way.

"I brought you chocolates," said Mineko. "Where's Alexis Vale?"

"She's in the corner," said Valerie. "But you don't want to disturb her. She's with somebody, and she doesn't like being interrupted."

Frowning, Gaspar emptied his glass onto the floor before turning to Kaori. "We have to do something about our daughter."

"Lachlan will take care of it." Kaori had a forked tongue, just like a snake, and scales down her neck. Someday, when Mineko was older, she'd remember to ask why. "Min, where are you going?"

"Social Ethics." Mineko stepped in the wine puddle as she walked away.

As she crossed the dance floor, the dancers whirled faster, becoming a frenetic blur of faces and limbs. Zeke took her hand and dragged her out of their way.

"Be careful, kid," he said, the lights glittering from his spikes. "Nobody's watching out for you over there."

"I want to see my friend. Alexis Vale."

"In the corner." Zeke lowered his voice to a whisper. "Like a roller coaster."

It was too far to walk, so she let Kade drive her. There was no road, and the wheel moved despite his hands not being upon it. That made sense, because it was really Mineko turning it.

"You going to Bare Hill?" said Kade. "They used to call it the Rail District."

Empty subway stations flickered by, separated by cement strips and ghostly panels of light. "I'm going to the mesa to watch the sunset." As she spoke, Mineko watched his face in the rearview mirror. "My friends are waiting for me there."

"Your old friend, Lachlan Reed? But he's right here."

Sure enough, it was Lachlan reflected in the glass, his face a glistening rictus. Shiny skin, shiny hair, shiny eyes.

"I'm not afraid of you," said Mineko, not looking away from his mocking gaze. "And this is my stop."

"Brave new world." Lachlan tapped the side of his nose. "Remember, Mineko Tamura, true resistance is involuntary."

No, that wasn't right, but he was already gone, leaving Mineko to follow the worn carpet to the corner of the lounge. Lexi and Callie were sprawled together on red leather, embracing while kissing. As Mineko stared, her body became weak in a pleasurable way. A way she wanted to remember.

"Alexis," she said. "Alexis Vale."

Lexi broke from the kiss and gave Mineko a glazed look. "Minnie-Min." She licked the length of Callie's neck from collarbone to jawline, and Callie smiled. "You'll have your turn, don't worry."

"I need to speak to you. It's about Project Sky."

Callie disentangled from Lexi, removed her tank top and tossed it aside. Her breasts were untanned, her nipples pink, her bare skin the promise of something soft and thrilling. "I don't give a shit about Project Sky." She sauntered closer. "It's you I want."

Mineko's breath became shallow. "I want you too."

Callie pulled Mineko close and kissed her. "Turn the key," she said, her breath hot on Mineko's lips, and she guided Mineko's hand down the front of her shorts. She wore no panties, nothing to stop Mineko's fingers plunging into that slippery heat...

Dizziness took her. She opened her eyes to find herself on the couch, straddled by Lexi's bare thighs. Lexi was naked, her body an exquisite wisp of white smoke, and her dark-rimmed eyes shimmered as she stared into Mineko's mind. As the music whispered, her parents drank wine and Kade drove the nowhere road to Bare Hill, Lexi fucked Mineko, fucked her lying on her back and dazed with lust, and Mineko writhed on the leather as she let it happen.

Now Callie was kissing her while Lexi rode her, and the music was becoming louder, a single steady beat repeated over and over, a rapid note matching each motion of Lexi's hips. Why was this happening? Despite her own best judgment, she still hungered after this pale apparition, this inscrutable cyborg, this herald of truth and shame...

Mineko woke, her body twisted in her sweat-soaked sheets. The sound from her dream was still there: a swift, chopping noise. She slipped from the blankets and padded to the window. A black helicopter was moving across the sky.

It was headed east.

CHAPTER 18

Lexi dreamed of railroads, and of smoke, and of Riva Latour.

She escaped her bunk before sleep could catch her again. Her hair had become a fluffy white mess in need of a wash and a little gel, and she fussed with it, to no effect, before dressing in yet another borrowed item from Riva's wardrobe: a white button-down shirt. The jeans were still her own. Good jeans never had to be washed. They were the cockroaches of fashion, designed to survive anything.

Callie mumbled. She was face-down, butt sticking out of the sheets. Sweat covered her bare shoulders. Something was seriously wrong with the way this girl slept.

Lexi touched Callie's warm forehead and searched for the odd, shifting shape of a mind dreaming. She was chasing roads beneath a black and orange sky. A dark shape swooped overhead, casting a wide, deformed shadow. Beyond the mountains, dead things opened their eyes to the night. Her mom was sitting in the back seat, and she didn't dare turn around, because that old bitch was dead too…

Lexi dissolved the nightmare and coaxed forth better memories, which mingled in the haphazard manner of dreams. Now the sun was out. She was following a trail near some abandoned mines, looking for little things—springs, screws, cogs. Mineko was helping, turning rocks and peering at dust. As she knelt beneath an overhang, the afternoon light streamed through the gaps in the rocks, dappling her thoughtful face.

Lexi stroked Callie's cheek as she withdrew her hand. "Sleep well, kid."

As she walked the silent halls of the bunker, it seemed at first that nobody but her was awake. She paused in the galley. The lights were on, suggesting she hadn't been the first to rise after all.

She took the steps to the surface slowly, tracing the rough wall with her fingertips as she climbed, and sauntered down the long hall.

The front door was open.

It was just before dawn, the sky still dark but tinged with an early hint of sunlight. Riva stood on the footpath, her arms folded against her chest and her face turned upward. She seemed somehow to belong out here, a thin, Mohawked silhouette against a black sky streaked with red. A natural element of this melancholy hour that was neither morning nor night.

Lexi held her from behind, and they watched the morning emerge. Even sunrise couldn't make this street attractive, but the shadows were deep enough to conceal the worst of the decay, and the glow rising above the fractured cityscape held a certain tragic grandeur. After all, the sun didn't give a damn what it rose on. It had risen on worse and would set on better.

"I didn't sleep well," said Riva, still staring at the sky.

Lexi planted a light, nuzzling kiss on her neck. "I hope you know it's dangerous out here."

"Don't worry. I'm still within shrieking panic of the front door."

Lexi tightened her hold on Riva's skinny waist. "I'm going to tell you a story. Three years ago, Callie had a girlfriend. A cute little brunette who worked behind the bar at Zeke's. Now, Callie loved this girl. Spoiled her rotten. But she's a smuggler, you know. Odd hours, long trips. And this girl, she wasn't immune to getting lonely."

"And that's where you come in?"

"I used to frequent Zeke's place back before him and me fell out. It's the best queer club in Foundation. The only one, really. The other places are just gay and dyke bars. Anyway, every night, this gorgeous girl served me, and of course I'd flirt, because that's how I'm wired."

"Oh, Lexi…"

"I thought it'd be harmless, but it turned out I hadn't read the girl right. She was out to detonate the relationship, and she used me. She fucked me so that she could fuck over Callie. I'm still not sure why."

"You didn't use that chip on her?"

"No. That would be disrespectful. A violation, in fact."

"And now, three years later, Callie still won't forgive you?"

"I won't apologize. That's why."

Riva looked toward the horizon, where a line of ruined towers was highlighted by a soft red glow. "Pride?"

"Principle. In the aftermath, Callie called me a slut. That crosses the line. A grown woman issued me an invitation to fuck her. I took it. Why should I apologize? The sex wasn't wrong. It was the woman's motive that was wrong, and that's not my problem."

"I said sorry to you last night, but not because I didn't have a good reason to react the way I did. I apologized because hurting me was the last thing you intended to do. Did you want to hurt Callie?"

"No."

"Yet despite your best intentions, you did."

"I get your point." Lexi sighed. "Did somebody hurt you?"

"In a sense. At first, I didn't have the words to explain why I was hurting. Then, when I finally found the words, nobody wanted to hear them."

"It's a new day." Lexi took Riva's hands and entwined their fingers, their cold palms finding warmth together. "Maybe that's nothing special. Happens every twenty-four hours. But if you want, you can make this particular sunrise mean something."

"I'm too scared. I don't want these memories to become so many scars. I love the way you look at me now, and if I confess to you, there's every chance I'll never see that look again."

"It won't end that way. Not with me."

Riva took an unsteady breath. "Those pills you saw in my room. Some were hormones. Estrogen. The others were anti-androgens. Do you know what that means?"

Yeah. Lexi knew. Would forever remember the day she'd found her best friend shirtless and weeping. *Lexi, they're coming through.*

Those dark, puffy nipples. They'd been coming through all right.

She'd put an arm around him, held him close. *It's no biggie. I'll get you a binder.*

It won't help. He'd cried the way people cried for the dead, choking and shaking. *I don't want Ash to see.*

"Lexi," said Riva, her voice broken. "Please say something."

"I understand. Babe, it doesn't make any difference."

Riva sobbed, and Lexi hugged her tight. "You can cry," she said. "I'm here." As she waited for Riva's weeping to subside, she felt the convulsions in that delicate chest and thought of the boy who'd used to cry the same way, held in these same arms.

It was just the right wall from which to observe a sunrise. They sat pressed close for warmth while the sun crested distant towers and the sky faded to a moody shade of gray.

"I once told a woman who then accused me of having lied to her," Riva said. "I couldn't make her understand that I'm living truthfully every day. Deception is what I've decided against."

"Don't feel you need to bring up bad memories. I'm not like the others. I already understand without you telling me."

"You do realize I have a…" Riva turned her face away. "I know you expected something else. That's one reason I was afraid."

With a gentle touch, Lexi tilted Riva's head until their eyes met again. "Every woman's body is different. For me, finding something unexpected is part of the fun."

"Most hate the unexpected. I'm comfortable with the way I look and dress, but all I get is abuse for it. I don't gender myself clearly enough for some people. They project their expectations onto me and get angry when they're wrong."

"Been there, done that, fuck them. We don't exist to satisfy anyone's expectations."

The emotions swirling from Riva were impossible to tune out—relief, tenderness, battered dignity.

"I don't hate my body," she said, "but I hate the way I'm treated because of it. And sometimes it's hard to tell those two things apart."

"I've never seen the big deal. If I play with a girl's finger, stroke it or suck it, that's obviously fine. So if I do the same with her dick, what's the difference? I hope to pleasure women, not body parts. I'm attracted to people, not organs. I'm sure there are some who see their partners as a collection of fleshy bits. They can keep the hell away from mine."

"Have you ever been with a woman like me?"

"Twice. They were nervous too, but you're something else." Lexi looked back to the sunrise—it was well and truly underway, a radiant birth of light on the ruptured city skyline. "You've had it bad, haven't you?"

"I just wish I'd trusted you earlier. When we had more time."

"Stop thinking like this was some dark, guilty secret. If I don't mention that my left nipple is a little smaller than my right nipple, that's not a secret. That's just me not telling strangers about my nipples."

Riva smiled for the first time since her confession. "I've seen your nipples. I didn't notice any difference."

"You won't notice until you get to play with them. I plan to sex you up, if you hadn't forgotten. We just have to find our moment."

"In the back of Callie's van, maybe? Or we could just do it in the galley."

"Not in Callie's van. She wouldn't speak to me for another three years."

Lexi gazed at the sun swelling on the edge of the world she knew, and nostalgia took hold of her—a lazy sense of solace accompanied by inarticulate regret. "There's something pure about a sunrise. We can't fuck it up the way we've done everything else. Can't deface it, can't tag it, can't break it just for fun. The sun's going to keep on being beautiful, if only to spite us."

"For about five billion years. Then there'll be nothing but vacuum."

Lexi grinned. "Let me enjoy a bit of sentimentality. I don't do it very often." She hugged Riva more tightly, and Riva squeezed back. "I had a cousin once. Ash. My only family. I lost her some years back."

"I'm sorry."

The sunlight gleamed on the antennas atop the buildings, turning them into unearthly rods of white flame. "She loved watching sunsets and sunrises. Forced me and Kade to watch them with her." Lexi hesitated. "We grew up together, by the way. Me and Kade."

"I know." Riva caressed Lexi's side, touching her neck, stroking her hip. "Last night, he came to my room to comfort me, and he told me that he loves you. That he misses you. And he said it with as much pain and grief as I felt when I confided in you just now."

Lexi closed her eyes. She'd had enough sunrise for one day.

———————

An hour later, Amity strolled up to the wall and glared at its cuddling occupants. "I see you two are quite comfortable."

"Good morning," said Riva, her feet swinging. "How'd you sleep?"

"Let me guess," said Lexi. "With a knife in your teeth."

Amity wrinkled her cute little nose. "Very amusing. Less amusing is finding you two sitting atop that wall like trophies on a pedestal. You're supposed to be in hiding, remember?"

"And we are. From you boring people." Lexi winked. "How are they?"

"Awake. Zeke complained to me for ten minutes about his sleeping arrangements." Amity broke into a perfect Zeke impression, bugging her eyes and waving her hands. *"Amity, I couldn't sleep! That fucking junkie smells so bad! C'mon, give me another fucking room!"* She grimaced. "Idiot. I offered him the toilet facility as an alternative sleeping quarters. Now he's sulking in the galley."

Lexi almost laughed herself off the wall. "I keep forgetting you have a sense of humor."

"She hides it well," said Riva. "When she's drunk, she's hilarious."

"I have more sense than to get drunk around Lexi Vale." Amity extended her hand to Riva. "Come down from there. I'll help you with breakfast."

"I'll push her, and you catch," said Lexi. "Ready?"

Chuckling, Riva let herself be assisted to the pavement.

"Me too," said Lexi. "Please. I can't do it alone."

Amity sighed as she offered her hand. Lexi took it, touched its knuckles to her lips and gazed into Amity's eyes. "You have the most enchanting nose, comrade. So petite."

With a swift yank, Amity pulled Lexi off the wall and sent her stumbling to the pavement. "Be quiet," Amity said to Riva, who had succumbed to a fit of giggles. "Some lowlifes may hear you."

"And lowlifes hate the sound of laughter," said Lexi. "It's blood in the water to them. There's a noseless monster in an alley right now, hunting around while growling, 'Is that some punk laughing? In my hood?'"

"Enough nonsense. Come have breakfast."

Upon descending into the galley, they found Zeke and Callie arguing around a table while Kade listened.

"He can't help it," said Callie. "The guy's been living on the street."

"But it was like sleeping inside an ass," Zeke said. "The ass of a dead man."

"Well, what did you expect from the guy? Spearmint?"

"Sure, be sarcastic. You didn't have to sleep holding your fucking breath." Zeke waved at the arrivals. "Lex, Riva. You guys been outside all this time?"

"I bet they were watching the sunrise," said Callie. "They're in love."

Amity nodded. "Confirmed. It looked very romantic."

"Guilty as charged," said Lexi. "If you'd only come out a little later, you'd have caught us fucking." She dropped into the chair beside Zeke, put her boots on the table, and yawned. "Where's that breakfast?"

"I'm on it," said Riva. "Amity, would you mind heating two pans for me?"

While Riva and Amity clattered in the kitchen, Lexi glanced at Kade. After years of avoiding him, it was still jarring to see him so close. He noticed her looking, and they stared at each other.

"Morning," said Lexi.

"Good morning." Kade gave a tentative smile. "You doing okay?"

Even though he'd changed so much, Lexi still knew that smile, but she couldn't yet bring herself to return it. Instead, she shrugged. "It was a good sunrise. She'd have loved it."

That emotional wall of his wavered—only for a moment, but enough to get a sense of how much he was hurting. Lexi looked away. She couldn't put herself through this. Not now. She needed to find that old resentment again, yet right now, it was hard to grasp...

A phone trilled. Amity plucked it from her trench coat. "Amity. Oh, it's you. Did you—" Her eyes narrowed. "I see. Yes, we're east of the University. Yes. Just the one, you said. No, it's not your fault. I understand. Did you want to talk to—I see. Very well. Thank you. We'll let you know." She lowered the phone. "That was Blue."

Callie jumped to her feet. "Is she in trouble?"

"We may be the ones in trouble. She's spotted a Codist chopper headed east, and intelligent woman that she obviously is, she's assumed that it's headed our way. We're certain they can't know about this bunker, but last night, she made a radio call."

"Damn it," said Kade. "Lachlan. He knew about the phone and used her to get our location. If there's a helicopter, that means there'll be agents on the ground soon. We have to leave now."

"What about Isaac?" Riva set down a half-opened plastic packet of food. "We can't leave him."

"He's an innocent bystander, not to mention near-incoherent. Lachlan won't trouble him." Kade took a pistol from his coat and inspected its safety. "You have maybe thirty seconds to grab whatever you've left in your rooms."

"We're fucked, aren't we?" Zeke wrung his hands. "A fucking shut-in helicopter, how do we get away from that?"

"By leaving as soon as possible," said Amity. "Lexi, stop lounging. It's time to move."

"But I'm hungry." Lexi held out her hand. "Riva, toss me one of those protein bars, will you?" Riva obliged, and Lexi caught the foil-wrapped bar with augmented ease. "What would breakfast have been if you'd had the chance to keep cooking?"

"Scrambled tofu," said Riva. "With my own special chili sauce."

"Motherfucker." Lexi stared at the unappetizing bar in her hands. "Lachlan Reed, you are a dead man."

Waite Street wasn't pretty. On its left side ran a long row of collapsed storefronts, while on its right loomed the steel skeletons of buildings picked apart by time.

Among the dreary scenery, the garage was easy to spot. It boasted a bright blue facade, and a cartoon animal had been emblazoned on its door. Maybe a pig, judging by the pink tint, though peeling paint had given it a rotted appearance. A zombie pig, then.

Amity unlocked the garage as Lexi stared down the street. A pair of dots were accelerating closer. They clarified into menacing shut-in bikes, two nasty pieces of work: shining white chassis, complex black under-bellies, sleek insect-like frames.

"Two riders coming," said Lexi.

Callie frowned. "I don't see anything."

"I have 20/5 vision. Trust me." A hundred meters back, three vehicles closed the distance. Low, black, sinister. "There're cars too. Three of them."

The door rattled upward. The garage had been intended for larger vehicles, transport trucks maybe, and Callie's van looked small and lonely parked at the back.

"I hear the helicopter," said Amity. "Do you see it yet?"

Sure enough, a repetitive thumping sound was drawing closer. Turning her head toward the noise, Lexi spotted a speck moving across the sky. "Yep, it's coming. Do you think that Lachlan guy is inside?"

"I hope so. I'm eager to put my fist through his face." Amity spun on her heel. "Let's get moving."

The group piled into the van—Zeke, Kade, Amity, and Lexi in the back, Riva in the passenger seat, and Callie behind the wheel. Amity pulled one of the rear doors shut, leaving the other ajar.

"All aboard?" said Callie. "Then hold on!"

She reversed while turning the wheel, and the van whirled to face the road. With a roar, it shot forward and took a sharp left, bringing it onto the street in the opposite direction of their pursuers.

"I see them!" said Zeke, pointing out the open door. "I see the fuckers!"

"Perceptive of you," said Amity.

The road became a blur beneath their wheels, yet the bikes continued to gain, as did the black vehicles cruising behind them.

"Not looking good," said Callie. "My baby here is quick for a van, but she'll top out a lot sooner than those shut-in cars will."

"What do you have back here?" said Amity. "Sniper rifle? RPG?"

"Um, no. Shotgun's under the seat, and that's it. If you wanted an arsenal, you picked the wrong smuggler."

"That's a pity." Amity took a pistol from her coat and offered it to Lexi. "You keep this. I'll use the shotgun."

She snatched the shotgun from beneath the seat, snapped back the handle, peered into the barrel, and slammed the handle shut, becoming ten times more frightening in the process. "We have a strategic advantage. They want Lexi alive, whereas I don't care if every single one of them dies."

Lexi brandished her unexpected pistol. "I've never fired a gun before."

"With your augmented vision, you should have learned." Amity glanced at Zeke. "I don't suppose you're secretly a crack shot."

"Nah," said Zeke. "Closest I ever get to crack is… Well, I can tell this ain't the time for jokes, so I'll just shut the fuck up, huh?"

Kade stood before the open door, his pistol drawn. The wind fluttered the hem of his trench coat and blew through his shaggy hair. All he needed was a pair of sunglasses to complete the image of a stern, gun-toting pain in the ass.

"Shoot the gas tanks on the cars," said Zeke. "Blow the fuckers up."

"Only in the movies," said Callie. "Sorry."

With a sudden burst of speed, the bikes tore up the remaining distance and drifted behind the van, separated by a distance of perhaps five meters. One of the riders held up a dark sphere.

"What's that?" Lexi said.

"Trouble," said Amity. "Kade."

Kade aimed. A gunshot erupted, and the rider slumped against their handlebars. The bike toppled, throwing the tumbling body to the road.

The other rider hunched, and their bike screamed as it veered to the right and shot past the van.

"He's in front of me," said Callie. The van swerved hard enough to send everyone in the back scrabbling for support. "He's putting down caltrops!"

Amity sighed. "So avoid them, Callie."

"I know that, you grumpy bitch!"

The slicing sound of rotors built to an immense volume, and a shadow rippled over the asphalt. The helicopter—black, of course—descended to hover above the road.

A dark figure hung out of its door and raised a megaphone. "Good morning, everyone. I regret to inform you that you're all on a Codist wanted list. Oh, and one of you is now charged with murder. Pull over and put down your guns, and some of you may enjoy lenience."

"That's Lachlan," said Kade. "Lachlan Reed."

"The guy that's been messing with Min?" said Callie. "Lexi, shoot the prick."

Lexi aimed, held her breath and pulled the trigger. The shot was loud enough, but the result was disappointing: no deaths, no explosions, not even one of those wacky *zing* sounds. "Sorry. Missed."

"I'm grateful for your appalling aim," said Lachlan. "As you prefer to do this violently, I suppose I must oblige you."

The helicopter hovered in retreat while the trio of cars glided forth beneath it. Lexi fired a series of shots, but despite her hitting the black windshields and tires several times, the cars didn't so much as swerve.

"They're too heavily armored," said Amity. "And the tires are airless, so save your bullets. Callie, we need to get off this road."

The van took a left, jolting Zeke and Lexi off their feet, and its engine thundered. Recovering her balance, Lexi turned to look ahead. Callie had swung them into a narrow side street littered with debris and shadowed by high buildings. As the van gathered speed, Callie worked the wheel, dodging craters in the asphalt.

"You really know how to drive," said Riva, and Callie grinned and took the van up another gear.

The steady chopping noise of the helicopter pursued them, and two of the black cars turned smoothly into the side street and continued their chase. The third car zipped past the intersection, its drivers presumably intent on cutting the van off elsewhere.

"I'd be careful if I were you," Lachlan said, his voice echoing from above. "I can see the road ahead, and it's not exactly in mint condition."

Zeke glared at the ceiling. "What an asshole."

Another sharp turn sent Lexi reeling, and she lunged for a handhold—Zeke, as it turned out. Callie had directed the van into an even narrower street, this one little more than an accidental bypass. Graffitied bricks flashed past, looking close enough to reach out and touch.

"Slow down," said Amity. "Let them get near."

Callie pulled a face in the rearview mirror. "If you say so."

The van slowed. As the first shut-in car neared the van's rear bumper, Amity leaned out of the door and fired. The tremendous shotgun blast consumed every other sound, and a compact pattern of cracks appeared on the car's windshield.

Amity cracked open the shotgun and ejected the spent casing. "Shell."

"Near the door," said Callie. "At Kade's feet."

Kade rummaged through a cardboard box and stood holding a shell, which Amity snatched from his hand. She pushed it into the barrel, flipped the handle shut, and fired again.

This time, the windshield became a crazed mess of glass, unbroken but certainly impossible to see through, and the car braked to a sudden halt. The second car behind it swerved and scraped the wall.

"Now speed up again," Amity said, and the van hurtled toward the next intersection. "That should slow them."

"You've added vandalism to the list of your offenses," said the obnoxious amplified voice pursuing them. "Do let me know when you feel you've sinned enough, won't you?"

The van shot onto a wider street, and Callie spun the wheel, reorienting them westward. The jagged teeth of the inner city dominated the skyline.

"This road leads home," she said. "I think we have a decent chance now, but I'd like to know where that other car is."

"Don't say that," said Zeke. "It'll burst out of the nearest street if you say that. Don't you know how car chases work?"

The van flew by several blocks, one ruined neighborhood vanishing after another. Lexi stood behind the mesh partition and surveyed the road.

"Burned out car coming up in the left lane," she said, and Callie nodded and shunted the van to the right. Maybe ten seconds later, the wreck passed them by.

"It must be incredible to have your eyesight," said Riva.

"It's wasted on me. I'm mostly indoors."

The helicopter's whir panned overhead. "Where exactly do you plan on going?" said Lachlan. "I can see everything from up here, you know."

Amity grimaced. "The bastard has a point. While we remain visible to him by air, there's no chance of us escaping. He'll already have agents setting up road blocks."

"Callie," said Kade. "Do you have a megaphone, by any chance?"

"Of course she don't have a megaphone," said Zeke. "Man, you might as well ask if she keeps a fighter jet or some dumb shit like that."

"Actually, I might." Callie spoke without taking her eyes from the road. "Try the crate next to Amity."

After scrounging through the box beside her, Amity held up a battered megaphone. "Holy fuck, keep searching," said Zeke. "With luck like that, maybe there really is a jet back here."

Gripping a door handle for support, Kade leaned out of the van while holding the megaphone. "Lachlan."

A chuckle boomed above them. "Hello, Kade. You really do go to extreme lengths to get a story. Tell me, is my target with you?"

"You know damn well she is."

"Would she like to surrender? In exchange, I'll spare the rest of you from detainment. You can all traipse home to plot her rescue."

"Of course she won't surrender. And it seems to me you've lost your touch. One of your people is dead, and this pursuit is out of control. The man I knew was significantly more competent."

There was a second of silence. When Lachlan's voice returned, it betrayed a trace of irritation. "I think you're judging my performance a little prematurely."

"It's hard to judge it at all, given your preference for hiding in the clouds."

"Believe it or not, there's some strategic value to being up here. As you know, they don't pay me to be an action hero."

"More likely you're scared of Lexi. She has Project Sky, after all. Is that why you're chasing her? To get that implant for yourself, to use it to carry out your schemes and manipulations?"

Another pause. "Hardly. I already scheme and manipulate quite well without it."

"We have a problem," said Callie, pointing to the road ahead. A black vehicle was parked across it, and two uniformed figures waited behind a barricade of razor wire. "Left or right?"

"Left," said Amity.

The van darted into a side street filled with refuse. Paper and cardboard scattered beneath the van's wheels, and Callie swore as she swerved to avoid the angular edge of a steel bin. Everyone in the back was flung off-balance, save for Amity, who remained steady on her feet.

"Keep goading Reed," she said. "Test his patience."

"No need," said Kade. "He's already brooding. He doesn't like his ability being called into question."

"So what's the plan?" said Zeke. "We can't keep driving around in circles. C'mon, Callie, you eat trouble for breakfast and wash it down with a glass of danger, right? You must have some ideas. Some wild smuggler scheme."

Callie shrugged. "We need to shake the chopper. Simple as that."

"Or destroy it." Amity patted the barrel of the shotgun. "If we can find a place to stand our ground, we'll be able to strike back. I've overcome greater odds than this. We just need the right opportunity."

"Fucking hell," said Callie. Everyone turned to stare at her, as people were prone to do after such outbursts. "He's forced us back to where we started." A familiar abandoned hotel flashed by. "He's going to box us in."

"Or maybe we're in luck," said Riva. "Callie, slow down. Look over there."

Lexi looked in the direction of Riva's finger. Isaac was on the pavement, staring up and down the street like a lost boy looking for his parents.

"Now there's a guy who must know his way around," said Lexi. "Let's offer him a lift."

Isaac buckled himself into the back seat and sat huddled, his head down.

"Isaac, we need your help," said Riva, and he gave her a meek look. "You must hear the helicopter chasing us."

"Yeah, I hear it." Isaac picked the skin around his fingernails. "Only the second time in my life I've heard that sound."

"Was the first time about twenty minutes ago?" said Lexi.

Riva shot her a stern look. "We have to get out of sight. Any ideas?"

Isaac wrinkled his face into a thoughtful knot. "Big parking complex on the north side. It could give you cover, maybe."

"How would Reed respond to that?" said Amity.

Kade shook his head. "You never know with him, but he'll be uneasy having us out of sight. It could spur him into doing something reckless. But we have to avoid driving ourselves into a dead-end."

"So how do we get there?" said Callie.

"Turn right here," said Isaac. "Keep going five blocks, then right at the big lights. Then left, but skip the first street. Road there's all fucked up."

"My very own GPS." Callie twirled the wheel and accelerated. "I wonder where that other biker went."

Amity paused from stashing shotgun shells into her coat. "We'll take care of that later. For now, drive."

Callie stuck out her tongue, and Riva laughed. The van picked up yet more speed, its wheels rattling over the uneven asphalt.

"The power still on in this parking place?" said Callie.

"Power's on," said Isaac. "Gangs meet there. It's neutral ground."

Lexi studied the pistol in her hand. She'd never owned a gun—it seemed crude somehow, a concession her smarts weren't always enough. Right now, the way she was being shaken about in the back of the van, it seemed all too plausible she might fire by accident.

"Kade, how do I put the safety back on?"

"Like this." Kade demonstrated with his own pistol, and Lexi imitated him, pushing back the small metal switch with her thumb. "Good idea, by the way."

"I don't know how Amity does it. We're all hanging on for life, yet she's just standing there, effortlessly upright, as if falling over is something that happens to other people."

Amity gave a grim smile. "It is."

The shadow of the helicopter flowed over the road, and the noise of its rotors intensified. "So you're going north," said Lachlan, his amused voice ringing from the heavens like some trickster god's. "Are you escaping or just circling the block?"

Isaac muttered another instruction, and Callie took a turn so sharp that Lexi almost lost her grip. "Calandre, be careful!"

"Hey, I'm trying to make us harder to follow," said Callie. "Don't hate the player, hate the game."

The road darkened as they sped between a series of high apartment towers. Strips of sunlight flickered across the asphalt, an eerie procession of light and dark, before the vehicle emerged onto a wide street.

"There it is," Callie said. A massive parking tower was visible on the horizon several blocks away. "Nice work, Isaac."

"Behind us," said Kade. Two black vehicles were cruising in pursuit, and the lone biker rode at their head. "It seems they're minus one car."

"You see?" said Amity. "We're making progress."

The van rushed through an alley, took another improbable turn, and blazed down a wide street strung with electrical wire. A faded sign had been erected at the next intersection: *Parking Next Left.*

"We really going to do this?" said Callie. "We might be driving ourselves into a corner."

"Do it," said Amity. "Good driving, Callie."

"Hey, a compliment! And here I was expecting you to snap at me again."

An intersection marked with a faded left arrow came into sight, and Callie took the turn without slowing. The van tilted but remained upright, though the same couldn't be said for Lexi's stomach.

"Jesus, Callie," said Zeke. "I'm gonna puke on Amity if you don't cut that out. And if that happens, I'm as good as dead."

The parking tower loomed ahead of them, layer upon layer of cement. At road level, a low entrance led into a dimly lit cavern. The boom gate had been dismantled, leaving just a sad yellow pole, and the toll booth was tagged with colorful gang signs.

Callie brought the van down a gear. "Anyone get the hourly rates?"

"Isaac," said Amity. Isaac raised his haunted eyes. "Describe the layout."

"It goes down three levels, goes up maybe ten. Four stairwells. Lift's all fucked up, don't use it." Isaac scratched his chin. "Overpass on the third floor, goes to the old mall. No power over there."

Amity tapped her fingers against the shotgun barrel, lost in some deep, murderous contemplation. The others in the back watched her, expectant, while

Callie drove the van down a long ramp and into a gloomy corridor lined with empty parking spaces.

"Standard practice is three agents to a vehicle," said Amity. "That makes seven in pursuit. Two in the helicopter, Reed and a pilot. That's a mere nine, and we have the tactical and psychological advantage."

"You're planning to fight," said Kade.

"A bloodbath would give Reed no choice but to intervene. And when he comes down here, I'll finally pay out justice for his treachery. Callie, park us on the bottom floor near a stairwell. Isaac, I'm going to require one final favor. I assure you that you won't be in any danger, and Open Hand will reward you for your assistance."

Isaac blinked. "Reward? What kind of reward?"

"If you want to be clean, we'll help you become clean. If you'd rather have your drugs of choice, I'll arrange that instead. All I need is your cooperation."

"Amity!" said Riva, and Amity flushed.

"Given the circumstances…" Amity cleared her throat. "I'm only trying to get us out of this alive."

"I'm not denying that." Riva touched her bandaged hand to the mesh, and a hint of emotion flickered in Isaac's bloodshot eyes. "Isaac, please think carefully before you answer."

"No more drugs," he said, his voice thick. "I want to be clean."

Kade patted him on the shoulder. "I'll fight beside you, Amity, but I can't condone bringing Riva and Zeke into this. They're non-combatants."

"There's a reason Nikolas allows me to stay as his second-in-command. Have a little faith, and I'll demonstrate it. However…" Amity averted her gaze. "I will need your help, Lexi."

Lexi smirked. "Obviously."

CHAPTER 19

Unsure of the plan, Kade watched as Amity held out the shotgun and a handful of shells. "Callie, have your shotgun back. Lexi, give me my pistol." The weapons were exchanged, and Callie stashed the shells into a small pouch on her hip. "It's better if you return to being unarmed, Lexi. Your aim is terrible."

"No arguments there." Lexi shoved her now-empty hands into her pockets. "I'll just throw myself at them, all rabid and snapping."

"Good plan. Callie, do you have alcohol?"

Zeke winced. "It's going to be that bad, huh?"

Callie retrieved a flask from the glovebox. Amity unscrewed it and took a quick sniff. "Is it because you fight better drunk?" said Callie. "Some kind of martial arts thing?"

"Don't be absurd." Amity handed the flask to Isaac. "Drink some and spill the rest over yourself. Kade, give him that old blanket from the back."

Now it made sense. Kade passed the woolen bundle to Isaac, who held it while taking frantic gulps from the flask. No doubt Amity could have told him to drink arsenic and he'd have been intimidated enough to oblige.

"Great plan," said Lexi. "Can't go wrong with blankets and booze."

"Shut up." Amity pointed to one of the parking level's gloomy corners. "Isaac, get comfortable over there. You're a drunk who's been sheltering here for days. You saw us get out of the van. We all ran through that door." She indicated the nearest stairwell. "All of us, do you understand? Too many people for you to count."

"I keep drinking this, that'll be true," said Isaac. "They won't hurt me?"

"They have no cause to. They're Codists, not cannibals. If they ask more questions, just mumble and feign stupidity."

"Feign?" Zeke said, and Callie swatted him.

"Okay. I'll do that." Isaac stumbled to the corner, lay wrapped in the blanket, and splashed alcohol on himself. With the heady aroma of booze added to his seedy appearance, nobody would think he was anything other than one of the city's many homeless. Which, of course, he was.

"Happy birthday, Isaac," said Lexi. "Amity, care to explain?"

"I want them to believe we've all kept together," said Amity. "In truth, Riva and Zeke will be escorted to safety while we prepare an ambush."

Zeke squealed. "You do know my name!"

"No time for foolishness. Kade, Callie, get them out of here."

"Quit ordering me around," said Callie. "Lexi, are you okay with this? I don't like your chances."

"I'll give it a shot," said Lexi. "But first, I need to talk to the media. Alone."

Kade followed her away from the group, his apprehension mounting with every step. They stopped and confronted each other. Her face seemed timeless to him, but it was likely Lexi saw him as a stranger—not just because he'd changed, but because her anger being what it was, it would be simpler for her to perceive him that way.

"Don't let Riva get hurt." Lexi spoke low and soft, without a trace of irony. "Look after her just like I used to look after you. Promise me."

Kade nodded. His throat and chest hurt, and the unexpected gentleness in her voice only made it worse. "I promise."

"Enough of your whispering," said Amity. "You'll see each other again shortly. Get moving now and find that overpass Isaac mentioned."

"Very well," said Kade. "Callie, cover me. Zeke, Riva, stay close to her."

His companions fell into step behind him, and they set off across the cement floor. Isaac raised his flask as they passed him.

Kade opened the first door he found. The stairwell beyond was lit, but the aroma of dust and mold suggested it didn't get a lot of airing.

They filed inside, Callie entering last with her shotgun at the ready. She'd be fine under pressure, but the strain was already showing on Zeke's and Riva's pinched faces.

"Let's go up," said Kade. "Your footsteps will carry, so walk light."

He ascended the first step, one hand on the blackened metal rail. "What floor did Isaac say the overpass was on?"

"Third," said Callie. "You think this is going to work?"

"Never underestimate Amity," said Riva. "I just hope she isn't going to gamble with Lexi's life. We can't let the Codists have her."

"You mean you're worried about her," said Zeke. "I bet she's worried sick about you. You ain't just another girl in her eyes. She don't watch no fucking sunrise with any random lay."

Riva blushed. "Yes, I'm worried."

"Lexi's scrappy when cornered," Kade said. "She put me on my ass a few times when we were kids, and she did worse to anyone who tried to pick on me. She may be richer now, but I can't imagine working for gangsters has allowed her to go soft."

"Plus she's got a reflex aug," said Callie. "I've seen cyborgs dodge bullets with those."

"Has she ever dodged a bullet?" said Riva.

"Lexi? I doubt it. Nobody's dumb enough to shoot at her. She's been given special protection by both Vassago and Contessa."

"Was given protection," said Zeke. "She can't rely on those gangland friends no more. They're all fucking pussies, scared of the shut-ins." He grinned. "But don't you worry. She and Amity are gonna kick some ass."

The next landing featured a sign: *Floor 3. Don't Forget Your Ticket!* Kade nudged the door open. Intervals of sunlight and shadow striped a long stretch of cement in front of him. Perhaps twenty meters distant, a low barrier overlooked a view of crumbled rooftops. The chopping sound of the helicopter remained audible, but the skyline was clear.

"You three hang back a second," Kade said.

"Okay." Callie hefted her shotgun. "Be careful."

Kade sprinted to the cover of a ceiling support. Just around the corner, a pedestrian bridge spanned the expanse between the parking lot's third level and a multi-story shopping mall.

He beckoned to the others, who dashed to join him. "We're going across."

"Okay," said Callie. "But as soon as I can, I'm going back to help out Lexi."

"Sure. I know how you feel."

Zeke took the lead, glancing around him as if expecting Codists to crawl over the railings. Kade followed with his pistol ready, and Riva kept close to Callie. When the group had made it halfway across the overpass, the sound of the rotors cut out.

"He's gone," said Zeke, staring upward. "Fucker ran away."

"More like he's landed," said Callie. "We'd have seen him flying off."

"Then a hundred bucks says Amity puts a bullet in his brain. Problem solved. Now can we get off this damn bridge?"

"I've never seen so much of Foundation." Riva stood by the railing, wondering at the westward view. In its prime, those skyscrapers and spires must have been an imposing sight. Now they were nothing but steel bones. "Does every major city look like this?"

Callie joined Riva at the railing. "Port Venn is nicer, at least. It has streets with controlled traffic, a proper power grid and everything. And there's those new townships built by the republics up north. Too many laws there, though. Easier to live here and steal from the shut-ins."

"I'd like to explore someday, but I don't know if I'd be brave enough. How would I survive without Amity and Nikolas?"

"Don't underestimate yourself," said Kade. "You seem capable to me."

"You'll see more of the world." Callie touched Riva's hand. "I promise."

"Um, friends," said Zeke. "Comrades. Guys. Can we have this poignant moment later? You know, when nobody is trying to kill us?"

"Yeah." Kade gave Riva a pat on the back. "Let's get inside."

<hr />

The mall's sliding doors had been smashed and the glass swept away. Callie took a cautious step through the frame. "No lights."

"Uh-huh," said Kade. At the other end of the darkened hall, a hint of daylight suggested the presence of windows, but the intervening shadows were far from inviting. "Guess we'll be careful."

"Or prepared." Callie took a stubby flashlight from her hip pouch and directed its beam down the hall. The light swept across chipped plastic tiles, exposed wiring and white walls smeared with dust.

"Or both," said Riva, and Callie giggled and shone the light at her.

One by one, the group ducked through the frame. Zeke entered last, his impatience apparently now eclipsed by his cowardice.

They advanced down the hall, guided by Callie's light, until they reached a balconied upper floor overlooking an abandoned shopping level. A cracked dome in the ceiling allowed sunlight to steal through the gloom, but it wasn't quite enough to disperse the darkness.

Storefronts lined the upper floor, opening into dirty, dusty chambers. Many of the signs were intact, from the glitzy facade of *Fashion Central* to the inert bulbs spelling *Game World*, but they only added to the place's mournful quality.

"There have to be stairs somewhere," said Callie, aiming her flashlight through the store windows. A sinister lump became a mound of sodden paper, and a hulking form turned into an office chair flipped on its side. In one store, broken mannequins were jumbled in the corner. A single plastic torso adorned the empty window display. Creepy.

"You're so brave, Callie," said Riva. "You're holding that light perfectly steady, whereas I can't stop my hands from shaking."

Callie gave her a sweet smile. "Trust me, chickadee, you're doing great."

"Only because you're here with me." Riva pushed aside a fallen light tube with her boot. "Kade, do you think Open Hand will last much longer?"

Kade hesitated mid-step. "Why do you ask?"

"Because of all the fighting lately. You're friends with Amity and Nikolas. Can't you convince them to work together?"

Kade studied her. Her appearance was reminiscent of Lexi: a tall, slight woman with angular, androgynous features. But unlike Lexi, who exuded confidence, Riva seemed somehow fragile. She moved self-consciously, as if she kept her head high only by an active effort of will. A shy person determined not to be.

"They're my friends," he said. "But they're tough to talk sense into."

"I can't stand to see them fighting. We're only strong together."

That was close to home. Those words had been Ash's perpetual refrain: *we're only strong together.* She hadn't believed in individualism—Lachlan had loved to tease her, calling her a 'bleeding-heart Codist'—but had unwavering faith in the capacity of a group to transcend any obstacle through unselfish solidarity.

Now that he thought about it, Riva and Ash had plenty in common. Despite being an Open Hand officer, Ash had spent her time working in the kitchens and medical bays. She too would have forgiven Isaac, pleaded with Rusalka, invoked the same arguments about common humanity.

Then again, Riva and Ash were different in one key respect—Ash had always been quick to judgment. She would have had little time for a smuggler like Callie Roux. Even less for a self-interested guy like Zeke...

"Kade?" said Riva. "Did I say something wrong?"

"No." Kade took a deep breath. "Just thinking."

The group reached an escalator, which mechanical failure had reduced to nothing more than an ugly set of stairs. The group descended to a dusty ground floor connected to numerous black tunnels. A single shaft of light offered scant illumination.

Zeke stared up at a map of the complex. It was obscured by graffiti. "Don't they know this stuff has historic value? Fucking tagger scum."

In the depths of one of the tunnels, something skittered. Callie aimed her shotgun at the opening. "You hear that?"

Zeke shrugged. "Rats. Gotta be. Or mutants. Mutant rats."

"This isn't one of those flicks you play in your lounge. I've done a lot more urban spelunking than any of you, and I know rats when I hear them. That was something being kicked."

"Shine the light down there," said Kade. "Let's take a look."

Callie pointed the flashlight. Despite several sweeps of the beam, nothing was revealed but dirty surfaces, broken fixtures, and refuse.

"If somebody's down there," Callie said, "you better come out. I'm a bloodthirsty badass, and I don't like being jerked around."

A slithering sound issued from a tunnel to Kade's left. He spun. Again, nothing but shadows. In the gloom, he could make out a sign—*Restrooms*—and a bulky shape that, hopefully, was nothing more than an old bin.

"It's just our nerves." He turned back to Riva and Zeke, who were standing by the illegible map. "Come on, let's keep—"

Something dark sped across the floor. Callie trained her beam on it, and light gleamed off its metallic surface. With a deafening eruption of sound, the object detonated. An intense flare of light swallowed Kade's vision, and the air compressed about his head, leaving him reeling.

"Put down your guns," said a heavily filtered voice.

Kade squinted toward the voice. His eyes stung on exposure to the light, but he forced them to remain open. Within the pink blur of his vision, two shapes formed into human silhouettes.

"On your knees," said the growling, robotic voice. "Resistance will result in injury."

"You can suck the shit out of my ass, shut-in," said Zeke.

A shadow rushed forward. Kade tried to aim, but it was impossible to discern between friend and foe. The crack of a baton striking bone rang out, followed by the sound of Zeke yelping.

"Disarm the other one," said the unseen Codist.

Something rapid swished through the air, and Kade's hands stung from a hard impact. He hissed and dropped the pistol.

"You fucker!" said Zeke. "You fucking hit me!"

Kade stumbled forward, fists raised. A heavy weight drove into his chest. He staggered, nausea sloshing in his guts, and Riva screamed.

Hands grabbed his shoulders and forced him to his knees. As he struggled to rise, his assailant struck him across the face. Cheek throbbing and thoughts scattered, he relented.

"Stay there." The agent looming over him wore a full mask—a standard Codist piece of gear that provided night vision, voice modulation, and environmental protection. Another agent, shorter and slimmer, stood a little further back. Zeke lay motionless at their feet.

Where were the women? Kade turned his head. There was Riva, trembling and isolated, but Callie was nowhere to be seen. Yet she'd been right there when the grenade had rolled in.

"Tell us where Vale is." The agent kicked Kade's gun aside. "I'm authorized to break a bone each time you say 'I don't know.'"

"I'm Alexis Vale," said Riva. "Leave my friends alone."

Shit. What was she thinking? And where the hell was Callie?

The agent inclined his masked face toward Riva. "You don't look like our photo. Your hair is different."

"Do you think I'm stupid? The first thing I did was change my hair."

"Her build seems right," said the other agent. The modulator on their mask had a subtly different timbre—less robotic growl, more mechanical crunch—and the voice beneath was higher pitched. "But didn't Vale have a fair complexion? I'm sure—"

Riva grimaced and clutched her temples. "Oh God. My head."

"Are you harmed?" Not even the voice filter could conceal the panic in the taller agent's voice. "Describe your pain."

"That flash of light hurt something in my brain. Maybe my chip, it doesn't feel right…"

"Oh, fuck!" The agent took a step forward, no longer paying attention to Kade—a mistake on their part.

He jumped to his feet, balled his fist, and drove it hard into the back of the agent's head. Fresh pain jolted up his arm, but the agonized cry from his target made it all worthwhile.

Drawing upon a second burst of aggressive energy, Kade tackled the agent to the ground. His adversary twisted around to claw for Kade's shoulder, but Kade grabbed the agent's arm and slammed it against the cement, pinning it there. "Your turn to stay down, you son of a bitch."

"Behind you!" said Riva. "Kade, he's got a gun! He's—"

A gunshot roared. Kade waited for the pain, the sensation of his insides falling out, the cold creep of death...but no. The shot hadn't been for him.

A shell tapped against the ground, followed by the hard click of another being rammed home. Callie stepped over the second agent's body, not glancing down, and pointed the shotgun at the agent in Kade's grip.

"Are there any more of you?" she said. "Answer quickly."

The agent remained silent.

"Riva, go check on Zeke. I think he's alive."

A muffled groan confirmed the diagnosis. "That ratfucker hit me on the fucking head," said Zeke, raising his face from the floor. "God fucking damn it. Probably knocked a fucking spike loose."

Riva knelt beside him and directed the flashlight at his head. From here, it didn't look like there was any blood. The agents had presumably been using minimal force, not wanting any accidental casualties. Even so, Zeke seemed to be reciting every expletive he knew.

"How'd you get away from the grenade?" said Kade.

"I'm quicker than you," said Callie. "You looked right at it."

Kade frowned at the body. "Your first kill."

"I don't want to talk about it. He was just a shadow."

Kade moved to the corpse and removed its mask. Sadness stilled his heart for a second. Far from being a shadow, the dead agent was a girl about Callie's age, but it would have done Callie no good to tell her so.

"I underestimated Reed," he said, turning the mask in his hands. "I should have known he'd cover the mall."

Riva and Zeke stumbled back to join the others, Zeke leaning on Riva's shoulder for support. "He has a huge bruise on his head," she said. "But judging from his rate of profanity, he's fine."

"I need some ice," said Zeke. "And a sexy nurse to hold my hand. Who wants to be my sexy nurse? Any of you three would do."

"Tough it out." Kade hunkered before the remaining agent. "Mask off."

The agent unclipped his mask and set it aside. He looked ordinary enough—round face, prominent nose, thinning hair. Riva pointed the beam at him, and he winced beneath the light.

"Is Reed getting all this?" said Kade. "Or are you switched off?"

"He's hearing it," said the agent.

"Bet you he's lying," Zeke said. "You know, we could really use a mind-reading cyborg right about now."

"You killed my partner." The agent's tone was flat. "Our orders were only to detain you. We don't execute people, not even murderers. It seems that's a mercy you uncodified scum don't bother to return."

"Don't take the moral high ground," said Callie. "Don't you dare."

"How can you talk about morality? You animals are the reason Codism exists." The agent closed his eyes. "She was only twenty-two."

Callie became very still. "Take the shotgun," Kade said to Zeke.

Zeke nodded. "Lemme hold that awhile, sweetheart." He eased the weapon from Callie's hands while she stared at the body, her face twitching.

"Don't look." Riva put an arm around Callie and hugged her close. "You had no choice, Callie."

"Yes, she did," said the agent. "She could have complied."

"And you'd have destroyed her mind," said Kade. "Tell me how many of you went into the parking complex."

No answer. "Is there something we can tie him up with?" said Zeke. "I mean, I don't want to ice the guy."

"Callie," said Kade. Callie murmured something inaudible in reply. "You and Riva go upstairs and find some cabling, ropes, wires, whatever it takes to restrain this man. Snap to it."

"Yeah." Callie blinked, and some of the strength returned to her voice. "Restrain him. I can do that. Riva, you keep the torch."

After the women had disappeared up the escalator, Kade shifted closer to his sullen captive. "I'm sorry about your friend," he said. "You misunderstand what we're doing. We're fighting and dying so that you can be the first generation of Codists to enjoy your freedom."

"We are free. And Codism will never fall."

"Yes, it will. The man who sent you here understands that as well as anyone. Better, in fact." Kade rubbed his forehead. The headache had gotten worse, a splinter digging into his brain. "You're the lucky one in all of this. Your other friends may already be dead."

That got his attention. "Dead? That's not possible. How many more of you could have been in that van?"

"It's not about numbers. You're up against some of the most dangerous people in Foundation. Nobody short of Lachlan himself stands a chance."

"What is it that makes this cyborg so special?"

"Trust me." Kade closed his eyes as fresh pain pulsed through his head. "Whether we win or lose, you'll find out."

CHAPTER 20

Amity stopped at the third landing. "This is high enough."

"Trust me, I'll never be high enough for this shit." Lexi relaxed against the stairwell railing. "So what we are doing?"

"Creating an ambush. If we await them here, the stairs will force them into an awkward single-file approach. There's a chance they may send someone from above, pincering us, but I'm confident I can handle that."

"Pincering? Sounds sexy."

"Be quiet. They'll begin their attack with batons or possibly stun guns, though they'll be hesitant to subject you to an electrical current. Unlike the thugs that comprise the so-called Codist military, Intel agents aren't killers by nature. Even Reed is soft on that score. I'll cut them down before they can find their resolve."

"You ought to get yourself augmented too. You'd be terrifying."

Amity pursed her lips. "Augmentations are expensive. Not all of us have blood money to spend as we choose."

"I wouldn't call it blood money. I make peace between the gangs. I've probably saved more lives than you have."

"Saved the lives of whom? Criminals?"

A door slammed below, followed by the noise of people ascending—not at speed, but with what sounded like a respectable amount of caution. Amity pressed a finger to her lips, perhaps assuming Lexi was so fucking stupid as not to realize silence was important.

Seconds later, a door opened above. Amity frowned, took Lexi's hand and pressed it to her forehead. Clever girl.

Lexi peeked into her eyes. Several fresh thoughts were there, waiting to be read. Lexi lying on the landing, feigning unconsciousness. Amity slipping through the door and sprinting to the level above...

Lexi nodded. Amity opened the door—its squeak was inaudible beneath the echoing footsteps—and squeezed through. As the door shut, Lexi curled on the cold steel and closed her eyes.

"I see something!" The excited voice came from above. "I think it's Vale!"

"Yeah, that's her," said a deep, cautious voice from below. "Is she dead?"

"She's not dead," said an irritated voice from the same direction. "Why would she be dead? Do you think the excitement killed her?"

"Easy. I'm just asking a question."

The agent above descended a step, and the steel beneath Lexi's cheek vibrated. "This isn't right. That drunk said the whole group went in here. So where are the others?"

"It was a trick, genius," said the irritated agent. "This is part of it. Get on the comm to Reed before somebody pops out and blows us away."

"Are you sure she's faking?" said the cautious agent. "I mean, this is definitely Vale. She's right there. Reed's just going to tell us to apprehend her. You know how he gets when people waste his time."

"She's breathing, fuckbrain, and I doubt she took this opportunity to dope up and pass out. It's a goddamn trap."

A fourth voice joined the assembly of idiots. "Guys, just call it in." The nasal tone suggested a young man, barely an adult by the sound of him. "Mr. Reed will handle the rest."

"Yeah, great," said Cautious. "He'll love that. 'We're too scared to touch her, sir. Please come down and collect her.'"

"Then you grab her," said Irritated. "Get the promotion."

"And maybe you're right, and she is faking." The cautious agent sounded even more nervous now. "We should just zap her from here."

"I'm not zapping her. You think I want to be responsible for frying that implant? Hell, fuck it." Feet clanged nearby, and a hand touched Lexi's shoulder and shook her. "Hey, you troublesome bitch. What are you trying to pull?"

Lexi opened her eyes and smiled at the agent, an ugly bastard with a broad face and a menacing expression. Before he could do more than widen his eyes, she trapped his head between her hands. His mind washed over her, a confused scattering of thoughts and a mounting sense of fear.

The agent on the steps above was a tired-looking woman. The two below were men, both looking every bit as hopeless as she'd imagined them.

"If any of you come closer, I'll wipe him," said Lexi.

"Wipe him?" One of the agents was, as Lexi had guessed, little more than a teenager, pimpled and bewildered. "How would you do that?"

"With this chip you're looking for. Didn't anyone brief you?"

"Call it in," said the agent in Lexi's grip. His forehead was damp with sweat, which slickened her palms and left her with a strong desire to wipe her hands. "Do it quickly."

The cautious agent—from here Lexi could see a bald spot on his scalp, which seemed tragically appropriate for his personality—snatched a mobile-comm from his belt.

"Sir," he said, depressing its button. "We have a situation. One of our agents is, uh… He's being held hostage."

Lachlan's voice crackled through the comm. "Explain."

"Vale. She's grabbed hold of his head, sir. She's threatening to wipe him."

There was silence. The agents exchanged worried looks. "She's holding his head?" said Lachlan.

"Yes, sir. In both hands, sir."

Another brief silence. "And where are the others?"

"We're not sure, sir."

"Then subdue her and find out, please. Just don't harm her."

The agent standing above unclipped a pistol—a stun gun, judging from its odd, squat shape—while the cautious agent took a nervous step closer, baton in hand. "Stay back," said Lexi. "I'm serious."

"You're bluffing," said the agent in her grasp. He lunged for her neck.

Lexi set his thoughts ablaze. His memories evaporated, spiraling out of the burning rupture Lexi had gouged into his mind, and his eyes rolled into the back of his head.

The female agent aimed her stun gun. A shot rang out, and she jerked, fell and slithered down the steps. Amity stood behind her, a wisp of smoke rising from her pistol. She fired again, and the baton-wielding agent crumpled, a bloody hole in his forehead.

"Holy shit," said Lexi. "Was that necessary?"

"They could have chosen to stay home." Amity glared down the stairwell. The remaining agent—the kid—stared back at her, apparently unable to move. Amity took aim.

"Fuck, Amity!" Lexi jumped to her feet. "Don't shoot him."

"Pity is a weakness. One we can't afford."

Lexi looked down at the dead agents—strange to be standing over the bodies of people who'd been talking just seconds ago—before placing a hand on Amity's forearm. "Executions aren't my style. This kid isn't planning on doing anything stupid. Right, shut-in?"

The young man nodded, and Amity lowered the pistol.

"Run home, okay?" Lexi said. "Before she changes her mind."

The agent fled down the stairs, taking them two at a time. Lexi scooped up his fallen mobile-comm, winked at Amity and pushed the button.

"Hello," she said in a suggestive purr. "Is this the sex hotline? I have shameful, naughty urges."

"Who is this?" Lachlan didn't sound amused. "Alexis? Is that you?"

"Call me Lexi. And I'll call you Lockie. I'm not one for formalities."

"What happened to my personnel?"

"Two are dead. One had a little memory lapse, and the other—well, never mind that. The point is that you fucked up, son."

"You're a sadist. Those were good people."

"I agree, it's a tragedy. Next time, send bad people." Lexi began climbing the stairs, and after nudging the comatose agent with her toe, Amity followed. "I hear you're a pretty nasty piece of work yourself."

"I suppose Kade was responsible for smearing my reputation."

"Fucking paparazzi, am I right?"

Lachlan sighed. "If I'd known you were so enamored of your own wit, I would never have accepted this assignment."

"You should've sent a hot femme fatale after me instead. Think of the sexual tension. Of course, she'd eventually fall in love with me, and you'd have to kill her. She'd die with betrayal in her eyes and my name on her lips. I'd avenge her and then carry her corpse into the sunset."

"You're quite deranged, Lexi. Are you really coming to the rooftop?"

"Certainly am, Lockie. Sorry to say that Kade isn't with me. I get an intuition that you two have been close in the past. How close, I wonder?"

"You do have a prurient turn of mind, don't you?"

"Not sure. I'd have to find out what that word means." Lexi turned to Amity. "What's prurient?"

"It's you," said Amity tersely. "Can you please stop bantering with the enemy and focus on the task at hand?"

"I need to go, shut-in. But I'll see you soon." Lexi dropped the mobile-comm over the bannister. "Why the scowl, Am?"

"You're treating this like a game. Reed isn't someone to be toyed with."

"This is my chance to meet the guy who's hunting me. I'm glad for it. If you're angry with me, sweetie, you can always punish me later."

"Don't adopt that tone with me. Don't think that what happened between us means you can take such liberties."

"No liberties. Understood. Just promise we get to do it again."

Amity blushed. "Of course it won't happen again. It was a moment of madness. I was confused, upset."

Even now, it was impossible to resist flustering her. "Felt good, though, didn't it?"

"Will you abandon the subject if I admit that it did? In any case, this isn't the time. We still have agents unaccounted for."

"And new friends to meet. I can't wait to see you kick this guy's ass."

"I have much worse in store for Lachlan Reed." Amity spoke with such coldness that Lexi's smile faltered. "And no more moments of pity. If any opportunity arises to kill him, take it."

"Not so quick. If I read his mind, we'll know what they're planning, and I can't read a corpse."

Amity nodded. "True. But once you've done that, I'm killing him."

By the time they reached the door marked *Roof*, Lexi's legs felt as stretched and limp as old rubber bands. She emerged into insipid morning light and a cold, persistent breeze. The helicopter sat twenty meters away, its blades still. A huge, impassive man in a black uniform waited beside it.

Amity drew her pistol and fired twice. Lachlan ducked aside, Lexi froze, and the windshield of the helicopter shattered. The pilot convulsed in his seat as a spray of blood misted the glass.

"What the fuck!" Her insides squirming, Lexi took a quick step back. "Jesus, Amity!"

"Now he can't escape." Amity gave Lachlan a disdainful smile. "This is your reckoning, traitor."

Lachlan gaped at the bloodied glass and the slumped shape behind it. He ran his palm over his greased hair before meeting Amity's pitiless gaze.

"Hello, Amity. If I'd known Nikolas had sent his rabid dog, I'd never have let that poor man wait in the helicopter."

"Draw your gun. Let me see it."

Lachlan unholstered the pistol at his hip, an inconspicuous little weapon with an oily black gleam. "And now what?"

"And now—"

Lexi interrupted. "And now you give both those nasty things to me. They're dangerous, and you two have proven you don't play nicely."

"Fine." Lachlan placed his pistol in Lexi's hand. "Your turn, comrade."

Unpredictable, Kade had called him. It seemed an understatement. She tried to penetrate his glittering brown eyes, but he was another one of those frustrating impervious types. "Aren't you afraid she'll shoot you?"

"No. You want to use Project Sky on me. It's no use on the dead."

"She could shoot you in the knees, though. I mean, she's capable of it."

"Trust me, I know. But she's a very smart woman. She'd be hesitant to subject me to any pain that might make your task difficult." Lachlan's broad lips formed a knowing smile. "I take calculated risks, Lexi. It's the nature of my profession. I'm sure you understand."

Fascinating. A professional manipulator with an excess of arrogance, a talent for bullshit and a healthy amount of brazen audacity—how very familiar. "I think we're in the same trade, you and me."

"An amusing comparison. Codism is certainly much like a drug, though I prefer dealing to partaking." Lachlan eyed the distant stairwell. "Where are your friends?"

"Let her read you," said Amity. "Or I'll make your death painful. I have no reservations about leaving you gutshot."

"I've no doubt. I was very sorry to hear about Ash, by the way."

"Don't you dare say her name."

"But it's a genuine tragedy. Your best friend cut down in her prime. Did you cry for her? Or have you forgotten how?"

"I'll shoot you, Reed."

"Do you know how a reflex implant works?" Lachlan tapped the back of his neck. "It's like a little brain devoted to keeping me alive. The chip monitors sensory stimulus and computes it in a nanosecond. Should something like a bullet come toward me, the chip forces a reflex action, and I move out of the way. It's rather like being on auto-pilot."

"He's exaggerating," said Lexi. "It doesn't always work. If you get attacked from behind, for example."

"Granted. Surprise attacks are something else." A metallic object shot from Lachlan's sleeve, hissing while it flew, and Amity grunted. A flechette quivered in her right shoulder. "I'm very good at them, as it happens."

Amity's fingers twitched, and her pistol fell to the ground. "Lexi, I can't feel my arm."

"I do apologize. But I have a healthy respect for your ability to tear a man, augmented or otherwise, into countless bloody pieces." Lachlan grinned at Lexi. "Now it's you and me. Shall we?"

The attack came sudden and swift—not the undisciplined lunge of a street brawler, but the precise strike of martial artist—and Lexi ducked just in time. He may have been built like a bruiser, but Lachlan was one fast motherfucker.

Lexi fumbled with the gun in her hands. Before she could do more than flick back the safety, Lachlan lashed out and struck her with the side of his fist. A single point of agony drove from her forehead to the back of her brain.

"Fuck!" Lexi dropped the pistol as she clutched her aching face. "You fucking asshole!"

"I hope I haven't damaged your looks. I suspect you're proud of them."

Lexi glared at him through her fingers. Her head still throbbed from the impact. "Amity, are you okay?"

Amity was fumbling with the flechette, but she seemed to be struggling to pull it free. "Going numb. Hard to breathe."

"Fucking hell. Lockie, I thought we were going to talk!"

"No, you were going to interrogate me and then kill me. I chose to play along with your ruse, but you're still the dishonest one, not me."

With frightening abruptness, Lachlan grabbed Amity and drove his knee into her chest. She gasped and doubled over. "That's for the innocent lives you took today," he said. "You haven't changed a bit, have you?"

He pushed Amity away. She staggered before dropping to her knees. Paralyzed though she seemed, her eyes remained bright with fury.

"Leave her the fuck alone," said Lexi, focusing through the biting pain. "You flew out here for the chip in my head. Why don't you come and get it?"

"You should have ended that taunt with 'motherfucker.' As in, 'come and get it, motherfucker.' It would have added a little more punch."

"Given who I was addressing, I thought the motherfucker was implicit."

There was a quiet thump as Amity fell forward and landed on her face. "Shit," said Lexi. "Tell me you didn't just kill her."

"She's not dead." Lachlan walked toward Lexi with a patient, measured stride that suggested he had plenty of experience in beating ass. "I wouldn't dream of killing an old friend."

"Something tells me she was never your friend." Lexi made a wary retreat while evaluating her enemy. Lachlan was a head taller, probably fifty pounds heavier and—worst of all—a fellow cyborg. Not great odds.

"Fill me in," she said. "You want to capture me. Then what? Dissect me?"

"It may be as insignificant a process as taking a blood sample."

"But if you had to take a brain sample, you'd do that too." Lexi raised a hand. "You come any closer than that, and I'll wipe you."

Lachlan stopped. "Will you now?"

"You know I'm capable of it."

"In that case, I'd better take you down quickly." Lachlan rushed her, and his full weight crashed into Lexi, sending her toppling. She landed with stinging force on her butt. "I'm sorry, did that hurt?"

Lexi scrambled to her feet, propelled by anger and panic. "You fucker." She unleashed a clumsy combination of punches. He laughed as he effortlessly evaded each one. The smug cybernetic bastard.

"I see you have no real martial arts training," Lachlan said. "You're completely reliant on your augmentations."

"I'm a sophisticated person. My hands are meant for finer things."

"You've had a good run with that undeserved implant, but it's over. Accept it gracefully. You'll likely live through our experiments, and even diminished, I suspect you're smart enough to continue in your career. In fact, given your ability to maintain order between the gangs, perhaps you could do some work for us."

Lexi glanced at Amity. Her eyes were closed, but their lashes fluttered as if she were still trying to force them open. "The moment you lay a hand on me, I really will wipe you. Think of me as radioactive. The nearer you come, the more dangerous I am."

"Then I won't lay a hand on you." Lachlan took a short black rod from his belt. A baton telescoped outward from it, and he gave it a quick swish through the air. "Far subtler than our standard issue."

He took a purposeful step closer, and Lexi tensed. Now that he had twenty inches of steel to keep her at bay, she really didn't stand a chance. Better to find Kade and Callie so that they could fill Lachlan with lead.

"Later, Lockie." Lexi was a decent runner, and urgency propelled her forward. Her boots beating out a rapid rhythm on the cement, she ran between a pair of striped barriers and descended to the level below.

How the hell had she ended up going this alone? Hadn't she boasted an entire posse just this morning? "Callie!" Her shout echoed back to her. Fuck, where was that fucking smuggler? "Help me out, you bitch!"

Behind her, Lachlan chuckled. Her very own arch rival. What a treat.

Lexi hurtled down a ramp and skidded around a corner. From this height, the view of the district gave the clearest sense yet of its devastation. Neglect and street warfare had reduced the suburb to a grid of ruined streets, collapsed bricks, and exposed metal, all laid out in the morbid pretense of a neighborhood. If this was going to be the last thing she ever saw, she wanted a refund.

"Kade!" Shouting wasn't conducive to conserving air, but it was better than dying with full lungs. "I need you, asshole! Come on!"

She flagged sooner than expected, already worn out from the stairwell climb. By the time she neared the next downward ramp, Lachlan had closed the gap to only a few meters. No gloating smirk on him now—his face was set in serious concentration.

Halfway down the ramp, Lexi stumbled and regained her balance only by flailing her arms. Her feet were aching, tired of being slammed against hard cement, and sweat had left a salty trail on her lips. She was fucked.

Engines growled in the distance. Lexi faltered to a stop.

Two bikes zoomed around the corner, one little more than a scooter, the other a big hog with tattered rags trailing from its handlebars. The riders—both men, both leather-clad, both as unattractive as a dog eating its own shit—whooped, and one loosed a bloodcurdling howl while whipping a chain above his head.

Behind the bikes, a rusted, graffiti-covered pickup bounced on its suspension as it tore across the parking level. A heavyset gangster sat behind the wheel, wearing a smile just about as pretty as a scar, while another gang member lolled in the seat beside her, playing with a knife.

Standing in the bed behind them, her black mane wild around her stern face, Rusalka looked like an Amazon having a bad day.

The bikers shot past Lachlan, accompanied by more hollers, before skidding to a halt. Lachlan stared up at the truck as it braked beside him.

"Hey, shut-in," Rusalka said. "I didn't give you permission to be in my district."

For once, Lachlan seemed speechless. A moment to treasure.

"You're late," Lexi said, trying to conceal her shortness of breath. "I already took out most of them."

Rusalka gave her an amused look. "You were running in our direction, Lexi Vale. Not his."

"I didn't want you to miss out, that's all."

"This is Code business." Lachlan brandished his baton. "Make yourself scarce, and I'll forget I saw you."

"Forget?" The truck's driver leaned out of the window and spat. "You're about to be dead, shut-in. You better believe you'll fucking forget."

Rusalka jumped out of the bed, and the bikers dismounted. "I decide who lives and who dies around here," Rusalka said, approaching with a sinuous gait. "Should've stayed behind your wall."

"Be careful," said Lexi. "He's a cyborg."

"Cool," said the biker with the chain. "Always wanted to meet a cyborg. Why don't his eyes glow?"

Rusalka paused beside Lexi. "There's a bruise on that pretty forehead of yours." She cradled Lexi's cheek in her hand. "Did he do this to you, my clever little broker?"

"Yes," Lexi said. "Now it's time to show everyone what happens when someone is hurt while under your protection."

"Oh, I will." Rusalka drew the knife from her belt. She was taller even than Lachlan, and the way he maintained a careful distance suggested he wasn't immune to her intimidating presence. "How do you want to die, shut-in? We can cut you. We can shoot you. We can drag you."

One of the bikers snickered. "Maybe we can mix it up. A little of each."

"Lexi, this is enough," said Lachlan. "Call them off. We'll talk, just as you wanted."

"Sorry, Lockie," said Lexi. "You're just not my type."

Rusalka and the bikers closed in. The chain whistled as it lashed Lachlan's back. He spun and drove the tip of his baton into the biker's eye, and the man reeled, clutching his wounded socket.

"That's one," Lachlan said. "I trust the rest of you aren't so expendable."

Rusalka executed a snakelike thrust. Lachlan pivoted, knocked the blow aside, and smacked Rusalka in the face with his free hand.

Without even flinching, she jabbed again. Lachlan easily twisted away from the flashing blade.

"He's fast for a big guy," said the truck driver, who apparently believed her role was to provide commentary. "No wonder you were running, Vale."

"Can't you just shoot him?" Lexi said. "You must have a gun."

The truck driver frowned. "Yeah, but I'd get in trouble with Rusalka."

Lachlan flicked his baton and struck the second biker in the mouth, spilling blood. The goon staggered back, leaving only Rusalka, who was visibly seething.

"Have I demonstrated my point?" said Lachlan. "Or must I break all of your minions before you understand?"

"You don't fucking stand still." Rusalka bared her teeth in an animalistic sneer. "You don't like fight like a man."

"I was unaware self-defense was so strictly gendered." Lachlan lifted his baton, and a drop of blood fell from its tip. "All this pain for the sake of a handsome ruffian you'll never see again. Is it worth it, do you think?"

"I gave her my word."

"I may have to kill you if you don't back down."

Rusalka growled. "You'd die with me, shut-in."

"Just hold him for a moment," said Lexi. "I'll do the rest."

"If you say so." Rusalka flipped her knife before sheathing it. "You're going to pay if you've blinded my boy there."

"You've already promised to kill me," said Lachlan. "How do you top that?"

"By choice of method." Rusalka flung herself at him, bearing him to the ground. As the two grappled, Lexi crept close and seized Lachlan by the head. He looked up, and she met his startled eyes.

Mineko.

She was everywhere in his mind, connected to every thought. The night before, she'd finally lost her temper, unveiling the woman he'd waited so long to see. She and Kaori looked so alike—the same slender, sensitive features—but Mineko was far greater, possessed of a deep richness of soul...

Older memories now. Reports of a Codist girl seen at a club. Dismissing the agent who'd brought the intel. Suppressing the evidence. Ensuring that nobody would ever know who the traitor was.

Another recent memory, still vivid. Mineko standing on a balcony with Valerie Wren, two silhouettes pressed close. A fearful sight. Kaori was a bigot, and Gaspar only cared about his position. A daughter with lesbian proclivities would do the Tamura lineage no favors at all. Yet how could he protect her without exposing himself and the crimes they shared?

Lachlan's mind was intense and chaotic, a dark current surging toward a waterfall. Lexi found herself swept through countless images, one sensation after another, all while Lachlan's anger smoldered around her...

A lifetime of nodding, listening, and lying. They all thought he wanted Gaspar's job, but little did they realize that to be seated behind that desk was a kind of death.

The current raged, tossing Lexi between frustration, confusion, and resentment, a wave of violent feelings that rippled across a bed of desires. Clearest among them was the face of the man they both knew.

Get out of my head. Lachlan's mind vibrated with the message, his entire will bent toward it. *Get out of my head, you bitch.*

Startled, Lexi retreated. The dark waters dried up. The current ceased.

Lachlan pushed Rusalka away and sprang to his feet. He whirled on Lexi, his face contorted into something primal. She flinched as she prepared for the inevitable blow.

He lowered his fist, gave her a rueful smile and ran toward one of the abandoned bikes. "Stop him!" said Lexi.

Too late. The gangsters in the pickup stared, slack-jawed, as Lachlan rode past them, whipped around the corner and vanished from sight.

"Is she dead?" said Rusalka.

Lexi knelt beside Amity and lifted her wrist. "Nope. There's a pulse." She tilted Amity's head. Eyes closed, breath shallow. "Can we get her into the back of the truck? Lay her down?"

Not showing the slightest strain, Rusalka lifted Amity and carried her to the bed of the pickup. "Hope princess here doesn't mind being handled by trash." She glowered down at Amity before looking away. "Mouthy cunt."

"I'm sure you've been treated worse."

"Yeah. But they didn't walk away." Rusalka loomed over Lexi, a hand on each hip. "We have unfinished business."

"Do we?"

"We do." Rusalka cupped Lexi's butt and planted a firm kiss on her lips. A pleasant ache built in Lexi's groin. Sure, Rusalka was a bloodthirsty colossus, but being handled this way was a definite turn-on.

"As far as women go, you're the type I like." Rusalka squeezed with both hands. "Nice tight ass."

"Sure you wouldn't break me?"

"I'm sure. I don't like to break pretty things."

The mobile-comm at Rusalka's belt crackled, and Rusalka kissed Lexi again before pushing her away. "Rusalka here."

Lexi managed not to laugh. The gang had fallen upon the comms with the enthusiasm of kids getting birthday presents. Rusalka had taken for herself an impressive black handset—presumably Lachlan's—that had been inside the helicopter. They'd even discussed stealing the chopper itself, not deterred by the broken windshield and the blood on the controls. That part hadn't been so funny.

"We found them," said the tinny voice of a gang member. "They're in the mall, like you thought. Two men, two women."

"Bring them over." Rusalka gave the mobile-comm a satisfied look before clipping it to her belt. "That shut-in's going to cause trouble now, isn't he?"

"I couldn't say. He's an odd one. But you might want to be careful."

"What were you doing touching his head? He stopped struggling the second you did it."

"Special fighting technique. Don't worry about it." Lexi stood on her toes to gaze at the unconscious Amity. If only she could slip a pillow under her head or put a blanket over her—anything to make her seem less like a body thrown in the back of a truck. "Thanks for the help back there."

"I didn't have any choice. My reputation was riding on it. Especially because I made that stupid promise in front of everyone." The corner of Rusalka's mouth lifted. "I can see why Vassago hires you."

"Because of my tight ass?"

Rusalka's laughter raised the hair on Lexi's forearms. "I doubt you'd go along with that. Something tells me you don't do dick."

"No, I don't do men. If you had a dick, I'd be on my knees blowing you right now."

"You're strange, Vale."

"You might even say I'm queer." Lexi grinned. "One of my friends is a doc. Kinda. He'll be able to help the poor bastard who got his eye poked."

"Good. That quick-shot journalist with you as well? I wouldn't mind having some unfinished business with him too."

"Uh, yeah, he's here." Lexi brushed a strand of hair from Amity's nose, just in case it was tickling her. "And he's all yours. I hear he likes it rough."

They waited together in silence while admiring the view. Standing high above the city, radiating savage grandeur, Rusalka looked like a warlord surveying her kingdom. Hard not to respect a woman who managed to survive in this wasteland while maintaining order among people as wild and ruthless as herself.

Callie arrived first, her auburn hair shining in the sunlight. Riva followed close behind, magnificent as ever, while Kade, Zeke, and a bored-looking gangster trailed them. The relief on Riva's face quickly became alarm. "Where's Amity?"

"In the back," said Lexi. "Don't panic, she's alive."

Kade touched Amity's forehead. "Her breath is erratic."

"Your friend Lockie had a needle hidden up his sleeve. She got a dose."

"A paralyzing toxin. It's commonly used to subdue defecting Codists and bring them home unhurt. It shouldn't do any lasting harm, but we need to get her some medical attention promptly. I assume Lachlan got away?"

"Yeah. But on the bright side, he's gone." Lexi prodded Zeke. "There's a guy downstairs who got his eye gouged. Want to take a look at him?"

"Uh." Zeke didn't even turn—he was too busy staring at Rusalka. "Wow, uh, sure. Um."

Rusalka smirked. "I like your look, little man. Nice tatts."

"Oh, uh, yeah." Zeke cleared his throat. "So anyway, I'm Zeke. Body artist and surgeon. Single, as it happens."

"A surgeon, huh? Not bad." Rusalka swaggered toward Zeke, who watched her every motion as if he were recording it on the seedy camera of his brain. She laid a hand on his spiked scalp. "This must have hurt."

"Nah, just a tickle. Now, this one here—"

Rusalka led Zeke away while he continued babbling and indicating his countless piercings and tattoos.

Lexi winked at Callie. No reaction. "Callie?" Lexi jostled her. "Did you see that? Zeke and Rusalka. Imagine those two together."

Still silent, Callie walked across the rooftop and stood at its edge.

"She shot someone back there," said Kade. "A young agent. A girl."

"And that's messed her up? I melted an agent's brain and then watched Amity shoot three people. I'm doing okay." Lexi bit her lower lip. "I think."

Now the action was over, a shivery sickness had crept into her stomach. Adrenaline crash, maybe. But it was hard not to dwell on the fact she'd wiped five people this week. Whole lives—dreams, memories, ambitions—gone in an instant of violent purgation.

"Hey." Riva put a hand on Lexi's shoulder. "I was worried about you."

Lexi smiled. There was something good about hearing those words and knowing they were sincerely meant. "Likewise, babe."

"And now I'm worried about Callie."

"Don't worry. She's a tough little butch. How are you holding up?"

"Besides being embarrassed about a little hysterical screaming, I'm fine."

"She did some quick thinking over there," Kade said. "She convinced the agents she was you."

Lexi laughed. "Seriously?"

"It was dark," said Riva. "And I have the right build. I guess it was luck."

"It's one hell of a compliment to me, that's what it is."

Riva smiled, but her attention had already strayed back to Callie. Lexi sighed. "Okay. I'll talk to her."

She joined Callie at the roof's edge. The smuggler was slumped against a barricade with her head in her hands, her palms squishing her chubby cheeks flat. It would have been adorable if she hadn't looked so sad. "Shit view," Lexi said.

"It's not so bad. You can see the mesa from here."

Presumably Callie meant the uneven, reddish-brown line on the horizon. "Ever been out there?"

"Lots of times. There's mountain lions."

"Huh. What do they eat?"

"Don't know."

That topic hadn't gone anywhere. Time to try something more contemporary. "Kade said you saved everyone's butts. He also mentioned you had to shoot somebody to do it."

"I've had that shotgun for five years. I've only killed dogs with it. Wild ones, you know, not nice dogs. I once fired at a guy trying to steal my van, but I missed on purpose."

"Well, smuggling's a rough gig. Ever considered being a plain old mechanic? You're handy with a spanner."

"She was only a kid." Callie closed her eyes, concealing—but not soon enough—her tears. "A girl told to wear a uniform and do as she's told. Just like Min. How am I supposed to fight shut-ins, Lexi? How am I supposed to hurt them? They're only scared. Like us."

A tear escaped Callie's lashes and crested her round cheek. The sight of that glistening trail hit Lexi in the gut and left her aching. This caring, lonely girl had been fucked over more times than anyone deserved. Fucked over by her mother, fucked over by her ex, fucked over by the shut-ins, fucked over by the world from the moment she'd been born.

Lexi put a hand over Callie's. "Can you forgive me, Callie Roux?"

"I forgave you a long time ago. I just couldn't forgive myself, so I pretended I still blamed you. Hoping I'd hate myself less. But I didn't." Callie's lips trembled. "Instead, you only ended up hating me too."

"I was selfish, that's all. I imagined it was all about me and my right to fuck whoever I wanted. I forgot to show you that it wasn't personal. To prove I never meant to hurt you." Lexi crooked an arm. "C'mon."

Callie stumbled forward, and Lexi hugged her close. Nosed through her auburn mane, nuzzled her neck, breathed her warm, scented skin. Callie squeezed back— soft body, strong arms—and held Lexi in a forgiving and protective embrace. No wonder Riva and Mineko found this so comforting.

Lexi's eyes prickled. How could she have hated this girl?

"It's been a long time since I had a friend," Lexi said. "I hope you'll help me change that."

That brought the dimples out. "I know we get on each other's nerves sometimes. But I'm glad you're here, Lexi, even if the reminder hurts."

"I could learn something from you." Lexi twisted a strand of Callie's hair between her fingers. "I've been a hypocrite all this time."

"You mean your grudge with Kade?"

"Something like that." Lexi took Ash's photograph from her pocket and held it to the sunlight. Callie craned to see. "Meet Ash, my cousin. No longer with us. She and Kade were a couple. Real lovey-dovey."

"He mentioned a woman. But he never said she was your cousin."

"My only blood relative, though she was smarter than me by a long shot. She was so calm, so decisive. You felt like nothing could go wrong when she was around. I mean, she wasn't perfect. But the three of us together, we came pretty close."

Lexi put away the photo—God, that fucking smile hurt to look at, like a hammer to the heart—and blinked away tears. "Anyway. Just wanted to show you."

"I had a weird dream last night." Callie stared at the distant mesa. "I was lost on the road, but your voice found me."

Lexi glanced over her shoulder. Kade still stood beside the van, talking to Riva. A lean, confident man. Nothing like the little boy who had trembled against her breast while trying to stammer out the truth he'd been hiding.

That night, she'd tried to comfort him by murmuring what she'd thought was his name. It had only made his distress worse. So she'd asked him the question that had changed both their lives.

What do I call you now?

Kade met her gaze. Lexi held it for a moment—the length of a single breath—before looking back to the sky.

CHAPTER 21

"Left," said Mineko. "The yellow jug."

Kaori swung left and caught the hold with her fingertips. "How did I miss that?" She vaulted to grab another jug on the overhang above. "I hope you're not bored. I'll be down soon."

"It's fine." Mineko couldn't have been further from bored, not with this fear crawling in her guts. "You're spilling chalk."

Kaori patted the dusty bag at her waist. "That's what it's for, child." She clambered across the overhang, tapped the ceiling and gave a thumbs-up.

Mineko let out the rope as Kaori descended. "Want to give it a try?" Kaori said, touching the ground. "I'll belay you."

"No. But thanks for offering."

"Are you sure?" Kaori unclipped her harness and wiped her chalky hands on her shirt. "You need to start being more active if you want to live a long, healthy life."

A longer lifespan would only mean more years of unhappy, subservient Codism, but Mineko didn't dare say so. "I promise I'll try next time."

The women left the gym and traversed the sunlit corridors to the foyer. The front doors were open, and several of the house staff were scrubbing tiles in the entrance hall.

"Let's have a quick snack," said Kaori. "Before you get back to studying."

The dining room faced the sun, allowing warmth and light, and the table was already set with midday treats. Mineko piled a plate with her usual favorites—a lemon slice, a chocolate cookie, and a raspberry tart—before taking a place at the end of the table.

Kaori sat beside her, having nabbed nothing from the feast but a slender finger of shortbread. "Are you confident about your exams?" she said. "Nervous, perhaps?"

"Apprehensive." Mineko took a sweet, crumbly bite of the tart.

"You do seem a little on edge." Kaori nibbled the corner of her shortbread. "Your father is the same way. It's this Project Sky business."

In the garden, tiny birds hopped among the hedges and perched on the decorative fencing. A fat crow watched them from the manicured lawn.

"Why are there so many birds but so few other animals?" said Mineko.

"Birds are natural scavengers. It's the same reason there are so many dogs around. They adapted well."

Mineko eyed the lemon slice. If she ate it now, after wolfing down the cookie and the tart, she might be reprimanded for greediness. "Those outside our enclaves must suffer terribly."

"That's a pointless thing to worry about." Kaori filled a glass with water, but instead of drinking merely set it aside like a prop waiting to become relevant. "It's time for you to find a man, Mineko. If you wait until your thirties, you'll discover they're only interested in your status. Meet someone while you're young, and there may even be a little passion there."

Mineko should have known this had been a trap. "Please don't. I'm too busy thinking about my exam for this."

"Surely you have time for a little mother-daughter chat. If you tell me what you want in a husband, I can set you up with a suitable young man. A ranking officer, perhaps."

To hell with it—Mineko needed that slice. With deliberate slowness, she consumed the soft layers of pastry and lemon and licked her lips clean.

"Are you stalling?" Kaori said, frowning.

"Maybe a little. To be honest, I haven't thought about it."

"Well, think about it now."

"I suppose…" Mineko ran a fingertip around the rim of her water glass. "I suppose I'd hope to meet somebody adventurous. They'd be good with their hands, clever and resourceful. A strong personality, but caring and considerate too."

"Now we're getting somewhere. There are plenty of men like that in the service, and any of them would jump at the chance to meet you. What other qualities do you long for? Physical traits?"

This was such an irritating discussion. It could be amusing to dance around the truth. "Maybe a redhead. With dimples."

"Aha! So you have been noticing men, you sly little thing. Perhaps there's somebody matching that description in one of your classes?"

"It's a secret." Mineko finished her lemon slice and wiped away the crumbs. "If you don't mind, I should do some reading in the study."

"There's no need to be shy. I know what it's like to have a crush. Is he older than you?"

"Gossiping is an ethical breach." Mineko stood, and Kaori produced a childish pout. "You shouldn't sulk. It's bad for your health."

"Fine. Go study, you tease. But I'll get to the bottom of this. I've been waiting too long to have this talk with you."

Mineko snatched another cookie on her way out. She returned to the lobby, contemplated for a moment her parent's bad taste in portraiture, and ascended the stairs.

Gaspar's study was unlocked and unattended. Though it was his private place of work in theory, the leather armchair in the corner was meant for Mineko. Her father liked being kept company while he worked, and she had spent many evenings curled in the chair, dividing her attention between him and whatever book she was reading.

She sidled around the desk to take a peek at his computer. For once, the screen had been locked, and she didn't know the code. No spying today, then. Instead, she unlatched the windows and inhaled the cool air.

In the rear garden below, topiaries jostled for space with statuary—animals, people, ugly abstract shapes—and flower beds formed colorful lines around trimmed hedges. Codists loved to plant trees and dig ornamental lakes. A tremendous waste of water.

Still facing the sun, Mineko closed her eyes and visualized Kade. He'd been handsome, articulate, impressive. What would it be like to kiss him? To feel his stubble against her cheek? It wasn't an unpleasant idea, but it didn't enthrall her like the thought of Lexi or Callie.

But why was that? Because they were women? Or was it just a difference of personality?

Mineko forced herself to stare at a hedge shaped like a horse. If she thought hard enough about horses, she'd stop thinking about Callie's tanned legs, or Lexi's fine-cheeked face, or how soft Valerie's lips had been. Horses, horses. Were there any still alive in the world? Did people still ride them? Could a horse win a fight with a dog?

Before she could consider the topic further, crunching noises suggested someone walking on the garden path below. Mineko ducked out of sight.

"I didn't think you'd be home this soon." It was Kaori, her voice coming from the direction of the hedges.

"Neither did I." Gaspar, sounding tired. "But Lachlan's made an unholy mess. He launched an operation without telling me, even requisitioned a helicopter. Now I have two cars, two bikes, and nine people missing. Lachlan logged it as a success, with a single comment: 'A promising start.'"

"Cheeky as ever."

"Given what was at stake, I thought he'd at least try to behave." Gaspar sighed. Mineko had seen him stressed enough times to imagine how he might look: hunched, frowning, his long fingers massaging his temples. "I have no doubt he'll get this woman in the end, but I have to explain his present stunt to the Committee."

"You could cover it up."

"I could, and then they'd have something to hang me with later."

"What if I initiate a coup? We'll parade the Committee through the districts in their underwear."

"Don't even joke about it. I'll have to reign Lachlan in, get him to come up with a better explanation for himself. He's earned plenty of leeway, but our personnel aren't expendable. This isn't the military."

"That's a low blow." Kaori's tone lightened. "Min's around, by the way. She didn't want to study at school."

"I'll have to say hello before I head out again. There're two more meetings this afternoon. District Affairs is hassling me. They think they should be the ones running the hunt for Vale."

"District Affairs couldn't run a bake sale."

"Whereas Lachlan would sell every cake and then burn the stall down." They both laughed, and the sound of footsteps resumed. "Maybe it's those implants of his. Who knows what the long term side effects are?"

"That reminds me. If we don't start implanting the troops, we're in for trouble. The Port Venn junta have entire squads of cyborgs these days. I wish you'd ride the Committee harder on it."

"In time, my love, in time..." Their voices faded.

Mineko retreated to her chair and sat hugging her knees. Was this good news? It sounded as if Lachlan had suffered a disastrous defeat. But that didn't mean one of her friends hadn't been injured. Or worse.

A chill spread through her. If only she could know for sure. Before she'd met these people, she'd had no role models. Now she could aspire to be as brave as

Callie, as insightful as Kade, as audacious as Lexi…whereas before, she'd simply wished she were less like Mineko.

If only she'd accepted Callie's offer.

Minutes passed uncounted in a cloud of numb regret. The door opened and Gaspar entered the room. "Min! You're all huddled up."

Mineko peered at him over her knees. "I'm just stressed about the exam."

"In a few months, you'll have forgotten about it." Gaspar frowned. "It's not the exam that's troubling you, is it? You seem very shaken up. Are you sure you're fine?"

"No." Mineko blurted the word, and by the time it had escaped, it was too late to keep back tears. "I'm scared."

Gaspar hurried to put a lanky arm around her. Mineko sobbed against his side, not crying for any one thing in particular but simply losing the strength to fight against what felt like the entire world.

"My poor little Min." Gaspar spoke too gently for a man responsible for so many terrible things. How ironic that he should be both the cause of her tears and the only comfort she could find. "Is your mother pestering you about marriage again?"

"Why do we live like this, Dad? Why is everything so unkind?"

Gaspar stroked her hair. "We're trying to make it better. Me and your mother, everyone around us. We're working hard."

"Would you ever hate me?" Mineko clutched his sleeve. "If they told you to hate me, would you?"

"Of course I wouldn't hate you. Why would you say that? Are you afraid you've done something wrong?"

"Yes. I was born a Codist."

Gaspar stopped stroking, and Mineko held her breath. She hadn't meant to say anything so extreme, but she'd become careless lately, distracted by impossible longings. And now she'd said the unforgivable.

"I thought this day would come. The clever ones always have doubts." Gaspar cupped her head in his hands and looked into her eyes. "You're ashamed because we have so much while they have so little."

Mineko nodded, and Gaspar patted her cheek. "I know you'll resist me saying so, but this is just a phase. As a Tamura, there are so many expectations put upon you. It's overwhelming, but you're strong. You just need to see it through. Then you'll view Codism as the glorious truth it is."

"Just a phase." Mineko was still numbed, and now she was empty too. After a lifetime of fear, she'd spoken her mind, yet instead of an explosion of anger she'd received only a patronizing dismissal. "Thank you. I'll try to keep my composure from now on."

"I did a bad job comforting you, didn't I? I'm sorry. You should talk to your mother. She wishes you and she would bond more."

It seemed Mineko had gone in an instant from being consoled to being lectured. "I'm sure that's a phase too."

"Is there anything I can get for you? Perhaps a new study tablet? I've noticed you're still hauling around that old model... No, that's not it. You want to become your own woman. You're resentful that there's so much attached to your family name. I can understand that."

"I know what my family name means. I just hope that wherever my future takes me, I'll make you proud."

Affection softened Gaspar's worried features. "I'm sure you will."

***

After an hour of reading, Mineko grew incapable of pretending to care about Social Ethics. She left the study and trekked through the house, descending the stairs in a pensive daydream, until she emerged into one of the side gardens.

The garden held her favorite statue, a sculpture of a warrior woman with a spear in one hand and an ornate shield in the other. Her helmet was Greek, Kaori claimed. Mineko loved the way the statue's hair had been carved around her shoulders in thick curls, somehow seeming wild and living despite being made of stone.

Mineko sat at the base of the statue with her tablet in hand. For a few idle minutes she played a game, tapping colored circles to form lines between them. A brown bird landed and stared at her, its little head tilted. She stared back. The bird gave the ground a rapid peck, glared at her and fluttered away.

"Mineko." At the sound of Lachlan's voice, Mineko's heart dove into her stomach and remained there, cowering. He advanced across the grass, a grim expression on his face. "Is your father around?"

"He left. He had a meeting."

"Fortunate for me." Lachlan scrutinized her. "You look very pale. Is something the matter?"

Mineko returned to her feet and gripped the warrior woman's leg for support. "I heard you had an incident."

"Word travels quickly." Lachlan slumped on a wrought-iron bench. He seemed tired, and his voice lacked its usual ironic quality. "That Vale woman is quite a character."

"You found her?"

"Oh yes. She wiped one of my agents. How does somebody with such inhuman power keep herself in check? Why isn't she living as a goddess, ruling over all Foundation?" Lachlan steepled his fingers and pressed them to his lips. "The woman clearly has no ambition."

Mineko's insides clenched into a queasy ball. "She wiped someone?"

"That troubles you, doesn't it? And people were shot dead, among them my helicopter pilot. Some of these revolutionaries are quite savage."

Wiped. Of course Lexi needed to defend herself, but a mind was such a precious thing, and to simply melt one away... "Did they escape?"

"I'm quite empty-handed." Lachlan smiled over his fingertips. "I'm sure you're relieved."

"Relieved? Why would I be relieved?"

"Because you want Project Sky to fail. You're afraid that Code Intel will use it to peer into the heads of the unrighteous, those like you and me. To convert the districts as though we were missionaries and Codism were our religion. And you're right. That is indeed their sick fucking end-game."

Not this again—not another test of her loyalty, another attempt to provoke her into saying something compromising. "Why are you saying these things?"

"I have no idea what to do about you." There was no trace of mockery in Lachlan's voice, not a hint of condescension. "If you flee, you'll be added to our list of traitors. Tamura or not, that guarantees you'll be Reintegrated when—and not if—you're caught. Yet you can't continue like this, can you? You'll break. You've seen too much. Experienced too much. Something like a kiss, for example, from little Dr. Wren."

Instead of fear, it was anger that surged to take hold of Mineko, the kind of indignant outrage she had often imagined would exist in the stone heart of the warrior woman. "Don't you hurt her."

"I'm not going to hurt her. It'll come as a surprise to you, but your father is much more dangerous to her, and to you, than I ever have been."

"Dad wouldn't hurt me."

"He would." Lachlan spoke with quiet conviction. "A decade ago, he gave me a special assignment, one that affirmed me as his greatest pupil. I was told to infiltrate the *Revolutionary People's Gazette*. I spent three years in that group, and when I came back, I was changed. Of course, even a few days would have been enough to change me. As it was for you."

"Leave me alone."

"My chief interest has always been preserving myself. But when one lives by choice amid ugliness, they're all the more liable to be stirred by a glimpse of beauty. You think I'm a terrible, unfeeling ogre. Life would be simpler for both of us if that were true."

"This is just part of your game. You're trying to coax a reaction from me or make me say something unwise. I won't."

Lachlan smiled with a hint of his old wryness. "I can't deny I've enjoyed myself. Setting you up with Valerie Wren, for example, just to confirm a little suspicion of mine."

His smile vanished. "Let me be clear, however. Yes, this is part of my game, but you're not one of my pawns. You're my queen, and I haven't the courage to sacrifice you. At least, not yet."

He rose and departed through the garden. Mineko remained flattened against the statue, her thoughts scattered. Nothing made sense. The Code, Lachlan, her parents, none of it. But one thing was certain—her secrets were no longer hidden, and Reintegration seemed more likely than ever. And then there would be nothing of her left. Just a body with her face. A stranger with her name.

CHAPTER 22

It had been more than a century since the last train had sped over the Rail District's corroded network of steel bars and spikes. Presumably, it had been headed in the only sensible direction: the fuck out of there.

Now, long after the final whistle had blown, the overland rail was nothing more than a map of scars connecting one abandoned district to another. Most of the tracks had been picked apart for scrap, leaving long troughs of earth crowded with weeds, rocks, and broken glass. The trenches of Lexi's childhood.

She rested her head against the van's window and watched the familiar scenery roll by. No doubt Kade was watching too, noticing places they both remembered—apartment towers with barred doors; stores where customers were served at gunpoint; diners with ancient plastic counters the color of pus; wide streets on which people gathered to sell trinkets, drugs, and human bodies, and narrow ones on which they lost their blood and lives.

Soil and cement fighting for superiority, weeds crawling up streetlights, windows without panes, houses without roofs, kids without hope in pairs or ragged packs—it was all here, the same as always, beneath a sky lit by the crimson hue of late afternoon.

"Bring back any memories for you guys?" Zeke was kneeling in the back of the van, peeling the bandage from Riva's hand. "I ain't never come here, personally."

"Yes." Kade slouched against the van's closed rear doors, his head down and his arms folded. "A few."

"It doesn't seem so bad." Riva stood swaying beside Amity, who was buckled into the van's lone rear seat. "The streets look pretty clean, and a lot of the buildings seem occupied."

"Well, it's not the worst district," said Lexi. "But this is Foundation. Being the worst district in Foundation is a little like being the worst strain of flesh-eating virus. Even being the best isn't something to brag about."

The van turned a corner. Far in the distance, tiny plumes of smoke marked the industrial district. It was possible to reach it by following the tracks on foot, but only at the risk of being devoured by the insects that floated in trembling bunches across the intervening wasteland.

"What is the nicest district, anyhow?" said Zeke. "Say I'm gonna move somewhere, start a family. Or steal one and raise it as my own, anyway."

"The University and the East Side," said Kade. "There are key enclaves in both, so the Codists protect them, and the local gangs are easygoing types. The Menagerie, Contessa, and so on. The Rail District falls under Vassago's thumb, and he doesn't have any serious rivals, so it's fairly safe on the streets. The worst areas are those where equally-matched gangs refuse to concede territory and everyone is caught in internecine conflict."

Zeke whistled. "Fun facts. What about the other way around? Callie, you tell us. What's the nastiest piece of corn in this big old shit heap?"

"Longway Falls," Callie said without hesitation. "It's way out. The same distance Rusalka's territory is from here, but south instead of east. There's maybe two thousand folks living in what used to be a rich suburb. It's next to an old golf course, which is just a forest with sand traps these days. A pack of skinheads runs the place. They're led by a piece of work who calls himself the King of Irons."

"King of Irons? He likes his shirts to be nice and crisp, is that his deal?"

"Nothing so cute. His gang kills anyone they think isn't 'pure,' which to them means white and straight. They've made the place into a nasty little enclave of their own."

"So they're scared of melanin and queer people? Riva, you'd be screwed twice over." Zeke gave a nervous grin. "We oughta set Amity loose on 'em. Go in guns blazing, wipe out the shitheads. I'd take the rear, obviously."

Riva raised an eyebrow. "But Zeke, taking the rear is what made you a target in the first place."

Zeke sniggered. "Damn, girl." He poked Amity in the arm. "You feeling any better yet, honey?"

No response. Though Amity had stirred a few times since the fight with Lachlan, she hadn't spoken save for a few irritated, incoherent mutterings. Her eyes remained glazed, her breath shallow.

"It's hard seeing her like this," said Riva. "How long until we get to these friends of yours?"

"Almost there," said Lexi. "Callie, see that big billboard ahead?"

Callie nodded. "Hard not to."

It had once been an advertisement for some kind of masculine product, maybe a watch, a suit or a cologne—hard to say for sure, as it had been tagged over

completely, with only the face of the groomed, smarmy male model spared from
the tide of graffiti. Somebody had painted an erect cock entering his mouth, and
the other graffiti artists had clearly found that too hilarious to cover up.

"The gas station behind it," Lexi said. "That's the place."

"You think they'll have what she needs?" said Zeke.

"If you can swallow, inject or snort it, Raffo has it. And if you have to insert it
up your ass, he'll even throw in the rubber gloves free."

Amity bared her teeth, and Lexi winked. "It's okay, babe. If it comes to that, I'll
insert it for you, how's that sound?"

Amity's fingers twitched. "If she could move, she'd have killed you," said
Zeke. "Talk about literally flirting with danger."

"These friends of yours." Isaac stared at Lexi from behind his lank mop of hair.
"They ain't gonna hassle me?"

"Nobody's going to hassle anyone." Lexi placed a hand over where she
assumed, without any medical certainty, that her heart resided. "I promise."

If extraterrestrials visited Foundation, they'd have taken particular interest in
examining Raffo, who swam in a gene pool all of his own. His gang was ugly as a
rule, but he was its crowning triumph, a man with more teeth than a denture factory
and eyes perpetually wet and staring. His scabbed, green-tinged skin seemed more
like the product of a chemical accident than natural evolution, and he had four
fingers on his left hand and seven on his right. In other words, a real looker.

He was already waiting outside the gas station, unaccompanied, his unique
body wrapped up in a long thermal jacket. "The great Lexi Vale." He extended his
four-fingered hand to shake. "Fancy you gracing us with your presence."

"Fancy you thinking I'd touch your claw. What's new, Raff?"

"Nothing, but I'm sure you're about to spoil my tranquility." Raffo motioned to
the gas station behind them. "Come along, children. Lift's in the back. Don't mind
the sentry, he doesn't mean to stare. He just lacks working eyelids."

They passed through the gas station and crammed into the service lift. As
it rattled into the earth, Lexi tried to maintain her smile. There was something
unnerving about smooshing so many bodies into an ancient contraption, especially
when it displayed a sign reading *Max. Capacity TWO PEOPLE*. Just as well Callie
and Isaac had stayed behind with the van.

The elevator landed, and its left door jerked open while the right remained where it was. "That was a smoo—" Raffo coughed a mass of sputum into his palm. He stared at the glob, sighed and wiped it on his chest. "As I was saying before my lungs intervened, that was a smooth ride down."

"Oh yeah," said Lexi. "I only shit myself the tiniest bit."

"It's been a long time since I saw you last." Raffo led them into a damp cement tunnel lit by a single sputtering bulb. "I see you've got a whole gang with you now."

"I only picked them up recently. They're not so bad. A few badasses, a few dumbasses."

"Which am I?" said Zeke. "A badass, right?"

"Oh, yeah. You're the muscle."

"And her?" Raffo singled out Amity, who was being supported by Riva and Kade. "Does she usually require aid to stay on her feet?"

"Nope. That's why we're here."

"It's a strange world that presents us to you as angels of mercy." Raffo rapped on a rusted door. "Pumpkin!"

The door squeaked open and produced a small, furtive gangster with a bulbous head. "Lexi? What happened with you and the Menagerie?"

"It's complicated," said Lexi. "Don't worry your pumpkin head."

"Okay." Pumpkin scuttled into the hall, his beady eyes fixed on Amity. "This one is sick, isn't she?"

"She needs our tender ministrations," said Raffo. "As to the specifics, I'm yet to be informed myself."

"Someone injected her with Codist neurotoxin," Kade said. "I've brought the dart, if you want to analyze it, but I'm sure it'll be their standard issue."

Pumpkin squeezed the pouch of flesh between his eyebrows while giving Amity an appraising look. "Yeah, I know the shit they use. Lemme go through my stash, see what I can come up with. Twenty minutes."

"Fifteen," said Raffo. "If you'd be so kind."

"Yeah, fifteen." Pumpkin retreated and slammed the door behind him.

"Excellent." Raffo beamed, a sight Lexi could have done without. "Now, may I treat my guests to a beverage?"

They walked under rusted pipes dripping clear fluid, across a grated pool of stagnant water, through a decaying archway and into the kind of place that only a subterranean mutant gangster could call home. Vinyl couches circled a television playing an action film, all guns and explosions, while a fridge covered in magnets buzzed like an eldritch altar beside a microwave coated with sludge. Two of Raffo's gang occupied one of the couches, their bodies oozing into the upholstery.

"Out with you both," said Raffo. "We've an honored guest."

"It's okay," said Lexi. "Let them stay. I feel safer with your deformed, menacing henchmen around."

"Very well, but volume down." The explosions quietened, and Raffo made a sweeping gesture towards a long couch. "Sit, and I'll go get you some lemonade. Do you like lemonade still, Lexi?"

"I'm fucking wild about it, Raffo."

As Raffo started toward the bar fridge, Lexi caught him by the sleeve—or a part of his anatomy that resembled a sleeve—and murmured into his ear. "Don't tell the boss I'm here."

"Uh." Raffo stared at her for a long moment, his big eyes not blinking, before giving a quick nod. "As you wish, dear. And I shouldn't ask why?"

"For your own sake, don't."

Raffo flashed his crowded grin, which sloped in the wrong direction and contained way too many canines. "Get comfy, then, and we'll talk about your friend. What's her name?"

"Amity."

"Not Amity White? The Open Hand enforcer?" Raffo gnawed on his blistered lip. "I'll have to ask Pumpkin to give her a sedative."

"Relax. I don't think she'll hurt anyone."

"That's not what her reputation suggests, but fine, I'll trust you."

While Raffo foraged for lemonade, the others settled onto the empty couches. Kade and Riva propped Amity between them—she was adorable, like an outraged life-sized doll—while Lexi sat on a stool opposite.

She crossed her legs, rested her chin on her fingertips and smiled. "Isn't this nice."

Somebody screamed on the television, and one of the gangsters made an approving gurgling sound. "Yeah, I'm real at ease," said Zeke.

"Can you trust these people?" said Kade. "There'll be a bounty on your head now. Probably more than one."

"I trust them," said Lexi. "When you and I were kids, Raff was my go-to guy for drugs. Of all the lowlifes I used to score off, I liked him the best. He was fair, none of his goons ever tried anything on me and, as far as I could tell, he wasn't much into hurting anyone. Later, when Vassago moved on the district, I convinced him to recruit Raff's gang rather than wipe them out. Since then, Raff has been living it up as one of Sammy's local lieutenants, and he has me to thank for it."

"Old friends, then?" said Riva.

"Sure, why not. He's handy to know. Specializes in medical drugs, can hook you up with anything. He'll fix Amity, no problem."

"No," said Amity, her voice slurred. "No gang drugs."

"Hey, she's talking again!" Zeke gave her a huge grin. "I was getting worried about you, baby."

"Shut up. You jackass."

Riva patted Amity's arm. "I've already spoken to Nikolas on the phone. He's sending someone here, but he wants you to get treated as soon as possible. We don't want you to suffer any lasting damage, Am."

Amity clenched her fists in her lap. "No."

"Is there a problem?" Raffo sauntered up with a bottle of murky lemonade in one hand and a stack of glasses in the other. "Your famously terrifying friend appears to be talking through gritted teeth."

"She's fine," said Riva. "We really appreciate what you're doing for us."

"Such civility! You get the first sip." Raffo poured lemonade into a glass, and the liquid hissed as it filled to the rim. "May I observe that you are one striking woman? That dashing Mohawk, those seductive eyes. Would I be wasting my time flirting with you?"

Lexi laughed. "Raff, forget it. She'd have to turn straight. And then she'd have to go blind."

"Lexi!" said Riva. "Don't listen to her, Raffo. Flirt all you like."

"Offended on my behalf?" Raffo fluttered his seven fingers beside his cheek. "I am helplessly in love. How's the lemonade?"

Lexi took a quick sip. The bubbling fluid scorched down her throat and fizzed in her stomach. "You sure this isn't cleaning product?"

"Ninety-four-percent sure." Raffo squinted at Kade. "You're Kade, aren't you? Lexi used to talk about you all the time. Kade this. Kade that. Me and Kade. Kade and I. She was so obsessed, I assumed you were her boyfriend. Quite a misunderstanding."

Kade smiled. "We were close in the day, but not that close."

"A pleasure to finally meet you." Raffo gave Lexi a reproachful look. "Lexi, hurry up and introduce me to the beauty."

"Her name is Riva Latour," said Lexi. "Unless you were referring to the tattooed loudmouth, in which case his name is Zeke and you need your sight checked."

"Zeke of Zeke's Lounge?"

"The very same."

"A celebrity. I'll have to get an autograph."

"I'll just ink it on you," said Zeke. "My groupies love that."

"Tattoos and I don't agree. My skin is brittle." Raffo twinkled at Riva. "Though I could imagine daring the needle in order to secure your enchanting name upon my body. Riva Latour. A moniker as captivating as its owner."

"Don't listen to him," said Lexi. "That's his mutated chromosomes talking. He just wants to drain your fluids and make a nest inside your skin."

"My wiles are clearly wasted here. Speaking of romantic things, I glimpsed Callie Roux up above. That strikes me as rather strange."

"Why? You think she's out of my league?"

"No, but the last I heard, you two weren't exactly on good terms."

"That's in the past. I'm crazy about her nowadays. Oh, and if you were wondering, the disheveled mass of rags and hair is Isaac Landon Hill. He's a junkie we just happened to pick up on the way."

"Is that right?" Raffo shrugged. "I'm not one to judge. I work with numerous colorful individuals myself."

As if to prove his point, Pumpkin lurched into the room with a needle in hand. "It's all ready for her, boss. One shot in the muscle."

"Make sure there's nothing sharp nearby," said Lexi. "She goes for the knives first."

Pumpkin waddled nearer, the syringe raised. Amity twitched. "No. Back off. Touch me and die."

"Amity, you need this," said Kade. "The sooner you get a counter-agent in you, the less chance of lasting nerve damage."

Amity hissed between her teeth. "I don't trust him."

"Pumpkin's handy with sharps," Raffo said. "Never killed anyone he didn't mean to."

"No." Amity turned her seething glare on Zeke. "You do it."

Eyes shining, Zeke clasped his hands to his breast. "Me? Does this mean we're friends?"

"Do it or I kill you."

"Sure!" Zeke snatched the syringe from Pumpkin and peered at the liquid suspended within. "What's this shit? I have to know before I put it in her."

"Half a milliliter of NeuroZex." Pumpkin sounded peevish, though his face remained inscrutably lumpy. "The real deal."

"And the needle, it's sterile?"

"Of course it's sterile. What do you take me for?"

"A man with a pumpkin-shaped head?" Zeke rolled up Amity's sleeve with a quick, practiced motion. "You just relax. Tough bitch that you are, you won't even feel this going in."

With a steady hand, Zeke performed the injection. Sure enough, Amity didn't even grimace.

"Thirty minutes and she'll have her mobility back," said Pumpkin. "She's not going to be happy for the next twenty-four hours, though. There might be vomiting, dizziness. She'll need to spend a day or two lying down."

"A day or two? This woman is our fucking lethal weapon, we can't lose her for a day or two!" Zeke shook the empty syringe. "You asshole. Help me get her to a bed. No mattresses covered in rat guts, either. I want your fucking penthouse suite, or else I'm setting Lex loose on you."

"Pumpkin, accommodate them." Raffo waited for Zeke and Pumpkin to escort Amity out before shaking his head. "So that's Zeke Lukas. He's as strange as his occupation might suggest."

"He's the excitable type," said Lexi. "As for the rest of us, we'd all like rooms too. We're not quite as fussy as Zeke, but it would be nice not to sleep in a pool of engine oil."

"I see." Raffo tapped his extra digits against his chin. "So, that's rooms for how many people? Seven?"

"Six." Kade gave a sheepish smile. "I'm cycling out. I have to report back to Sarabelle, and I've work to do."

He wasn't staying? Lexi stared into Kade's eyes—the most familiar part of him; warm with good-natured intelligence. "But it's late."

"I know this district as well as you do. I'll be fine."

"But..."

Lexi hesitated. If she admitted that she didn't want him gone, that she was concerned for him, that—fucking hell—she maybe even missed him... Well, that would summon feelings she couldn't deal with. "Whatever. We have Isaac to train up as your replacement, so it's no real loss. We just have to find him a trench coat and a philosophy textbook."

Raffo clapped his hands together and nodded. "Six beds, then. Perhaps somebody should run up top and let Roux know the situation. We have a place to hide her van, so she won't need to keep watching over it like a mother bear."

"I'll go tell her," Riva said. "That okay?"

"Sure, go," said Lexi. "Keep her company a while too. She gets lonely. Kade, care to escort Riva topside?"

As she departed with Kade, Riva stroked Lexi's nape in passing. Lexi's hairs rose, and a pleasant tingle spread down her spine.

"Not bad," said Raffo, gazing after Riva. "Not bad at all, Alexis. How long have you known her?"

"A few days."

"In your case, that makes it a long-term relationship. I must say, I didn't expect Kade to be quite so serious."

"He's always been like that. It was cute when he was a kid. Now he's all grown up, it makes him a pain in the ass."

"You were looking at him rather wistfully just a minute ago. Which reminds me of another, related subject. What the fuck happened to Ash?"

An explosion marked the beginning of some new theatrics in the film behind them, and the gangsters whooped. It was too reminiscent of the real violence Lexi had seen today—the helicopter pilot twitching in his bloodstained seat, the agents shot in the stairwell, the sensation of a living mind melting under her will, the brutal way Lachlan had taken out Rusalka's bikers—and a sour taste filled Lexi's throat.

"Forget about lemonade," she said. "Get me a real drink."

Garlic-rich aroma rose from the frying pan. Callie waited, a plate held out, while Riva scooped up a mound of food. "This one is for Raffo."

Callie pouted. "Isn't it my turn yet?"

"You and Lexi will eat soon, don't worry."

Callie exited with the plate. Lexi watched her cute butt wiggle away. "Stop ogling her," said Riva. "Or at least try to ogle while helping."

"Hey, you're the one who volunteered to cook dinner for a gang of hungry mutants. I'm only in this for the company of gorgeous women." With a spoon handle, Lexi prodded the steaming contents of a pot. "Raff said he had some dog meat in the freezer. Why didn't you cook it?"

"The same reason I wouldn't cook you."

"Vegetarian, huh? Doesn't surprise me somehow. Growing up, I had to eat rats and dogs a few times, but it wasn't for fun. It was that or starve."

Riva thumped a spice bottle, sending a puff of sand-colored powder into the food. "I understand that. But soy is plentiful and cheap."

"Sure. Plus meat's hard to catch, and then there's a good chance it'll get you sick. Though Kade told me that people used to eat it all the time."

"It's true. Massive fields of soy were grown purely for use as animal feed. Over ninety percent of the global crop never found its way into human diets. Just one of the many ways we consumed the planet."

"So you really do read that little column he writes."

Riva smiled through a cloud of steam. "Every fortnight."

"Does Amity read it?"

"Usually, but she doesn't agree with him on everything. She respects his views regardless. Just like she respects Nikolas's and mine."

It seemed a decent opportunity to ask a question Lexi had been carrying for some time. "She knows about you, doesn't she?"

"How'd you guess?"

"Two nights ago, she cornered me in an alley and threatened to hurt me if I didn't keep away from you. I thought she was just being a bitch. Now I realize that she was trying to protect you."

A new emotion bloomed in Riva's eyes—devoted, wistful affection. "She's protective towards all of us. The gangs see the purple palm as her mark, a symbol they fear more than any other tag in Foundation."

"I believe it. But she's got a special connection to you."

Riva nodded. "It was five years ago. I was twenty-two, homeless, and searching for a warm place to sleep. An alley that seemed promising proved a dead end. When I turned around, three men were blocking it."

Lexi's breath stopped. "Tell me they didn't."

"They tried. They forced me down and stripped off my jeans. Then they started laughing. Soon the laughter stopped, and they began kicking me. Calling me... well, you know what they called me."

Her remembered humiliation ignited the air between them. "Please tell me this is when Amity intervened."

"At that very moment. A shot rang out and the men ran, leaving me lying beside a gutter. Degraded. Naked from the waist down. And after having seen the contempt and disgust in their eyes, I shared their revulsion. I found myself wishing that Amity's warning shot had been aimed straight at my head."

"Oh, babe..."

"Amity reached me before I could cover myself. She looked down, just quickly, but she saw. Then she held out her hand and said, 'You're a strong woman. You'll survive this.' Those words saved me, I think. She brought me back to Bunker One, and I've been with Open Hand ever since. She still brings me my pills and watches over me. My guardian angel."

What was it Nikolas had said? *I alone saw the fallen angel...* "When I first met her, I never would have guessed she had a soft side."

"She terrifies me too, but I love her more than I've ever loved anyone."

"Reed said something about Ash being Amity's best friend. I can picture that, actually. Ash was always drawn to strong personalities." Lexi breathed in the wafting cloud of sauce and spices, but her appetite had long gone. "Even as violent and unfriendly as she is, I can't help but find Amity sexy."

"She told me you'd done something sexual with her."

Surely Lexi had misheard. "She told you about that?"

"She only said, while blushing to her ears, that you performed a 'sex act' on her. I asked if she'd enjoyed it, and she told me to shut up." Riva giggled. "Don't look so startled. She knows I have feelings for you, so she considered it her duty to inform me. She didn't want to feel that she was betraying me somehow."

"And did you feel betrayed?"

"Of course not. I'm just happy she let her guard down to you. And amazed, to be honest. I can only imagine what the circumstances were."

Before Lexi could think of a response, Callie bounced through the door. "Hey, cute things," she said. "I'm surprised you both have your clothes on."

Lexi grinned. A timely interruption. "We were waiting for you."

"So this is going to be that kind of friendship, huh?" Callie dumped the empty plate into the sink. "Get out some candles, then, and seduce me over dinner. I'm so hungry."

"First, Amity needs her soup." Riva tapped a spoon against a bowl of white, watery goop. "I've made it specially for her."

"Lucky Amity. By the way, I popped my head into her room. She, Zeke and Isaac are watching some film together."

"What the hell would those three watch together?" said Lexi.

"It's a cartoon with lots of talking birds and ghosts and things. Amity seemed peaceful. I guess she must be on some serious drugs."

"In that case, Zeke and Isaac can have their meals now too." Riva laid two more bowls on the tray. "Would you mind?"

Callie hefted the tray. "Anything for you, chickadee." She winked at Riva and strutted from the room.

"She's definitely into you," said Lexi. "You tempted?"

"And explain again what I keep in my panties? I can't bear to think about it. Too many girls react like I've just turned into a spider."

"I wish I could say she'd be okay with it, but I don't know her well enough." Lexi poked a finger into the nearest pan and tasted the warm, salty sauce. "But if you keep cooking her food this good, I don't think anything could stop her falling in love with you."

"I thought she was in love with Mineko."

"Nah. Well, maybe." Lexi shrugged. "I promised I'd help rescue the kid tomorrow. Damned if I know how, though."

Riva gave a slow nod. "I'd like to help. Even though I haven't met Min, I know how she might be feeling right now. I understand what it's like to be trapped in a self-preserving deception, afraid the people you love will turn against you."

A touching sentiment, but there was no way. "Shut-ins are bad news. Leave the dangerous work to me and Amity."

"Amity can't do anything that might take her into an enclave. It'd get her in serious trouble with Nikolas. I'm sure he feels sorry for Mineko, but he'd never take the risk of helping her defect."

"Wait, seriously? Wouldn't rescuing someone like Minnie be a big revolutionary victory?"

"Protecting you is the victory he's looking for right now. Lexi, you can't enter an enclave either. Not even for Mineko. Tomorrow, you and Amity should return to Bunker One. Take Isaac and Zeke with you."

Being commanded around by Riva was so unexpected, it took Lexi several seconds to grasp for an objection. "But Callie…"

"Won't be left on her own, I promise. I'll help her to free Mineko."

"Babe, you can't—I mean, you might—I shouldn't—" Shit. Usually, Lexi was never short of a reply. But what could she say?

"Mineko's backed into a corner," Riva said. "She must feel the world is against her. I know what that's like, and I have to prove to her it's not true."

Funny. After so many years brushing eager women away, here Lexi was, clinging to the first one she wasn't sure she could keep. "But you'll get hurt. They'll wipe you."

"I did well enough today, didn't I?"

"That was different. You had…" *Kade.* Now there was an idea. If anyone could talk Riva out of doing something stupid, it would be him. "If you're going to do this, make sure you find Kade first. Ask him to help you." At which point he would talk her out of it. Surely.

Riva bowed her head, and a shy smile lifted her lips. "You're really worried about me."

Unexpected heat climbed Lexi's neck. "I just don't want to see you hurt."

Riva looked up. The gleam in her eyes hinted at what might be coming, but it gave no warning of the intensity of it—a sudden, forceful kiss that pinned Lexi to the bench behind her. Their mouths joined hard, their lips and tongues moved, and Riva's thigh pressed into Lexi's groin. To ensure it stayed there, Lexi grabbed Riva by her small, firm ass and pulled her even closer.

God, Lexi had been aching for this. She wanted to fuck Riva right now, to stroke, grip, and squeeze every part of her body—the soft curve of her tits, the bony edges of her hips, the cock stiffening under her tight jeans…

A wolf-whistle shrilled from the doorway, and Lexi and Riva separated, gasping and flustered.

"That was hot," said Callie. "Do it one more time?"

CHAPTER 23

He rode into the evening, his bike shuddering as it rattled down corrugated lanes of earth where rails had once rested. When headlights pierced the night and an engine roared behind him, Kade braced for the worst.

An Open Hand jeep, military green with a purple palm on its door, pulled up alongside him. Nikolas rolled down the window. "I suppose you assumed I was a Codist."

"It crossed my mind. How'd you find me?"

"Alexis suggested you might take this route home."

"The tracks make good bike paths. I rode them all the time as a kid."

"Will you accept my offer of a lift? It's much warmer in here."

"The cold's no problem." Not quite true. The longer Kade sat still, the more the chill insinuated itself under his coat, cooling the sweat on his skin. "When Riva said somebody from Open Hand would be coming, I didn't expect it to be you."

"I wanted to speak to Amity personally. Now, please, get in. I have a passenger who may be comforted by your presence."

Truth be told, Kade hadn't been looking forward to plunging into the district's dark streets, and it was with some relief that he stowed his bike in the crowded storage area just behind the jeep's rear seat. The vehicle was well-stocked with tools, a spare tire, medical kits, and dried food: Nikolas never went anywhere unprepared.

Warm air cloaked Kade as he settled into the front passenger seat. Isaac was sitting in the back, looking as miserable and evasive as ever. A short, slender Open Hand revolutionary sat beside him. Her taciturn features, dark-green eyes, and chestnut bob were familiar. Audra. One of Nikolas's most trusted guards, a quiet woman who never carried a gun and rarely spoke.

"You'll be fine, Isaac," Kade said. "This is a friend."

Isaac nodded his unkempt head. "Okay."

Nikolas accelerated, slowly, with one hand on the wheel. "Amity was surprised to see me." He kept his eyes on the road, his gaunt features lit by the glow of the dashboard. "She seemed heavily sedated. Calandre Roux, on the other hand, was very lively. When I refused to help rescue the Tamura girl, she had more than a few choice words for me."

"I can imagine."

"Alexis narrated the day's events. Battling Codists in the streets. Besting our turncoat comrade. Quite an adventure for you, old friend."

Kade stared at the darkening sky. It seemed wrong that the sun still set on Bare Hill, as if Ash hadn't been the reason it shone at all. "Mineko risked her life for us."

"So I was told. Many times. With increasing amounts of profanity."

"We owe her, Nikolas."

"I can't get involved." The jeep bounced over a rough section of road. "I've lost Riva Latour over this. She insists on helping them."

"Is it really such a terrible thing to rescue an innocent girl?"

"You don't understand how volatile Foundation is. Only patience will ensure a minimum of suffering in the days to come."

There seemed no point arguing with him. Instead, Kade continued to look out the window. The sun trailed downward, its red light gleaming on the rails...

He started from his reverie as they cruised by the wrong intersection. "Where are we going?"

"I'm taking a detour." The darker it grew, the stranger Nikolas became in profile, with his rangy shoulders, mad mop of hair, and the odd smile skewing his lips. "I've been meaning to do this for a while, but I'm always occupied elsewhere. Monitoring the streets, the Codists, my people..."

"How is it you keep so well informed?"

"I exchange stories with Lachlan Reed."

It was as unexpected as a knife in the dark. "What do you mean?"

"Every month, he and I meet to talk. Nobody knows but Audra, who accompanies me as a precaution."

"What could you two possibly have to talk about?"

"A mutual interest in stability. Amity makes him nervous, so he places infiltrators in our ranks. But he also agrees that Open Hand plays a vital role in our city's delicate balance."

"Why tell me this? I'm the last person who should keep it secret. I'm a reporter, for Christ's sake."

"I want you to understand how far I'll go to keep Foundation stable. I can't permit the Tamuras, who I understand love their daughter very much, to tear this city to its...well, to its foundations."

Once again, Kade gazed out the window. A confusion of light, shade, and broken stone had supplanted the sensible waking world. "Are you seriously telling me that Lachlan gives you insider Codist information? And that you give him intelligence in return?"

"Yes. He's already told me, vaguely, about Project Sky. Not the specifics of the chip, what it does, but merely that it was a present Codist interest. He advised me to expect some intensification of our warfare."

"Did you tell him about Lexi?"

"Of course not. I only reveal to him such information as is mutually useful. In particular, information on gang activity, which is an irritation to both of us. If a gang conflict threatens innocent lives, Lachlan often warns me ahead of time, allowing me to intervene however I can."

"But Code Intel is allied with the major gangs. Lachlan acts as mediator."

Nikolas frowned. "I despise his lack of conviction, but he's not an evil man. He won't be turned away from Codism, because it affords him the greatest possible power and luxury. But he understands that Codism itself is a pernicious doctrine, and he's as keen to rein in its excesses as we are. Thus the duplicity, the deception, the double-dealing. He's a figure for our troubled age."

"But not a role model, I hope."

"No." Nikolas nodded at the road. "Stay alert. We're almost there."

***

Kade should have guessed.

He watched, huddled in his coat, as Nikolas laid a bouquet upon her grave. "I've only come here once," Nikolas said. "Is she in fact buried down there, or is this all purely symbolic?"

"She's down there."

Nikolas knelt and touched the slab. "I miss you, comrade."

A familiar, desperate tightness seized Kade's throat. The evening had become oppressive, its shadows too dense, the tinge of night above the glowing band of horizon somehow unsettling. "Is there anything else you haven't told me?"

"Audra is pregnant. Six weeks. Is it old-fashioned I'm hoping for a son?"

"Yes. Let the child be what it will."

Nikolas gave a quiet laugh. "Consider me properly chastened."

"This morning, Lexi and Riva woke to watch the sunrise, and Lexi thought of Ash then. Now here I am, thinking of her as the sun sets. Lexi's at the beginning, while I'm facing the end." As much as Kade tried to keep his voice level, he couldn't keep it from wavering. "Please help Mineko. Do it for me."

"Ash would have moved the heavens for that girl, but I'm not her. She was the future taken from us. We'll never know what might have been. Now I can only do what I feel is right." Nikolas's cheeks glistened where the dying light met the trails of his tears. "I'm so tired."

"It's been a hard week for all of us."

"Perhaps none more so than you. You almost seem bereaved again."

"It's seeing Lexi. The more time I spend around her, the more it sinks in that we can't ever be friends again. At most, she'd learn to tolerate me." Kade breathed out. "And that hurts."

Nikolas remained silent, his head bowed. If someone didn't know the man, they might have thought that he was praying.

Westward, the night sky was suffused with neon—the radiance of the club district where Lexi's life had taken its recent turn. Beneath that colorful shimmer, Foundation's more fortunate inhabitants would now be gathering, dressed for enticement and hungry for oblivion. Strange that even on the brink of extinction, the rituals of a dead age continued.

"They'll make an example of you," Nikolas said. "The streets are restless. The Committee are afraid. Even Vassago is nervous."

"Good. That thug deserves a few sleepless nights."

"Do you even care if you live or die? Or is it all the same for you now?"

"No. I'm not fatalistic." Kade stared down at the grave. Lexi had paid for it, and though Ash would have disliked that blood money was responsible for her resting place, Kade had chosen not to protest. "I prefer to live."

"If that's true, then leave Foundation with the others."

"I can't. Ash loved this city, and someday, I'd like to understand why."

The last thing Kade needed at this bone-wearying hour was to run into Sarabelle. Yet there his editor was, sitting at Kade's desk, eating a chocolate bar and frowning at the unfinished article on subway safety.

"I don't like your opening sentence." Sarabelle pointed to the screen with the half-chewed bar. "The participle phrase makes it clunky."

"I suspect the revolution will survive." As Kade left the stairs, Goldie perked his ears. "Goldie's here, but no Mahesh?"

"You know how he was researching restaurant hygiene? He did some firsthand investigation. Result: food poisoning." Sarabelle grinned. She was only in her mid-thirties, but the creases in her brown skin and the gray flecks in her messy black hair betrayed the rapid aging that came with leadership of a revolutionary cell. "I'm looking after the big pup, though I'd much rather you were doing it, given my allergies."

"Hint taken." Kade patted his knee, but Goldie only buried his snout deeper in his blankets. "I'll watch him tonight."

"I hear you've been hanging around with Open Hand."

"Solidarity, that's all. And some personal business."

Foil crackled as Sarabelle reached the end of her chocolate bar. "Careful. Amity is batshit."

The timeworn shot at his friend rankled more than ever. "I can assure you she isn't."

"Bat-fucking-shit crazy, Kade." Sarabelle balled the wrapper and tossed it across the room. "A helicopter was spotted at dawn this morning. And now there're rumors, nothing I can verify, that a Codist operation went wrong. Agents killed. You know anything about that?"

Kade made a non-committal sound. "I did hear Lachlan Reed is back and throwing his weight around."

"Don't mention that scumbag." Sarabelle stood, still scowling at the article. "Now you're here, I might take off. I promised Mahesh I'd bring him some medicine." She wagged a finger at Goldie, who opened one eye. "Behave for Kade, you questionable sentinel."

"Nikolas sends his regards, by the way."

"I'd rather he sent money, but I'll take what I'm given." Sarabelle retrieved her beloved fedora from the hook by the door. "You aren't in some kind of trouble, are you? You look a little ragged."

"No more than usual."

"Then take some time tonight to finish this damn article." Sarabelle reached the first step and looked back with reproach in her eyes. "And just when are we going to have that drink?"

He'd been waiting for it. They'd had one date, just one. Sarabelle had ranted about grammatical pet peeves, abused the waiter and, after Kade had escorted her home, tried to drag him into her bedroom. During his escape, he'd promised to someday take her out for drinks. It was an event now marked in her mythology, as significant a moment as the return of a messiah or the end of all things.

"I'll let you know," he said.

Sarabelle gave him a skeptical look before retreating up the stairwell. "You're lucky to be a dog," Kade said to Goldie, who glanced up with an expression that was surely the canine equivalent of a shrug.

Kade entered the kitchen and liberated a container of suspicious-looking chunks from the fridge. He struggled to remain awake while the meal whirled in the microwave. A concluding *ping* drew him back into alertness.

Yawning, he deposited the steaming contents into a plastic bowl. He ate in front of his desk, stabbing one rubbery lump after another, and stared at the article on his screen.

Had Sarabelle been tinkering with it in his absence? The fifth paragraph seemed different somehow—

Goldie snuffed, a powerful, explosive sound.

"Dust in your nose, boy?"

Goldie snorted in frustration and batted his snout. A puppyish gesture that evoked memories of the way Ash had used to play with him. She'd loved to roll him across the floor, turning him into a squirming, black-and-brown ball of fur and claws...

Why the fuck had Nikolas taken them to the grave tonight? Her name seemed so apt now that she was choking him, making his eyes sting. Even the food seemed flavorless on his scorched tongue.

He would have loved to show her this stupid article. She'd have laughed at his subtle jokes, frowned at his poetic excesses, noted where his arguments were unclear. Even a week later, she'd have sprung on him with some unexpected contribution.

I was thinking about another way you could end that article, if you still weren't happy with it...

Though Lexi had never cared much for his writing, she too had found ways to build up his pride. She'd let him into her rough, adventurous lifestyle, taken him to clubs, introduced him to people she knew. *This is Kade,* she'd say, *he's my best friend.*

If they'd laughed—which they often did—she'd snarl at them. Sometimes, there had been violence on his behalf, and he'd watch the ensuing skirmish with a mixture of horror and gratitude. But sometimes, they hadn't laughed. Sometimes, Lexi had introduced him to girls who smiled as if they didn't know. *This one's straight, Kade. Trust me, I've tried. Definitely into guys only. You should go for it.*

He was crying now. Couldn't pinpoint when he'd started.

He opened a drawer, took out a flask of something, tasted it. Sharp in his mouth, hot in his throat. Maybe more would muddy his mind. Dull the ache.

Goldie's big, melancholy eyes reminded him somehow of Callie Roux. What would she say about his past? Would she stammer and stumble on all the wrong things? *So you were born a... When did you decide... What did your parents call... So, do you have a, uh, you know...*

No. Not Callie. She'd say: *That's cool. We're all a little different.* Something nice like that. He'd still never tell her, but it was reassuring to imagine.

Poor, daredevil Callie, with her selfless loyalty to Mineko. What could those two really have in common? Callie was instinctive, expressive, and content with small things, whereas Mineko was cerebral, reserved, and ambitious. She'd stunned Kade with the breathtaking intelligence in her cool green eyes, the quiet resolve in her voice. She was reminiscent of Nikolas, Ash, Lachlan. Rare people with the quality of leadership.

Lachlan...

Did he ever feel guilty? He had duped Kade, Sarabelle, and Mahesh for three years, yet he had always been honest about his disdain. His Codist education often made him sound arrogant, even pompous, but under all his verbosity was a bitter lyrical streak. Like Lexi, he had an eye for absurd detail, a determination to speak his mind and an incisive quickness of wit. Betrayer though he was, it was tough not having him around.

Codism was like an infection that never quite healed. There were several ex-Codists in the underground, and all of them were eccentric—forever haunted by their social blueprint. It was the reason Nikolas was afraid to trust Mineko. The reason Amity wouldn't be satisfied until she saw the enclaves burning.

Bat-fucking-shit crazy, Sarabelle had said.

It couldn't have been further from the truth. There wasn't a drop of madness in Amity, not a hint of anything but remorseless sanity. Besides, it wasn't as if Kade were a saint. He'd taken two lives himself this week. A brutal, racist gangster and some anonymous Codist on a motorcycle.

So much violence. Enacted by him, enacted for him. Starting from the very beginning, when Lexi had fought on his behalf, so lithe that not even the biggest street bullies could take her. She slipped right out of their hands, came back so fast and vicious they didn't know how to respond.

Don't come back here again, or I'll fuck you up twice as bad...

But Ash had never hurt anyone. She'd been too gentle. He'd loved to stroke her long blonde hair, feeling the delicate shape of her head, while she tilted her face nearer and murmured his name.

His name...

They'd been waiting for Lexi outside an old rail station. Ash had looked him in the eye, begun to speak, and then faltered. Paused. Taken a deep breath. Kade had understood in a terrible instant: Lexi'd told her.

He'd frozen, longing for some escape that might deter his humiliation.

But then Ash had smiled.

Why didn't you tell me your real name was Kade?

A nose bumped his leg. A quiet whimper. Goldie.

"Hi, puppy." Each word rasped through the pinhole of his throat. "Don't worry about me."

CHAPTER 24

As a child, Mineko had spent many nights under her blanket, hiding from the agents who'd wiped her tutor. She remembered his forbidden stories even if he didn't, which surely meant they'd come for her next.

Now, with nowhere else to turn, she'd returned to her old sanctuary.

It should have felt absurd, an adult swaddled like a baby, but the snug darkness proved as comforting as before. If only she could be buried this way forever. How had Valerie managed to endure this nightmare for so long? What stopped her leaping off that balcony of hers?

The door opened. "Min?" said Kaori. "Is that you under there?"

"No."

"What are you doing? Are you masturbating?"

Mineko flung back the blankets. "I am not."

"You're a funny thing. I'm glad you've decided to stay the night, even if you're wasting it fantasizing about that red-headed boy of yours."

"I told you, I wasn't masturbating." Mineko slipped from the bed and smoothed her blanket flat. "I was thinking about my exams, in fact."

"How disappointing. Anyway, your father has a date with the Committee, so it's just you and me at dinner. Maybe we can bring out a bottle of that juice you like so much and watch a good movie."

"A romance movie, you mean."

"There's a new one with a very hunky male lead. I was involved in the production, believe it or not. The lead plays a young officer, and I had to give permission for the fictional portrayal. Including use of the uniform. Not that he's always wearing it in the film, if you know what I mean..."

"You make it sound pornographic."

"The camera is on his naked torso for about five seconds. But when you see those abs, you'll agree they're the finest five seconds of a woman's life." Kaori leered. "I could always arrange a date. I'm not sure how I feel about an actor being a Tamura, but your children would be gorgeous."

Mineko stopped fussing with the blanket—it was all an act anyway, as if she gave a damn about how neat the bed was—and moved to the window, where she stood with her arms folded. No doubt her mother assumed she was sulking like a child, unable as always to distinguish between petulance and justified indignation. "I don't care for abs."

"Daughter, you're raving."

"Lachlan was here earlier. His manner seemed odd."

"He was around? I must have missed him. Something went wrong with an operation, and he's likely to get a slap on the wrist."

"Is it related to those strange people he showed us at dinner?"

"Yes, it is. Though I have to say, you're not usually so interested in the family business."

"The family business isn't always so colorful. I recall a man with spikes on his head. And a white-haired woman."

"Lurid characters, yes. But quite depraved."

"Not like you, with your healthy love for abs."

"Mineko." Kaori spoke her name like a word of reproach. "You've always been so reserved. Some of my friends would say sullen. Yet I know you've a generous heart, an insightful mind and a deep love of learning. Maybe you'd be happier if you directed your instincts in a more fruitful direction. All this philosophy is only making you doubt yourself."

"The Code is an ethical system. How is it not fruitful to study ethics?"

"The Code is…" Kaori fell silent, her gaze moving between the gray-breasted birds flitting in the garden. "The Code can be misleading. We Tamuras are more important than other Codists. Think about it this way. The little finger and the thumb both belong to the hand, but if you had to lose a digit, you wouldn't choose the thumb."

"I don't think that analogy would go down well in my exam."

"If the Code is a hand, we Tamuras are the thumb. Obeying ethics, let alone studying them, only diminishes us. We exist to wield power."

Did Kaori really not realize how sinister that sounded? "I don't care for wielding power either."

"Why not? Our ancestors fought for it. They were Codifiers. Their name means something, and when I married your father, I only allowed him to take it because he had the right character." Kaori squeezed Mineko's shoulder. "So do you."

"What have I ever done to deserve anything? I was born into this."

Kaori released Mineko only to grip her again, as if unwilling to relinquish that small contact. "You should tell me more about your world. Your life. Lachlan says that you and I look like sisters, the shameless flatterer. I think we ought to behave like them. You shouldn't have secrets from me."

"What's the point? I spoke to Dad before, and no matter what I said about my feelings, he told me it was part of a phase."

"He means well, but he's a man. They tend to be thoughtless."

"If men are so thoughtless, what's the appeal?"

Kaori chuckled. "Do I really have to spell it out?"

Treat me like a sister, she had said. Don't keep secrets. Well, fine. It hardly mattered anymore.

"To be truthful," Mineko said, "I find men very boring."

"What about that redhead of yours?"

"Maybe I invented him to cover some dark secret." It was like talking with the barrel of a gun in her mouth, the trigger tightening with every word. "Maybe it's women I find interesting."

The playful smile slipped from Kaori's face. "That isn't funny, Mineko."

"But I'm the thumb, remember? If I want to see a woman with her shirt off, nobody should be able to stop me." Mineko laughed—having leapt off the edge, nothing was easier than to keep falling—and gave Kaori a teasing nudge. "If only you could see your face right now."

"Are you teasing me? You are teasing me, aren't you?"

"I'm only trying to get a direct answer from you. If we Tamuras are diminished by ethics, why can't I marry a woman?"

"Because the Code—"

Mineko arched an eyebrow. "The Code can be misleading."

"Oh, very funny. The fact is, two women aren't designed to—"

"Designed? Are you a theist now?"

"You know what I mean! This is one of your awful classroom thought experiments, isn't it? You know very well you're being absurd, but you want to see me struggle to prove it."

"Yes, Mother. I've trapped you in a web of logic and doubt, because I'm a Tamura, and I reign over whatever my dominion may be. And ethics is mine. So please stop questioning my choice of vocation and instead concede that I'm suited to it."

"You're so like your father. You look like me, but you speak like him. And you've always been so stern." Kaori's smile made a tentative return. "I was always so afraid I'd done something wrong raising you. My mother called you 'the little grump.' I longed for a smile, a laugh from my baby girl. Tell me, Min, have I lost you? Have you really grown old so fast?"

Only moments before, Mineko had hated Kaori. Now she pitied her so deeply, her chest hurt from it. "I'm still your little grump, Mom."

Kaori fumbled for Mineko's hand and held it tight. "I'm sorry if I made a bad impression. I just so badly want things to work out for you. You have so much potential." She took a deep breath. "I need to instruct the staff about dinner. What do you want? It can be anything my clever girl likes."

"I don't mind. Surprise me."

"I have a few ideas." Kaori smiled with more assurance, and Mineko's ache intensified. This infuriating, interfering mother—impossible to live with, impossible to imagine a life without. "And I'll decide on a different movie. Now that I think about it, I'm tired of always watching romances."

Mineko waited for the door to shut before letting her grief escape in a single sob. There was nothing she wanted more than to escape from all this, but God, how she loved them.

Dawn striped the shutters. Mineko had dreamed, but she recalled nothing but a sensation of loss.

She took the watch from her writing desk, walked to the window, opened the shutters—if a gardener happened to glance up and see the young Tamura in her underwear, good for them—and inhaled. The air harbored a frost that stirred her blood as her lungs expanded.

As she breathed, she stroked the watch's cover. Memories of her friends returned in vivid detail. Paradoxes, all of them. Selfish, gentle Zeke. Brooding, joyful Callie. Arrogant, protective Lexi. And Kade, who had entered her life as a terror and left as an inspiration—a man suggestive of quiet mysteries, depths Mineko would never know.

How many mornings could she hold this timepiece and keep from crying? What was the point of all her courage if she never directed it toward what she truly wanted?

Beyond the floral hills and groves of the district, past that towering wall, was the sky she'd seen on the day Callie had driven her through the desert: a brilliant dome above a wasteland, from which Foundation appeared only as a line on the horizon. There was no grass there, only soil dried to dust the color of sand and bone. Yet it was beautiful because it was endless. Because nobody had yet thought to enclose it.

Yes, Mineko loved her parents, which was why she had to save them from the prison they'd created. Yes, she was a Codist—a Tamura—but that only made her responsibility all the more pressing. She had to flee, but not to save herself.

It was her duty now to liberate everyone.

She dressed. Each button she fastened seemed to increase the constriction in her throat, and sealing the collar left her breathless. But when she looked at the mirror and saw herself consumed again by formless blue fabric, a rush of air filled her chest. The time had come.

Callie would rescue her. It had been a promise. And as Mineko closed her hand around the watch and felt it tick in her palm, she had no doubt that promise would soon be kept.

For the first time, the cleanliness of the campus subway station appalled her. Plastic and steel surfaces gleamed under light panels that emitted a warm, constant glow. Not a trace of dirt. In fact, the platform's blue and silver tiles—laid out as an ornate spiral mosaic—were being swept even as Mineko walked through. The janitor, an elderly man in a dark brown overall, seemed aware only of the broom in his hands. A sharp whisk to the left, a quick sweep to the right, a pointless repetition on a spotless floor.

The escalator carried her upward, as monotonous and unthinking as the world around it, and she tasted the sharp scent of the white blossoms that dotted the trees around campus.

What kind of trees were they? Why had Mineko never thought to wonder that before? Did they exist anywhere else in the world or had Codism alone preserved them? If there was one upside to her people's ecological excesses, it was that they kept alive species that would otherwise be extinct.

A student walking alongside her stopped short. Mineko glanced ahead. Oh, God—what were they doing here? Two Intel agents stood where the path curved around a flowerbed, both youthful but still suitably grim and officious in their black uniforms.

The duo nodded at Mineko, and she gave them a smile that trembled on her lips. No good. She had to focus.

The main lawn, usually a place of chatter and play, was silent. A dark figure sat upon a stone wall, watching a group of students who kept a respectful distance. Everyone looked glum. Little wonder. Nothing was more frightening than seeing these creatures in the innocent heartland of Codist learning. Wherever a black uniform was sighted, it meant somebody had misbehaved, and what if that were a friend, a study partner, a tutor? Had a wrong answer been expressed in some essay, an inappropriate thought raised in a seminar?

Steeling herself, Mineko marched across the lawn. The agent on the wall looked in her direction. She knew this one—Jasmine Turani, a quiet, serious young woman who had been working her way up the ranks. She'd even earned the privilege of attending several dinners at the Tamura household.

Mineko gave a curt nod. "Hello, Jasmine."

"Good morning, Ms. Tamura." With her penetrating topaz-brown eyes, flawless copper skin, strong jaw, and regal nose, Jasmine looked—at least in Mineko's imagination—the way the stone warrior woman might if some sorcerer had brought to her life. Despite her sultry good looks, however, she was unfailingly modest and polite.

"I can't imagine why my father has you here, of all places."

"It wasn't his order, ma'am. We've been posted by Mr. Reed."

An indiscreet answer, but not unexpected. Intel agents often showed deference to Mineko, no doubt assuming it would benefit their career at some point. Today, that dynamic might work in her favor.

"Is Lachlan so determined to ensure we all study for our exams?"

Jasmine smiled. Her teeth were imperfect, which was just as well—she would have been despicably beautiful otherwise. "We're trying to be discreet."

"Well, you're a distraction here. You're intimidating the students. Look at this bare section of lawn around you."

"If they've nothing to hide, they don't need to be afraid."

Mineko's face must have shown her disdain, because Jasmine blushed. "That's a foolish response, Agent Turani. They're afraid you'll imagine indiscretions they haven't committed. A healthy, rational fear."

"Yes, Ms. Tamura."

It was fascinating. Students barely ranked higher in the Codist hierarchy than the old man sweeping the station, but Agent Turani clearly didn't see a student in front of her. She saw the girl who sat at Gaspar's right hand while drinking wine without reprimand. The daughter of the most powerful official in the Codist military. The young woman who could address Commanding Agent Reed by his first name.

"My mother would suspect you'd invented this as a cover story," said Mineko. "An excuse to come here and ogle." She pointed out a group of sweaty students chasing a football across the lawn some distance away, and Jasmine blushed deeper. "But my mother has a lurid imagination."

"It's not like that at all. I've been told to apprehend anyone matching a certain description. Infiltrators, Mr. Reed says. Revolutionaries." Jasmine adopted a resolute expression. "I'm diligently doing my job, ma'am. Duty means everything to me."

Mineko's lips twitched, but she kept her amusement constrained. "Of course it does. I'll convey to my father your commendable attitude."

"Really, would—I mean, how kind of you. May I wish you the best of luck in your upcoming exams?"

"I don't rely upon luck in my pursuit of success, agent."

At the frosty retort, Jasmine flinched, adding to Mineko's satisfaction. She was enjoying this exercise of power a little too much. But why not? She'd finally stopped caring about projecting an image of quiet humility. The tumultuous week had taken care of that.

Mineko continued on her way, leaving Jasmine to her surveillance. It seemed that, knowing Mineko to be complicit, Lachlan was using her as bait. Perhaps he sensed that a rescue operation might take place and that this would give him the opportunity to obtain fresh clues in the hunt for Lexi. Hence this pervasively menacing atmosphere, this frisson of apprehension spreading through campus at Lachlan's behest.

But Mineko was unafraid. She was a Tamura, and she would make her parents proud even as she broke their hearts. And then she would reject her birthright and be free.

CHAPTER 25

Waking up next to two gorgeous lesbians should have been the stuff of fantasy, but not this early in the day. Not when they were chattering away like two lyrical birds on a wire, just begging to be shot.

"Go back to sleep," Lexi said.

"Are we bothering you?" said Callie. "We thought you were awake."

"Why would you think that?"

"You groaned," said Riva. "We asked, 'Lexi, are you awake?' And you made a groan that sounded like a yes."

Lexi sighed and struggled upright. The grubby underground bunkroom was tiny, and each slim bunk barely fit its single occupant. "If you want to hear a groan that sounds like a yes, crawl into bed with me."

The radiator plinked. It was still blazing, its bars bright orange, and a comfortable heat filled the room. That had been Callie's idea, of course. Lexi's suggestion for keeping warm would have been a lot more fun.

"You shouldn't sleep with your makeup on," said Callie. "You look like somebody gave you two black eyes."

Tempting though it was to bludgeon Callie with a pillow, Lexi refrained for Riva's sake. She was especially pretty this morning, her Mohawk down and its pink strands swept to one side. "Did you rest well, Latour?"

Riva's mascara-smudged eyes crinkled at the corners, intensifying Lexi's urge to hug her. "Just fine. With you two here, I wasn't even a little bit scared of the dark."

"You're too cute," said Callie. "I might have to steal you from Lexi."

"She's not mine," said Lexi. "So go right ahead. Give her a passionate good-morning kiss."

Callie glanced at Riva's lips, blushed, and bounded to her feet. "Time to take a shower. I'll check on Amity too, see if she's better."

"Tell her I said good morning." Riva watched, smiling, as Callie departed the room. "And how did you sleep, Lexi?"

"I had nightmares," Lexi said. "But seeing Raffo always does that to me."

"Did you hear Callie crying last night?"

"What?" Lexi's cheerfulness evaporated. "No."

"I don't know if she was dreaming or awake, but she was definitely crying."

"Well, she did kill someone yesterday." Lexi wriggled down the bed and scooped her clothes from the floor. She took her time dressing until—zipper drawn, buttons fastened—she had no choice but to look at Riva again. "She's not a happy kid, okay? You already knew that. Don't show me that accusing face."

"I gather she doesn't have a lot of friends."

"Everyone likes Callie, but no, she doesn't have what you'd call friends. For one thing, she's not always easy to track down. She's like a stray dog. There's a few places she haunts, people pet and feed her, but you can't ever be sure where you'll find her day to day."

"A stray dog? That's an awful comparison."

"But it fits. And even though you want to adopt every stray you see, you eventually realize you can't. That's why she doesn't have close friends. It'd take too much emotional investment."

"I'd be her friend if I had the chance. Having just met you both, it's sad to think you're going to be leaving so soon."

Awkward subject. To buy time, Lexi popped a mint, sucked its coating off and chewed it into powder. A knock at the door rescued her from responding. "I'll get that."

Lexi found Raffo lurking in the corridor, his looks unimproved by sleep—assuming, of course, that he slept. "What's up, Raff?"

"You and I need to talk."

"Let me guess. Callie clogged the pipes."

"This is serious, I'm afraid."

When Raffo described something as serious, he meant it. Lexi leaned back into the room. "I've got to take a walk, babe. You going to be okay?"

"Sure." Riva faked a smile. "I'll fix breakfast."

That was one of the worst things about Lexi's chip—seeing all the unhappy emotions she had no business knowing about. "Get Callie to lend you a hand, all right?"

She rejoined Raffo in the corridor, and they set off without apparent direction. "What's the deal?" Lexi said.

"I had a phone call twenty minutes ago," Raffo said. "Rather than expect you to rely upon my own memory, I recorded it." He set a phone in Lexi's palm. "Listen, my dear, and then explain to me what the hell is going on."

Lexi tapped the screen.

"Hello?" Raffo, answering the call.

"Raffo." The deep, rhythmic voice of Samuel Brink, better known to the hapless people of Foundation as Prince Vassago. *"Where's Lexi Vale?"*

A short pause. Raffo should've known better—Vassago could read more from a pause than most people could from a full sentence.

"Raffo. You have a duty to me."

"I don't know, boss. I haven't seen her for years."

"Callie Roux's van was seen in the Rail District yesterday. I'm informed the two women are together. They didn't come to you?"

"No, boss." Raffo's reply was quicker this time, but there was no missing the tremor in his voice. "I can send some people out looking if you want."

"She's shrewd as they come. She won't go to somebody she doesn't trust completely, someone who might even be stupid enough to lie to me. And I can't think of anyone in the Rail District who fits that description but you."

Lexi glanced at Raffo. His battered face was unreadable, but—she crept inside—it was jittery concern that consumed him, not guilt. However this conversation had ended, he hadn't sold her out.

Raffo's voice piped again from the phone, hoarse with anxiety. "If I see her, my prince, what do you want me to do?"

"Tell her to get out of Foundation. The shut-ins are coming for her. Several of her friends have betrayed her already, and others are waiting on an offer. If she whines, remind her that she's one of my best investments. I don't like to see my investments put at risk."

"Tell her to leave? But boss—"

Vassago cut in. *"Has Contessa tried to contact you?"*

Shit. Lexi had forgotten about Contessa. The self-styled Queen of Foundation would flip her shit over this. She and Lexi had a special working relationship. One that Lexi wasn't expected to walk away from.

"No. Should I expect her to?"

"Yes. And I need you to lie to her just as you've lied to me."

The recorded conversation ended. Lexi passed back the phone.

An uneasy silence ensued. Raffo waddled. Lexi prowled. They glanced sidelong at each other. The silence continued. Raffo cleared his throat. Lexi adjusted her collar. Raffo licked his lips.

"How long is this fucking corridor?" Lexi pointed down its endless darkened length. "We've been walking forever."

"No idea. It's part of a maintenance grid that runs under the entire district."

Lexi stood facing him, hands in her pockets, and stared him down. "What do you want to know?"

"A crumb of truth, perhaps?" Raffo held out a cracked palm, his seven fingers bent upward. "A morsel of confidence, something to explain why our high and mighty master is shitting bricks on your behalf? If shut-ins are hunting you, why didn't you go to Vassago?"

"Raff…" Lexi probed his thoughts a little deeper. His mind was actually quite attractive—animated, vibrant, sparking with an earnest desire to help, warmed by nostalgic fondness for her. Much nicer than the exterior would suggest. "I've kept something from him."

"Like what?"

"Like the fact that I have the only working suicide chip. I'm unique, baby. A one-of-a-kind cyborg. I can't tell you what the chip really does, but when Vassago and the others find out, they'll be very pissed off."

"So you've betrayed him, is that what you're saying?"

"Not exactly. Maybe I played by my own rules, but I've still gotten him everything he wanted. There's peace in the inner districts, and I made a lot of people rich in the process."

"Yourself included."

The pointed observation gave her pause. Here was a heavily disfigured man who chose to skulk inside disused tunnels, a gangster who embraced his grotesque image because it gave him street cred. Why else had Lexi been drawn to Raffo and his crew if not because of her instinctive desire to be among misfits?

And as a forbidden cyborg, wasn't she now a pariah herself?

"Listen." Lexi took out her wallet. "I'm getting out of the city, just as Sammy wants. I know things might get a little hot around here, so take this." She peeled off half the notes she owned and forced the wad into Raffo's claw. "You might need it."

Raffo squinted through the half-light at the money. "This is more cash than we get from our business in three months." He riffled the notes. "Why give it to me?"

"You lied to him. We both know that's not easy."

"Of course I lied. He's the chief, but you and me go back further." Raffo folded the notes before tucking them into his pocket. "I can't afford to refuse this, but let's say it was for services rendered, shall we? Accommodation, garage rental, that sort of thing. My conscience winces at taking money simply for keeping my word."

"Deal." Lexi stuck out her hand. After a moment's delay, Raffo shook it. "Funny. All these years refusing to touch you, and this feels just like any other hand."

Grinning, Raffo wiped his palm on his shirt-front. "And to my horror, yours feels disgusting."

Lexi laughed. "Fuck you."

Amity pushed her plate across the plastic table. "I don't want this."

"You gotta eat." Zeke looked meek but hopeful, like a tiny animal trying to befriend its natural predator. "I know you ain't feeling so great, but you need it. Force some down."

"If I eat, I'll vomit. And I refuse to vomit."

Zeke held out a fork. "C'mon. Here comes the airplane."

Amity narrowed her eyes.

"This is ground control," said Callie. "Conditions too hazardous. Abort flight. Return immediately to the tarmac."

On the opposite side of the table, Riva and Lexi laughed, and Amity gave a grudging smile. "One bite." She allowed Zeke to put the fork in her mouth. Adorable.

Breakfast had been surprisingly enjoyable, despite the dining venue: an ancient vault filled with rusting, unidentified machine parts. After a quick investigation, Callie had deemed the scrap to be useless, though with Raffo's permission she'd pocketed a weathered cube with prongs on one side. An auto part, Callie had told them. It could have been a sex toy for all Lexi knew.

"I hope Kade made it back." Callie swung on her chair, ate from her plate and talked all at once—it was even money whether she'd choke on her food or fall over first. "Do you think he could convince Nikolas to help Min?"

Amity shook her messy blonde head. "The Commander has spoken."

"You don't have to listen to him, though, right? You could still help us."

"Don't force her to choose loyalties," said Riva. "Besides, she needs to stay by Lexi's side. And Lexi certainly can't go."

Nobody seemed inclined to disagree with that. Not even Lexi. In fact, it had begun to dawn on her just how much trouble she was in. It was one thing to have oddballs like Min and Nikolas trying to scare her out of town, but when even Vassago said it was time to run…

"So, I'm in a mood to save my ass," Lexi said. "Assuming we allow time for Callie to rescue Minnie, what's the earliest we can split?"

"You could leave Foundation today," said Amity. "It's a little earlier than we had planned, but time isn't on your side. You all need to come to a decision among yourselves."

Zeke raised his fork. "I vote for today. After that raid on my lounge, my life here is a fucking lost cause anyway."

Lexi nodded. "I'm with you."

"Works for me," said Callie. "I'll drop in at Bunker One, grab Min from the University and high-tail it back. A quick service of the van, and we're on the road by late afternoon."

"I'll come with you to the University," said Riva. "I want to help."

What little color Amity had regained drained from her face. "What?"

"I know what you're thinking. I don't have the skills you four do. I'm the weakest of us physically. But even so, I can make a difference." Riva smiled at Callie, whose mouth hung open, showcasing the last of her breakfast. "I'd hate you all to think I'm just the girl who cooks and cleans."

"I'm sorry, but no," said Amity. "I order you to come back with us."

"I told Nikolas my intentions. He said he wanted me to reconsider, but I insisted, and so he finally gave his blessing."

"I don't care what he says. You aren't going."

"Hey, don't boss her around," said Callie. "She makes her own decisions, okay? And she's coming with me."

Riva gave Callie a shy smile. Under her asymmetric pink bangs, her blue-gray irises were bright and untroubled, evoking the quiet clarity of a cloudless winter sky. "Thank you, Callie. And Amity, please don't worry about me. We'll ask Kade to join us."

"Good idea." Amity latched on to the suggestion with as much enthusiasm as Lexi had the night before. "Go to him first and explain in detail what you have in mind."

"But…" Zeke jittered in his chair, as agitated as Lexi had ever seen him. "Look, I want Min out of there too, but this is so fucking risky." He gave Callie a pleading look. "I still remember how you used to swagger into my lounge as a little kid, cheeky as all fuck. You'd hit on the women, make 'em laugh. They thought you were the most adorable fucking thing. We all did. Hell, you still are."

Callie blushed. "C'mon."

"But it's true. You'd take some junk out of your satchel, old chips and mods, and I'd give you money and a hot meal. You kept coming back. You grew older. The women stopped cooing and started swooning instead. But you never stopped being a sweetheart. The most honest smuggler I ever met. You give me a fair price, never let me down, always keep your end of a deal."

"Of course. You've always been good to me too."

"But that's not true. I've ripped you off every chance I got. I've shortchanged you on so many fucking deals, and you just shrug and trust me. And now you're going out there today, risking it all. If we lose you, I'll never get to pay you back." Zeke broke eye contact and stared at the wall. "What kind of—" His voice broke. "What kind of fucking world would this be without you in it?"

As Riva comforted Zeke and Amity awkwardly offered Callie a tissue, Lexi focused on eating the last of her breakfast. She'd lost her appetite, but she couldn't look these people in the eyes right now. Not if she wanted to maintain her tough reputation.

Raffo flicked through a set of keys while Lexi and her crew suffered the freezing air. The high, skewed walls of the alley blocked the morning sun, and frost sprouted from the weeds that wound through the brickwork. In her big black coat, Amity seemed unaffected by the cold, while at the other extreme, Callie hopped from boot to boot, bare legs bristling with gooseflesh.

"Here it is." Raffo flourished a small key. "And may I say, it's been a pleasure having you."

"The pleasure was unexpectedly mutual," said Amity. "You may be an amoral gangster, but you have a very civil manner."

"And you may be a sanctimonious Open Hand stiff, but you have very persuasive friends." Raffo inserted the key in the lock. "Damn thing always sticks. Give me a second to get the door open."

The man waiting behind the garage door held a shotgun. "Hi," he said, pointing the gun at Lexi. "Don't move."

Two more figures emerged from the darkened garage. One was a leather-clad, motorcycle-booted, shaven-headed ugly bastard wielding a semi-automatic. The other...

Well, how about that. It was that oily fucker the Viper, his face twisted in what he probably believed was a tough-guy smirk.

"How long were you waiting in there?" said Raffo.

"Too fucking long." The Viper flourished a chipped samurai sword. "You want to keep out of this, Raff. Ooze back into your hole."

He whistled. Four more armed gangsters emerged into the alley behind them. One loomed above the others—that hulking moron, the Squid.

Raffo stared at the approaching thugs. "Is the Zookeeper really so desperate that he'd make war on Vassago?"

"Well, his name *is* the Zookeeper," said Zeke. "Not the mark of a guy with good judgement."

The Viper scowled. "Watch your mouth. You're the Zeke who runs the body-modder lounge, aren't you?"

"Nah, that's some other Zeke. I'm the Zeke that fucks your mother."

Lexi snickered. "Take the Taipan seriously. He's a real bad man."

"It's the fucking Viper!" The Viper growled. "You know that. Don't fuck around." He paced while tapping the blade against his palm. "You're coming with us, Lexi. We need you for a trade."

"You loser." Callie sneered at the Viper, who sneered right back. "Working for the shut-ins. How pathetic can you get?"

"Fuck off, Roux. We've got to pay up to some guy called Reed. Otherwise, the boss says, our ass is mincemeat."

"Your collective ass?" said Lexi. "Or your ass, singular?"

"I ain't fucking singular. Who the fuck told you that? I got a girlfriend. You saw her."

The gangsters in the alley menaced their way closer, the Squid lumbering at their head, while the Viper continued to pace. Raffo and Riva seemed terrified, Callie looked pissed, Amity remained calm, and Zeke...well, like Lexi, he was having trouble keeping a straight face.

"Do you know who we are?" said Amity, toneless.

"Uh, let's see. Callie Roux. That Zeke guy. Raffo the Mutant. Lexi Vale. Pink-Hair Girl. Trench-Coat Bitch. Is that right? Did I get that right?"

"I'm Amity White."

"Oh," a gangster said, very softly.

The Viper glanced at the Squid. "That mean anything to you?"

"I think she's the psycho Open Hand enforcer." The Squid eyed Amity with evident respect. "Their best heavy. She's the one who took out the Inferno last fall."

"Shit, you were the one who iced Inferno?" said Lexi. "He was over four hundred pounds of muscle. I always assumed he overdosed on roids."

"Fine, whatever," said the Viper. "If she's going to cause trouble, just shoot her now. Jesus. We're not some fucking supervillains that've got to talk this shit to death first." He stopped pacing and leaned against the van.

"Hey!" The way Callie exploded, the Viper might as well have taken out a photo of Mineko and pissed on it. "Don't touch my fucking wheels."

"They're nice, aren't they? Can't wait to get the keys off you."

Callie stormed into the garage and shoved the Viper hard against the van. The gunmen switched their aim, but if Callie noticed, she didn't seem to care. "Like hell you'll get my fucking keys."

"Don't touch me, you fucking dyke." The Viper pushed Callie back. "Was your ass always so fucking big, or have you been comfort eating?"

"You dumb fuck. Your name isn't even the Viper. It's Ralph Jackson, and you once got so drunk at a bar you shit yourself in front of everyone."

"Back the fuck off, Roux. I don't want to have to kill you. It'd be bad for my reputation."

"What reputation?" said Zeke. "You mean the one you have for shitting your pants?"

The Viper snarled. "That's enough. Next person says anything, they're dead, okay? You're all disposable. Even Lexi fucking Vale."

"Idiot," said Amity. "Kill her, and the Codists will come for you next."

The Squid cracked his knuckles. "Let me take a shot at White. Everyone knows she's a bad motherfucker. If I take her clean, it'll be good for my rep."

The Viper nodded. "If you want. But don't take too long about it."

The Squid's stupid face contorted into an even stupider grin. "I heard they call her the Bloody Hand, because when she kills a man, she puts her hand in his blood and leaves a palm print on the nearest wall."

"I don't remember ever doing that," Amity said. "But it's a compelling idea, so perhaps I should adopt it. I'll start with you."

"Please, stop," Riva said. "There has to be a better resolution to this."

"I agree," said Raffo. "Vassago will know it was you boys behind this. The only way you can come out alive is to tell your boss Lexi wasn't here."

"Shut your ugly mouth." The Viper smirked. "Worst thing your gang could do is breathe on us. Squid, hurry the fuck up."

The Squid shambled over to Amity, looked her up and down, and grinned. "Just hand-to-hand, okay? No guns." He patted the pistol on his hip. "That means I won't use this."

Amity stared at him with contempt. "I understood what you meant, you troglodyte."

The gangsters formed a curious semi-circle, jostling for the best view. "Get the bastard," said Zeke, as enthusiastic as if he were Amity's hype man. "Fuck him up, Ammie!"

The Squid closed in, his fist shaped into a wrecking hammer. He might as well have tried to punch a waterfall. Amity slipped the blow and, with a violent burst of speed, drove her elbow into the Squid's solar plexus.

The gangsters released a sympathetic groan. "Jesus," said Zeke.

The Squid wheezed and pawed the air. Amity's right hook burst open his left eyelid. He roared, only to be silenced by an elbow strike to the face—a sickening crack. Then a wet moan as blood gushed into his mouth, pouring down his chin like scarlet vomit.

"Fuck!" said the Viper. "Squid, are you okay?"

The Squid growled, lurched, and grappled Amity in a bear hug. She reached for his hip and took the handle of his pistol.

"Riva, Zeke, get down," said Lexi. "Get—"

Amity drew the gun and fired.

The gangster holding the shotgun dropped, his face a bloody hole. A second later, the semi-automatic rattled. Amity turned her living shield, and the Squid's jacket wept blood while his body convulsed beneath the impact of countless bullets.

Callie pounced like a wildcat. Her snap kick knocked the sword clean from the Viper's grip. He fumbled for his pistol. Before he could free it from its holster, Callie swept his feet out from under him. He yelped. Tumbled to the cement.

Gangsters scrambled. Gunfire popped. Zeke leapt at Riva, covering her as he brought them both to the ground. Somebody shouted. A knife flashed. The Squid fell, still twitching.

Amity snarled. Whirled on a second opponent. The Viper tried to stand. Callie smacked him in the face, sending him back onto his ass. A gangster trained a pistol on her.

Shit. Callie's back was turned. She hadn't seen it.

"Callie!" Lexi rushed at the gunman, who spun and fired. Her torso twisted, an unconscious reflex. Something whistled by her cheek.

Lexi charged onward, caught the gangster's face in her palm, drove him hard against the wall of the alley, and smashed his head into the bricks as she gouged out the contents of his mind.

The hollowed gangster went limp. His gun smoked in his hand. Shit, she'd dodged a fucking bullet...

"Riva!" Callie. Screaming.

Lexi spun. A weedy, machete-waving gangster loomed over Riva. She huddled, hands over her head. Callie was struggling to reach her, but the Viper had seized her by the ankle.

The gangster raised the machete. Lexi's next heartbeat drove through her like a rail spike. Callie shrieked again. Amity shouted. Lexi moved, but she was too far away...

A long piece of metal in hand, Zeke stepped up to the gangster and, to the sound of iron striking bone, drove the teeth from his head. The man landed face down amid a spatter of blood.

"Shit." Zeke stared at the gore-soaked clump of hair clinging to the metal bar. "That's sick."

Callie limped over to Riva. Helped her up. Which was nice, but it meant nobody was watching that son of a bitch behind them...

"Hey, you fucks." To put it poetically, the Viper looked like shit. Crimson trickled from one nostril, his chin was smeared with blood, and a purple bruise puffed his temple. Callie had really worked the bastard over.

If only she'd killed him. The Viper held Raffo at gunpoint, the pistol pushing so deep it indented his cheek. "Give up or I shoot the mutant."

"Ignore the little bastard," Raffo said. "Do what you have to."

Besides the Viper, there were three gangsters still standing: the asshole with the semi-automatic and two of the thugs who had come into the alley with the Squid. One held a knife, the other a pistol.

"This sucks." Zeke adjusted his grip on the bloody iron rod. "You assholes made me kill someone. I never killed anyone before."

"Don't worry," said the Viper. "Your pangs of conscience will ease once I fucking add you to the body count. You bunch of fucking queers. Two dykes and a faggot. The shut-ins have the right idea about you people."

Lexi opened her mouth, but Callie was quicker. "You shut the hell up."

"Callie Roux, you stupid fucking whore. Everyone laughed when they heard that Lexi screwed your girl. She was pretty, that one. I bet she looked even prettier with her face buried in Lexi's pussy." The Viper leered. "Or maybe the rumors are true, and she was choking down Lexi's dick. Is that how it is, Lexi? Are you a fucking tranny? Do you have to tuck when you get into those tight jeans of yours?"

"Yeah, I do," said Lexi. "You have a problem with that?"

"Problem?" The Viper wiped the blood from his chin. "Nah. I already knew you were a sick freak. This just clinches it."

"Don't you dare talk to her like that," Callie said. "The only freaks around here are you and your chickenshit friends."

"Ignore him," said Lexi. "He's dead already. His boss sent him because he's a natural fuck-up, a perfect scapegoat."

"Bullshit." The Viper wore a spasmodic grin, but he was sweating anxiety. The other gangsters were just as nervous, their emotions bare as they struggled to comprehend the dead friends at their feet. "I'm in for a promotion."

"Nah, you're fucked. If you kill me, your boss gives you to the shut-ins by way of an apology. If you take me alive, he gives you to Vassago as a peace offering. Like I said. Scapegoat. At least it fits your dumb animal theme."

"Fuck you! You killed Squid. You killed Tarantula. You even took out Yellowjacket, and he was just a newbie. You're dead, Vale. Reprisal. Even Prince Vassago can't say shit when it's about reprisal."

Lexi probed the remaining gangsters. The nearest was a wreck, his mind a churning cauldron of fear and anger. The young thug beside him could barely keep a grip on his pistol. And the third wasn't even listening to any of this—he was staring at the blood…

"Reprisal?" Lexi smiled. "You really want to play that game, Anaconda?"

"Don't fucking smile. I'm this close to blowing Raff's head off."

"I'm a sick freak. Why would I care?"

"I'm serious." The Viper's face glistened beneath a sudden outbreak of sweat. "I'm done being laughed at, you fucking queer."

Lexi closed her eyes. "So am I."

She reached out. The hum of their minds returned. Memories tarnished and seedy, yet sometimes startlingly pure. Fighting, fucking, taking drugs that ran wild through the bloodstream, broken glass on rain-slicked asphalt, lights pulsing in the hearts of clubs, women screaming and begging. Slamming cartridges into guns, oiling knives, making deals in alleys. Soft bags of powder. Money, beautiful fucking money. A mouth wrapped around a dick. The rewards of power.

A guttural drone of thoughts. *I know this bar where you can't even move for pussy... The bitch cheated on me... Cut his fucking throat... We're going tonight so bring your sawn-off... Hotwire that bitch, it's on... We got the junk, we got all the shit...*

Heads like hives, teeming with impulses. *He's dead, she killed him, he owed me twenty fucking dollars.* Bodies clammy with sweat. Nostrils choked with the stench of blood. *We're supposed to take this bitch back alive, who the hell put Viper in charge...*

Her vision darkened. Their minds receded into single points. Candles of dumb meat with fragile wicks. Three screaming flames.

Lexi puffed them out.

In the same instant, the gangsters dropped. Sprawled limbs, blank faces. Even Amity looked horrified, while Raffo swallowed air like a goldfish.

"This is my district. I grew up on these streets." Lexi swaggered toward the trembling Viper. Her head was clear. Her heart felt still. "I'd give anyone a beating, no matter how big they were, no matter how mean their gang was. Over time, people learned not to fuck with me and mine. Now, dumb prick that you are, you come here and threaten five of my friends all at once."

"I'm sorry." The Viper released Raffo, who scrambled to the cover of a garbage skip. "I didn't mean any of the things I just said. I was only trash-talking. You know how it is..."

"Snakes slither on their bellies. They're cold-blooded, creepy fuckers. Why the hell would you pick the name of a fucking snake?"

"You know why. Vipers are lethal. One bite and you're dead." The Viper was sweating fear, rivulets of mortal dread.

"No, they're weak. They hunt little things. Rodents. Other snakes. Even the meanest serpent is prey for something bigger, and you're about to learn where you rank on the food chain."

"Please, Lexi. I'll tell you anything. I'll sell out the boss, anything, just don't hurt me. I couldn't tell him no. Don't hurt me..."

"I'm not going to hurt you. I need you to take a message home." Lexi leaned closer still. With a bit of luck, in this gloom, the Viper would be able to see the ghostly light deep in her irises. "Tell the Zookeeper that if he fucks with my friends again, I'll introduce him to the principle of natural selection."

The Viper fled more like a rabbit than a snake, cowering as if expecting Lexi to suck out his soul at any second. Zeke spat in the direction he'd ran.

"Well, shit," said Raffo. "So this is what you were hiding from Vassago."

Amity strode through the carnage. "How did you do that? You said you had to look into their eyes. You certainly didn't tell me you could reach multiple people at once."

"I never tried it before." With her boot, Lexi prodded one of the limp gangsters. "They came here expecting to kick ass. Instead, they watched their friends die. It made them vulnerable. The rest was just me pushing where I hadn't yet dared to go."

"I saw it, but I still can't believe it." Callie had one arm around Riva, who still seemed dazed. "To be honest, it scares me a little."

"You and me both, babe. Raff, you need to clear out. Get your gang somewhere safe."

"I'm staying put until I see you drive out," said Raffo. "But I will call some of my boys to come up. For one thing, free guns."

"Hey, Lex." Zeke was crouched by a fallen, bloodied gangster. The man's chest was moving, but in a feeble way that suggested it wouldn't keep doing so for much longer. "Can we take this guy back with us? I might be able to save him."

Lexi nodded. "Let's get going. Riva, front seat, and stay close to Callie. Amity, you help Zeke with the patient."

"Why?" Amity grimaced. "We don't have time for this."

"Because we're all comrades. Lesson of the day."

On her way to the van, Lexi stepped over a body and hesitated. She'd seen a lot of grisly scenes, but this one had the unique distinction of being mostly her own handiwork. The city's gang lords valued her negotiating skills, but things would change the moment they understood how powerful she truly was. Vassago didn't enjoy having rivals.

She touched Callie on the forearm. "Take me far from here, okay?"

Callie smiled back. "You got it."

CHAPTER 26

At seven a.m, the last paragraph clattered into place. Kade sent the file to the printer. It howled a garbled electronic screech. Paper jam.

As he fumbled inside the machine, yanking torn strips from a hungry roller mouth that resisted all attempts at paper liberation, it struck him as absurd that despite astounding human inventions—Project Sky, for Christ's sake—printer technology hadn't changed in over a hundred years. In fact, printers were at risk of extinction. The *Gazette* had once owned two, but the other had perished while jetting precious ink like arterial fluid. Sarabelle had wept as if it were her own child.

"Damn it." Kade pulled again on the trapped page. "Come on."

Goldie sat upright, ears quivering, and released an immense bark. Tensed for trouble, Kade opened his desk drawer and took out his revolver. It was either that or the stapler, and at least the revolver was loaded.

"Hey!" Callie bounded into view, taking the stairs two at a time. Riva descended with more decorum behind her.

His tail thrashing, Goldie hurtled across the room and buried his nose in Callie's groin. She laughed as she patted his flanks. "Look at you, you giant silly thing! What's your name, friendly fellow?"

"Goldie," said Kade, returning the revolver to the drawer.

"Goldie! You're a big old Goldie, that's what you are!" Callie crouched and treated Goldstein to a barrage of affectionate thumps and pats. He gave a joyful whine and placed a paw on her shoulder.

"I suppose you can guess why we're here," said Riva.

"Yes, I can," said Kade. "Though I expected Lexi rather than you."

"I'm her stunt double, remember?"

Callie looked up, giving Goldie an opening to lick her cheek. "We want to see Min. Can you get us into the University again?"

"It's easy enough under normal circumstances," Kade said. "But the codes will have changed, and they may have agents watching the entrances. We have to assume Lachlan has anticipated this."

"So you won't help us?"

"Just the opposite. You need my help more than ever. So let's figure out a way to proceed." Kade frowned at Riva. Even with her Mohawk down, she looked an unlikely infiltrator. He'd need to find a way to discourage her before matters became too serious. "This is very dangerous, comrade, and I doubt you have much field experience."

"Don't you start," said Callie. "Riva's already proved she's plenty tough."

For now, it was easier to play along. "Then let's discuss logistics. It's exam time, so Mineko won't have classes. The first place to look is her room, but realistically, she could be anywhere on campus. "

"Can I use my disguise from last time? It suited me."

"I have a superstition about wearing the same disguise twice. You two could pass for students. Being a little older, I'd be better off as a lecturer."

Kade opened the cupboard that contained the *Gazette*'s collection of stolen uniforms. He passed the women a pair of dark blue overalls before taking a teal-colored lecturer's uniform for himself. "Just put them on over your clothes. They're very loose-fitting."

Riva knelt to unzip her boots. Goldie trotted over and stuck his nose in her ear. She giggled. "Callie, call him off."

"Goldie!" Callie clapped her hands, and Goldie dropped to his haunches and gazed at her in adoration. "That's a good boy."

"I'm surprised you don't keep a dog," said Kade. "Something to guard your salvage."

"Dogs don't live long out my way. Either they get injured and die, or something wild takes them. And plenty of wild things walk on two legs."

"Port Venn might be different," said Riva. "You could get a puppy there."

"Maybe. I'd love to have my own little pup." Callie kicked off her left boot, and Goldie sniffed it. "You are coming with us, right?"

"Um." Riva began to remove her facial piercings. "As much as I might like to, I'm not sure Lexi would want me along."

"Who cares? I want you to come, isn't that enough? You'd always have a place with me."

Riva gave her a stern look. "You shouldn't make promises to people you barely know."

"I know you well enough." Callie wrestled her way into the student uniform. "Anyway, I think Lexi would let you follow her anywhere. What do you think, Kade?"

The question set Kade itching for a beer, but he managed to resist the call of the fridge. "Where you go in this world shouldn't be decided on the basis of how she feels. I learned that lesson many years ago."

"It's hard to have found her, only to lose her," Riva said. "But it'll hurt so much more to follow her and then be pushed away."

"Don't take her attitude too seriously. She's not as superior as she wants you to think, but she's a better person than she'd like you to believe."

Riva grimaced as she buttoned up her stolen uniform. "It's ironic. We spend our whole lives trying to find an authentic way to live, yet we always seem to be forced into some new disguise or other."

Words that could have easily been his own, spoken with a measure of despair he understood too well. If only Kade dared to tell her the truth, so she could understand that nobody was brave enough to walk through this world entirely naked of deceptions.

Not even Lexi Vale.

Parked in an alley offering a view of the University's eastern wall, they sat in the back of the van while passing a printed schematic between them.

Riva inspected the page before handing it to Callie, who subjected it to much closer scrutiny. "I count eleven entry points," she said. "How many do you think he'll have covered?"

"Agents work in squads of three," said Kade. "Lachlan wouldn't involve more than two squads, for fear of drawing rebuke from his boss, so let's assume he has about six agents on the inside."

"Okay. And he's not going to have them all stand at doorways, because that'd be dumb. He'd put some in central areas." Callie prodded the blueprint. "Like this open section."

"The campus lawn. It offers line of sight to all three major school buildings."

"Science, Medicine, and Politics."

"Right. By the way, if anyone asks, you study Mechanical Engineering. Riva, you're doing a major in Family Ethics."

Riva stuck out her tongue. "Nasty."

"And I'm a lecturer in Environmental Politics. Don't be afraid to bullshit. Remember, Codists are deferential by nature. They're taught that people outside the wall are primitive, savage simpletons, so they'll never believe for a moment you might be an outsider."

Callie held the blueprint to the light. "Some of these entry points are too convenient. These two near Min's dorm, for example. There's no way Reed will leave those unguarded. And this one here opens into the back streets, which would make it perfect for a getaway. He'll cover it for sure."

"I'm suppose you're right."

"You know I am. Now, clear something up for me. You said you don't wear the same uniform twice."

"Not if I can help it."

"I bet you have a similar superstition about breaking in through the same door twice."

Kade nodded. "Got me there."

"You seem to know Reed inside and out. My hunch is, he feels the same way about you. Probably prides himself on it. And he'll tell himself, 'I can't know exactly how Kade will get in, but I do know one thing for sure. He never uses the same door twice.'"

Callie circled an entrance point with her finger. "The door we entered by last time. He won't put a guard there."

It was remarkable to see Callie in her element—confident, mature, and completely focused on her task. "Maybe," he said.

"Count on it." Callie tapped the thick black line that demarcated the enclave wall. "Why aren't there security cameras on the perimeter?"

"The Code forbids the use of security cameras within enclaves."

"Really?" said Riva. "I thought they were a surveillance society."

"In a sense. But Codists can't spy on other Codists without it seeming grossly hypocritical. Their doctrine champions blind trust."

Callie frowned. "But what does Min's dad do if not spy on people?"

"Code Intel collects data and monitors suspicious behavior. But camera networks are both indiscriminate and indiscreet. Even if you automate them, many kinds of middlemen are involved—architects, electricians, maintenance people. You can't necessarily control who has access to footage or who gets watched. That's why Code Intel relies on human agents as its eyes and ears."

"How do you know all this stuff?"

Kade gave a rueful smile. "Traitor or not, Lachlan told me things about the Codists I would never have learned anywhere else. He once admitted that there's

almost nothing to stop the enclaves being raided. These walls are potent symbols
of impenetrability, but there are plenty of explosives capable of breaching them.
He was immensely curious why Nikolas and the others had never tried it."

"The Codist military," said Riva. "They number in the thousands."

"Sure. But they're stationed on the outskirts, ready to stop Foundation from
being invaded by the coastal republics or the Port Venn junta. It'd be simple for a
lone revolutionary to assassinate one or more members of the Committee before
being stopped. Lachlan once said that we ought to arm Amity to the teeth and send
her in. I thought it was funny at the time. Now I'm not sure he wasn't trying to
drop a hint on me."

Callie held out a battered backpack. "Is it okay if I wear this?

"That's fine. It looks a little rougher than the nice satchels the students have,
but you're an engineering major, after all. There is something I'm worried about,
however. Riva, I think you already know what it is."

Her guilty look was confirmation. "My hair," she said.

Callie stared at Riva's head of pink hair. The fallen Mohawk concealed some
of her shave, but she was still visibly clipped almost to the scalp. Certainly not a
style in vogue among Codists.

"She can wear a cap," Callie said. "I wore mine last time."

"A cap's not going to cover that," Kade said.

Riva took a deep breath. "I could shave it all off."

"Hell no," said Callie. "You're not giving up your gorgeous 'hawk on my watch.
Lexi would kill me." She dragged a plastic box from the surrounding clutter. "I'm
a smuggler, remember? I carry disguises."

Well, shit. Kade tried not to look dismayed as Callie held up a shoulder-length
black wig. "I'm not sure that would be convincing," he said.

"It's a good wig, and you yourself said that shut-ins are mostly dumb."

Riva gathered up a handful of the hanging tresses. "This is funny. I swore I'd
never wear one of these."

"You swore never to wear a wig? Why?"

"Reasons." Riva flashed a cryptic smile. "Just promise not to laugh at me."

"Funny you say that. My ex was the last person to wear this wig. The girl the
Viper was talking about." Callie turned the hairpiece in her hands, smoothing the
glossy strands. "She put it on as a joke, and I giggled until my chest hurt. It didn't
even look strange or anything. It was just the way she did it. She always knew how
to make me laugh."

This conversation didn't seem intended for Kade. He set the blueprint on his knees and feigned studying it.

"I'm sorry you had to listen to that Viper asshole," Riva said. "He really was a disgusting person."

"Not so long ago, his words would have hurt. But things have changed." Callie wound the wig's black hairs around her finger. "When my ex broke my heart, I figured I'd let it stay broken. If someone that kind and funny could hurt me so bad, then anyone could, right? But then I stumbled into a girl so sweet, generous, and beautiful, I'm starting to think I could risk anything for her."

Riva smiled. "We'll get Min out of there. Don't worry."

"Sure. Right." Callie blushed and glanced at Kade, who quickly looked away. "Let's get this wig on you…"

⁓

The University's wall dwarfed every other structure in the district, and the trio walked in silence beneath its shadow. After a few minutes, they arrived at the maintenance entrance, a nondescript steel door within a shallow alcove.

Callie pointed to a steel box inside the alcove. "So the keypad is under that hinged cover?"

"That's right. It's not locked, though. You can just flip it up."

"Forget that." Callie dug into her satchel and emerged with a pair of thick gloves and a standard screwdriver. "I'm going to take the whole thing to pieces. Better safe than sorry."

"You're certain you won't break it?"

Callie gave Kade a long, level look. "Please."

She jammed the screwdriver into the gap between the box and the wall. "Just gotta pry this off, and… See, there's the screws, hidden behind this strip of metal. If there's a monitoring circuit, I'll bypass it. Then I'll overload the security circuit and the door will pop open. All shut-in doors default to open when a security circuit is jammed."

With fascinated eyes, Riva watched over Callie's shoulder. She looked conventionally beautiful now, with her piercings removed and her features softened by straight black bangs and luxurious locks that seemed a natural complement to her olive-brown skin.

"Somebody should watch our backs," said Callie. "Would you mind, chickadee?"

"No problem." Riva walked some distance from the alcove and stood looking up and down the street. In her uniform and wig, she appeared every bit a Codist. Lexi would have been heartbroken to see it.

"Come over here." Callie beckoned to Kade, and he moved deeper into the alcove, wedging himself between the control panel and the door. "You're a prick, you know that? There's no way in hell you didn't think of her hair when we were back at the *Gazette*."

Damn it. He'd thought he'd gotten away with it. "Callie, I—"

"You kept quiet because you wanted to spring the problem on her late. Scare her into changing her mind at the last minute. Admit it."

"It's true, yes, but you can't blame me for trying. Lexi told me to look out for her. Letting her go into an enclave is in direct contradiction to that promise."

"You're all so stupid." Callie eased the box from the wall, exposing a panel covered in electronics. "Everyone treats her like she's made of glass, and it pisses her off. She'll never say so, but it does."

"How did you get so good at reading people?"

"I don't understand all people, Kade. Just the ones who are like me." Callie chipped away at a soldered board. "Staying strong means taking chances. Otherwise we forget what we're capable of. When I'm on a bike, I don't ride fast because I want to die. I do it to prove to myself that if I ever need to fly, nobody will be able to stop me."

"Do you have any idea how unique you are?"

"Unique is just another word for lonely, isn't it? Now stand back. I'm going to connect this battery to the terminals."

The circuit sparked beneath Callie's gloved fingers. An acrid smell choked the alcove, accompanied by gouts of smoke. A second later, the door hissed into the wall, moving smoothly along a narrow track carved through the brick. Behind was a short tunnel.

"Safety regulations," said Kade. "Proof the Codists aren't all bad."

"Riva!" Callie waved, and Riva rejoined them. "Check it out."

"You're so clever." Riva admired the blackened circuits. "Where would we be without you?"

Callie dimpled. "Stuck waiting for a ride, that's where." Shouldering the satchel, she set off down the tunnel.

It was cool inside the hollowed brick. Dust coated the floor, a fine layer marked with footprints and trails indicating where items had been dragged or wheeled.

The overhead bulbs were dim. If not for the wedge of sunlight behind them, it would have been hard not to feel entombed.

Steel steps rose to a tarnished metal door. Callie opened it with a nudge of her boot. A fragrant rush of air carried the sound of conversation and laughter. "Oh my God," said Riva. "It's beautiful."

From this elevated section of campus, almost everything in the enclave was visible—trees clustered around dormitories, the high white towers of the Politics building, the golden dome atop Medicine, glimpses of lakes and fountains joined by intricate pathways, blue-uniformed students strolling through the scenic landscape...

"Those are the three school buildings." Kade indicated Politics, Medicine, and Science one after another. "That's the elite dorm over there, in that clearing." He gestured to a four-story building that rose above an encircling barrier of white-blossomed trees.

Riva shaded her eyes as she looked down the hill toward a group of students playing football. "Do they know how lucky they are?"

"They're taught from an early age that they're lucky, but they don't understand what that truly means. Privilege is just a word to them."

"And you think Min is willing to leave all this behind?"

"Sure," said Callie. "What's the point of a beautiful world if you can't ever be happy in it?"

"How perverse. A paradise built for a society forbidden to enjoy it."

Kade hadn't yet stepped from the shadow of the wall. It was hard not to feel exposed here, even though none of the students below seemed to be paying any attention.

"Let's go join our fellow utopians," he said. "Just keep an eye open for anyone in black."

They didn't make it far.

Two agents cut across a lawn with a determined stride. It soon became apparent that neither was interested in Riva, who continued to walk down the path unimpeded.

Callie wasn't so fortunate.

"Student, please stop for a moment." The agent was young, maybe early twenties, but his pale face was stern. "May I see inside your satchel?"

"My satchel?" Callie looked convincingly puzzled. "Why?"

"A precaution."

"Excuse me," said Kade. "What's going on here?"

The other agent, a dark-complexioned girl with iridescent green eyes, glared at him. "Don't get involved, please."

"This student is attending my next exam preparation seminar. You'll be delaying everyone."

"We won't take long. Student, the satchel."

Callie shrugged off the backpack. The first agent took it from her and glanced inside. His forehead furrowed.

"What's this?" He flourished a battered yellow device trailing two leads.

"Multimeter," said Callie.

Kade slipped his hand inside his pocket. The revolver was concealed within its baggy depths, safety engaged but fully loaded. "This seems a waste of your valuable time, agents."

"We'll be the judge of that," said the green-eyed young agent. As she spoke, she studied Kade closely.

The man took a set of tools from Callie's backpack. "Explain this, please."

"I study mechanical engineering."

"These look like lockpicks. Why would you need lockpicks?"

"To open locks."

Riva had stopped some distance ahead, sheltered by a blossoming branch overhanging the path. Kade shook his head at her as subtly as he could. Riva didn't move. Kade motioned with a little more urgency, and Riva resumed walking until she was out of sight.

"Turani," said the young man. "Do students need lockpicks?"

"I don't know," said the girl. "I think we should call this in."

There was a moment of silence, broken by the shrilling of a bird in the trees above—a harsh, penetrating double-whistle. The agent licked his lips slowly. "You think it's them?"

Callie yanked back her satchel, and the young man grunted as he instinctively gripped its straps. While he reeled off-balance, Callie shoved him in the chest, and he fell on his ass with a startled yelp.

Kade drew his revolver and flicked back the safety. "Don't move."

Ignoring him, Turani reached for her gun. Kade fired a single shot into the air. Several nearby students screamed, and the young agent on the ground cringed and covered his ears.

Impressively, Turani barely flinched, but she stopped short of drawing her own weapon. Instead, she raised her empty hands.

"Shit," said Callie. "What do we do now?"

"First, take her gun," said Kade. Callie took the pistol from Turani's holster. "Talk to me, agent. Lachlan is on campus, isn't he?"

Turani didn't respond.

"You," Kade said to the other agent. "Find your boss and tell him we have an agent hostage. He already knows my terms."

The young man scrambled upright and sprinted across the lawn. Callie gave Kade an uncertain look. "What's the idea?"

"We're buying time. Keep that gun pointed at Agent Turani here while we move to a defensible location." Kade singled out the long flagstone avenue that ended below the Medical building. "Move this way."

Turani glowered at him. "You're Kade August. *Revolutionary Gazette*. Aren't you afraid of Commanding Agent Reed?"

Kade held her accusing gaze. Despite her defiant attitude, she was surely too young to be completely indoctrinated. "I'm not afraid of him, no. But *you* are. Tell me, don't you ever get tired of living in fear?"

No reply, just the sullen silence he'd expected.

"Time to go," he said. "Callie, keep her covered."

Callie bit her lip. "But—"

"Uh-uh." Kade raised his finger, and she fell silent. "Don't worry about that. Things will work out."

Of course, he had no way of knowing that to be true. He'd failed his promise to Lexi. Riva Latour was now on her own.

CHAPTER 27

Lexi lay on her bunk while trying to find pictures in the cracks and stains on the ceiling. Unfortunately, her imagination had flagged, and they looked like so many cracks and stains to her. Except for the blotch in the corner that looked like a spider, but there was a decent chance it actually was a spider, so it hardly counted.

An aggressive series of knocks jolted her back to reality.

"Come in." The door inched open. "Hey, hot stuff."

Amity sidled into the room and closed the door. "Zeke sent me to ask about your wellbeing."

"He sent you? Why didn't he come himself?"

"Because he was afraid that you might bite his head off."

"And get spikes in the roof of my mouth? No thanks."

The mattress sagged as Amity seated herself at its furthest end. She cupped her head in her hands. "Nikolas was also concerned about you."

"Fuck him. He could at least have given Callie a machine gun." Lexi sighed and sprawled back. "It's stupid, you staying here to guard me. As if Lockie is going to bust out of a cupboard and snatch the chip right from my throbbing brain."

"Do you trust Callie to take care of Riva?"

"Sure, I trust her. But the truth is, I'm worried about her too. The silly little smuggler thinks she's an action hero."

"She handled herself well this morning."

"Yeah, but Lockie would still eat her whole. I've glimpsed a lot of minds in my time. Criminals. Psychopaths. Murderers. I even know what it's like inside Vassago, all twists and turns." Lexi closed her eyes, remembering. "Reed's like that, but worse. That fucker chased me out of his head. Nobody has ever done that to me before."

"He's an unusual creature. He came to Sarabelle, Kade's editor, around ten years ago, and claimed to have escaped from an enclave. He identified as a former member of Code Intel who'd been monitoring the *Gazette* and had been convinced by its oratory. He was persuasive. Charming. Deception is his gift. So they believed him."

Intrigued, Lexi wriggled down the bed. "How long did he keep the act up?"

"Three years. He and Kade became friendly enough that Ash grew quite jealous. I never liked him, but I understand why Kade did. Reed considers himself a political moderate, and moderates have a weakness for timidity veiled as cynicism."

"You read a lot, don't you?"

"We all do down here. Education transforms us. And nobody was more educated than Reed. He knew Codism inside and out, and he made it seem absurd, something we could laugh at. It gave him a reputation as a morbid jester, somebody incapable of taking human suffering seriously, but he also wrote and spoke very well. He was witty. Incisive."

"In other words, an asshole."

"Some people would say the same about you." Amity smiled, a sight Lexi would never get used to. "Kade defended Reed to the last. And it was Kade who persuaded us to protect you. That's the kind of man he is. He lost his lover, his closest friend betrayed him, you abandoned him, yet he never gave up hope in humanity. He's the most honest person I know."

"I felt that way about him once. I even trusted him with my cousin." Lexi couldn't keep the emotion from her voice, though whether it was anger or grief, even she couldn't tell. "You know how that ended."

"That isn't his fault and you know it. Apportion blame where it belongs." Amity laid a hand on Lexi's wrist. "Talk about the living. Tell me about Riva. I don't fully understand her, but she tells me that you do."

"I can't talk for her. Only for myself."

"Then tell me why it is that you understand."

How ironic—Amity had unwittingly taken their conversation back to the subject they'd just abandoned. But what did it matter now? More likely than not, after today, Lexi would never see Amity again.

"I was once close to a trans man," Lexi said. "Closer than I've ever been to anyone. And whenever he was called a woman, it hurt him in ways I couldn't bear to watch." Tears were suddenly on her cheeks, salting her lips. "I would have done anything to spare him that."

"What happened to him?"

"I guess you might say we failed each other."

Amity's green eyes, usually so steely, took on a softer light. She stroked the back of Lexi's hand. "I'm sorry."

"I have my own secret. Something I've only told a few people. Including that stupid fucking Zeke. Another best friend who let me down."

"He seems to be remorseful. Perhaps you should consider forgiving him."
Amity hesitated. "May I ask what your secret is?"

"It won't make sense to you. Even so, I'll tell you anyway." Lexi fumbled for
Amity's fingers and squeezed them. "I don't think I'm a woman or a man. I'm just
Lexi. But there's no way to express that. People see a butch woman or, sometimes,
a pretty man. You can't get them to see outside that binary. Not when they're wired
to think it has to be one or the other."

"You're right. I don't understand, though I wish I did. You know, I once offered
to help Riva obtain surgery. She refused. Yet most of her personal disappointments
seem to have resulted from the…" Amity looked away. "The male part of her
anatomy."

"It's not the male part of her. There isn't a part of her that isn't female, okay?
Even her fucking Y-chromosome is female."

"I'm sorry. I didn't mean—"

"Gender is like love, okay? It's a human concept, a way of talking about
pheromones, hormones, whatever. But because it's not *real* doesn't mean you can
choose not to fall in love. And when your heart is broken, that's as fucking *real* as
anything in life ever gets."

"Having never been in love, I can't comment."

"I've been in love. It sucked."

Amity shifted Lexi's hand to her lap and clasped it tight. "I'll tell you something
in return. My own story. If you're willing."

"Please."

"I was born in a rough district. Rougher than this." Amity stared, unblinking,
into the burning filament of the bulb overhead. "I lost my virginity when I was
twelve. I told myself I'd consented to it. A lie to keep myself sane. At fourteen, I
found myself in a gang, not as a member but as a girl to be passed around for sex.
The day before I turned eighteen, the gang's enforcer decided he didn't want to
share me. I was declared his exclusive girlfriend. Believe it or not, I was grateful."

"Holy shit." Lexi's guts churned. "Amity…"

"Their speciality was prostitution, and my boyfriend kept the pimps in line.
Being his property meant I was protected. For a few years, I kept my head down,
gave him what he wanted, and tried to stay clean. I'd seen girls wrecked by the
drugs they took to keep from breaking down. I found other ways to go numb."
Amity drew her hunting knife and held it to the light. "This was his knife."

She turned the blade. Its cutting edge shone, almost as bright and hard as the gleam in Amity's eyes.

"I had a day job serving drinks. One night I came home early to find him with one of his pimps. They had two girls with them. Until then, I hadn't known they sold children."

"God…"

"I ordered the girls to run, and I blocked my boyfriend's path while they escaped. He was furious. He pushed me into a wall, slammed me against it while screaming. So I took this knife from his belt and gutted him. Then I killed the pimp. And with the knife's tip, I carved my name into their foreheads. I wanted the gang to know it was me."

Amity ran a fingertip down the knife's back. "The gang hunted me. I killed three more. Others joined in the hunt. It didn't matter. Nobody could stop me. Killing had become a way to cleanse myself. I'd been granted a bloody purgatory, and I didn't want it to end."

"Nikolas told me you'd murdered someone, but…" Lexi gave a nervous laugh. "Let's just say he left out the finer details."

"He was the one who took me in. At that time, he was only a lieutenant in Open Hand. The others didn't want me. They thought I was an animal. But he convinced them I was a victim deserving of their help and, under his wing, I found my bloodlust cooling. He rewarded me with responsibilities and my education."

After a final wistful glance at its edge, Amity sheathed the knife. "Even so, I never did become human again. I can kill and not feel a thing. Death is all I know how to give a person."

"That isn't true. You saved Riva."

"It wasn't really a conscious decision. It was instinct. I'm nothing but an impulse, an unthinking reflex toward violence. Reed called me a rabid dog, and it's true. Nikolas holds my leash. Without him, I'd go back to what I know."

For some time, they sat in silence. Amity stared at their joined hands while Lexi studied Amity's face. Despite all her suffering, there was still plenty of beauty in her tired features.

"I couldn't understand why I enjoyed it so much," Amity said. "I watched you between my legs, and it thrilled me. Ever since that moment, all I can think about is your mouth. Your eyes."

With a delicate touch, Amity cradled Lexi's face. "I was confused, because I'd never been attracted to women. Now I understand you aren't a woman. Nor a man. You're neither, and you're beautiful."

Lexi kissed her. Amity responded with intensity, forcing Lexi to the bed and pushing her tongue deep into Lexi's mouth. Stunned into limp submission, Lexi shivered as Amity kissed, nibbled and bit toward her ear.

"I was afraid of being intimate again." Amity's breath was soft, heated. "But you're nothing like the men who hurt me."

Watching Amity undress was like being witness to the unveiling of a mighty goddess. Her shoulders were broad, her arms powerful, her chest muscular. Fine veins decorated her large breasts, and her torso was marked by numerous scars. A few burn marks too. She bent over Lexi to kiss her again.

"I want to make it better." Lexi murmured the words while nuzzling Amity's cheek. "I don't want you to suffer the way you do."

Amity stared back. Her blonde, shaggy mane shadowed her face, but her emerald eyes remained brilliant and penetrating.

"I don't expect you to agree to this." Amity's voice was soft, but that hint of danger remained—a tension in her face and muscles, suggestive of someone always ready to strike. "But all my life, I've longed for somebody to know what they did to me. To understand why I have to fight. To kill."

"Okay." Lexi touched Amity's cheek. "Show me."

As their minds met and Lexi felt the first traces of alien thought and feeling, Amity trembled. "I feel it again. A chill in my spine."

No time to wonder about that now. Lexi drifted through the uppermost layer of Amity's mind—lust, anxiety, the blazing anger that was always there—and into her recent memories. The shame of defeat. Fury at Reed. Fear for Riva...

Deeper now, memories of blood and injury, killing and survival. Cutting, beating, breaking. Everyone faceless as they died. Her name carved into an anonymous forehead, drawn in lines of split, bleeding flesh. *AMITY.*

Lexi had never gone this deep into anyone before. Opaque as mist, hard as diamond, a blur of resentments, pains, losses. She was being dragged around, spat on, screwed. Cutting herself. Burning herself. The other girls were faceless. The men who abused her were faceless. All but him, the first life she'd ever taken, a ghoul whose face was a knife wound. Even as he raped her, there was no face, just a wound...

Her anger surfaced like a beast breaking from water, a killer baying as it was birthed from a cold sea. She no longer cut herself but cut them instead, abused their flesh to show them how it felt, stood in the spray of their blood and imagined it to be rain. Cleansing their filth from her skin. Washing her pure.

Such solace as she'd never known. A gift tied up in ribbons of flesh.

Lexi became disoriented, her own thoughts fleeing from the phantoms of Amity's mind. She began sobbing. It was dark, she was lost...

As if vision and reality had blurred, as if the implant had glitched, bloody letters were carved on Amity's forehead. She was branded by her own name. Marked by the knife she couldn't let go.

Lexi blinked, and the letters disappeared. "I saw." She wiped her eyes. "I understand."

Amity released a long breath, and her shoulders sagged. She lifted Lexi in her strong arms and, with a soft touch of her lips, kissed away Lexi's tears.

———————

Amity fucked with enthusiasm, gripping tight enough to leave crescent marks in Lexi's skin, kissing with such force that Lexi's lips came away stinging. At times, she showed hints of tenderness—a sensitive touch here, an unexpectedly loving caress there—but mostly it was like having sex inside an active washing machine.

After a bout of especially vigorous grinding, it became clear Lexi needed to finish the encounter if she were to escape serious bruising. She cupped Amity's pussy, pressing hard, and Amity gasped. Lexi slipped a finger inside while rubbing her thumb against Amity's swollen clit.

One final convulsion later, Amity shuddered and went limp.

Lexi nestled close, still held in Amity's arms. Sex was one thing, but sharing a lifetime of trauma was more than she usually signed up for. There would be no forgetting those images of fear and blood.

Yet Lexi had no regrets.

She still brings me my pills and watches over me. My guardian angel.

"Was Ash really your best friend?" said Lexi.

"Yes. But I didn't know she had such an attractive cousin."

Lexi smirked. "Keep that up. So what did you two do for fun?"

"We got drunk. I had to carry her home more nights than I can count."

"She could put them away, that's for sure. Did you notice how after five or six, she'd only seem tipsy, but then she'd have one more and keel over? One second, chatting away, the next, face down on the floor."

They laughed, and Amity cuddled closer, her fingertips drifting up and down Lexi's side. "She never once mentioned you."

"I told her not to introduce me to her revolutionary friends. I hated you all for taking her and Kade away from me. If only she could see us now, fighting shut-ins and fucking our brains out."

"A perfect existence. Are you so sure you want to leave?"

"I'm not staying in Foundation if it means getting wiped. I know how that feels. I've done it to other people. And I feel sick whenever I think about it." Lexi touched the tip of Amity's nose. "Snuggle me?"

The entire city was hunting Lexi, and everyone from Kade to Vassago had told her she stood no chance of survival. Yet as she lay on tangled, sweaty sheets, her head on the breast of her watchful angel of vengeance, Lexi felt an impossible conviction.

Right now, in these arms, she was safe.

CHAPTER 28

Even in a week filled with impossibilities, the sound of gunfire on campus seemed too shocking to be true. Mineko ran to her window and leaned out. Silence. Had she imagined it?

The first scream was followed by a distant uproar. Propelled by a jolt of fear, Mineko dashed out of the room and down the corridor. Several students stood in the hall, engaged in excited babble.

"Mineko!" A student stepped into her path. "What's going on?"

Mineko stumbled to a stop, barely avoiding knocking the younger woman over. "Why should I know?"

"Because you're Mineko Tamura."

"Oh, get out of my way." Mineko shouldered the girl aside. The carpeted floor thudded beneath her feet as she made her rapid way to the stairwell. One hand grazing the bannister, she flew down the stairs.

Reaching the bottom, she slammed through the swinging doors and into the lobby. It was swarming with panicked students. As Mineko stopped and stared, the elevator popped open to disgorge another helping.

"Ms. Tamura!" A lanky student dotted with acne waved at her. "They say there's lunatics with guns!"

"Why are you telling me?" Mineko took a nervous step back as students hurried toward her, a jumble of familiar and strange faces. They crowded close, talking at once, buoyed by the energetic kind of fear that was indistinguishable from excitement. "Stop pushing me!"

"Call your father," said an older boy with a pinched, bug-eyed face. "Tell him we're in trouble, that the district people are invading."

A girl grabbed Mineko's arm. "Somebody told me they shot an agent on the lawn!"

This was anarchy. Where was a lecturer, somebody official to set this frenzied mob in their place? Mineko stood on her toes, peering above the crowd of agitated faces. There, skulking in the corner, was the dreaded lecturer in Social Ethics.

"Sir," she said, waving at him. "Tell everyone to stop crowding me and get to safety. Take control."

"I don't…" The lecturer pressed his knuckles to his mouth. "I, um, I think if we just…"

Someone screamed outside, and the lecturer shrieked as he plowed through the crowd and into the dining room. Students scattered, some running up the stairwell, some beating on the elevator doors, others even venturing out the front doors only to run back inside gibbering.

"They're going to kill us," said a tiny student brandishing a marble bust of a Codifier—an unlikely weapon if Mineko had ever seen one. "Somebody has to tell the military."

A pallid boy thrust up his hand. "My father is a captain."

"Who cares about that?" An accusing finger was pointed at Mineko. "Her mother is General Tamura! Mineko, help us!"

"Let me through." Using her elbows to break apart the crowd, Mineko waded into the mass, only to be impeded by yet more beseeching students. "You're in my way, get out of—" Her foot erupted in pain as a big student stepped on her toes. "Damn you all, go back to your rooms!"

It seemed hopeless. These students had never experienced real panic in their lives, and now they were doing what they knew best: reaching for someone in authority, or in this case, someone in close proximity to it.

"He's coming for us!" A female student stood in the entrance, wildly gesticulating. "He's already shot three students, he blew their heads right off! I saw it happen. He's on his way. Save yourselves!"

The students exploded in selfish survival instinct, swarming to wherever they might be safe—fleeing up the stairs, running onto the lawn, escaping into the kitchen. One enterprising student hurled herself through a window. Seconds later, they had dispersed, though pandemonium still echoed through the building.

The only student left was the one who'd shouted the warning. Having caused so much havoc, she now seemed unaccountably calm, even shy. Mineko didn't recognize her, though she looked memorable enough: a strong nose and cheekbones, glossy black hair, unblemished olive skin, gentle blue-gray eyes.

"Hello, Mineko," the girl said. "Kade and Callie need our help."

"What? Who are you?"

"I'm Riva Latour. We don't have much time."

Wasn't that the name Callie had mentioned on the phone? The woman who had been laughing with Lexi in the background? "You're the person who works for Nikolas."

"Yes. I'm with Open Hand. But I'm here as a friend."

"Over here. Tell me what's happening." Mineko ushered Riva toward a storage closet. Opening it, she discovered the cowering lecturer in Modern History. "Get out."

The lecturer whimpered before fleeing. "And your classes are bullshit," Mineko shouted after her. "I hope you trip and break your neck."

Riva gave a startled laugh. "Callie said you were unceasingly polite."

"People change." Mineko pulled Riva into the closet. No doubt Lexi would have made some snide remark about her choice of conference space. "What did you last see?"

"Kade and Callie have an agent held hostage. I saw them taking her in the direction of a building with a golden dome on it. I don't know what they're planning."

An agent held hostage? It seemed like a desperate, irrational act. But no, Kade wasn't stupid—he'd have some kind of strategy. Mineko just had to think what it might be.

"Lachlan can't afford to lose any more agents after yesterday," she said. "Therefore, taking a hostage applies pressure where he's most vulnerable. He's in trouble already, and he has to maintain face... He can't call for backup until he's resolved the situation himself. In other words, Kade is buying time for us."

"But buying time for us to do what? What can we do?"

A good question. But Kade had put his trust in Mineko, counting on her to take advantage of an opportunity made at great risk to himself. If he and Callie were to survive, Mineko needed to work something out.

In a society like yours, truth is subordinate to power. You have powerful parents and that makes you powerful too. Never forget it.

His parting words to her. There was her answer.

Mineko smiled. "I know exactly what to do."

⁕

The Administration building was a dumpy structure that looked a little like a slate-gray pear. Trees with coarse, black bark stood around its perimeter, and thick leaves filled the gutter beside the stone path leading to the building's double doors.

Mineko strode under the dark branches while Riva kept pace. "How did you get here?" said Mineko. "Did Callie drive you?"

"Yes, she did." Riva peered at a chipped fountain. Perhaps all this was as strange to her as the outside world had been to Mineko.

"May I ask why you chose to come? It's very dangerous for you."

"Because you needed my help."

A stray leaf lay on the path. Mineko crunched it without hesitation. "Didn't you only meet Kade and Callie recently?"

"Yes, but Callie is my friend now. And I owe it to Lexi to bring Kade back."

"Lexi? I thought she hated Kade."

Riva smiled sadly. "Only so as not to love him, Min."

The doors slid open at their approach. The entrance hall was stuffy and thickly carpeted, and its walls had been painted a visceral dark red. The same strange silence that had fallen over campus was here too, hanging like a moment between breaths.

"We need to go to the top floor," said Mineko. "Let's take the stairs."

Riva gave a wry smirk—like Lexi, she seemed able to suggest a great deal with nothing but a twitch of her lips. "I'll be fit by the end of this."

The stairs ran three flights up a drab shaft decorated with Codist portraiture. Though it was tempting to run, Mineko restrained herself to taking the steps at a steady pace.

"Have you ever been in an enclave before?" she said.

"No." Riva frowned at the ornate bannister beside her. "I never expected it would happen, either."

"What do you do?"

"Mostly I help care for Foundation's destitute. When I'm not following wayward cyborgs into hiding, that is."

Yet another landing, yet another sinister Codist depicted in oils. Mineko sneered at the painting as she passed beneath it. "What's your opinion of Lexi? Do you like her?"

Riva laughed, a husky, self-conscious sound. "To be honest, I'm a little in love with her. But I'm sure I'm not the first."

The door to the top floor was ajar. Mineko bumped it open the rest of the way. Another bland hall ran past several closed doors and ended at an arched window overlooking the campus lawn.

Somebody was speaking from within the Head Office, their voice agitated. "That's completely unreasonable." It sounded like the Dean of Politics—that nasal shrill was hard to mistake for anyone else.

"Your opinion is noted," said a deep, calm voice.

"At least tell me why our outbound calls are blocked."

"Imagine all these students contacting their parents at once. Think of the panic that would ensue."

"Then you should let me on the speaker to reassure everyone."

"The speaker is off-limits, sir."

"How dare you order me around in this way. Don't you realize who I am?"

The other speaker chuckled. "I think you're the one who's lost sight of who is who, professor. Don't take that tone with me again."

Mineko nudged Riva. "I need to get inside that office, but I can't let this agent see me. He'd inform Lachlan."

The Dean stalked out of the office. He was a large, middle-aged man with an impressive jaw and a wide mouth that tapered into the most disapproving frown on campus. Right now, he looked more irate than ever. "What are you two doing up here? Get to your rooms."

"Shh." Mineko touched a finger to her lips. "Don't talk too loudly, please."

"Tamura, it's not safe to be roaming campus. At least, according to these friends of your father. And they won't let us call for help. It's ridiculous."

Riva surveyed the hall before pointing to a nearby office kitchen. "Do you have the key to this room?"

"Me?" The Dean scratched one of his jowls. "Yes, I do."

"May I have it?"

"Absolutely not. Go back to your dorm."

Time to assert some authority. "Give her the key," said Mineko. "Now."

The Dean produced a startled croak. "You can't talk to me like that."

"I damn well can. I'm at this institution purely by choice. I could just as easily enter the service, be granted official rank overnight and return tomorrow qualified to demote you to cleaning cupboards. So don't you dare ignore me. You'll do as I say, or else I'll remember your name when I inherit my father's place on the Committee."

And with that, the man who strutted about campus like an overlord became a meek, obliging servant. "Yes, Ms. Tamura. Ma'am." The Dean fumbled in the breast pocket of his uniform, took out a key ring and handed it to Riva. "It's this one, the copper one."

"Thank you." Riva entered the kitchen, peeked into the cupboards, stood on her toes to investigate the smoke alarm and tested the window.

"What is she doing?" said the Dean. Fair question.

Without a word of explanation, Riva stuffed the microwave with an odd assortment of items: a ball of aluminum foil, several forks, a sheet of baking paper. Apparently satisfied, she shut the microwave and began prodding its control pad.

"Mineko, get out of sight," she said.

Despite her curiosity, Mineko ducked into a small study. She closed the door, leaving it slightly ajar, and waited.

First, a ping—the microwave turning on. Then a steady whirling sound—the microwave in motion. A sparking noise. The heavy thud of something banging against plastic. More sparking. A hint of smoke in the air. A whooshing sound, as of paper catching alight. A high pierced shriek repeated over and over—the fire alarm.

"Help! Somebody help!" said Riva. "It's a bomb!"

Mineko peeked through the doorway as the agent dashed into the hall. He was a young, surly henchman: a little Lachlan-in-training. He drew his pistol and ventured into the smoke-filled kitchen.

Riva shut the door behind him and locked it. Furious knocking erupted from the other side.

"That's him taken care of," Riva said. "I do hope he opens the window."

The Dean looked ashen and distressed, as if he'd accidentally started swallowing a live frog and realized he had no choice but to finish it. "I find it hard to believe this is acceptable behavior."

"Shut up," said Mineko. "Come with me."

She'd only been inside the Head Office twice before, both times for minor administrative matters. Still, she knew where to find what she was looking for: a chunky terminal with an attached handset, the system used to broadcast messages campus-wide.

She made an imperious gesture to the Dean. "Turn this on for me."

"Yes, yes, of course." With a chubby finger, the Dean poked in a security code. The fire alarm fell silent—thank God. "What shall I tell them?"

"Say that I'm here with you. Let them know I'm about to speak."

"If you say so." The Dean depressed another button. "Staff and students, this is the Dean of Politics. Attention please. I have with me Mineko Tamura, who has a message to convey about the situation on campus." He scowled into the distance, perhaps struck by how implausible his situation had become, before releasing the button. "It's all yours, Ms. Tamura."

"Thank you." Mineko closed her eyes, inhaled, and took the microphone.

CHAPTER 29

On the path outside the Medicine building, Callie faltered. "I'm going to be sick…" She doubled over and stared at the ground while heaving air into her lungs. Turani watched the spectacle, expressionless.

"Are you okay?" said Kade. "Is it adrenaline?"

"No. I just can't…" Callie wiped sweat from her forehead. "I can't hold a gun on her like this."

Shit, of course—Callie had only yesterday been traumatized by that shooting in the mall. Now here was Kade, forcing her to move another young woman at gunpoint. "Christ, Callie, I didn't think. I'm sorry."

"No, I'm sorry. I should be tougher than this."

"You scout ahead. I'll take your place." Kade gripped Turani's shoulder and pressed his gun into the small of her back. "Keep moving, agent."

Turani treated Callie to a scornful look. "I'm surprised a Codist-killing rat like you has already lost her nerve."

The last thing Kade needed was for Turani to have any hope that her captors might lose their resolve. He jabbed her with the revolver, pushing her forward. "My friend doesn't want to see you harmed, but me, I'm not so sure. You Codists live privileged, comfortable lives. Perhaps having them cut short is a proper reckoning for your wealth. A brief lifespan would be some small measure of justice."

Callie looked horrified, but Turani relented and let herself be steered into the building.

Several nervous students in the lobby scattered at the sight of the intruders, leaving the pristine marble space empty. "They act like we're here to kill them all," said Callie.

"That's what they're taught. We're rabid wolves circling the enclaves."

Callie roamed the lobby, gaping at the vaulted ceiling and walking through patches of soft sunlight cast through circular windows. "I've never seen a building like this that wasn't in ruins." She gawked at a portrait of a stern woman clutching a book. "Who's the grumpy lady?"

"A Codifier." Kade nudged Turani in the direction of the elevator. "One of the first Codists."

"How long ago was she alive?"

"Over a century." Kade thumped the elevator call button. An arrow above the doors turned green.

Callie whistled as she admired the chandeliers that glittered above, their artificial candles tipped with incandescent bulbs. "Where'd they get the money to build all this?"

"The Codists seized their wealth during the plunder of Europe. They brought it here after the collapse. In the brief peace, they built the first enclaves, and then somehow they rode out the apocalypse."

A blue shape moved on a balcony above. Just a student, staring at them over the railings. Kade waved the kid away, and the poor thing retreated.

"I suppose you pride yourself in knowing about us," said Turani. "However flawed your knowledge might be."

"Studying Codist history is instructive. It shows us what happens when people sit on riches rather than share them. It explains your stagnant, repressive system, in which the elite are free to flout a moral code that holds absolute for those at the bottom. A system where—"

Just as Kade was warming to his speech, the elevator opened. Its interior was mirrored, and it confronted him with the image of himself holding a subdued woman at gunpoint. Hard to feel righteous looking at that.

He sighed. "Get in, Callie, and keep an eye on Turani's hands. She might try to hit the emergency button."

The ride up was tense, silent, and aromatic—pine-scented, if Kade was any judge. Finally the elevator reached the top level, marked *O*, and the doors jolted open.

The Observation Dome, as it was called, offered a view of campus from behind a glass wall that spanned half the hemisphere of the room. The circular space was sterile, with clean, white tiles and chunky plastic furniture. The only other entry point was an emergency fire exit with a plain blue door.

"Sweet view." Callie stared through the curved glass. The Dome was lower than the enclave wall, which obscured much of the cityscape, but the campus was still visible in full. "You'd think from here that the world was perfect."

"And here comes the man responsible for the illusion."

An imposing figure in black strolled down the wide avenue toward the building. Several students approached him—the kids were everywhere, hiding behind trees, lurking beneath gazebos, peering out of windows—only to be ignored.

"Callie," said Kade. "I need you to break the elevator."

"What, with my bare hands? I'm buff, sure, but not that buff."

"You know what I mean. Sabotage. And you, agent, go stand in the corner and keep quiet."

"Jesus, lay off her. Power trip much?" Shaking her head, Callie ducked into the elevator. After some consideration, she took a screwdriver from her pocket—did that girl ever run out of screwdrivers?—and tapped it against the control panel. "I can probably yank this off and mess up the insides, but I have no tools, so once it's broken, it's broken. You sure?"

"I'm sure."

"So our plan is to trap ourselves in here?"

"Essentially, yes." Without taking his eyes off Turani, Kade retreated to the fire escape door and set the bolt. "As far as I know, this is the only spot on campus that's defensible and that offers a scenic view."

"Sure. Don't want to die without a scenic view."

There was an immense clang as the elevator panel fell to the floor, followed by the tearing sound of Callie taking apart wires. "Mind if I fill my pockets? This is good copper."

"Sure. Take anything that isn't nailed down."

"Pssh. You think nails could stop me?" Callie poked her head out of the elevator. "Let the poor woman sit down, you asshole."

"If you insist." Kade indicated a study table. "Take a seat, agent."

Instead of sitting, Turani leaned against the window with her arms folded. "Why do you people call yourselves revolutionaries? What are you in revolt against? We don't claim authority over you."

"Have you actually read the Code?"

Turani looked away, scowling, and Kade allowed himself a smile. "Well, I have. Your Code is the embryonic doctrine for a single world state. It dictates a future in which there are only two possible outcomes. You'll either try to convert us or you'll wipe us out to prevent contamination. It all depends on whether you have a gentler or more brutal Committee on the day you decide to make your move, and frankly, I don't like the outcome either way."

"You can't predict the future."

"Predictions aside, you already rule over us through collaboration with the city's gangs. You imagine we can't see the strings that bind Gaspar Tamura to Samuel Brink, but we can."

"I don't know who Samuel Brink is."

"If you were in District Affairs, you'd know the name, but you still wouldn't know what I'm talking about. That ladder you're aspiring to climb, Agent Turani, you don't really want to know where it leads."

Callie emerged from the elevator, stuffing bundles of copper into her stolen uniform, and approached a vending machine. "Anyone want a snack?" She peeled back the maintenance panel and poked at something inside. The machine spilled a cascade of foil bars, clinking bottles, and brightly colored bags. "I won, I won!"

"That doesn't belong to you," said Turani as Callie snatched up a chocolate bar. "Leave it where it is."

"You can afford to lose a few candy bars." Callie stripped back the wrapper and smiled at the dark stick of chocolate in her hand. "I once found a whole box of these in one of your supply trucks. Four days of gorging later, I moved up a belt size." She devoured her trophy and licked the brown mess from her lips. "No regrets."

"Try to stay focused," said Kade. "Lachlan will be here at any moment."

"Don't you 'stay focused' me. I know the score." Callie shoved a handful of bars into her pocket before picking up two bottles of soda. She cracked one open, took a sip and sidled across the room. "Would you like a drink, shut-in?"

Agent Turani glared at the bottle without replying.

"Try not to stand too close to her," Kade said. "Code Intel trains all agents in martial combat. They're usually quite good at it."

"I bet they still get thirsty, though." Callie waggled the bottle, a persuasive smile lighting her face. "Come on. This one's on me."

Still glacial, Turani looked away. "I'm not interested."

"Well, do you have a name?"

Fascinating though it was watching Callie try to befriend an agent, Kade couldn't let himself be distracted for long. Lachlan would be in the building by now, making his cautious way up the stairs. The thought set a steady drum of apprehension beating in Kade's chest.

"I bet you know my name," said Callie, perching on a desk. "I suppose you have a file on me. Given all the things I've stolen from you guys, it's probably as big as my butt."

Turani's lips twitched. "You already know my name. Agent Turani."

"You sure you don't want one of these chocolate bars? They're so good. I don't know how you shut-ins don't walk around stuffing your face with candy all the time."

"If you'll stop hassling me, I'll take it." Turani swiped the bar from Callie's hand. "But unlike you, I intend to pay for this afterward."

Callie's cheeky grin widened. "Hey, sure, me too." She swung her boots onto a chair and took a swig from her soda bottle. "Come on, you must have a first name. Or did your parents name you 'Agent'?"

It was the first time Kade had seen someone angrily eat a chocolate bar. Turani paused from her furious chewing to give Callie a look of focused contempt. "My first name is Jasmine. Now I suppose you'll pass that information to your revolutionary friends."

"Jasmine. That's a beautiful name. And just so you know, I'm not a revolutionary." Callie tipped her bottle in Kade's direction. "I love this dude, but I haven't understood a single word he's said since we got in here. No offense, Kade, but it's true."

This time, Turani couldn't conceal her confusion. "If you don't agree with his twisted worldview, why are you here with him?"

"Ah, you know. Because I like the guy." Callie took another sip of soda. "I don't see why we can't all get along. Look how rich you shut-ins are. What's the harm in sharing a little?"

A thump at the door interrupted them. Kade jumped to his feet while Callie set aside the bottle and drew her pistol. Turani disposed of the silver foil in her hand, perhaps afraid to be caught in her larcenous indulgence.

Kade raised his voice. "Can you hear me, Lachlan?"

"Of course," said the familiar voice behind the door. "I'd rather not have to shout, though."

"We have Jasmine Turani. We'll trade her for our freedom."

"Granted! Unless you mean 'freedom' in that improbable wider sense of 'freedom from all oppression.' I'm afraid that's rather beyond my means." Even through the doorway, there was no mistaking Lachlan's distinctive deep chuckle. "Open the door, then."

"Not just yet."

"Please? I'd break it down, but it's property of the University. I'd have to fill out a form afterward." Another thump. "Pay heed to my indignant battering and let me in. Didn't you just hear me say I'll accede to your demands?"

"Forget about me, sir," said Turani. "Don't negotiate with these people. I'll die for the Code if I have to."

"Good God, agent, why would you do that?" The handle turned and the door shifted as weight was put against it, but the bolt held firm. "If you're anxious to know, Kade, I'm here by myself. I didn't want to run the risk that Amity was lurking on one of the landings, an ill-tempered spider waiting to devour my agents whole."

It seemed unlikely that Lachlan could break the bolt, but he'd always been impressively physical, and there was no knowing what augmentations he'd picked up in the last few years. "I don't believe you," Kade said.

"No, you do believe me. You're just stalling. Though for what, I have no idea." The handle rattled. "Is that notorious smuggler inside as well?"

"Callie Roux is with me, yes."

"Here's something I haven't figured out yet. Why is she involved in this? I'd assume a romantic motivation, but I know her tastes don't run to rugged men like yourself."

Callie beamed. "They really do have a file on me."

"Let me provide a proposition of my own. I'll trade myself for Agent Turani. You can hold me at gunpoint instead, and we'll talk."

Kade glanced at Turani, who remained motionless by the window. "I don't know about that."

"What's your alternative? You aren't going to hurt her. I know you, Kade, and maiming hostages simply isn't your style. If you were cold enough to smear Turani's cranial contents across that picturesque view behind you, you'd also have been cold enough to ignore a certain young woman's plea for help."

In the ensuing silence, a bird shrilled. The same abrasive double note that Kade had heard earlier. Callie took a quiet sip from her drink.

"And speaking of that young woman, you've wasted your time." Lachlan's voice had grown softer, harder to make out through the intervening barrier. "She's not on campus. In fact, she warned me you were coming."

"That's bullshit," said Callie, jumping to her feet. "She never would!"

With silent speed, Turani rushed her. Callie spun, aimed her pistol—and hesitated. Turani lunged, tackling Callie to the floor. With the sureness of a trained wrestler, she pinned Callie down and grabbed the fallen gun.

Kade stood frozen. He hadn't even had time to shout a warning.

"Stay there." Turani pointed the pistol at Callie's crestfallen face and returned to her feet, keeping Callie in her sights. "Move and you die."

"I'm sorry," said Callie, still flat on her back. "I couldn't shoot her."

"You shouldn't have let me see your weakness earlier, Roux."

"Maybe. But nothing's easier than pulling a trigger when you're scared." Callie gave a regretful smile. "What's really tough is stopping yourself."

Turani blushed, but didn't lower the gun. Helpless, Kade watched as she circled the room, reached the door and released the bolt.

Lachlan entered smiling, empty-handed and alone. He patted Turani on the shoulder. "Good work. Let Roux get up and keep your gun on her. Comrade August isn't afraid to risk his own life, but he tends to be more cautious when his friends are at stake."

Far from putting on flab, it seemed Lachlan had gained muscle, filling out the black uniform that he'd sworn to Kade he'd never wear again. Only a few new lines marked his handsome face, which still seemed to possess a million muscles for him to flex in sarcastic ways. Just as familiar was that raised left eyebrow, as if his wit were a firearm with the safety off.

"Look at you, Kade," he said. "Unkempt as ever."

"And I see you're still drowning yourself in that damn grease."

"We're all slaves to habit." Lachlan smoothed back his oily brown hair. "Though it must be said, you two proved especially easy to predict."

"I hate the way you talk," said Callie. "Like you're sucking off every word that comes out of your mouth."

Lachlan laughed deep from his chest. "The great and daring Callie Roux. I'll ask again. Why is someone of your reputation working with an unsavory gang dealer like Lexi Vale?"

"You're in no place to judge. All I hear is what a major jackoff you are."

"Oh, if jackoffs had military rankings, I'd be a general at the very least."

"Stop trying to be funny and zap my brain already. It's not like it makes any difference to me. I'll still have my hot body."

Lachlan produced his cunning smile, the one Ash had always complained made her uneasy. "You're very engaging in a brash sort of way. I'm lucky to have been given such amusing prey."

"You get off on being the villain, don't you? I'm surprised you didn't come through the door in a big black cape."

"Brilliant. I could continue this all day, I really could. Unfortunately, I need to talk to the mastermind alone." Lachlan gestured to the dim stairwell behind him. "Agent Turani, please detain this smuggler outside while I negotiate."

"But sir," said Turani. "You're unarmed, and August has a gun."

"Just trust in my judgment, please."

"Very well. Roux, move."

Callie shrugged, took another gulp from her soda bottle, and trudged out of the room. Turani followed, pistol raised. Lachlan shut the door and set the bolt.

"Would you mind not pointing that revolver at me?" he said. "It's not liable to be the solution to your problems."

As reassuring as the revolver was, Lachlan had a point. Kade engaged the safety and placed the gun on the nearest table. "Now I suppose you'll race across the room and snap my spine."

"You know I'm not that kind of cyborg." Not even sparing a second glance for the gun, Lachlan walked to the window. "It's a nice view from here. Look, there's a student trying to hide up a tree."

"Is tree climbing a Code-approved activity?"

"So long as they're not competing to reach the top, I see no objections." Lachlan's expression softened. "You admirable idiot."

Somehow, the mood had shifted. It was still Agent Reed by the window, of course, the fearsome enemy of the people, the most unpredictable operative in Code Intel. But it was also someone else. An imposing physical presence that, once, had been so reassuring. A broad face with a sarcastic cast that, once, had been so endearing. Lachlan.

Kade joined him by the window. Sure enough, there was a student clawing at the limbs of a stout tree not far from the base of the hill. "People died yesterday, Lachlan."

"Well, you did bring Amity with you."

"I shot somebody on a bike. I assume they're dead too."

"Very dead. By the way, he had an infant daughter. Or should I not mention that?"

"I wish you hadn't."

Lachlan gave a sympathetic smile. "I've been keeping tabs on you, so I won't ask tedious questions about what you've been up to. I'm happy to field your tedious questions, though, if you have any."

"I know you've been planting moles in Open Hand. Amity told me about the incident a few days ago."

"A little fun, that's all."

"Did you really know something about the mole's daughter?"

Lachlan glanced away. "She's dead. A drug overdose. I didn't have the heart to tell him."

"So instead you exploited the tragedy, sold him false hope and turned him into a spy."

"When you put it like that, I sound like a real bastard, don't I?"

Kade sighed. Shameless as ever. "Speaking of your character defects, why did you lie just now about Mineko? We know she didn't tell you we were coming."

Lachlan moved his shoulders in an almost imperceptible shrug. "I was trying to provoke a reaction. The truth is, I often can't help myself. Imagine you'd found a string that, when pulled, makes people dance. How much strength of will do you think it takes to refrain from pulling it?"

"More than you possess, it seems."

A group of students crept across the lawn below. Lachlan chuckled. "Look at them. They have no idea how to react to disruption in the order of their lives."

"Disruption is the order of life." It was time to see how much research Lachlan had really done, and how much reality he'd decided to ignore. "Did you know that Lexi is Ash's cousin?"

"I did find that out, yes."

"I used to ask myself how it was that Ash could die while someone like you kept living. Then I realized it's a pointless question. She died precisely because she wasn't like you. Cowards live. Heroes die. That's why those words have the meanings they do."

Kade waited, but Lachlan didn't rise to the provocation. "Tell me why you're protecting Mineko."

Lachlan laughed softly. "You won't believe me."

"That's true for anything you might say, so don't let it stop you."

"I've watched her since she was a child. She's always studying the world around her, that somber little face hiding a mind like a cutting edge. She has her mother's iron will and her father's labyrinthine intellect, but unlike them, she's capable of empathy. And humility."

Lachlan's smile returned, though now it was more wistful than anything else. "Where is our savior? The one who'll truly set us free? Amity wants us all dead.

Nikolas is timid. Sarabelle is just a loudmouthed opportunist. Even you, Kade, you're too reluctant to be a leader, even though you're the only worthy one. No, nobody out there is going to tear these walls down."

"But Mineko? You can't mean it."

"I do, comrade. There'll be a new Committee someday, and a Fourth Moral Code. The natural successor to the throne of Gaspar Tamura is his beloved daughter. I just have to ensure she makes it that far. Then I'll show you a revolution."

"But she's not a tool for you to use. She wants to be free."

"She's the only chance I have. She hates me, but that's just as I intend it. My role is to fuel the fire inside her, the one building out of control. When it comes out, I want to see them all burn."

"She'll burn first."

"You underestimate me. I've persuaded Code Intel that you're no threat, convinced them it's instructive to simply monitor your pathetic efforts. A few years ago, Gaspar floated the idea of purging the districts of the so-called revolutionaries, and I alone argued otherwise. Something else would arise in your place, I said, and might even prove competent. Better the enemy we know. You can guess whose argument prevailed."

"You're a true hero of the cause." Yet Kade couldn't put any venom into his sarcastic reply. What if it were true? Did he and his friends only still live because of the intervention of Lachlan Reed? Was he still fighting for them in his own selfish way? God, what an irony...

Lachlan glanced sidelong. "I learned something about you while researching Lexi's past. I assure you that until then, I had no idea."

As if Kade hadn't endured enough unpleasant surprises today. "My history is none of your business."

"I fully agree, which is why I omitted that detail from your file. I'd never let those bigots degrade you. The language they use to describe men like you is utterly dehumanizing."

Kade's mouth had become dry. He took a sugary sip from Callie's abandoned soda bottle. "If you're looking for gratitude, you're too optimistic."

"Don't worry, I won't mention it again. Though I can't help but wonder if it's the reason you're so damn handsome."

"No. That's just my winning personality coming through."

Lachlan smiled. "Project Sky is only the beginning. We're already thinking of imitating the genetics work they're doing in Port Venn. Clones. DNA splicing.

All the things banned before the war. It's almost as if nobody had ever read a dystopian novel."

"And I thought cyborgs were bad enough." Kade sipped the soda again. Tasted like a purple sugar explosion. "I can't let you hurt Lexi. I love her."

"I realize she must feel like the last link you have to Ash. But she's too dangerous to leave to her own devices. I have to get to her first." Lachlan drummed his fingers on the window, his face thoughtful. "Here's what will happen. I'll report that you and Roux were sent to the nearest security outpost for interrogation. Sadly, the van arrived empty, Roux having picked the locks en route. We shake our fists, curse the heavens, and get on with our business."

"So what's the reality?"

"I escort you outside, scold you both and tell you to run along. But if Roux tries this again, I'll have no choice but to send her on for Reintegration."

"And if I try it again?"

"I'm hoping you won't make me contemplate an answer to that question."

"Just let Min go. She deserves the chance to live her own way."

"There's no life out there. The good die like Ash died, while the bad join together and oppress the merely inadequate. If you think——"

Lachlan's mobile-comm crackled. "Mr. Reed," said an irate male voice. "I'm trapped in a kitchen."

There was a brief moment of silence. "What?" said Lachlan.

"A student trapped me in here, sir. She lit a fire and tricked me."

"Describe this student."

"About five-seven, long black hair, light brown complexion..."

Oh, shit. Kade looked away, but it seemed Lachlan had already read his face. "You know this person, don't you?" He turned off the comm, silencing the agent mid-ramble. "So that's why you're buying time. There's a third invader on campus."

"I don't know what you're talking about."

"Don't be obtuse. Listen to me, Kade. Mineko is dangerous. If you encourage her fantasy of escape, it'll backfire. You're only giving her an outlet through which to destroy herself, and then we'll all be——"

A nasal, uncertain voice boomed from a speaker in the ceiling. "Staff and students, this is the Dean of Politics..."

CHAPTER 30

Beyond the office window, the harsh disc of the sun crested the distant southern wall, forcing Mineko to squint as she looked at it. The campus had become entirely hushed. Even the birds observed the silence.

If she went through with this plan, she could never go back. Was it too late to change her mind? She could step away…

No. She couldn't. This moment had been inevitable from the day she'd walked into her room to find Callie Roux waiting for her.

A girl like you deserves the world.

"Fellow students, this is Mineko Tamura. I speak to you at a moment of crisis. Enemies of the Code are among you. Disguised as agents of my father, they have come to abduct me."

The Dean made a strangled sound and covered his mouth.

"These imposters intend to take me hostage and escape to the districts from which they came. But they didn't count on our bravery. Some of us have fought them all the way to the Medicine building, where even now the counterfeit Codists press their threat against our harmonious lives."

How easily the rhetoric flowed. Those grandiose lectures, the manipulative passages in her textbooks, they were all so simple to emulate.

"You know my father, Gaspar Tamura, the great man who ensures the stability of our society. You likewise know my mother, Kaori Tamura, the decorated general who keeps us safe from wasteland savages. I am their daughter, and today I will make them proud. Join me and earn their favor. Prove that no insurgent can stand against Codified brothers and sisters. March with me to the Medicine building. We are the boldest generation yet, and when our time comes to be custodians of this planet, we will be fearless. This is your true exam."

Mineko set down the microphone and nodded to the Dean, who disabled the speaker system with shaking fingers. "Find somewhere safe to hide," she said. "You're too old for this."

Before Mineko could make it more than halfway down the hall, Riva caught her by the arm. "Min, what are you doing? If you send these students to fight against agents, they'll be hurt, even killed."

"Don't preach at me." Mineko glared at Riva. Who was this woman, to emerge from nowhere and try to impede a realization of purpose? "For my entire life, I've been forced to suppress all that's true about myself and inhabit a sickening lie. Believe me, in my position, you'd do the same."

"I'd do a lot of things. But not this."

"How could you even know? Besides, anyone who believes what I said is already a lost cause. The clever ones will stay hiding in their rooms."

"You're lying to yourself. The bravest will be the ones who follow you."

Idiot. Cowardly idiot. "Callie and Kade will be wiped if we don't act. Are you telling me these stupid students are more important?"

"It's wrong to have innocent people fight our battles."

How absurd and galling this was, given the patient self-sacrifice Mineko had adhered to until now. But it was futile to take out her temper on some well-meaning—albeit utterly infuriating—stranger. "Tomorrow, we'll consider what we might have done better," Mineko said with as much patience as she could. "But today, we must fight to protect what we have. Please trust me."

"Do you really think Callie would be comfortable with this?"

Now that crossed the line. "Emotional blackmail is something I'm very used to, Latour. Don't waste your breath trying it on me again."

Riva flinched. "I didn't—"

"If it helps your conscience, rest assured that Lachlan won't hurt any of the students. It'd be the end of his career."

"The agents I saw yesterday seemed brutal enough."

"Those were different circumstances. Are you following me or not?"

Riva averted her eyes. "Yes. I'm sorry."

Presumably she hoped for some gentle word, some sign of forgiveness, but Mineko wasn't in the mood. Instead, she nodded and continued on her way. After a second of hesitation, Riva fell into step behind her.

Mineko descended the stairs in a state of brooding uncertainty. It seemed she had become a hypocrite—she had relished seeing others submit to her authority: Jasmine, the Dean, this Riva woman. It had been pleasurable to overwhelm their weaker resolves. Did that speak to some dark strain in her own nature?

Well, if so, she would be prudent in her use of that power. And Lachlan Reed would be the first to feel it.

CHAPTER 31

For some time after Mineko's announcement, Lachlan kept silent, though the glint in his eyes suggested his mind was working in a frenzy. Kade had learned to both admire and fear that look.

"What are you going to do?" said Kade.

"I'm..." Lachlan rubbed his forehead. "I'm thinking."

"You have to admit, it's clever of her."

"I'm swelling with pride, believe me. But the part of me that doesn't want either of us to be Reintegrated is very pissed off."

Lachlan pressed a button on his mobile-comm. "Agents, listen. Do not interact with any students. Keep your distance, even flee from them if necessary. Try not to let them harm you, but if you value your careers, do not under any circumstances harm them." He switched off the comm and exhaled. "Hell."

"You're taking her threat seriously, then?"

"Very much so. She's astute. The Code encourages ambition even as it stifles competition, allowing for very few routes to the top. So when these students see a golden opportunity... Well, let's just say I'm lucky we don't keep pitchforks and flaming torches anywhere on campus."

"What's your plan?"

"Short of whimpering and running? I'm not yet sure. I could call Gaspar and tell him what's happened, but that would be the first step to forfeiting my memories and personality. Still, I'll figure something out."

"You can't seriously believe you can cover this up."

"Of course I can, at least to an extent. The challenge will be doing so while protecting Mineko. As I told her yesterday, she's my queen, and I'm very reluctant to sacrifice her. Though she didn't appreciate the remark."

"Most people aren't pleased to be compared to game pieces."

"I think it's a compliment. Without them, the board is meaningless."

The mobile-comm buzzed. With a weary look, Lachlan reached for it. "Reed here. Talk."

"The students are mobilizing, sir," said a nervous voice. "They're behaving strangely. One of them saw me and made an aggressive gesture. Should I talk to them?"

"Did you not hear me before? Keep your distance." Lachlan put away the comm and opened the door. Callie and Turani blinked at him. "Get inside, you two. And for God's sake, agent, put that gun away."

Turani frowned. "But sir, how will I stop Roux escaping?"

"I don't give a damn if she does escape. The worst she can do is steal more confectionery."

"With all respect, Commanding Agent, enforcing the Code is our duty. And this woman is a murderer and a criminal."

Lachlan sighed. "Agent Turani. Forget whatever they're teaching you now in the academy, leave the law enforcement to District Affairs and focus on your priority, which is to maintain social cohesion."

"But we should at least subdue them."

"Then go ahead and tie Ms. Roux up. She might well enjoy it."

Turani's mouth fell open. "Sir!"

"Don't be so distressed. I'm permitted a sense of humor. It's a liberty I've earned from loyal service."

"Whatever you say, sir." Turani matched his mocking gaze. "Why did Mineko Tamura tell all those lies?"

Lachlan's smirk vanished. "I expect somebody forced her to express those absurd sentiments. Our responsibility now is to take her to safety."

"So that's our objective? Find Mineko Tamura?"

"Yes, but I'd rather handle it myself, if you don't mind. This is a delicate situation that only I'm qualified to deal with."

Turani lowered her dark lashes, turning her eyes into suspicious slits. "Because of your augmentations?"

"That's a little insubordinate of you, but yes, if you like. Because I'm a terrifying cyborg." Lachlan said the word cyborg with such theatrical emphasis that Kade was unable to keep back a chuckle, much to Turani's obvious irritation.

"Look down there," said Callie. At the base of the hill, a group of perhaps fifteen students had gathered. "This kinda fucks you over, doesn't it, Reed?"

"I wouldn't myself have found such a poetic way of saying it, but yes."

"May I suggest something?" said Turani. "We could strip the uniforms from these two. You wear August's and I take Roux's. Then we force them to wear our old uniforms. The students will target them instead."

Callie grinned. "You just want to see my panties, don't you?"

"I didn't ask for your opinion." Turani flushed, clenched her fist and impotently opened it again. "Mr. Reed, your thoughts on my plan?"

Lachlan shook his head. "It would only feed the possibility of violence, not to mention disrespect our uniform codes."

"I see." The chastened Turani hung her head. "I apologize for my inappropriate suggestion."

"Cheer up, Jasmine," Callie said. "I thought it was clever."

"Don't talk to me!"

"Agent Turani." Lachlan spoke with the forced patience usually directed at unruly children. "If you'd be so kind as to reconnoiter the ground floor."

"Sir." Still scowling, Turani clanged down the fire escape.

"I should ask for her number," said Callie. "I think she likes me."

Lachlan chuckled. "That would explain why she seems so determined to pull your hair."

"By the way…" Callie picked up Kade's revolver and flicked back the safety. "If I shoot you now, I solve all our problems, right?"

It was such a casual invocation of violence, it took a moment for its importance to sink in. Kade stared at her, mouth open to speak, but not yet able to articulate an objection.

"Hardly." True to form, Lachlan seemed unfazed by the gun pointed at him. "Anyone else would have hauled you straight to Reintegration. I'm the only Codist who'd prefer you keep smuggling. Spreading the wealth."

"But you're hurting people I care about. What if I let you go and you kill Lexi? How would I forgive myself?"

Lachlan tensed. "A fair question."

"I killed a shut-in yesterday. It was the worst moment in my life." Callie took aim. "But for Lexi, I'd do it again, because I'm sentimental that way. She's my friend, and I won't let you hurt her. So close your eyes and think of something clever to say before you die."

No. Kade had to act. Whatever his sins, Lachlan didn't deserve to die here. Nor did Callie need to live with yet more blood on her conscience.

"Put the gun away," Kade said. "As much trouble as Lachlan has caused for us, he's the only one who can command these agents."

"Exactly." Lachlan visibly relaxed. "Turani is next in rank. Shoot me and she'll report what's happening. Your charming insolence inclines me to show you lenience, but it won't get you any further with her."

"But still, you'd be dead," said Callie. "And you're the kind of guy who can't imagine a world without himself in it, aren't you?"

"Why threaten me? What can I do? You'll find there isn't any prize available to you. Shall I give you Mineko?" Lachlan held out his empty hands. "She's not mine to give. She's out there raising a rabble to overthrow me. Shall I let you walk out? I already have no intention of stopping you."

"I don't fucking get it. You keep giving up your advantage, and I can't figure out why. No matter what happens, you act as if you planned it all along. If I didn't know better, I'd think you were a total lunatic."

Lachlan shot Kade a quick, knowing smile. "You're confused only because you believe what you've been told, that I'm a bad man. The truth is, I'm not a bad man, and I want what you do. I think Mineko should be happy, safe, and successful. We just disagree on what those words mean."

"And Lexi? What about her?"

"Honestly, I have no desire to see her hurt."

"I saw that bruise on her forehead from where you hit her. You stuck a dart in Amity. Your thugs beat up Zeke and Kade."

"Did I say I wasn't a savage? You know Foundation is no place for the weak. Lexi built the brutal crime syndicates of Vassago and Contessa. Amity and Kade have killed countless Codists, and unlike you, they don't lose sleep over it. I'm no different from any of your friends. No better, yes, but certainly no worse."

"You are worse. How can you say you aren't worse?"

"Well, I've never taken a woman hostage. Nor have I ever tried to trick naïve students into attacking armed agents." Lachlan's lips shifted in a faint smile. "And I've never broken into a vending machine."

Callie looked to Kade. Her big, dark eyes expressed heartbreaking doubt. "Do I shoot him?"

"I don't want you to," said Kade. It was terrifying how much he meant it.

"Riva wouldn't want me to either."

"No. She wouldn't."

"But if I can't shoot him, how can we ever end this?"

"Your mistake is thinking it ends with me." Lachlan sounded almost gentle. "I'm big, but not as big as you think. If you want to protect Lexi, take her somewhere I can't find her. Shooting the hunter won't stop the hunt. It'll merely ensure they send out a nastier hunter."

"The way the others tell it, the shut-ins don't have anyone nastier than you. Kade, you pretty much said so yourself."

Potentially true, yet the lesser of the truths here. Hadn't Amity been shunned once, hated by comrades and criminals alike? Kade, Ash, and Nikolas had befriended her and shown compassion, and time had proven their decision to be wise. Kade knew what it meant to be offered a reprieve—an opportunity to try again from a new perspective. Lexi had given him a similar gift once. A new life. A new name. A second chance.

Could that someday be Lachlan? Who knew?

Kade held out his hand. "Give me the gun."

CHAPTER 32

Kaori Tamura could have been a desk officer, protected by her family name, yet she'd never shied from combat. Mineko had seen all her battle scars—where a bullet had grazed her ribs, a knife had cut her shoulder, an explosive had burned her back.

Mineko was her daughter. She had the same blood. And now she had her own army. They waited for her at the base of the hill, a group of young men and women, all students. That wasn't surprising. Codist academics were typical propagandists. Derivative, insipid cowards.

A skinny girl with a chestnut bob spoke first. "Is what you told us true?"

"Yes. My father warned me to expect a kidnap attempt. It seems that today, his fears came true."

A heavyset young man cleared his throat. "But they looked like real agents."

"Anyone would, in a black uniform."

"I don't understand how they got in," said a short, spectacled student with a threadbare uniform and scuffed boots. Presumably the daughter of low-ranked parents. "There's no way in but the subway."

"They broke in through the service doors," Mineko said. "We're not as safe as you all think."

The revelation sent a shudder through the assembly, save for one boy, a wide-eyed, pale creature with a sprinkle of freckles. He was a fellow sufferer of Social Ethics, a quiet student who always sat in the back while seeming on the verge of sleep. He stood apart from the others and watched Mineko with obvious skepticism.

"This doesn't explain what's going on," he said. "Everyone says they saw an agent taken at gunpoint by students. How does that fit your story?"

"I'm sure there was exchanging of uniforms to cause greater confusion."

"How can you possibly know that?"

"That's enough!" Riva turned on him with an impressively convincing scowl. "This is Mineko Tamura. Don't you know who her father is?"

"I know who her father is. But she's not her father. If she and her father were so close, she wouldn't be here studying to be an ethicist."

If not for the inconvenience he was causing, Mineko could have hugged this wonderful, stubborn boy. As things stood, however, she needed to shut him down quickly.

"My parents aren't impressed by imitation," she said. "They're impressed by people who choose to think and act boldly. It seems to me I have a group of students here who fit that description. All except for you."

The other students frowned at the doubtful boy, who licked his lips, clearly conscious of his diminishing position. "What do you want us to do, then? Run up there and toss rocks at them?"

"If necessary. We have to capture these false agents, tie them up, and stand guard over them until backup arrives."

"Are they violent?" said the girl with the bob. "These district people?"

Another student snorted. "Of course they are, stupid. They aren't codified. Violence is the natural state of a world without the Code."

"You've been rehearsing that line for the exam," said the freckled skeptic, but all he won for his cutting observation was a disapproving look.

Time for Mineko to play her trump card. "I'll be sure to tell my father your names. You'll be remembered as the students who saved my life."

That did the trick. The students began to climb the hill, and even the skeptic relented and followed the pack. Mineko gave him a triumphant smile as she hurried to take the lead.

The Medicine building was a compound of cuboid buildings around a dome-capped central tower. Its marble walls boasted decorative balconies, vine-coated trellises, curling stone eaves, and embellished ledges—a full excess of architectural flourishes.

Fifty meters from the entrance, Mineko stopped short. Heavy dread uncoiled in the pit of her stomach. Lachlan Reed was waiting before the doors. Kade stood in an alcove behind him, looking grim in a lecturer's uniform, while Callie sat on a nearby stone ledge.

"We'd like to talk, Mineko," said Lachlan. "Inside."

Where was the hostage? More to the point, what were Kade and Callie thinking? Was Lachlan exerting some invisible threat over them, or—surely too absurd—were they sincerely expecting her to negotiate?

She wouldn't have anticipated such gullibility from either of them. Every second they allowed Lachlan to act unimpeded, they were furthering whatever covert intentions he held.

"I don't think so," she said. "Students, help me detain this imposter."

Several of the larger students moved to Mineko's side, including the big youth who'd spoken earlier, but they hesitated and went no further.

"Well done," said Lachlan. "You've all performed well on this training exercise. We don't need any further demonstrations of loyalty, so please return to your daily affairs."

"Training exercise?" said the girl with the threadbare uniform.

"That's right. Ms. Tamura has been helping us coordinate a tactical evaluation of the student body. I'm very impressed by what I've seen."

"Don't listen to him," said Mineko. "He's lying to you."

She and Lachlan stared each other down. Amazing to think Project Sky could penetrate that deliberately relaxed face of his, peeling away every layer of deceit, and leaving him helpless. Little wonder the Codists coveted Lexi's power, even though cybernetics was forbidden...

Of course. Cybernetics was forbidden. There was her solution.

"I can prove to you this man is no Codist," said Mineko. "In fact, he's not even a human. He's a cyborg."

"That's an inventive scenario," Lachlan said flatly. "Very clever. But I don't think we need to embellish the exercise any further."

"It's the truth. I'll prove it to you all."

Mineko took a smooth stone from the garden bordering the path, weighed it for a moment and tossed it at Lachlan. He twisted away with superhuman speed— pure reflex, the sort only made possible by a chip firing stimulus straight down the spine. The students gasped.

"Nothing human moves like that." Mineko was unable to keep the satisfaction from her voice. "And now I'll give him a chance to prove me wrong. If this one strikes him in the chest, he's not a cyborg." She scooped up another rock. "All he has to do is let himself be hit."

This time, Lachlan's smile was unconvincing. "Why would I do that?"

"A reflex implant forces a body to move away from incoming threats. As a cyborg, you have no say over whether that happens or not. The chip compels you. Because, as I said before, you're less than human."

"Min!" Riva's hiss was reproachful, even angry. Presumably she was offended on Lexi's behalf, not understanding that if it meant destroying Lachlan, it was permissible to say or do anything.

Kade took a step forward. "Mineko, don't do this."

"No, let's see him dodge it." The skeptical boy had moved to the front of the pack and was studying Lachlan closely. "If he's not a cyborg, let's see him do it. I've never seen anyone move as fast as he just did."

"Sure," said the big student. "Let her hit you with the rock."

"Everyone, observe," Mineko said. "And remember that no Codist can be a cyborg. If he isn't a Codist, he's no agent either."

She threw the rock. As before, Lachlan dodged, and the rock sailed past. Aghast, he watched it strike the bricks behind him.

"There's our confession." Mineko grinned, exhilarated. She'd outwitted him, this man who'd sought to rule her. "Not an agent. Not a Codist. Not even a human being. Now take him down. Together, you can subdue him."

The students surged, jostling to be first, and Lachlan retreated with his hands raised. "Students, this is a mistake…"

Mineko yelped as a hand caught her arm and spun her. It was Kade, his eyes wide. "You need to tell them to back down. If this continues——"

"Get away from her!" The big student pulled Kade from Mineko and shoved him. Mineko swallowed hard, her triumph obliterated by the horror of seeing Kade handled so viciously on her behalf.

"How dare you come here," said the skinny girl with the bun. "How dare you!" She hurled a large stone, missing Lachlan and nearly striking Riva. Callie leapt at the girl and grabbed her wrist.

"Be careful, you idiot! You almost hit her!"

The girl growled as she pushed Callie back. "Out of my way."

It was chaos. Each student wanted to receive the fullest measure of the adulation and glory Mineko had promised them, and so they fought among each other while Lachlan, clearly unwilling to defend himself, backpedaled to the front doors. Meanwhile, Callie, Riva, and Kade ran from student to student, trying to prevent them throwing stones, only to be jostled and bumped themselves.

And Mineko—she was helpless. Her student army was no longer under her control, and her friends seemed to be supporting her enemy…

A gunshot rang out, and the students screamed.

"Back!" Jasmine Turani stood on a ledge two stories above, holding a pistol aimed at the crowd. "Students, stand down. This is Commanding Agent Lachlan Reed. If you harm him, you're as good as Reintegrated."

"Agent, put down that gun," said Lachlan. Mineko had never seen him so shaken. "Don't fire another shot."

"You can't let this riot continue, sir." Jasmine pointed the pistol at the big student, who stared up at her. "You! Step away!"

The freckled skeptic tore a big stone from the earth, shedding soil, and raised it above his head. "Fucking uncodified!" He hurled the stone, which clattered against a gutter. "Bring her down!"

In a renewed frenzy, the students dismantled the garden for missiles. Another stone whistled through the air, followed by a half-brick that flew high enough to strike the roof below Jasmine's feet.

"Stop." Mineko struggled to raise her voice above the commotion. "That's enough."

A rock smashed a tile beside Jasmine's left foot. She stepped quickly to avoid a second, and her heel skidded on the ledge. She shrieked as she slipped and tumbled down the sharply angled tiles. Mineko's guts compressed into a sickened knot.

Jasmine slithered across the roof, fell into empty air, twisted, and caught the edge of an ornamental gutter. She swung one-handed, kicking while she flailed for a second grip that wasn't there.

She screamed again. An inarticulate and desperate sound.

"Turani!" Lachlan shoved through the wall of students, knocking them down, no longer showing any care for their safety. "Hold on!"

But Callie was quicker.

She threw herself onto a trellis and scampered up it with as much ease as if it were a ladder. The ivy-woven grid stopped short of the second floor, but Callie, without hesitating, reached for a jutting piece of masonry, found purchase, and—heels pressed flat against the wall—hauled herself onto a decorative ledge.

"Oh my God," said Riva, articulating in three faint words everything that Mineko felt.

A sizable gap separated Callie's ledge from the one Jasmine was dangling from. Callie studied the distance and flexed her fingers.

"Don't!" said Kade. "Even you won't make it across that."

Callie put a foot off the ledge and, with both hands, took hold of the brickwork. Clinging close to the wall, she climbed horizontally until she reached the opposite ledge. It was every bit as impressive and baffling as the times Mineko had seen Kaori scale the hardest routes on their indoor wall, fingers wedged in holds that seemed little more than pockmarks.

In seconds, Callie was beside Jasmine. "Don't be scared." She crouched and took hold of Jasmine's wrist. "I've got you."

"I can't pull myself up. Please don't let me fall."

"You won't fall, I promise. Give me your other hand."

Jasmine waved into the open air. "I can't reach."

"Swing for me, then."

"I'll only drag you down." Jasmine's voice was barely recognizable, every vowel thickened by tears and terror.

"Just trust me, Jasmine. I've got you."

With a desperate sob, Jasmine lunged for Callie's extended hand. The contact yanked Callie off balance, but after a terrifying second of teetering, she righted herself and pulled Jasmine up to the ledge.

The students all murmured. Even Lachlan seemed stunned.

"We're going back to the window now, okay?" Callie put an arm around Jasmine. "You're still wobbly on your feet, so hold onto me."

Mineko's relief was soured by an irrational twinge of jealousy. She'd imagined all that selfless heroism and beautiful generosity had been intended just for her. But no. It was simply how Callie Roux was.

A shadow fell over her. Lachlan. "Are you satisfied, Mineko?"

Mineko avoided his eyes. The muttering of guilt inside her had to be crushed. "I didn't mean for that to happen."

"It's been a long two days. Please tell me you're done causing trouble."

"Yes. We'll talk. You and me, with Kade present to keep me safe."

"Exactly the arrangement I would have suggested."

The students continued to watch in fascination as Callie helped Jasmine through an open window. "Stay calm," said Mineko, though her recruits didn't seem to be listening to her anymore. "I'm going in to negotiate."

Kade was waiting in the doorway. His expression was severe, and a fluttering feeling rose into Mineko's throat and left her queasy. Soon there'd be reprimand. Disappointment.

"Don't be afraid," he said, and the kindness in his voice brought her to the edge of tears. They'd all been so good to her. Would they understand she had only done what was necessary?

Yet what a scene she had left in her wake. A wrecked garden, scattered rocks, a crowd of students still puzzling at the roof from which Jasmine Turani had nearly fallen…and walking away from it all, Riva Latour, silent but somehow accusing.

CHAPTER 33

They found Callie and Agent Turani waiting in the lobby. Turani hung her head. "Commanding Agent," she said. "I lost self-control. I'm ashamed."

"We'll talk soon," Lachlan said. "For now, gather the other agents and have them assemble in the Administration building."

"But we should arrest these—"

"I said, we'll talk. You and me. Don't worry about repercussions yet."

Turani glared at Mineko. "Why did you do it, Tamura? What could these district people possibly offer you?"

"One of these district people just saved your life." Mineko spoke with her usual quiet firmness. "Perhaps you should take time to reflect on that."

For a second, Turani seemed about to respond. Instead, she shook her head and continued on her way.

As soon as Turani had left, Callie dashed to Mineko and squeezed her in a bear hug. Mineko gave a breathless laugh. "You scared us," said Callie. "You and your angry mob."

Mineko giggled, momentarily a happy young woman rather than a figure of self-control. "You've been unwise to trust Lachlan."

"If he tries anything, I'll beat him down."

"No. Stay here. If he does try something, you'll have time to run."

"Have you forgotten I'm right here?" said Lachlan. "I can assure you, if any of your friends wish to flee, they're more than welcome to do so. I'll even close my eyes and count to ten."

Callie grinned. "You're one sneaky shut-in, Reed."

"Compliment or insult?"

"Fifty-fifty." Callie bounded over to Riva, who still stood in the doorway, and hugged her tight. "Chickadee! I was so worried about you."

Riva smiled back, her hand lingering on Callie's hip. "You were amazing out there. How did you pull yourself up?"

"Hidden muscles." Callie flexed her right arm. "I practice bouldering out in the canyons, and I'm a beast at parkour."

"You just keep getting sexier. I should get myself in trouble so that you can come rescue me."

Lachlan chuckled, but Mineko glared at Riva with such naked animosity that Kade quickly intervened. "We don't have time for banter. Keep watch down here, and if any more agents show up, let us know."

"Very good," said Lachlan. "Don't leave your back unguarded, especially around evildoers like myself. Now, perhaps we might conclude this in one of the seminar rooms. Objections?"

"No, that's fine." Kade reached into his pocket and touched the handle of his revolver. Reassuring though the gun was, it was unlikely he'd have to use it. The time for violence had passed. "Min, let's go."

They left Riva and Callie still chattering and walked down a corridor to the seminar room—small, sunlit, and filled with motes of dust. Mineko stood on an illuminated patch of carpet, her upturned face catching the sunlight, while Lachlan lounged against the lectern.

"You didn't tell them I was lying." In the light, Mineko's green eyes seemed impossibly bright and clear. "Instead, you invented a further lie that would have exonerated me. Why?"

"As I told you before, you're important to me," Lachlan said. "You have a unique opportunity to inherit real power and liberate other Codists. People like sweet, hopeless Valerie Wren."

"Don't bring her into this."

"She's not going to forget that kiss, you know."

Mineko blushed. "You still take pleasure in mocking me, even now."

"Whatever you're looking for, you won't find it outside. Trust me. Stay in the enclave. Participate in the future rather than flee from it."

As much as Kade wanted to offer some input, to influence Min, he kept himself in check. This was a debate between Codists, and nothing he said now would hold sway.

"I don't want to live under the Code," said Mineko.

"There's always a code. Out there, it's the code of human baseness. Most district people are covetous, hateful, and vindictive. Codists, in contrast, tend to be timid, well-meaning, and troubled by thoughts of disorder. Like Dr. Wren. Like those students, when they're not being goaded into acts of hate. Like Agent Turani, desperate to perform her duties well. That's Codists for you. Meek and obliging."

"Are you trying to persuade me or to arouse my contempt?"

"Believe me, I also despise these cowards. I just don't restrict my contempt to the fortunate." Lachlan produced a humorless smile. "Kade, why don't you tell her who killed the woman you loved?"

Would that memory ever stop being a physical blow, a fist right into Kade's chest? "It's irrelevant," he said.

"It could hardly be more relevant. This is the life you're offering her. When Mineko too lies in some district grave, will you then be satisfied?"

"For God's sake, Lachlan. She's on the verge of being caught and Reintegrated. For that matter, so are you. You have nobody to protect you."

"That's fine. The devil always stands alone in the end."

Nobody could ever fault Lachlan his gift for melodrama. "The devil doesn't win, though."

"Perhaps not. But he knows full well what he's doing." Lachlan looked back to Mineko. "Just do what I do, Mineko. Inspire fear, and you'll no longer be afraid. Laugh whenever you feel like crying. Then you'll survive."

"I want to follow Callie." Mineko spoke softly but with conviction. "I want to see the sky."

"The sky? You can see it from here."

"Not the horizon." Mineko took a phone from her pocket. "You enjoy manipulating me. Now it's my turn. Discover what happens when you provoke a Tamura beyond the point of tolerance."

She tapped the phone. Several trills later, it emitted a quiet click. "Mineko?" said a deep, puzzled voice. "Why are you calling me at work?"

"Dad." Mineko sobbed as tears—perhaps real ones—formed in her eyes. "You have to help me."

Blackmail. But it was no surprise that Mineko knew that art form. Her entire life, she'd witnessed her father's craft, and now she was putting the lessons to work…

Lachlan paled and gripped the lectern. Apparently, he was beginning to understand how it felt when somebody else held the strings. Mineko smirked at him, a contemptuous, superior twist of her lips.

"Help you?" said the astounded voice of Gaspar Tamura. "What's wrong? Are you in trouble?"

"I've been taken hostage. They're district people. Lachlan tried to save me. Him and Agent Turani, they risked their lives for me…"

Now that was one hell of a game-changing move. Sparing Lachlan, yet forcing him to remain complicit in order to enjoy mercy. Judging from Lachlan's dazed expression, the implications hadn't been lost on him either.

"Who has you?" said Gaspar. "Where are you? Describe anything you can see. Stay on the line, we'll track you."

It was time to do what little he could. Kade held out his hand. Mineko frowned at him but surrendered the phone. "Agent Tamura," Kade said. "This is Kade August. I have your daughter."

"What do you want from me?" The fuming tones of a powerful man in a situation outside his control.

"I want you to stop exploiting us for cheap labor. I want you to break the gangs instead of lending them your support. I want your internal oppression to end, for your caste system to be dismantled, for Codists to be allowed to express themselves as they choose. I want you to join us as comrades. To share the burden of a broken world."

"Radical drivel. What do you really want?"

There was only one path to take now. Kade took a deep breath. "I did this alone. That's all you need to know for now. I did this alone and nobody helped me." He ended the call with a tap from his thumb.

A second later, Lachlan's breast pocket buzzed. Still staring at Mineko, he answered the call.

"Reed here. Yes, sir. It's true, sir. Yes. He was heavily armed, I couldn't—yes, I'll be there straightaway. Yes, every detail. Of course. We'll get her back, sir. I'm sure August wouldn't harm—yes, I know. Yes. I was wrong. Clearly. Yes, sir."

He lowered the phone and locked gazes with the unsmiling young woman opposite him. "Your mother will be heartbroken."

"Someday, she'll understand," said Mineko. "Meanwhile, I hope you appreciate what I've done for you and Jasmine. My father will never doubt my version of events. You'll be pardoned, and Jasmine will get the promotion she's been craving. Be sure to remind her often that she owes it to my lie. Ambitious as she is, she'll understand her career now depends upon supporting our version of events."

Mineko ejected the battery from her phone and tossed it to Lachlan. "They'll try to track me through this, so take it and dump it in the street. Now you've spoken to my father and endorsed my deception, it's impossible for you to turn back. Furthermore, if you harm my friends, I'll call home and let them know you facilitated my escape. You've lost, Lachlan."

"To think I've been refusing to blackmail you, and now I'm the one being blackmailed. It's like I told you, Kade. Her father's mind."

"Did you plan this?" said Kade. "These choices, this outcome?"

"I've reacted to circumstances." Mineko clasped her hands behind her as she stared out the window. "I've long committed myself to the project of overcoming my own weakness, unlike Lachlan, who tries to delude himself that he has power inside here."

Lachlan pressed his fingers to his temples. "Get out. Leave me to clean up your mess."

Mineko inspected him the way a bird might contemplate an insect. "I know you intend to kill Lexi or to sabotage the Project in some other way. One of my parents will catch you in the end."

"Be warned. Your family name means nothing out there."

"Don't think I'm running. Remember, breathing is an involuntary act. Resistance must be chosen."

Where the hell had Mineko read Beatrice Abramo? But there was no time to ask, and she was already halfway to the door.

"I'll meet you outside," Kade said. "Five minutes."

"Five minutes." Mineko closed the door behind her.

Kade glanced over to Lachlan. "She outplayed you."

"Yes." Lachlan moved to the window and stared out. "Gaspar will have squads all over campus within the next half hour. They'll rake over her room and interrogate students. I have to admit, covering it up will be a challenge."

Kade joined Lachlan by the window. "But you do love a challenge."

"I've seen for myself how Callie Roux can drive, so I suppose they might even make it to Port Venn. Will Amity be going with them?"

"I doubt it. Foundation is her soil."

"Which she fertilizes with blood. Dear Amity. Did she recover quickly?"

"Very quickly. You'd best hope your paths don't cross again."

Lachlan shrugged. "Perhaps she'll come to forgive me."

"Unlikely. What about the gang boss who interfered with you yesterday? Do you plan on hassling her?"

"That she-colossus? Of course not. It would be a sin to remove such an astonishing specimen from Foundation's ecosystem." Lachlan breathed a soft, weary sigh. "You noble idiot."

The window sill was made of real wood, coarse, warmed by the sun. Kade pressed his palm to it. Hard to believe the entire world had once felt as alive and honest as this. "Noble doesn't seem the right word."

"You gave your name to Gaspar so that he would focus his search upon you. Desperate to regain Mineko, he'll devote the majority of our resources to that pursuit. Lexi will have every chance now of escaping the city. In other words, you've sacrificed yourself for her. It's far from a fair trade."

"You don't know her." Kade traced a whorled knot on the sill, following its wild shape. "She and Ash adopted me. A family distilled into two people. Lexi was a sister and a brother both, and Ash was our caretaker."

"It's hard to imagine you irresponsible enough to need a caretaker."

"Ash was older than us by a year. Mature as she was, it felt like a decade. That didn't stop me falling in love. And somehow, she returned my feelings."

The room brightened. Ironic that just as his heart was hurting most, the clouds outside had chosen to disperse, fully unveiling the sun and leaving the sky clearer than he'd ever seen it.

"Love," Lachlan said. "In times like these, you'd think we'd have moved on from that concept, yet here it is, still commanding us."

"I want Mineko to know what love feels like. Yes, it can be cruel, but my scars are the map I follow whenever I'm lost and frightened. Amity and Nikolas ask me why I never seem to despair. It's because I know that Ash died loving me. As love is deathless, that means she loves me still."

"And so she's the hero, while I'm the coward. You all claim to be repulsed by my treachery, yet when you thought it was only my own people I'd betrayed, you all admired me. In truth, I've betrayed nobody. There's no betrayal in ensuring one's own survival."

"A useful rationalization, I'm sure."

Lachlan stared at Kade with unguarded intensity in his eyes—an emotion somewhere between desperation and anger. "You grieved for Ash. You always will. But did you ever once grieve for me?"

"Only until I felt like a fool for doing so."

"Do you really think I never considered staying? I longed to. But Ash saw my motive, and she hated me for it."

"What are you talking about? What motive?"

"She's the one who reported me to Sarabelle. Never once letting me defend myself. She hated me because she saw from the beginning what you're too stupid to see even now." Lachlan touched Kade lightly on the cheek—a moment of fleeting contact that left a warm and lingering imprint on his skin. "I know very well how cruel love is, you arrogant son of a bitch. Had Ash only let me, I would have stayed for you."

He strode from the room. Kade stared after him, unable to speak. Confusion like an ache winding around his ribs. All these years, and he'd never even guessed.

Mineko peeked through the doorway. "Lachlan just stormed out. Why?"

"He said goodbye." It seemed truth enough.

"Good. Let's leave before the situation changes. We can take a rear exit to avoid the students outside."

"Sure. We'd better grab Callie and Riva first."

"Do you think Callie is disappointed with me?"

The plaintive question instantly exposed the vulnerable young girl beneath the armor. Kade inspected her with renewed sympathy. Her eyes were penetrating, true, but it was her mouth that made her seem so thoughtful. Her fragile lips curved slightly upward even in rest, as if they bore the imprint of some past happiness that refused to entirely fade.

"Don't worry about Callie," he said. "It takes time to really understand someone, and you two will have plenty of it."

"But will I ever get to know you? You aren't coming with us. I can tell."

"I'll be staying in Foundation. But just because I'm not physically beside you, that doesn't mean I'm not with you in every moment that matters."

"I don't understand."

Kade laughed, and Mineko gave him a bright, puzzled smile. At her age, he wouldn't have understood either. But now there was no fact he understood with more certainty or intimacy.

True, the price had been too great. Even so, it was paid.

CHAPTER 34

A titanic, gleaming monster swept aside the remains of a fallen skyscraper. With a grinding roar, the giant robot caught a fighter plane and smooshed it.

"How much do you think that cost?" said Zeke. "The robot, I mean."

From her comfortable position at the other end of the couch, Lexi frowned at him. "It's not real, dumbass. It's a special effect."

"I know that. I mean, how much do you think the effects cost? These old movies seem so fucking expensive. Cars blowing up, buildings falling down. And look at that dude in spandex spinning around shooting beams from his fucking hands. How much did *he* cost?"

"How the hell would I know? It probably didn't matter back then. They thought this was art."

A tank rolled down the street, shells spitting from its turret, only to be smashed beneath the robot's left foot. A second robot—bulky, green, covered in lights—hurtled into the first. The spinning dude promptly fired another sparkling beam from his hands.

"History. I don't get it." Zeke nabbed a peanut that Lexi had dropped between the cushions. "I'd take a good porno any day over this shit. Hell, we oughta watch one together right now. Bond over it."

"Surely by now you know I'm never going to sleep with you."

"C'mon, admit it. I'm your guilty fantasy."

Lexi flicked a peanut at him, and it pinged off his bald head. "When's the last time you got laid?"

"Hey, I get laid regular." Zeke took his electronic cigarette from his jacket pocket. "Granted, fifty percent of my sexual congress is people blowing me for a discount, but it counts." The blue light flared at his lips. "I hear Port Venn has good clubs. You gonna come with me when I check out the scene?"

"Sure. We'll take Riva and Callie, show them a fun time."

"What about Min?"

"I guess the kid can come too. But I'm not going to babysit her."

"Huh." Zeke sucked at the cigarette. "You don't think she and Callie are going to be soulmates or whatever?"

"I fucking hope not. Min's packed with neuroses. Doesn't know what the fuck she wants. At this point in her life, Callie needs someone mature. Sensitive. A babe who's able to articulate her own dreams and desires."

"So…we set her up with Riva, then?"

Lexi stretched back, grinning. "I don't think we'd have to do much. Just leave them both in the same room, close the door, check back in an hour."

"Can she come with us, Lex? She wants out."

"I don't make the decisions. Don't ask me." Lexi popped a peanut into her mouth. "If you and Callie like the girl so much, you two ask her."

"Don't play dumb. You know she won't come unless you want it too."

The more Lexi thought about Riva, the more her stomach felt like a scorpion pit. It had been hours since Riva and Callie had left, which meant Kade hadn't succeeded in talking them out of it. And that meant…

"Let's not talk about Riva right now," Lexi said. "I'm anxious."

"Yeah, me too. But I got faith in Callie to bring her back. I saw her catch a rattlesnake once."

"No kidding?"

"Fucking thing was in my lounge. I didn't know what the hell to do about it, so I called her in. She corners it, catches it, and I swear to God, starts patting the slithery son of a bitch. She thought it was cute."

Gazing into Zeke's eyes, Lexi took an idle trip through the memory. Callie holding the writhing snake behind its head, laughing as it coiled around her wrist… *Jesus, Callie, put that fucking thing in the cage already…*

Zeke pouted. "You're reading me, aren't you?"

"Not really. Just skimming the surface."

"Why can you read me from over there, but some people you gotta touch on the face? I never understood that."

"People are different. And to be honest, I'm getting better at it. Like this morning when I wiped all those gangsters at once." Lexi stared at the erratic light bulb above them. "I wonder what the limits are. Usually when I hit a wall, I stop, but lately I've been tempted to keep pushing. See what happens."

The bulb's filament trembled. Sometimes it was hard to believe she wasn't controlling such things too, willing the world to bend or break.

Zeke twirled his cigarette between his fingers. "Scary to think what a bad person might do with that power of yours."

"But I am a bad person. Gang scum. Vassago's flunky. Contessa's bitch."

"You think Contessa knows anything about all this?"

"Sure she does. She's the Queen of Foundation. And she's not going to be happy when she finds out I'm gone."

"What's she like in person? Is she sexy?"

"Yeah, but she's got a huge fucking ego. Take that fancy penthouse of hers. Her gang fixed up an entire luxury hotel, made it just like it used to be. Except for the view. Not even Contessa can make that pretty."

Zeke leaned closer. "You ever fuck her? If it ain't too sleazy to ask."

Sleazy in the extreme, but that had never stopped Lexi before. "In the course of our usual business, sure. And to tell you the truth, I don't much enjoy it. She calls all the shots. Likes to dominate me. Pushes my head between her legs, bends me over her desk, that sort of thing."

"She bends you over her desk? Like, with a strap-on?"

"That, or just to spank me." Lexi frowned. "I once got offered a hundred thousand to ice her. I said no, tipped Contessa off, and the gangster who suggested the deal ended up in a dumpster. No wonder Ash stopped wanting to have anything to do with me."

Zeke reclined again, his eyes thoughtful. "I remember when Ash would come to pick you up from my lounge, way back in the day, before you fell out with her and Kade. She was drop-dead fucking gorgeous. Smiled at me once. It was weird how good it made me feel."

Why had she let the topic shift to Ash? She didn't need any more another reasons for her stomach to twist inside out. "What's that got to do with anything?"

"The day she died, you told me that you had nothing left. Then you cried on my shoulder. I'd never seen that side of you before. I've never seen it since, but once was enough. Now I know it's bullshit when you act like you don't need people. You ain't pushing us all away because you don't want us. It's because you're scared of this shit. This needing people."

Lexi stared at the glowing tip of the cigarette. Fucking Zeke...

She was rescued from answering by the dramatic arrival of Amity, who rushed wide-eyed into the rec room. "They've come back. Kade phoned ahead and told me they have Mineko Tamura. I had to force Nikolas to open the garage door."

"Force?" said Lexi. "You mean he tried to turn them away?"

"He was conflicted, so I made the decision for him. They should be driving in now."

Zeke jumped to his feet. "Are they all okay? Nobody got hurt?"

"I don't know much." Amity gave a breathless laugh. "Mineko Tamura is coming here to Bunker One. Do you have any idea what that means?"

"The kid needs a better agent?"

"No, you idiot. It means all hell is about to break loose."

Callie's van rolled down the ramp, a grubby white box on wheels that just happened to contain pretty much all the people Lexi gave a damn about.

Open Hand had turned out to meet the arrivals. Nikolas looked even more ragged than usual, his ginger hair disarranged and his body language agitated. He moved without rest, pacing and fidgeting. In contrast, Amity exuded all the grim triumph of someone who'd just dug themselves out of their own grave.

A tanned, black-haired woman stood with Nikolas and Amity. Her scuffed brown coat, tilted fedora and casual stance set her apart from the Open Hand stiffs around her. Her creased face suggested somebody more likely to frown than laugh, and she didn't seem in the mood to smile now.

Lexi nudged Zeke. "Who's the tired-looking woman in the hat?"

"She came in earlier. That's Kade's boss. I forget the name."

Callie jumped out of the van. Whatever disguise she might have worn on her little adventure, she'd already ditched it. She took off her cap, brushed back her messy hair and grinned at Lexi. "Miss me?"

Riva emerged a second later. She flicked her pink bangs from her face, clearly attention-shy but smiling nonetheless, and waved.

After a deep breath to compose herself—it was important to look cool in front of the sexy girls—Lexi sauntered across the garage. "You took your time, Latour. I was beginning to think I wouldn't see you again."

"Don't be dumb." Callie gave Riva a fond look. "Of course I was going to bring her back."

"You're my hero, Callie Roux." Lexi cupped Callie's chubby cheeks and kissed her on the mouth. Her full lips proved enticingly soft, and it was impossible not to feel a stab of regret when she wriggled away, dimpled and blushing. "Now pass that kiss to Riva."

Callie giggled and twisted the cap in her hands. "Shut up."

The van's rear doors opened. Enter Kade and Mineko. The shut-in hadn't changed—same solemn little face, same perfect posture. It was surprisingly gratifying to see her again, and Lexi smiled without even meaning to. "Heya, Minnie-Min."

Mineko gave Lexi a long, studious look. "Hello, Lexi. I'm eager to talk to you, but I think I should speak with Nikolas first."

Odd. Lexi had expected more excitement, something like the childish interest with which Mineko had first taken in the sights and sounds of the streets. "Uh, sure."

Kade and Mineko resumed walking. As Kade passed Lexi, he glanced sidelong, and her smile faltered. He looked so lonely. So tired. And so much like the boy he'd once been. It was a jarring interruption in a moment that should have been pleasurable, like having sex with a girl only to find a lump in her breast.

"Min's been quiet the whole way," said Callie. "Hasn't said a word since we left the enclave. Even putting on the music didn't get a smile."

The revolutionaries converged, only to split into two separate discussions—Nikolas and Mineko holding one, Amity, Kade, and the unfamiliar woman holding the other.

"That's Sarabelle," Riva said. "She'll be chewing Kade out."

"What'd he do wrong?" Lexi said.

"He didn't tell her about Project Sky. And he certainly didn't get her permission to go into the University and rescue Mineko."

"Who cares what she thinks?" Callie seated her cap back on her head. "I've got to start prepping my baby for the road. You two want to help?"

"Ask Zeke instead." Lexi put an arm around Riva. "I'm going to borrow our favorite comrade, if you can bear to let her go."

A nervous excitement flared inside Callie, though anyone without a mind-reading chip might have been fooled by her casual grin. "Go ahead. Just make sure you bring her back to me."

"Will do." Lexi bumped Riva with her hip. "Can we go back to your place? I want to hear all about your adventures."

"Sure." Riva played with one of her earrings while giving Lexi a smile that trembled at its edges. "I'd like that."

Lexi peered up at a poster of a spindly, spiky-haired woman standing on the edge of a stage, singing toward the silhouetted heads of an audience. "It's weird to think all the musicians in your posters are dead."

"It sinks in sometimes." Riva faced the mirror and fussed with her hair, adjusting the strands to fall more neatly across her face. "The books we read, the films we watch. The entertainment of the dead. The streets we walk on, the apartments we live in. Built by the dead. We imitate their fashions, speak their languages, recreate their machines. Obsessed by what we've lost, we mimic them instead of starting again."

Lexi touched the glossy surface of the poster. Good condition, given the tour had taken place in 2043. "I wonder what she sounded like."

"Listen." Riva tapped a few buttons on her stereo, and a lethargic melody crept from the speakers. Beneath layers of guitar drone, a bass line shivered like a heart on the brink of dying, while a keyboard pierced the sonic cloud with ethereal high notes and somber low ones.

"I like this." Lexi listened, transfixed, as vocals joined the mix—sometimes a husky crooning, other times a sensual growl. "I really like this."

"She was trans too. The singer. I didn't know when I first discovered her music, and when I found out…well, it was a moment." Riva closed her eyes as she swayed to the music. "It's so easy to feel I'm the only one."

"You're not."

"I know, but most of us hide it. There was once a brief period when we didn't have to, when people like me could be proud. Imagine if things had gone differently."

Lexi settled onto the edge of the bed. "Are you happy with yourself?"

"My body isn't always what I want it to be, and it's rarely what others prefer, but I've grown to fit it." Once again, it seemed as if Riva were staring through her reflection, seeing something on the other side. "It's like I survived a violent crash, a collision between the person I am and the one I was expected to be, and then pieced myself together from the fragments."

"Seems to me you did a pretty good job."

"Maybe. But while you can fit broken pieces together, you can't always hide the lines where they meet. Some days, that's all I can see."

"My chip." Lexi felt for the scar on her scalp. "The shut-ins would use it on people like us, wouldn't they? Straighten us out?"

"Yes. That's the plan." Riva turned from the mirror. "When Codists wipe someone, they call it Reintegration. That's a lie. True reintegration means finding yourself in fragments. and when that happens, Lexi, it's beautiful. We should never be ashamed of our patchwork selves."

Lexi stretched on the mattress. The drowsy music washed over her. "Will you take my boots off?"

"I'm powerless to refuse." Riva crouched at the foot of the bed and began unlacing Lexi's bootlaces. "Are you going to talk to Kade before you leave?"

"Maybe. By the way, if you're wondering about the bruises on my neck, that was Amity. She bites."

"You got your wish, then?"

"Yep. It was nice. Rough, but nice." Lexi shifted onto her side. "You aren't even slightly upset that I had sex with your best friend. That's one of the many things I like about you."

Riva reclined on the bed and wriggled close. "Amity deserves intimacy. We all do." As she spoke, her breath warmed Lexi's nape. "Did you make each other happy?"

"I hope so." Lexi rolled over, bringing her face-to-face with Riva. "Sex means a lot to me. We're so vulnerable when we're naked together, and I need to be reassured that it's normal to be afraid of each other. And of ourselves. Especially ourselves."

Emotion welled from Riva's eyes, a sensory accompaniment to the hazy music. Tenderness. arousal, fear, stricken anticipation. The certainty that Lexi would be leaving and that all this would be lost…

With the tip of her index finger, Lexi traced the indented outline of Riva's upper lip. "Can we?"

Riva flushed. "I have to take something off first. I'd rather you not see me do it."

"Okay." Lexi shut her eyes. "But dress again once you're done, so that I can undress you myself."

Riva shifted on the bed. The clink of springs was followed by the sound of a zipper opening. Elastic snapped. Clothing rustled. "It's done." Riva sounded weak. "I'm sorry about that."

Lexi opened her eyes. Though she remained dressed as before, Riva sat differently. her legs crossed and her hands folded in her lap.

"You're the only one who still sees those broken lines," Lexi said. "All I see is you."

Their lips met, and a strange fluttering filled Lexi's chest. It was familiar somehow, yet distant too. Like a memory from a long time ago. Like the fading trace of an old dream.

Lexi admired her own reflection as she undressed. She knew the terrain well: flat stomach, barely-there breasts tipped by pale pink areolas, broad shoulders, narrow waist, elegant prominences of bone at hips and collar, slender legs curving up to a compact behind. For the sake of a little mystery, she kept her panties on.

"Your turn, babe," she said.

Riva removed her shirt. Underneath, she wore a plain black bra. Lexi unclasped it with a single expert pinch. Riva's breasts were barely large enough to be cupped, and her tiny, dark nipples were already erect. Lexi teased one with her fingertip, and Riva twitched.

"We need to jump right to the part that's terrifying you," said Lexi. "Otherwise, you'll never relax."

"I know. But I'm terrified for a good fucking reason."

"Swear more often. It's cute." Lexi took hold of Riva's zipper. "May I?"

"Yes." Riva exhaled. "Do it."

Together, they removed Riva's jeans. Her pale green panties were stretched taut over a subtle bulge, which she moved to conceal with her hand.

"It's okay." Lexi gently brushed Riva's hand aside. "I want to touch you."

Riva closed her eyes and nodded. If there was ever a time Lexi wished her chip had an off-switch, this was it. The tumult of dread spilling from Riva was almost impossible to think through.

Lexi put a hand on Riva's crotch and smirked as the soft shape moved under her palm. Nothing quite like giving a pretty girl a hard-on. "Think about it this way, babe. You'd still do me if I had a dick, wouldn't you?"

"In a heartbeat. But people are entitled to have preferences."

"There's preferences, and then there's making women feel like they're only as important as what's between their legs. Now, are there any rules?"

"Um. I don't use it to penetrate."

"That's fine by me. I was hoping to grind. Is that okay?"

Riva managed a nervous smile. "It's okay."

Lexi settled into Riva's lap. She moved her hips, rubbing herself against the growing hardness compressed inside Riva's panties, and at the same time, Riva explored Lexi's body with her hands—traveling the lines of her ribs, brushing the arc of her collarbone, following her inner thighs, touching each bump of her spine.

They kissed. Riva's erection pushed free of her panties, a slender cock forcing through a band of tight elastic, and she stopped kissing and fumbled to hide it.

"Leave that alone." Lexi caught Riva by the wrist. "You're here to play with me." She redirected Riva's hand into her own panties, and Riva blushed as her fingers glided through Lexi's wetness.

With her free hand, Lexi gripped Riva's cock. This felt so fucking good—the agile fingers thrusting into her pussy, the gorgeous, gasping woman whose dick she was pumping, the soft breast in her mouth, the stiff nipple she was flicking back and forth between her teeth...

Fuck, fuck, she needed to settle down. There was still one more thing she had to try. "I want to eat you out," Lexi said.

"What?"

"I want to suck your dick, babe. Is that okay?"

"I didn't think you..." Riva gave a quick nod. "Okay."

Lexi took Riva into her mouth and began sucking, moving her lips across tightly-stretched skin. Riva murmured. Lexi kept sucking, slickening that firm shaft with her mouth. Riva gave a quiet groan. Probably faking it.

Lexi flicked her tongue, and Riva clutched Lexi's shoulders. That seemed like a good sign. Lexi sucked faster. Any minute now, she'd have Riva in helpless convulsions—

With a loud, wet pop, Riva's cock slipped out of her mouth.

"Oh, shit." Lexi's face burned. "I'm sorry. I have zero blowjob experience."

Riva giggled. "It's okay."

Lexi gave her a rueful smile before lowering her head again. Wasn't fellatio supposed to be easier than cunnilingus? Maybe if she tried—

"I said, it's okay." Riva lifted Lexi's head from her lap. "Come back."

"But babe..."

"Don't be greedy." Riva slowly licked her upper teeth. "It's my turn."

Now that was a compromise Lexi could accept. She laughed, sprawled back on the bed and angled her knees apart. "Go on, then. Show me how it's done."

They curled together, as entangled as two people could be without the aid of a freak transporter accident, and nuzzled one another. Sweat cooled on their bodies and the bunched sheets beneath them.

"I'm not your first," Lexi said. "You've definitely eaten pussy before."

"I'm glad you could tell."

"Can I ask how many women you've been with?"

"Less than two. More than none."

Lexi grinned. "What was she like?"

"Gentle. Funny. But she wouldn't touch it. She explained that it was just her own sexual preference, that she wasn't attracted to penises. I still couldn't help but feel like I was disgusting to her. She never even liked to feel it against her when we slept."

"But she did let you pleasure her."

"Yes. She had no complaints about my mouth." Riva kissed Lexi's shoulder. "If I wanted to come, I had to do that myself. And afterward, I'd feel queasiness and a desperate need to hide. I'd call it shame, except I don't want to use that word."

"Did you feel it this time too?"

"Yes. I was hoping I wouldn't, but I did." Riva pressed her cheek into the hollow of Lexi's neck. "But then you put your arms around me, and the sick feeling went away. I'm going to miss you."

The fluttering was back, beating in Lexi's chest like a trapped bird. She sat upright. "You're coming with us, though. Aren't you?"

Yet more emotions poured from Riva's startled blue-gray eyes. Lexi blinked, trying to sever the connection, but they kept coming. Wonder, joy, bewilderment, adoration, apprehension, doubt…a storm of confused, contradictory feelings.

"But Port Venn is so far away," said Riva. "How can I trust you won't abandon me there? You've told me that you don't do relationships."

"That's true, but you're not someone I want to move on from." Lexi took Riva's hand. "I'm not suggesting you be my exclusive girlfriend or anything. I don't think that'd be right for either of us. But we can still have something special. We can hold onto this."

"What does 'this' mean?"

"You're my friend. I care about you. I want to have sex with you. And I promise to never leave you stranded. If Port Venn isn't for you, if you get sick of us, I swear I'll find a way to get you back here."

"I don't have words." Riva blinked tears from her lashes. "But I don't need them. Not with you."

Lexi pulled Riva back to her, and they wriggled until they were perfectly interlocked, a warm jumble of limbs. Vulnerable together. Strong together.

As much as it hurt to face it, Ash hadn't respected Lexi before the end. She'd become distant, scornful, prone to scolding. *Everyone needs a cause, Lexi. If you aren't fighting for change, you're bequeathing all this to the next generation. The struggle, the squalor, the bullshit.*

But now, as Lexi held Riva close to her bare skin, it was never more evident that she did have a cause, a camaraderie of defiant bodies and unrepentant desires. It was the same struggle that had made Kade so patient, Zeke so tolerant, Callie so gentle, Riva so generous...

And if a moment like this were still possible—if people like Lexi and Riva could create together such a perfect instant of warmth, solace and solidarity—then it meant that the queer revolution had never ended.

It had only gone underground.

CHAPTER 35

Sarabelle was angrier than Kade had ever seen her—including the time an edition had gone to print with a typo in the main headline. "Keeping company with Codists, gangsters and smugglers," she said. "Dealing with Reed. Who are you loyal to, anyway?"

"Don't question his loyalty." Amity loomed over her. "There's a limit to the slander I'll endure hearing."

"Oh, keep out of it, you thug. He doesn't work for you, he works for me. Not that you'd know it, the way he's been carrying on."

A few meters away, Nikolas and Mineko continued their quiet conversation. Kade would have given a great deal to know what they were saying to each other. Unfortunately, he was stuck listening to his incensed editor.

"The shut-ins will tear the press to pieces," Sarabelle said. "They'll march in and smash my printer."

Kade shook his head. "I told Gaspar Tamura I was solely responsible. Lachlan will do his part to ensure my lie is believed."

"Why would he do that? Why would he?" Sarabelle flung up her hands. "And you spoke to Gaspar Tamura? For God's sake!"

"Certainly the biggest scoop I've ever had."

"You son of a bitch. I ought to use your blood as ink for the next edition."

Amity scowled, and Sarabelle took a nervous step away from her. "I didn't mean that literally, you brute. You look like you're one primal instinct away from snarling at me."

"No," said Amity. "I passed that point a few minutes ago. I'm now one primal instinct away from tearing out your throat."

"It's that girl you should be menacing. That little Tamura monster. If you have any sense, you'll take her right back to her parents wrapped in a big bow with a gift card that says 'I'm so very, very sorry.' And maybe some fucking chocolates just in fucking case, you fucking idiots."

Kade chuckled. "All my years of service have been erased in an instant of your white-hot temper, I see."

"I can't believe you kept this a secret from me. The Codists are making mind-reading cyborgs. That headline writes itself, Kade."

"Nobody would believe you," Amity said. "It sounds like science fiction."

"Science fiction? We live in a dystopian nightmare! People traipse around with chips in their spines while a cabal of reclusive ideologues develop evermore-sinister technologies to exert their control over the drug-fueled gangsters who run riot in the districts! There is no such thing as science fiction anymore. An alien could land in the street and it would be business as usual. Hell, somebody would try to fix it up with some junk and a hooker."

Amity blinked. "I beg your pardon?"

"You just—" Sarabelle took a deep breath. "Fine. I have to remind myself that you aren't creative types down here. No, you're goose-stepping paramilitary morons with sticks wedged so firmly up your asses, the act of shitting freely is but a distant memory."

"I suggest you watch your tongue."

"Oh yes, I'm sure you'd love to tear out my ovaries and then hang me with them, you bloodthirsty ass." Sarabelle flailed a hand in the direction of Lexi, who was ascending the stairs with one arm around Riva. "Somebody tell that cyborg to get back here. I need to interview her before it's too late."

"You know her name," said Kade. "Don't 'that cyborg' her. And I can guarantee you she's not interested in an interview."

"Of course not. She's dragging off that pink-haired woman, hoping for one last explosion of Sapphic passion before the Codists run her out of town. Her reputation does her justice." Sarabelle clenched her fists. "Damn it, she's getting away. Kade, call her back."

"You could always talk to Zeke. I'm sure he'd love to be interviewed."

"The body-modder?" Sarabelle glanced at Zeke, who was snooping on Nikolas and Mineko's conversation. "I hear he's weird, though."

"He's a charming man," said Amity. "Go talk to him." She placed both hands on Sarabelle's back and pushed her in Zeke's direction. "Go on. Get."

"Don't you handle me. I'll talk to whom I please. His surname is Lukas, right?" Taking her recorder from her pocket, Sarabelle approached Zeke with the furtive gait she always assumed when stalking her prey.

Amity gave Kade a wry look. "You and your infinite forbearance. Now, let's go see what nonsense Nikolas is putting into that girl's head."

Mineko and Nikolas were still in intense discussion, each appearing as serious as the other. They broke off as Kade and Amity approached.

"Hello," said Mineko. "Are you the woman I spoke to on the phone yesterday?"

"Yes. I'm Amity White. You warned me about the helicopter, and for that, I'm grateful."

"It was my fault they located you. I don't deserve any praise."

"I said you had my gratitude, not my praise. In any case, if Lexi has vouched for you, then the question of your worth is entirely resolved. Nikolas, I suggest we give Ms. Tamura whatever she requires, assist Callie with the servicing of her van, and send these people on their way."

"In time." Nikolas flashed a boyish grin. "First, we need to compose some kind of message to accompany our brave voyagers. I was just now telling Mineko about our friend Kristiano Iglesia and how he should perhaps not be informed of Mineko's true identity. It would put her at considerable risk."

"You don't trust your own man?" said Kade.

"He does believe in the cause. The Port Venn chapter has always remained loyal. But his broader values are questionable."

"Lieutenant Commander Iglesia is an excellent soldier," said Amity. "But that's the extent of the kind words I have for that bastard. Keep Mineko's identity secret, and even more importantly, conceal Project Sky from him. He'd use Lexi as a weapon."

Nikolas raised an eyebrow. "Wasn't that your own intention?"

"I've since learned the error of my thinking."

"Excellent. Now, I have a further proposition. I believe we should send a loyal comrade of the Foundation Chapter to act as my official delegate. I've considered the options and have decided upon Riva Latour. Naturally, Amity, I require your approval."

That was a serious promotion—from kitchen hand to Nikolas's proxy. Amity seemed taken aback, but the strongest reaction came from Mineko, who looked as though somebody had forced a lemon into her mouth.

"Min," Kade said. "Why don't you go help Callie with the van? She could probably use an extra pair of hands."

Mineko gave a curt nod. "I'll do that. When will you be leaving?"

"Well, I'm a liability here. My presence puts all these good people at risk. But I won't leave without saying goodbye."

"Please don't." Mineko pivoted on her heel and headed toward the van. Callie looked up, smiled and waved.

"Interesting." Amity continued to frown in Mineko's direction. "She clearly disapproves of Riva. Why?"

"They may need to warm to each other," Nikolas said. "It takes time for Codists to adjust. Even so, she's a charming girl. Controlled, understated intelligence. Wonderfully poised. Don't you agree, Amity?"

"Yes, she's impressive, especially when you consider her age. But she also makes me uneasy. There's a remoteness to her."

"She's just lost her parents. I'm sure she's not quite herself."

"I'm sure you're right. Let's rescue Zeke from Sarabelle and bring her to help take care of the paperwork. She may actually be useful for once."

"Ah, yes." Nikolas rubbed the creased flesh of his forehead. "Sarabelle."

They found the unlikely pair consulting behind a jeep. Far from needing rescue, Zeke seemed to be reveling in Sarabelle's attention.

"…right at the windshield," he said, complete with frantic hand gestures. "Bam! Shatters the fucking glass! And then Amity pumps the shotgun and says, 'Bring it, bitches, I'll put the next one right up your ass—'"

"I did not say that," said Amity. "Be quiet, you ridiculous little man."

"Oh, sure, not exactly. But that was your attitude, right? And then we were on the road again. Callie's like a fucking demon behind the wheel. Shut-ins roaring behind us in hot pursuit. Lexi's clutching me and screaming—"

"What about the helicopter?" Sarabelle appeared to have absorbed Zeke's manic energy. "Was it still chasing you?"

"Oh, yeah. That fucker was zooming over the road like some kind of angel of death. And that Reed guy, he's all leaning out its door, shouting abuse, you know, saying, 'I'm gonna get you, I'm comin' for you, you're all dead meat!'"

"Lachlan Reed said that?"

"No, not exactly, but I was paraphrasing, you know? And then—" Zeke mimed shooting. "Lexi takes a shot. Pow! And she misses!"

"You have it out of order," said Kade. "She fired at Lachlan before Amity broke the windscreen."

"Man, fuck the shut up, huh?" As usual, Zeke didn't seem to care whether his words made sense to anyone but himself. "Linear conceptions of time do not do this madness justice. Now listen. A guy rides up on a fucking bike, all ready to hurl a grenade. I'm shitting myself. Feces pooling around my feet. And Lexi's like,

'Someone save us!' She's in tears. And then Kade gets out his gun and just ices the biker. One shot. Boom! Dead shut-in."

"Kade killed someone?" Sarabelle glowered at Kade. "I don't pay him to kill people." She tapped a button on her recorder. "Can you all go away? You're interrupting my interview."

"I don't got to stop yet, do I?" said Zeke. "I want to tell the part where Rusalka throws down with Reed. The shut-in cyborg versus the biggest woman to ever lick blood off a switchblade. You coulda sold tickets to that fight. Wish I'd seen it."

Amity took hold of Zeke's shoulders, and he gave an indignant yelp as she forcibly moved him aside. "Go play elsewhere," she said. "I'm sure Mineko would love hearing your absurd stories."

Zeke brightened. "Oh, yeah, she would! I could tell her about the thing that went down at Raffo's place."

"The Mutant?" Sarabelle brandished her tape recorder again. "What does he have to do with this? Is Vassago involved as well?"

"Later," said Kade. "We have duties, comrade. Correspondence needs to be written, people have to be notified. Zeke, we'll see you around."

"Yeah, sure." Zeke gave Amity an insolent grin before scuttling off.

"An amusing man, but entirely mad," said Sarabelle. "Kade, you'd better give me a clear and lucid account later."

"I can't promise it'll be comprehensive, but I can guarantee it'll make more sense than anything Zeke just told you." Kade clapped her on the shoulder. "Cheer up, boss. Maybe we'll finally have that drink."

"You know that'll never happen now. Not with the target on your head." Sarabelle sighed. "Come on, then. Let's get this over and done with. "

After an hour of arguing—Amity griping at Nikolas, Sarabelle griping at Amity, Nikolas griping at both of them, Kade trying not to laugh—the worst of the formalities were concluded. Nikolas sat at his desk, looking weary, while Sarabelle frowned at the letter they'd written for Kristiano Iglesia.

"Are you really sure about this last sentence?"

"Yes," said Nikolas. "Yes, I am sure."

"Fine. Commit crimes against the English language. Take the final step into anarchy."

"With great pleasure." Nikolas opened his drawer, took out a flask and set it on the table with a resonant tap. "Excuse my rudeness, but I'm not offering this to anyone else."

"I don't think anyone else would want it," Amity said. "Knowing you, that's straight vodka in there."

"A little taste of reality." As Nikolas unscrewed the flask, he gave Amity a level look. "There's something else on your mind, isn't there?"

"Yes. Commander Reinhold, I formally resign my position."

Sarabelle gasped. No doubt Kade looked as stunned. Amity loved her ranking position. This was as impossible as Lexi Vale giving up women.

Yet Nikolas didn't seem surprised. "Elaborate."

"All of Foundation will be hunting for Kade. He needs a bodyguard who can stand fast against an entire city."

"Amity..." Kade faltered. He'd intended to make this sacrifice alone. It was unimaginable that someone else would make it with him.

Nikolas stared at his hands—those large, strong hands that Kade had never seen used for violence. "Your request is granted. I'll sleep better knowing he's in your care. But I hope you understand that I'll be unable to replace you."

A faint smile softened Amity's tired face. "You were always threatening to demote me."

"I never would have done it." Nikolas motioned to the door. "I'm going to say farewell to you now, Comrade August. Sarabelle and I need to talk in private about the future of the revolution."

"I'm sorry about the trouble I've caused," Kade said. "But I don't think the Codists will come after you. Lachlan's looking out for us."

"I know you want to believe that, but he's only looking out for himself." Nikolas took a swig of vodka and set the flask aside. "One last thing. If Audra is carrying a boy, I'd like to name him Kade. How do you feel about that? And if it's a girl—"

Kade smiled. "You'll name her Ash."

"Please be careful out there, comrade. We need you."

Kade and Amity left Nikolas still drinking and Sarabelle glaring at the letter. Amity set off down the hallway at her usual brisk stride, and Kade tried to keep pace.

"Who do you trust?" she said. "That's the first thing we need to establish."

"I have a friend at the *Gazette* I can count on. Nice guy. Fond of animals. He knows the city as well as anyone, so he might be able to think of a place for us to hide."

"Good. We need to distance ourselves from Open Hand for a time." Amity licked her lips, for the first time betraying a trace of anxiety. "In my absence, I hope Nikolas reinforces his personal guard. Especially given one of his better soldiers is compromised."

"Compromised? That's the word you use for pregnant?"

"I consider it an accurate term. Nikolas is too gentle to protect himself, which is why he keeps me at his side." Amity gave a sharp laugh. "It's strange. I despised his weakness even as I admired him for it. He never would have risen to the leadership of Open Hand without my backing, yet without his kindness, I wouldn't even be here. I'd be a bloodthirsty creature on the street, another ghoul feeding on death and chaos."

"I'm glad you aren't. There are more than enough of those."

"They exist in Port Venn too. If Lexi is complacent even for a moment—"

Before Amity could finish speaking, Riva walked around the corner with a cardboard box in her arms. Her Mohawk had been restored to its towering splendor, and she wore a smile heartbreaking in its intensity. As she noticed Kade and Amity, the smile wavered.

"Riva." Amity nodded at the box. "What's this?"

"My belongings. I'm going to Port Venn."

"I'm glad." Amity took the box from Riva's unresisting hands and set it on the floor. "Tell me about this decision of yours."

"Lexi asked me to come." Riva's smile returned, wide enough to set her eyes shining. "These people are incredible, Am. Callie's so beautiful and brave, and Zeke's sweet and funny. And they're all queer like me. I feel comfortable when I'm with them. Like I belong."

"And Mineko? How do you feel about her?"

"I don't think she likes me. But I'm not completely fragile, you know. I've lived on the streets."

"And that didn't end well." Amity spoke softly, even gently. "We'll always be here if you need us. Open Hand is your family."

"You are, and I'm grateful, but this is still the most exciting day of my life. I can't wait to tell Callie."

"I wish I could be there to see her reaction. Unfortunately, this is our goodbye. I need to get Kade to safety."

"Right now? But I'm still not ready. How am I supposed to say goodbye? Amity, I love you…"

"I love you too." Amity embraced Riva and squeezed her hard before letting her go. "See Nikolas before you leave. He has an important instruction for you."

Riva scooped up her box, wiped away tears, gave Kade a desperate, apologetic look—he lifted a hand in recognition, tried to convey as best he could that she didn't need to say a word—and vanished down the hall.

"You seem surprised," Amity said.

"I've not seen you hug anyone before."

"My greatest regret is that I never once held Ash. I never even told her that I loved her. I refuse to make the same mistake again."

Shit. If Kade didn't control himself, he was going to be the next one in tears. He took a measured breath. "Then you'd best say farewell to Lexi before you leave. You may not see her again, and I know she's grown fond of you."

"About that." Amity hesitated. "You know her better than anyone."

"In all honesty, yes, I do."

"Then you know that she has a secret. An anxiety. Something relating to her identity."

Was it really possible Lexi had confided in Amity? It had been a strange week, after all. "I think I know what you're referring to, but I don't want to be specific if there's a chance I'm wrong."

"We can talk around the specifics. My concern is that Riva may get hurt. She wants to be loved by a woman, Kade. Note my emphasis. A woman."

So they *were* talking about the same thing. Amazing. "Lexi isn't sure about her gender. Strict categories are stifling to her. But keep in mind, much of what we admire and love about her comes from that inner rebellion."

"And you think Riva will be able to accept it? That inner rebellion?"

"I think she's lived it." Kade tried to meet Amity's gaze, but for some reason, she kept averting her eyes. "I have to ask. Why did she tell you this? How did the topic even come up?"

"We were talking about transgender people. I don't recall the reason why. She told me she was once very close to someone of that nature. Being her oldest friend, I suppose you might have known them too."

"Did she say who that person was?"

"No." Amity stared down the hallway, distracted. "She didn't."

Did he dare? His fear, as always, was of the terrible switch being hit. That inevitable reassessment. *So that's why his hands are so small and his shoulders so slim.* As though men never had slight builds. *So that's why he has those cheekbones.* As though no man had ever been pretty. Every time he divulged, his body was dismantled into clues for those hell-bent on refashioning him in the image of a woman. Yes, that was his fear. The moment they dismembered him with their eyes.

Yet, besides Lexi, he had nobody with whom he could share his life without eliding its most shattering dynamic. And if anyone knew what it was like to carry the weight of the unspeakable past, it was Amity.

So what the hell.

"Amity, I am that person."

It didn't seem to sink in at first. Then Amity's eyes widened, and the light caught the tears filling at their rims. "Just between us," said Kade.

Amity nodded. She touched her knuckles to her lips and blinked until the tears were gone. "Did Ash know?"

"Of course."

"I always thought I understood how you must have grieved for her. But now I realize that I wasn't even close." Amity bowed her head. "I can't say goodbye to Lexi. There's no way to keep secrets from her, and I need to part from her with dignity. So go say your farewells, and I'll wait for you in my room."

Just when he'd thought the day had exhausted its surprises. "You've fallen in love with her."

Amity glanced up. She was blushing but smiling too, with a radiance that cut through her customary shadow. "Just between us."

———

Callie had extracted a gadget from her van and was showing it off to Mineko and Zeke. Kade walked over, and the trio looked up. "Heya!" Callie had managed to land a dab of grease on her cheek, and more dirt smeared her left arm. "How's it going?"

"I was hoping you could direct me to Lexi."

"She drifted past us fifteen minutes ago. Said 'hi' and kept on moving."

"I think she'd gotten laid," said Zeke. "She had that little wiggle she gets. No prizes for guessing who the lucky girl was."

"Her and Riva make a hot couple, but I'm sad I wasn't invited." Callie wiped her hands on her shorts. So that was how the grease traveled. "Min says you were handling paperwork."

"We're finished," Kade said. "Now it's time for me and Amity to go into hiding. She's sworn to be my full-time bodyguard."

"That's reassuring news," said Callie. "Nobody's going to mess with you and the A-Bomb. Where is she? Do we get to say goodbye?"

"She can't make it, but she wishes you well."

"Aww, really?" Zeke's lower lip drooped. "But I was just getting to know her. I swear she was warming to me."

"This is kinda hard on me, Kade." Callie fixed him with her soulful eyes. "You're in trouble now, and I can't help you. I won't even know if something happens to you. That's not how I like to part from my friends."

Parting. The word felt real now, a concept with solidity, a bitter taste. "It's going to be rough," Kade said. "But this is the fight I chose."

"It's my fight too," said Mineko. "I'll be back someday to join you."

"Don't come until you're ready. You made it this far by biding your time."

"Speaking of time." Mineko took an old-fashioned watch and a tiny key from her pocket. "Lately, the ticking of this watch has been more real to me than the beating of my own heart. It's something from an uncodified place and time, and it's beautiful. Truthful. Just by being real, ticking in my palm, it proves Codism to be a lie."

She held out the watch and key. "Wind it every morning and think of us."

Kade accepted the watch, studied its embossed surface, and opened the cover. Two slender hands glided over a pale white face decorated by a series of gold digits. One more gentle motion of the hands and, suddenly, it became too beautiful to endure. He shut his eyes for a moment until the pain passed. "I don't know if I can take your watch, Min."

"Most of us had some prior connection with Project Sky. Lexi wields the implant. Zeke installed it. Callie stole it. My people built it. But you became involved purely by choice. It wasn't money, power, or survival that drove you, but loyalty. Friendship. I only wish my father was the man you are. Please take the watch, Kade."

Kade closed his fingers over the watch and nodded. "Thank you."

Mineko glanced at Callie. "That's okay, isn't it?"

"Yeah." Callie smiled—the same dimpled, roguish smile that had secured Kade's affection all those years before. "It's exactly right."

The sound of raucous laughter led Kade to a barracks crowded with young revolutionaries. Lexi lounged in their midst, her deep purr commanding the room's attention.

She raised her handsome head and smiled at him, her eyes seeming to glow beneath her lashes. She was never more otherworldly than when exerting her seduction. "Join us, comrade."

"Be warned," Kade said. "She's notorious for stretching the truth."

"Says the journalist. I suppose you're here to spoil everyone's fun."

"No. Just to say goodbye."

Lexi's smile faded. She made a languid gesture with her fingers, and the revolutionaries trouped from the barracks—bizarrely, given that it was their room to begin with. "So say goodbye, then."

"If it were that simple, you wouldn't have sent them away."

They contemplated one another in silence. Kade had once been so envious of her appearance, the way she confused assumptions of gender. Everything about her sustained that ambiguity—the lithe, assertive way she walked, the graceful gestures she made when she spoke, her sprawled manner of sitting with boots apart and legs outstretched. A delicate performance of strength.

For years, Kade had tried to copy her elegant swagger, yet for him the feminine had been far more than just a suggestion. He'd had the wrong hips, the wrong torso, and as he'd matured, it had only become worse. All the while, Lexi had stayed tall, narrow, and flat-chested. It said a great deal about their friendship that he had never once resented her for it.

"Remember that bomber jacket?" said Kade. "The one from the bar?"

"I remember. You wanted it so badly."

"It was far too big. Ash was right to give it to you."

"You were a late bloomer. You sure did bloom, though."

"Thanks to you."

"I just got you the drugs. The hard work, that was all you." Lexi inspected her fingernails. "Is it weird that I miss those fucked-up days?"

"I don't miss them." Not the days when his clothes didn't fit, when his body seemed to belong to someone else, when meeting someone new was an exercise in humiliation. "I just miss you, Lexi. Sometimes I miss you more than I miss Ash. At least she died still loving me."

"It's funny being in her old workplace. It wasn't Nicky running the show back then, though, was it?"

So they were finally going to talk about her. Well, it was about time. "No. Her commander was Nathan Bastian."

"The old boss. I vaguely remember the name."

Kade couldn't—refused to—forget. It was Bastian, that ruddy, sweat-stinking beast, who had ignored Ash's report that an Open Hand shelter was being used for forced prostitution. Kade, idiot that he was, had suggested they could expose the ringleaders by going undercover. Just like the journalists of old.

"We were naïve," he said. "We never imagined it might end the way it did."

"What always gets me is how fucking stupid you both were. Playing detective when lives were at risk. Like you were making a game of it."

"Yes. I was fucking stupid, Lexi."

A tear spilled from her left eye, cresting her high cheekbone, cutting through her dark eyeliner. "It was me who brought you two together. I introduced you to her, and I helped her to understand that you were a man. Not just any man, but her man. I did that, did it all for you, and what did I get? I lost you both. You chose her, while she came to hate me."

"She never hated you. And I never chose against you. You and I, we simply grew apart."

"She never mentioned me to Amity. Not once."

"You know why that is. Because you told her not to. Not because she was ashamed of you." Kade steeled himself. "On the subject of Amity. We detained the killers, intending to try them. I went to visit them that same night, only to find that Amity had gotten there first. She was in a frenzy, soaked in gore. When I told her to stop, she broke down and cried."

"She'd killed them herself?"

"Yes. And the next morning, Nikolas admitted he'd given her the key."

"Nikolas? I thought he was opposed to that sort of thing."

"It shows you how much they loved her. Afterward, Nikolas challenged for the leadership, blaming Ash's death on Commander Bastian. He won, not because everyone admired him, but because we had all respected Ash. She's a hero in the underground, and she's still part of it, fighting through us. Even in private, she called me 'comrade.' It's why I keep going. She'd never have wanted me to walk away."

"You two should have come to me. I'd have sorted those fuckers out."

"Vassago and his cronies are our enemies as much as the Codists are. Ash blamed them for the suffering of children. That was what drove her. The thought of little Kades and Lexis she couldn't keep out of trouble."

"Sometimes when I wake up, I think I see her at the foot of my bed. Watching over my sleep the way she did when we were little." Lexi gave a wan smile. "Back before we had you."

"She always read everything I wrote. I couldn't write for a year after she died. It seemed pointless." Kade tried to take another breath, but his lungs refused him air. "I was in the middle of an essay when it happened. She was so excited to see how it would end, and she never—"

It was the breaking point, but Lexi was there. She held him to her chest while he sobbed against her shirt, each breath convulsive and futile. Her body was warm, her embrace unyielding, her murmurs gentle.

"It's okay, Kade. I'm here now." She ran her fingers through his hair. "We're strong together, remember?"

Be careful in there, he'd said. Ash had smiled at him. Given him a thumbs up. And he'd laughed, and he'd never seen her again.

"The day you came to me with your secret, I was wrestling with telling you mine," Lexi said. Still holding him tight, still stroking his hair. "You spared me having to get it out, but I never did let myself fall in love again."

She smiled, her eyes distant. The same way she'd looked at him when they were kids, sitting by the old tracks at evening, passing bottles and sharing little secrets. Finding covert ways to admit to the big ones.

"I'm taking Riva with me," she said. "I don't want to lose her. Do you know why?"

"Because she reminds you of Ash. I feel it too."

"No, stupid." Lexi spoke with a tenderness he'd never expected to hear again. "She reminds me of you."

She kissed him on the forehead, a light imprint of her lips, and walked away with a confident stride. She didn't once look back. Just like the Lexi he knew.

CHAPTER 36

It was a treat to see how deftly Callie worked on the van, a pleasure to hear her lively comments and explanations. And yet…

Petrified of appearing childish, terrified of saying the wrong thing, Mineko did little more than stare, nod and mumble. It turned out that catching a dream was far easier than knowing what to do with it.

"See here?" Callie held up a stick taken from the van's cryptic inner workings. "It's called a dipstick. It measures the oil level."

"Oh. What is the oil for?"

"It keeps the engine from wearing down. The parts create friction when they move, and if they're not oiled, the engine doesn't last long."

"Yeah, I get that problem too," said Zeke. "Gotta go heavy on the lube."

Callie laughed, though Mineko had no idea why. "Grow up."

Mineko faked a smile. Perhaps one in ten of Zeke's interjections made any sense to her, but they did prevent the conversation from lapsing into an awkward silence. For that much, she was grateful.

"So what happens when we have to stop for a toilet break?" Zeke said. "Do I get a bottle to piss in? I don't want to go in the desert and have to worry about some hyena eating my dick."

"Relax," Callie said. "No animal is that desperate for food."

"Callie, I'm curious," said Mineko. "How did you learn to drive?"

"I taught myself." Callie rummaged in her toolbox as she spoke, only briefly glancing up. "When I was fourteen, I traded everything precious I'd scrounged for a shit-heap of a car. A rusted hatchback with all these faded Christian bumper stickers. *This Car Runs On Faith*, that sort of thing. Even a little cross hanging off the rear-view."

With a pious smile, Zeke pressed his palms together. "Praise the Lord."

"Well, not to brag, but a few girls did find God in the back seat."

Zeke sniggered, and heat rushed up Mineko's neck. With Callie's attraction to women so casually confirmed, her every glance and interaction now seemed fraught with sexual significance.

She jumped as Callie nudged her. "You've gone bright red."

"Of course she has," Zeke said. "She ain't gonna shake off the shut-in thinking overnight. They don't even fuck each other, I don't think. They grow babies in hydroponic pods."

Mineko stared at him. "That's not true."

"You're right. It's probably vats. Big, dripping vats." Zeke shot up his hand, startling Mineko yet again. "Sexy babe alert!"

Riva Latour approached them with a box in her arms. Her hair had been shaped into a bizarre series of spikes that divided her shaved scalp—the most uncodified hairstyle Mineko had ever seen. The dark makeup around her eyes was smudged, and faint lines scored her cheeks.

"What's in the box?" said Zeke. "Tell me it ain't a head."

"Are you okay?" Callie hurried to her. "You've been crying."

"I'm sorry," Riva said. "I should be happy, but…"

Callie took the box, set it down, and put an arm around Riva. "Come here. Tell me what's wrong." She steered Riva to the back of the van, where they sat between its open doors.

Riva inhaled a short, sharp breath, pressed her forehead to Callie's neck and wept. "I said goodbye to Amity," she said between sobs. "And Nikolas too. I've always relied on them both. Now Nikolas has given me a huge responsibility, and I have to do it all myself…"

Was this woman seriously mewling about having responsibilities? Mineko dealt with that every day.

"Oh, chickadee." Callie cupped Riva's cheeks and leaned close—any observer might have assumed they were about to kiss. "You'll be just fine. You're smart and brave, and on top of that, you aren't alone. I'll be here for you no matter what. That's a promise."

What was this *chickadee* nonsense? Why did Riva get a pet name? Maybe they really *were* about to kiss. Callie certainly looked like she wanted to, the way she was stroking Riva's face and gazing into her eyes.

"It's just so sudden," said Riva. "I don't know if I'm ready."

Pathetic. Mineko had sacrificed everything. She'd even lost her parents. Where was her comfort? Her caresses?

"I have a feeling you're coming with us," Callie said. "And you have no idea how happy that makes me. You're going to see the world now. We'll do it together, okay?"

Oh, yes. They'd take a bike ride and watch the sun set over the basin. They'd sit cuddled close, fickle Callie Roux and this bitch of an intruder. Fucking Riva Latour with her stupid angular face, obnoxious piercings and infuriating hair. A sanctimonious idiot. To think she had tried to lecture Mineko—an ethics student, for God's sake—on morality…

A hand touched her arm, and she flinched.

"Take a breath," said Zeke, his voice low. "If Callie were to look over here right now, she'd have a fucking heart attack. You look ready to kill someone." He gave her shoulder a squeeze. "We're gonna take a little walk. Maybe have a beer or two."

Mineko frowned at him. He wasn't without charm, despite the spikes and his perpetually frantic manner, yet it was hard to admire him the way she did Kade. Codists valued the impression of emotional indifference, and Zeke's excess would have been deemed a mark of immaturity.

And yet his eyes were so very kind…

"Come on, Min," he said. "We'll catch up, just you and me. Before we're stuck in a van with a bunch of weirdos."

It was impossible not to smile, and when Zeke grinned back, her anger abated. "Okay."

The revolutionaries relaxing in the recreation room seemed unhappy about Mineko's arrival. One of them, a muscular man with a scarred cheek, blocked the doorway and crossed his arms.

"You got a problem?" said Zeke. "You're kinda in our way."

"We don't want that Codist in here. Go somewhere else."

"Hey, I've been using this room all morning. Amity even told me I could help myself to the fridge. You telling me you got higher authority than her?"

"It's the Codist we have a problem with, not you."

"Listen to me, fuckface. Yesterday, I survived a car chase, fought in the streets with shut-ins and bunkered down in what was practically a fucking sewer. This morning, I smashed a gangster over the head and killed him. An hour later, I performed surgery to save the life of a second one. Plucked a bullet out of his goddamn lung. So if you want to fuck with me, go ahead and do it now, because I'm one busy son of a bitch."

The revolutionary backed down, and Zeke nodded. "Yeah, good choice." He directed Mineko to a pair of facing armchairs. "Sit down, kid."

Mineko settled into the frayed chair. It didn't seem to have any springs, and its cushion had been permanently indented. Still, a lack of comfortable furniture was presumably among the least of the things she'd have to become accustomed to.

Zeke opened a bar fridge, took out two cans, glanced at the action on the television—a man was somersaulting over a tank while several robotic soldiers unloaded machine guns—and returned to Mineko's side.

"I've never had beer before." Mineko tasted the frothing liquid. Her mouth puckered shut. "It's bitter."

"Yeah, real nasty shit. You drink it to spite yourself." Zeke sat and cradled the can in his lap. "Let me remind you of something. Riva and Callie just risked their lives to get you out of that enclave. They didn't have to do that. They don't know you from anyone. Coulda ended up wiped for it."

"I feel like you're accusing me of something."

"I'm only telling you to slow down and think. Sure, you're jealous because Callie thinks Riva is the best thing since sliced bread fucked a toaster and gave birth to self-toasting bread. But don't take it personally. Those two click, that's all."

"They click?"

"Yeah, click." Zeke snapped his fingers. "Don't compare yourself to Riva. She knows how to flirt and make Callie laugh, while you're scared just to open your trap. She can look Callie in the eye, while you struggle to stare at the tips of your fucking shoes. That's part of your charm, kid. Quiet, shy, friendly. That's you. The more you give Riva them fucking death stares, the more likely Callie's going to get second thoughts about you."

"Why do you swear so often?"

"Some people pause for breath. Me, I pause for fucks. And that's another thing you gotta learn. A lot of things that you've thought of as forbidden, we do without even thinking."

"So I've noticed."

"Physical contact is gonna throw you. Hugging, kissing. It ain't strange for us. I know it's different in shut-in land, where you only touch somebody if you're trying to shake a black widow off their sleeve, and even then you ask nicely first and wear a fucking condom on your hands to do it."

"You think I'm jealous." Mineko took another mouthful of beer. Somehow, the bitterness was more palatable now. "I do think Riva was being melodramatic, but I'm not jealous."

"Yeah, you are. There's not been a lot of love in your life. You've felt like an outsider among your folks, yeah? Well, we know that outsider feeling too. That's why we band together. That's why, when Callie sees Riva upset, she wants to make it better. Because the thing is…"

Zeke looked Mineko in the eyes. "The thing is, too many people have torn through Callie's life and left her feeling worthless. So next time you see that she's happy, don't ask whether it ought to have been you that made it happen. Just be glad, okay? And trust that she ain't going to forget you."

"Nice speech." Lexi stalked across the room, silent as a panther, and stood smirking with a finger beside her lips. "Is that beer she's drinking?"

"Hey, Lex." Zeke raised his can to her. "I'm corrupting the kid. Gonna get her on nicotine next."

"Corrupting her, you say? I have a few ideas myself."

Aware she was blushing, helpless to do anything about it, Mineko shifted her attention to the movie. The hero had managed to leap a building while the robot gunners marveled at his escape.

"What's this film?" said Mineko. "I've never seen anything like it."

"*Death Droids*," said Zeke. "Actually, *Death Droids III*, but it's a prequel. You see that guy in the spandex? Just an hour ago, he turned out to be a different guy we thought was dead."

"How is that possible?"

"Face transplant." Zeke gave a satisfied nod. "By the way, Lex, Riva's in the garage with Callie. She got a little emotional. There were tears."

"Is she okay?" Lexi said. "Did Callie take care of her?"

"Yeah, it's a love-in. That's why we're here. All that sappy shit made us want to throw the fuck up, right, Min?"

Mineko didn't dare look Lexi directly in the face. "Right."

"Uh-huh." Lexi sat on the arm of Mineko's chair, crossed her long legs and rested her chin in her hands. "So how are you feeling?"

"I'm fine. Thank you."

Still smiling, Lexi took the can from Mineko's hand and drank what was left. "She's just as cute as I remember."

"I was thinking," said Zeke. "We could fix her up with some new clothes. Get her out of that overall."

"Sure. A new wardrobe for the new Minnie. There's a place down the hall where they keep clothes and things. Outfitting room, Riva said it was."

"Yeah? You check it out?"

"Of course I did. Lots of trench coats. I might borrow one of the black ones, see if it suits me." Lexi played with a decorative button on Mineko's shoulder. "How does that sound to you, sweetie?"

If it meant Lexi would stop bending over her, provoking all kinds of unfamiliar sensations, Mineko would agree to anything. "I'd like that."

"We'll pick out something in red," said Zeke. "To match your face."

Mineko glared at him. "Shut up, Zeke."

The devilish smirk returned to Lexi's lips. "I think she'll turn out okay."

The outfitting room's sole occupant was a revolutionary shaving over a basin. Lexi pointed to the door, and he left, wiping foam from his cheeks.

"People just do anything you tell them to, don't they?" Zeke roamed the room, peering into closets and flicking through racks of clothing. "Check out this cool hat." He took a fedora from a peg and seated it on his head. "Zeke Lukas, Private Eye. Gonna solve some mysteries."

Laughing, Lexi opened the doors of a large wardrobe. "Focus. We need to find something that will transform our shut-in into a sex goddess."

"I don't want to be a sex goddess," said Mineko. "Practical clothes, please."

"I'll meet you halfway." Lexi pawed through the clothes. There were lots of trench coats, as predicted, but also shirts, blouses, trousers, boots and—novelty of all novelties—a skirt. It was a peculiar thing, an open tube of shiny synthetic leather closed at one side with a zipper.

Lexi held the skirt aloft. "This is what you need."

"I don't think so. I mean. I don't know."

Zeke examined a label sewn to the skirt. "Nice. A fashion piece."

"What do you mean, a fashion piece?"

"I keep forgetting you were born yesterday. A fashion piece is clothing that's expensive because some asshole said so. People wear this stuff so that everyone knows they're King Shit."

"Like my jacket." Lexi tugged at her lapels. "It cost me a fortune, even though you could buy something far sturdier for a handful of cat's teeth and a bag of bottle caps."

It was frustratingly hard to tell when Lexi and Zeke were being serious. "But isn't everyone out here struggling for survival?" said Mineko. "How can you afford to place a symbolic value on clothing?"

"Decadence and decay ain't contradictions," Zeke said. "In fact, they're fucking bedfellows."

Lexi whistled. "Profound. Kade-worthy, even."

Zeke's lean face sprang into a smile. "That's a compliment, right?"

He held out a worn, spike-studded brown jacket. "This'd go well with the skirt. Give her that rough and tumble look, you know, but with an urban edge."

"Sounds hot. She'll need combat boots. And tights."

Mineko stroked the jacket's dark sleeve. Her fingertips bumped over the tiny studs. "Do you think it's appropriate to take anything we want?"

"It's for the purpose of disguise," said Zeke. "Revolutionary business."

Lexi bundled the garments together. "Try these on. It doesn't look like they have a privacy screen, so we'll ask Zeke to turn around."

Mineko glared. "Both of you will turn around."

Exchanging an amused glance, Lexi and Zeke turned. Mineko counted silently to ten—she wouldn't have put it past Lexi to fake some excuse to spin around and leer at her—before slipping out of her overall.

Cool air touched her bare, blushing skin. She struggled into the tights, an impossible task until she realized it was easier to begin with them rolled up, and tried to open the skirt. The zipper stopped short. It appeared she had to step inside.

Well, fine. She could handle that.

The next piece, however, was impossible: a plain black shirt. It might as well have been a puzzle box. It had no buttons or zippers, just multiple holes and twisty, stretchy fabric that bunched and caught whenever she tried to insert part of herself into it.

"Lexi, how do I wear a shirt?"

"Pull it over your head and put your arms through the sleeves."

How? How did anyone do that? Mineko studied the holes before trying to shove her head through the largest. The shirt tried to choke her. Wrestling through it, she managed to locate an opening. Far too small. Fabric clung to her face, blinding her. Did she have it back to front? God, was she trapped like this?

"Do you need a hand, Minnie?" Lexi said.

"I think it's backwards. Or inside out. Or I have the wrong opening. Or all of the above." Mineko tried to retreat from the shirt. No use. It had captured her left arm. "I'm stuck!"

An external force eased the shirt away, and Mineko found herself face-to-face with Lexi. One eyebrow raised.

"Don't look." Mineko folded her arms over her breasts.

"I'm not looking." Without glancing down, Lexi aided Mineko into the shirt and deftly guided her arms through the holes. "There you go." She held out the jacket. "Add the final touch and then look in the mirror."

Mineko obeyed. The jacket added unexpected weight and movement, while the tights beneath her skirt followed the shape of her legs and thighs. Freed from that formless blue fabric, she looked like a different woman. A far stronger one.

"You look good," said Zeke. "The skirt suits you."

"I don't care whether it suits me." Mineko considered herself from a different angle. How thrilling to see her bust outlined under thin cloth. "What matters is that it's uncodified."

"Oh, yeah. Uncodified as fuck."

"Zeke, go tell Callie we're almost ready," said Lexi. "I need a word in private with the new girl."

If only Mineko hadn't been looking in the mirror—she wouldn't have had to endure seeing herself turn red.

Zeke gave an amiable wave and exited. To make matters worse, Lexi shut the door behind him.

"You look good." She circled Mineko, her eyes glittering with a light that seemed too pale to be natural. "You'd fit right in down here, wouldn't you? A head full of big words and bigger ideas, a massive chip on your shoulder. Comrade Minnie-Min."

"I've yet to reach a decision about these Open Hand people. But if Kade respects them, I'm inclined to do so as well."

"Put all those serious thoughts aside for a moment. When we get to Port Venn, I can see about hooking you up with a cute girl. You'd like that, wouldn't you?"

"Don't you dare tease me."

The sharp reply seemed to take Lexi by surprise. She shoved her hands into her pockets and pouted, looking like a chastened child. "I didn't mean it that way. I'm just playing."

"You're as bad as Lachlan."

"Quite possibly. But still, why not let me help you explore your sexuality?"

All the blood in Mineko's body seemed to have relocated to her face. "This is no time to proposition me."

"Sorry, sweetie, but I wasn't. You're a little too complicated for my tastes."

It stung. It shouldn't have, yet it did. And instead of the sullen defiance she wanted, plaintive hurt was the only response Mineko could muster. "You think Codism has damaged me?"

"I know it. I've been inside, remember." Lexi tapped her temple. "Callie would have you, if you asked her. Please don't. You're on track to make a few mistakes, and that girl deserves better than to be a trial run."

What could Mineko say to that? She hadn't even had time to consider these questions herself, and now she was being openly challenged by the one person she could never hope to deceive.

"Trust me, Min. You don't know if you want love, sex, or just a chance to rebel against your fucked-up society. You're a virgin in more ways than one."

"You don't know everything. Since we last met, I've kissed a woman."

Lexi's eyebrows jumped. "You move fast, don't you?"

"Once I saw what was possible, I had to find out how it applied to me. The truth is, I do have feelings for Callie. I don't see what right you have to warn me away from her."

"No right whatsoever. I'm only looking out for my friends, and that includes you. In Port Venn, you'll get to experience all kinds of uncodified things. Don't be angry with me for wanting to set one or two limits. Be excited that the limits are so few."

"Who appointed you my guardian?"

For several seconds, Lexi remained silent, her mouth open. "Oh, God." She laughed, took Mineko by the shoulders and bent low, bringing their faces level. "I know exactly how you feel right now. There was once a pushy bitch in my own life who refused to let me make decisions. Ash, my cousin. She sure could preach. I resented her, not least because she took the only man I've ever loved."

"You were in love with a man?"

"I didn't know it at the time. I thought…but when I knew, Min, it didn't change anything. And that shook me. I loved him just as I thought I'd loved her. But it was never *her*. Not really."

There was an urgency in Lexi's voice that deserved to be respected, but God only knew what she was talking about. "Lexi, I'm confused."

"Sorry. I'm just using you to get something off my chest."

Lexi brushed Mineko's bangs aside—her fingertips felt cool as they skimmed over Mineko's forehead—and smiled. "I'm going to be that pushy bitch for you now. You'll kick and scream. I did. But I hope you'll learn to love me for it, even though I'll fuck up as well."

Love. The one thing her parents had given her even as they'd denied her everything else. "I don't know what you're saying, yet I feel like I want to believe you."

Lexi took Mineko's hand and kissed it. A warm, comforting sensation. "Trust me, I know how hard it is to believe in anyone. We're at the same point right now, you and me. We're facing down futures we never thought we'd let ourselves have. And we'll do it together."

The passenger seat was just as Mineko remembered it, right down to the rumpled bag of sweets near the gearstick. Callie snapped on her seatbelt and inserted the key into the ignition. The roar of the engine banished the last of Mineko's uncertainty. This was really happening.

Riva occupied the van's rear seat. Lexi sat nearby on the floor, her eyes closed in pleasure as Riva caressed the back of her neck. Zeke huddled in the corner opposite, a blue light at his lips. The scent of nicotine vapor filled the van, a mild, cloying aroma.

The garage lamps flashed overhead. A trail of light to the surface.

Callie touched the dashboard, and the music arrived with a frenetic cascade of drums. She tapped her hands on the wheel while Riva hummed. Daylight flooded the van's interior, and the tunnel fell away. The shattered architecture of the city took its place.

They drove through the shadows of splintered towers, navigating streets that carried the last, thin blood of humanity. Mineko pressed her hand to the window as the asphalt blurred. Though this was a spectacle of neglect and decay, it was also a poignant reminder of the enduring past. In time, this would be dust, but not today. Not yet.

The buildings became sparser, road signs streaked past, and the van plunged down an ancient off-ramp without slowing. They screamed through the dead heart of suburbia: faded paint, scuffed plastic, rusted iron, stripped wires, fallen fences, scorched cement...

And then Foundation was behind them, and there was only horizon.

This place takes many things from you, and hope is one of them. Valerie had stared at the stars in the undirected way of the blind. *I've given up dreaming, Mineko.*

If only Valerie could see what Mineko saw now—a highway to a dream, beneath a sky without end.

About Eden S. French

Eden S. French is an award-winning novelist, a graduate researcher at the University of Tasmania, and nothing but trouble. The only thing she enjoys more than writing about queer cyborgs is the certain fact that, someday, she will become one.

Despite being some sort of frightening vegan-lesbian-goth person, she has received a Goldie Award and an Alice B. Lavender Certificate, both for her 2015 debut novel The Diplomat. She currently lives in Hobart, Tasmania with her enchanting artist girlfriend, at least one cat, and a sense of foreboding.

CONNECT WITH EDEN:

Facebook: www.facebook.com/eden.soph
Twitter: www.twitter.com/edensfrench
Website: www.edenfrench.com

Coming from Queer Pack

www.queer-pack.com

Queerly Loving

(Book 1)

Edited by G Benson and Astrid Ohletz

Queer characters getting their happy endings abound in this first book of a two-part collection. Discover pages upon pages of compelling stories about aromantic warriors, trans sorceresses, and modern-day LGBTQA+ quirky characters. Friendship, platonic love, and poly triads are all celebrated.

Lose yourself in masterfully woven tales wrapped in fantasy and magic, delve into a story that brings the eighties back to life in vibrant color, get lost in space, and celebrate everything queer.

Get ready for your queer adventure.

Queerly Loving

(Book 2)

Edited by G Benson and Astrid Ohletz

In part two of *Queerly Loving*, our authors bring you short stories with characters across the fantastic queer spectrum, with endings that will leave you warm and smiling. Trans love interests, demisexual characters trying to find their way in the world, bisexual characters dealing with a heartbreak in the best way, and lesbians on escapades.

Dragons roar into life, dystopian futures unfold, mermaids enjoy space voyages, and modern-day adventures will curl your toes and make you cheer. There are first kisses, friends that are like kin, and aromantic characters discovering their place among a queer-normative family.

Get ready for your queer adventure.

Reintegration
© 2017 by Eden S. French

ISBN: 978-3-95533-926-5

Also available as e-book.

Published by Queer Pack, legal entity of Ylva Verlag, e.Kfr.

Ylva Verlag, e.Kfr.
Owner: Astrid Ohletz
Am Kirschgarten 2
65830 Kriftel
Germany

www.queer-pack.com

Second edition: 2017

Credits
Editor: Zee Ahmad
Coverdesign: S. Achilles (Dreamstime/Kts, Depositphotos/mppriv)

CPSIA information can be obtained
at www.ICGtesting.com
Printed in the USA
FFOW02n0531190318
45715646-46559FF